I WILL MEND YOU

PEN PAL DUET

GIGI STYX

GIGI STYX

I WILL MEND YOU

AUTHOR'S NOTE

This dark romance thriller contains graphic depictions of torture, psychological abuse, deviant sexual acts, non-con, and torture. If you are offended by such content, do not continue reading.

TRIGGER WARNINGS

This is a dark romance that includes dub-con, graphic depictions of torture and violence, and sexually explicit scenes. If any of this content is triggering for you, please do not read this book.

Triggers include:

- Abduction
- Abortion (backstory)
- Anal sex
- Arson
- Assassination
- Attempted sexual assault
- Blackmail
- Bukkake
- Bullying
- Cannibalism
- Captivity
- Car accident
- Castration
- Child assassins
- Child porn (secondary character backstory)
- Child murder
- Child sexual abuse
- Child trafficking
- Choking
- Drugging
- Dismemberment
- Elder abuse
- Execution
- Exhibitionism
- Fear play
- Financial abuse
- Forced abortion (backstory)
- Forced feeding

Gang rape (to side character)
Gaslighting
Grooming
Hallucinations
Humiliation
Immolation
Imprisonment
Inappropriate use of medical equipment
Infant death
Interrogation
Medical abuse
Medication tampering
Memory loss
Mental illness
Murder
Mutilation
Organ trafficking
Online harassment
Poisoning
Pornography
Primal kink
PTSD
Rape
Sexual harassment
Snuff movies
Somnophilia
Sororicide
Stalking
Suicide
Torture
Trafficking
Trauma
Victim blaming (by antagonist)
Vigilante justice

Reader discretion is advised. If you find any of these topics distressing, please choose a different book. Your mental health matters.

For everyone who ever needed a villain
to burn down the world for you.

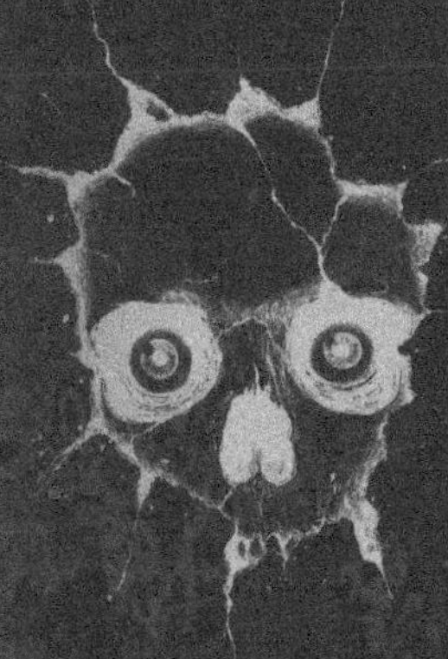

ONE

AMETHYST

My life flashes before my eyes like a kaleidoscope of fractured memories. The first ten years are black, the ones following are muted. When I meet Xero, the colors turn vivid, at first. Then red with his betrayal. And finally flames, when I set him on fire.

Now, I'm here, in Mom's kitchen, staring at her corpse.

The monster in the mirror got to her first.

She also shot Uncle Clive in the chest.

How did that thing escape her glass prison? She isn't real. She can't be real. But her breath mists in the air, her eyes gleam with life, and her hands drip with blood. She's too terrifying to be a nightmare.

I step backward through the kitchen, my feet slipping on Clive's freshly spilled blood. My heart beats so hard that its vibrations reach my fingertips. That only excites the doppelgänger, who advances on me, her chest rising and falling with excited breaths.

The afternoon sun streams through the kitchen window, highlighting the golden flecks in her green eyes. She looks nothing like me, even though everything about us is identical from the scars on our chins to the way only the left side of our curls is bleached. She even lightened her right eyebrow to match mine.

Which means she isn't a mirror image.

Another sign that she hasn't crawled out of the mirror is her clothes. While my hoodie, leggings, and tank top are covered in mausoleum dust, she's clad in an over-bust corset and black miniskirt identical to what I wore for shooting videos for the fan club.

But that doesn't mean anything I'm seeing is real.

This has to be an immersive hallucination brought on by overwhelming stress. I just watched Xero invite a bunch of men to rape me while I was unconscious. Then I burned him alive and escaped through the catacombs. My trauma doubled when I went to the vicarage for help and ended up fighting off Reverend Tom.

It's no wonder my brain is glitching.

On the journey across town, I kept hallucinating smoke. Maybe my mind conjured up an empty road, and I crashed the car. Maybe the real me is lying in the wreckage, imagining this creature wearing my face has crawled out of a mirror dimension to murder my family.

"What's wrong, Amy?" she asks, her grating voice forcing me back to the present. It's melodic, mocking, menacing, like she's merely a parody of a human. "Aren't you happy to see me?"

Her green irises dance within the whites of her eyes. It's like locking gazes with a predator that wants to eat my soul. Nausea clogs my throat, and my stomach twists the way it usually does when I look in the mirror too long.

This creature is nothing like me. She's hateful. Murderous. Insane. She's everything Mom and Dr. Saint feared I would become—a remorseless killer.

Blood roars between my ears, drowning out the frantic beat of my pulse. The kitchen spins, rooting me in the center of a carousel of delusions.

I swallow hard, forcing down a surge of panic, and my gaze bounces to the monster's gun. When the kitchen timer chimes, something inside me snaps. This is too vivid to be a hallucination. Too visceral. This has to be a grand mal delusion.

"Tongue-tied?" she asks.

"What..." I gulp. "Who are you?"

Her laughter rings in my ears like alarm bells, warning me to turn around and run. Run now before I become her third victim.

"What kind of question is that?" she asks, her voice hardening. "Don't tell me you've forgotten the sister whose life you stole."

Ice fills my veins, making my breath catch. I glance at the floor where Mom lies unmoving in a puddle of congealed blood. She never mentioned any siblings. I would know if I had a sister, let alone a twin. And I sure as hell didn't steal anyone's life.

The creature flutters her lashes, tilts her head, and stares like I'm the curiosity. "You don't remember?"

"Remember what?"

"Me," she snarls and raises the gun to my head.

My heart flips. I still can't believe this is real, yet she's advancing on me, her fury mounting with each sticky, wet step.

Terror clogs my throat, and I swallow over and over, trying to dislodge the knot of paralysis keeping me rooted to the spot. She keeps coming, those uncanny features twisting into a rictus of rage.

Move, Amethyst.

MOVE!

"If you've forgotten your sins, then I will make you remember!" she screams.

Her shrill voice triggers dormant prey instincts, and every nerve in my body screams at me to flee. The tendrils of fear tethering my feet to the kitchen floor snap, and I turn on my heel and run into the mud room.

One foot catches on Uncle Clive's leg, while the other slips on his blood. I stumble through the narrow space, my arms flailing as I hurtle out of the door.

The doppelgänger's maniacal laugh follows me through the mud room and out into the manicured garden. Juniper-scented air fills my nostrils but does nothing to clear the scent of death. It clings to my sinuses, my throat and lungs... down to the very depths of my soul. Mom... Uncle Clive... murdered by that monster.

I stumble over the gravel patio, my gaze darting across the garden. Beyond the hedge maze, flowerbeds, and lawn stands a border of evergreens separating Mom and Dad's property from the neighbors.

Scenarios flicker through my mind like strobe lights. I could escape through the trees and run for help or rush around the house to where I left the car. Either way, I risk being shot in the back before I get even close to help.

I sprint toward the driveway, but two familiar-looking men emerge around the corner, both clad in navy blue uniforms with gold badges. Even though the visors on their flat-topped hats obscure their eyes, I can tell they're here for me.

"Where are you going?" rumbles the man on the left.

He's an oversized brute with a broken nose and a jaw covered in dark stubble. Spreading his arms, he charges at me like a linebacker. His partner, a golden-haired pretty boy with sparkling blue eyes, pulls out a taser and grins.

Alarm punches me in the chest, knocking out my air.

Change of plan.

Pivoting, I bolt toward the hedge maze, putting as much distance as I can between me and the men. If I can reach the trees at the end of the lawn, then maybe I can catch the attention of a neighbor or circle around toward the car.

"Come back, Amy," says a smoother male voice that probably belongs to the blond. He sounds almost kind, but there's no mistaking his sick joy.

I quicken my pace, not stopping to work out their uniforms. They aren't the police, even though they're both wearing body cams. Gravel crunches underfoot, threatening to drown out my thoughts. Are they connected to the other men who broke into my house? Does it even matter? I need to focus on escaping, not speculating.

"Don't damage her," the doppelgänger yells.

Her voice provides a fresh surge of adrenaline to pump my arms, forcing my body to run faster, harder, and escape this nightmare. As I round the maze at full speed, heavy footsteps thunder closer. Before I know it, a large arm encircles my waist, lifting me into the air.

My stomach lurches. Cold alarm forces out a scream.

"Got you!" The brute spins around so we're facing the back of the house.

The doppelgänger stands in the mud room door with the blond, both flashing me dazzling grins.

"Help—"

The brute clamps a hand over my mouth.

"Put her in the van," says the doppelgänger.

"Sure thing, Dolly."

Dolly.

Stiffening, I turn my gaze back toward the monster wearing my face. Dolly is the name of the woman from X-Cite Media. The one who sent men to my house. The one who arranged for Lizzie Bath to be raped and murdered for a snuff movie.

Dolly is also married to Xero's father.

As the large man marches me around the back of the house, her eyes burn into my profile, but I can't withstand her stare. I thrash within the brute's grip, even though each futile movement saps my strength.

I refuse to believe this is real. My real body must be out there, trapped in a car wreck, or strapped to a gurney while I hallucinate this horror to escape the truth that I killed Xero.

But if I can't break through this illusion, then I'm facing a nightmare that will make me wish I was dead.

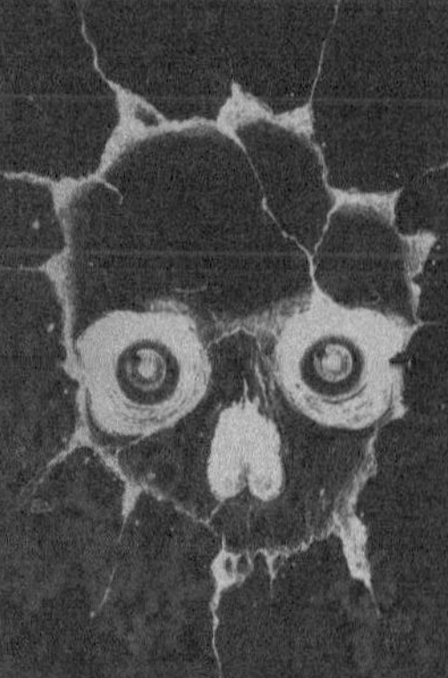

TWO

XERO

An alarm rings through my ears, piercing the thick veil of unconsciousness. I jerk awake, my senses assaulted by an oppressive heat and the acrid stench of smoke.

Flames flicker through the haze, accompanied by the sizzle and snap of burning wood.

The crawl space is on fire, but my hair and clothes are drenched. Jynxson must have installed a sprinkler system in the bedroom to stage a prank.

I grope around the mattress, trying to awaken Amethyst, but she's not there. In a frenzy, I roll off the bed and inhale lungfuls of cooler, more breathable air. The smoke down here isn't nearly as thick, giving me a view of the fire raging through the door.

After pulling down the bed sheet and holding it over my nose, I crawl around the bed's perimeter.

"Amethyst?" I yell, my lungs exploding into a riot of coughs.

My answer is the crackling of flames and the popping of burning wood.

Where the hell is she? Did she already escape?

My palm lands on a piece of broken glass, reminding me of the bottle Amethyst smashed over my head. There was no explanation—just a cryptic conversation about a video of us shot in the graveyard.

The dizziness, headache, nausea, and fatigue I'm suffering could be symptoms of smoke inhalation, but the chemical scent hints at chloroform or somnochlorate.

That makes no sense. I'm the only thing standing between Amethyst and her enemies. She wouldn't set her only protector on fire and escape... unless someone or something affected her mental state. Pushing those thoughts aside, I rush around the bed, checking that she isn't lying somewhere on the floor, unconscious.

Heat crawls under my skin, and my breath comes in ragged gasps. If I don't leave this crawl space soon, the flames will overwhelm the room. I grope around in the dark, but there's no sign of Amethyst. I hurry across the space to the panel by the bathroom door and stand, hoping to hell that the heat hasn't warped it shut.

The metal lever sears my palm even through the protective sheet, but I force it open just wide enough to squeeze through and tumble into a darkened hallway.

I stagger forward, choking, coughing, groping my way through the smoke-filled enclosure. Up ahead is another hatch that leads to the space beneath Mrs. Baker's house.

Betrayal burns through my gut, filling the back of my throat with bile. The woman I went to such lengths to protect left me to burn.

She knows too much: our hiding places, our personnel, our plans. Hell, if she told the police I was still alive, or even a fraction of what she's observed of my operatives, then every asshole with a gun and a grudge against our group will invade the catacombs.

My fingers find the section of the wall that opens into number 15 Parisii Drive, and I push. The small door swings open, letting in a rush of cool air. I clamber inside, cross Mrs. Baker's crawl space, and continue into the tunnel leading to the catacombs.

Footsteps echo toward me through the dark. I straighten, already on guard for an attack.

"Xero?"

The overhead lights flicker to life, illuminating a small group of people in black. I can't make out their figures with my vision still hazy, but I recognize the voice.

It's my hacker, Tyler.

I stumble, only for him to rush to my side and catch me before my knees collapse.

"Your computer system went down," he says. "I checked the cameras, but there was nothing. What happened?"

My lungs burn, and my throat is raw, but I force out, "The crawlspace is on fire. Amethyst is missing."

"Were you under attack?"

I don't know what stops me from saying that the woman I once forgave for betraying me left me unconscious to die in flames. Maybe it's disbelief. Maybe it's the shame at having been fooled twice. Maybe it's the futile hope that this was all just a misunderstanding. Either way, the truth clogs my gorge.

"Evacuate the catacombs," I say through ragged breaths. "At least until we assess the threat level."

Tyler and the others speak at once, but their voices fade in the rush of blood between my ears. As my vision turns black, the last thing I think about is the raw fury twisting Amethyst's beautiful features as she hit me over the head with that bottle.

Time passes. It could be hours, considering every muscle in my body screams as if I've forced it through four marathons. I wake up in one of our above-ground infirmaries, overlooking a garden. The last vestiges of sunlight stream in through the windows, telling me that I've lost most of the day.

My chest is tight, with smoke still lingering in the back of my throat despite the oxygen mask. There's an IV attached to my arm delivering a clear fluid that I hope is just saline, because I don't have time to hang around.

Amethyst is gone, and I passed out before I could order Tyler to track her movements.

With a grimace, I remove the oxygen mask and force myself to sit up. As I reach for the IV, a small hand grabs my wrists.

"What do you think you're doing?" a female voice snaps.

I turn to lock gazes with my sister. Her hair, which is usually pulled off her face in a neat bun, is disheveled, and her brown eyes are swimming with concern.

"Camila, I—"

"Isabel says you can't leave." She places the mask back on my face and yells, "He's awake!"

Grinding my teeth, I make a mental note to kick Tyler's ass for his choice of babysitter. If anyone other than my two sisters were keeping me restrained, they would have landed in the wall.

The door opens, and Isabel strides in, her features stern. "Hear me out before you tear apart the room."

My nostrils flare, and I clench my teeth.

One would think Isabel would be the kinder of my sisters. She's a year older than Camila with delicate features framed by loose curls. She's more maternal and chose to heal people rather than kill. But the training she's endured under our Chief Medical Officer has polished her soft edges to stone.

"We performed a bronchoscopy to remove small particles from your lungs. You need to rest for at least the next few days until we receive the results from your arterial blood gas analysis. That'll give us more information to work out a treatment plan."

"I don't have twenty-four hours, let alone seventy-two," I say through gritted teeth.

Camila places a hand on my arm. "Everything's under control. We evacuated the catacombs. All operatives are in above-ground safe houses across the city. Tyler and Jynxson are both in the waiting room with information on Amethyst's movements."

My heart skips a beat, and I shuffle up to sit straighter. "Bring them in."

"Wait." Isabel raises a hand.

"What?"

"Mobilize the team from your bed, but don't leave this room. Do not make me have to sedate you." She levels me with a glower.

I give her a sharp nod.

"Alright." She reaches across the bed and gives my hand a gentle squeeze. "And welcome back."

Guilt settles in the pit of my gut, and my chest tightens with regret. I was so preoccupied with finding Father and the boys he'd confined in the underground facility that I hadn't thought to make time to celebrate my escape from prison with my sisters.

Then there was my obsession with Amethyst. It was so all-consuming that I didn't even notice the red flags. Maybe fucking her in the Ministry of Mayhem's screen room was the step too far that finally made her snap.

The events of last night are still hazy from having inhaled a large quantity of nervous system depressants. I need to find her before she destroys my operation and—

Jynxson steps into the room, interrupting my thoughts. Isabel slips out of the door, letting in Tyler. They're both downcast, and Tyler's eyes are red-rimmed, making me dread the worst.

I inhale a sharp breath into the oxygen mask and brace myself for bad news.

"Report," I rasp.

"Two operatives are dead," Tyler says.

My stomach plummets. "Who?"

"Port and Bowker," he replies.

"Was it Amethyst?"

He shakes his head. "Doubtful. Police found Melonie Crowley murdered at her home with her brother-in-law, Clive Bishop. When the forensic team searched the grounds, they found our men parked in a car nearby, with bullet wounds through their heads. Whoever took them out used a long-range rifle and knew what they were doing."

I grind my teeth. "What did the surveillance footage show?"

"About twenty minutes after the fire started, someone triggered a localized EMP burst around the Crowley house, taking out all the surveillance cameras and communication networks."

My jaw tightens. The timing is too much of a coincidence to be anything other than intentional. Whoever killed Port and Bowker had to be connected to Amethyst's disappearance. The question is whether she was working with the killers.

"What kind of device?" I snarl.

"We think it's connected to a truck that's been circling the highways surrounding Alderney Hill." Tyler glances at Jynxson before adding, "It entered the hill just before the communications went dead."

Clenching my fists, I glance over at Jynxson. "Did anyone track Amethyst?"

Jynxson steps forward. "We found footage of her exiting through a mausoleum and running toward the new vicarage."

My breath catches at the thought of her running to that bastard. "So, she's with the priest?"

He grimaces. "She entered the vicarage with Reverend Thomas. Shortly afterward, she drove his car into the EMP-affected region on Alderney Hill."

"And where is he now?"

"Simon's Memorial Hospital," Jynxson mutters, "but that's not the worst part.

"What?"

"We recovered footage from the vicarage of Reverend Thomas attacking Amethyst. It looks like he's connected to X-Cite Media."

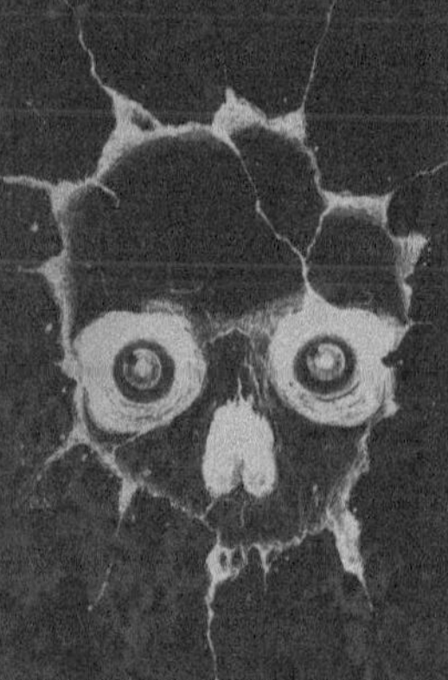

THREE

AMETHYST

Nothing will pull me out of this nightmare. Not biting the inside of my cheek, not closing my eyes and opening them again, not even throwing myself against the wall of this vehicle.

My doppelgänger's brute and pretty boy wrestled me into a straitjacket and tossed me in the back of a truck. The bastards placed a gag and some sort of harness around my mouth so I can't scream. All I can do is kick at the door like a mule.

My arms are bound tight within the thick fabric secured by bands at the wrists, elbows and biceps. It's not as uncomfortable or as confining as the zip ties, but I think that's the point. Strait-jackets are supposed to be snug, offering a deceptive form of safety to stop you from attempting to escape.

How the hell would I know a thing like that?

I roll my shoulders, trying to loosen the restraints, but I'm bound tight. The belts at the back of my jacket are attached to a hook in the truck's interior, so I can barely even reach the doors.

Xero taught me how to escape ropes, handcuffs, cable ties, and locked trunks, but he didn't teach me how to break out of a contraption like this.

Shit.

Why am I even thinking about that betrayer at a time like this? He's worse than my shitty music teacher, Mr. Lawson, who at least kept me to himself. Xero wove an entirely different reality where he was protecting me from snuff moviemakers, only to share my body with multiple men.

Pain lances through my chest, making me double over and gasp. In the end, Xero was just like any other backstabbing man, which is why he needed to die. But even knowing that—even after all the betrayal—my traitorous heart still aches with grief. Grief for what could have been. Part of me wonders if I could have changed him. Or even saved us

The truck stops, and the engine goes silent, pulling me out of my thoughts. If I'm stuck in a lucid dream, then I need to take control. Maybe I can even muster up some superpowers so I can escape the doppelgänger and her cronies.

I wiggle my fingers, trying to create bursts of flame to burn through the fabric, but nothing happens. Footsteps echo outside the truck, accompanied by tinkling laughter that makes my skin erupt in goosebumps. My pulse pounds through my eardrums as the locks creak.

The doors swing open with a screech, and daylight pours into the truck's interior, making me squint. The brute's silhouette looms in the entrance, blocking out most of the sun.

He stares down at me and grins. Without the hat, he's not so terrifying, with gray eyes set within the rugged masculine features of a boxer or an action movie star.

"Are you going to be a good girl for me?" he growls.

I shrink into the wall.

"Fen," Dolly snaps, her voice making my spine stiffen. "Stop fucking about and get her out."

Fen's smile dissolves into a tight line. He climbs into the truck and unfastens the belts holding me to the hook.

I skitter backward, but he lunges forward, grabs my middle, and carries me out of the truck into the blinding afternoon. Eyes burning, I blink over and over until my vision clears.

We're on the runway of an airport with small jets parked in neat rows. Dolly and the pretty boy are already striding toward a set of boarding stairs.

My stomach plummets.

Dream or not, I can't let these people transport me to another location. Any fan of true crime knows that's when the worst happens to the victims. Thrashing within Fen's grip, I scream through the head harness, but the sound is muffled.

Grunting, Fen adjusts his grip around my arms to suppress my struggles. "Just relax," he growls into my ear. "Then you won't get hurt."

I jerk my neck forward, then back, delivering a head butt. Pain explodes across the base of my skull, but Fen releases his grip with a roar. I crash to the tarmac, landing painfully on my tailbone, yet it's nothing compared to the agony of what I need to escape. Scrambling back onto my feet, I tear away from the brute and sprint across the runway toward the building.

"You incompetent fuck," Dolly shrieks. "Get her!"

Gritting my teeth, I pick up my pace, my legs pumping harder. The building looms closer with each approaching second. It's a steel-and-glass structure with reflective windows that mirror the planes and the surrounding tarmac.

Behind me, Fen gives chase, but I focus on the double doors, which slide open for a security guard, a red-haired man who can't be more than nineteen. He stops in his tracks, his mouth falling slack, but doesn't make any move to help.

"Stop her!" Dolly yells.

When the guard reaches into his pocket, my hopes soar, but he pulls out his phone and starts recording.

Tears prick my eyes, but I continue toward the door, not having the time or mental bandwidth to curse his callousness.

A large weight barrels into my back, knocking me onto the ground. My head hits the tarmac with an explosion of agony, and my vision fills with stars.

"Good try." Fen hauls me off the ground and tosses me over his shoulder. "You won't get another one."

"No!" I buck against his bulk and scream for help, but everything comes out muffled through the fabric covering my mouth.

Fen turns around and marches toward one of the private jets. No matter how desperately I struggle, his grip tightens until I can't breathe.

"Let me take a look at her." Dolly appears at my side, grabs a handful of my hair, and wrenches my head back. I flinch, partially from the pain, but mostly at the flash of those malevolent green eyes. "Ugh. You've damaged the face."

"But she was getting away," Fen mutters.

"It's going to take days for her to be camera ready," she screeches. "Now, I'll have to stand in for her until she's healed."

Fen falls silent. "Sorry."

Camera ready?

Oh, shit. Please don't tell me this is about a snuff movie.

"Load her up on the fucking plane," she says.

Fen's burly frame sags, and I feel him nod. His dejection is only a fraction of the dull ache of despondency weakening my will to live. Dread rolls through my gut like thunder at the prospect of ending up like Lizzie Bath. Without another word, he carries me toward the steps of a private jet.

Behind us, the pretty boy laughs. "You should have sedated her."

Dolly huffs. "I wanted her to feel the whole experience of her life turning to shit."

The pretty boy says something that makes her giggle.

"Alright then." She snaps her fingers. "Hold on a minute. Locke wants to give her a little something."

Fen stops walking for the second it takes for the pretty boy to saunter over and order the larger man to cradle me in his arms. I squirm within Fen's grip, trying to break free again, but he holds me so tight that I can't breathe.

I used to think Xero's eyes were cold, but that was only the color. Locke's irises are an inky blue, completely devoid of humanity. They're set within perfectly proportioned features that belong to a Ken doll. He advances on me with a syringe filled with clear liquid.

Every fine hair on the back of my neck stands on end. I shake my head, my eyes stinging with tears. I don't want to lose consciousness and let these bastards subject my defenseless body to even more atrocities. I can't let that happen again.

"No need to struggle, little impostor," he drawls, his lips curving into a smile. "We'll take really good care of you when you're asleep."

The confirmation of my fate unleashes a torrent of adrenaline, sparking a frantic struggle. Thrashing from side to side, I scream into the gag, my eyes darting toward the building where the security guard just disappeared.

What happened to him? Where's the alarm?

What kind of airport allows innocent people to be abducted into private jets?

A needle pierces my neck, and I whimper, my eyes filling with tears. Nightmares usually end at this point, when the terror becomes unbearable. I should wake up in a bed, drenched in sweat, with my heart pounding.

But I'm still here.

Darkness swarms the edges of my vision, turning the world into a blur. As my body goes limp, Locke turns away from me and pulls Dolly into his side. In my periphery, the pair of them continue toward the private jet. My mind battles to stay awake, but my limbs succumb to the drug.

Before I can even consider what the hell this means, the world goes black.

~

I wake up again, collapsed at the back of a school bus racing through a landscape of woodlands. Beyond the trees are rolling hills peppered with sheep. The setting sun paints the sky in hues of tangerine and lilac, turning their wool peculiar shades.

My neck throbs, and my tongue is coated with the faint taste of chemicals. I try to move, but dizziness and the straps of my restraints keep me rooted to where I slump.

Up ahead, Fen is in the driver's seat with Dolly and Locke canoodling in front. I can't hear their conversation over the drone of the engine, but I'm sure whatever they're planning will make me wish I'd perished at the hands of Reverend Tom.

I glance up to find cameras mounted on the bus's ceilings, with blinking red lights indicating that they're recording. The bus drives over a hump in the road that brings up a wave of nausea. I double over and groan.

"She's awake." Locke's voice cuts through what's left of my haze.

The pair approaches, and my insides twist into painful knots.

"Do you recognize this place?" Dolly asks.

I shake my head.

"What's wrong, impostor?" she asks.

"Maybe she's shy," Locke says with a chuckle.

Dolly sits beside me and scoots so close that her body heat soaks through my straitjacket. Locke settles into the seat in front, his lifeless blue eyes scanning our features.

"You're so identical, it's spooky," he says, his voice breathy with wonder.

"She's got that bruise on her temple," Dolly mutters.

"You can cover that up with makeup." Locke leans over, his fingers reaching for my face. I recoil, but Dolly slaps his hand.

"No one touches her without my permission," she snaps.

"Fine," Locke mutters before offering me a wink.

I shrink against the window, trying to put as much distance as I can between Dolly and me, but she edges closer, like a predator admiring her quarry before moving in for the kill.

These people aren't just murdering rapists, they're gleeful. They remind me of bullies on a school trip. They want so much more than to film my degradation and death. They want me to suffer for sins I can't even remember.

Dolly's breath reeks of acetone as she closes in, her fingers tracing my jawline in a mockery of affection.

"How about now?" she asks.

My brow furrows.

She grips my jaw with harsh fingertips and turns my head toward the front of the bus. "Do you recognize it now?"

I turn to look out through the windshield, my chest tightening with unease. We're now on the unkempt grounds of a Victorian building. Its crumbling red bricks hide under a thick layer of ivy. Nature has taken over its courtyard, which is now overgrown with weeds as tall as saplings.

My mind flickers through a state of déjà vu that knocks my sanity off balance. Despite not knowing what the hell is happening, there's no denying this chilling sense of familiarity.

"Well?" Dolly snaps.

I shake my head, not wanting to give her any satisfaction.

"Those photos I sent should have refreshed your memory."

Gasping, I reel forward in my seat. All this time, I thought the polaroids were the work of an older man.

"This is the Saint Christina Lunatic Asylum." She wraps an arm around my shoulders and pulls me into a hug. "Welcome back to your former home."

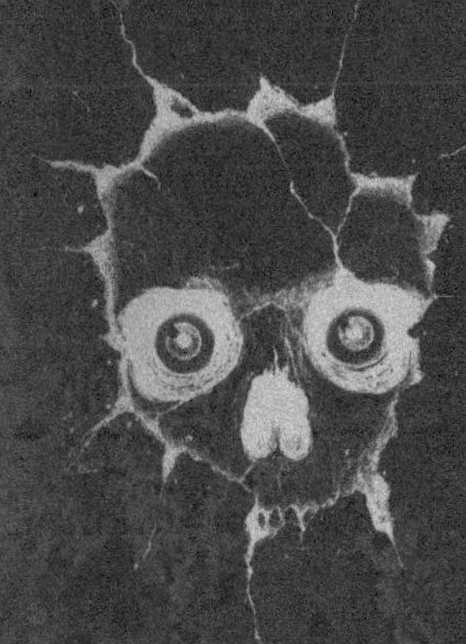

FOUR

XERO

I rise off my cot, only for Jynxson to grab my shoulders.

He shoves me back down. "What are you doing?"

"Going to interrogate that priest." I push against him, but in my weakened state, he may as well be a boulder.

"Stay down," he snarls. "We have people watching Reverend Thomas's hospital room. Someone will seize him the moment he gets discharged."

The door opens, and Isabel storms in, her eyes flashing. "I told you what would happen if you tried leaving."

My glare drops to the syringe she's wielding like a pistol. I clench my jaw, forcing myself to lie down. It isn't like me to be so impulsive, but the situation with Amethyst is fucking with my mind. I don't know why she attacked, if she's having a psychotic break, or if she's fallen into enemy hands. One thing is for certain: fighting Isabel head-on will set back my recovery.

"Fine," I snarl. "Give me a laptop. Let me reach out to the operatives at Simon's Memorial."

Jynxson turns to Tyler, who reaches into his messenger bag and pulls out a computer. I lie back, fix my gaze on Isabel, and force my features into a neutral mask.

I can disable Tyler and Camila in a few moves. If I fight dirty, I might be able to take Jynxson in my shitty condition, but Isabel is the most likely to hit me with a tranquilizer. Out of every operative in the room, she's the most dangerous, and the most familiar with my moves.

Tyler approaches with the laptop, and I focus my attention on the screen. Isabel remains in place for several moments before leaving. My friends and family are already reeling from the loss of Port and Bowker. I won't worsen their grief by acting out.

"Alright then." I turn to Tyler. "I need someone tracking the movements of that truck. Where did it go after the EMP attack? Check the recruiter's house and its surroundings to see if Amethyst went to that location downtown and put me in touch with the operatives you assigned to Reverend Thomas."

Everyone in the room exhales a collective sigh and launches into action. My people at the hospital inform me that the reverend is being kept overnight with a concussion and an eyelid laceration.

Tyler set up my room at the infirmary as the headquarters of the investigation into what happened to Amethyst. It's no coincidence that she went missing the day her family and two of our operatives were murdered. The truck is registered to a salvage yard north of Beaumont City, a common tactic criminals use to hide illegal activities.

We scour X-Cite Media's website for any mention of Amethyst, but it's still hyping up the production they made of Lizzie Bath's murder.

The footage of Amethyst in the vicarage with Reverend Thomas shows her scared and confused. She tries to talk her way out of the locked room, but he attacks first.

When he grabs her throat and pins her to the wall, it takes every ounce of self-control not to throw aside the laptop and fight my way to his hospital bed. When she injures his eye and clubs him over the head with one of his cameras, my heart soars.

Camila grabs my hand. "You taught her well. Wherever she's gone, she'll survive."

My chest squeezes. "But what about her mental state?"

"I can set up a camera in Dr. Saint's cell. You can interrogate the psychiatrist over video chat."

"Do it," I rasp.

She kisses me on the cheek and leaves the room.

"Xero," Jynxson says.

"What?"

"Did Amethyst start that fire?"

I lock gazes with my oldest friend. Most men find me intimidating, but not Jynxson. We've known each other since we were both ten at the underground facility, then we were roommates at the Moirai Academy.

Jynxson had been on my team during the graduation run, and joined the Moirai with one of my tokens, yet he was one of the first to defect once I started my small resistance group. Despite the length of our friendship, he wouldn't understand what I have with my little ghost.

"Did she or didn't she start that fire?" he asks again, his voice hardening.

"No," I say. "Not on purpose."

His eyes narrow. "Then by accident?"

Common sense plus eight years of training as an assassin says I shouldn't protect a woman who tried to kill me in a house fire, but Amethyst has gotten under my skin. I know her well enough to understand there's more to her actions than petty revenge or even a psychotic episode.

"Xero?" Jynxson asks.

"That's what I'm trying to find out."

Our standoff continues for several tense seconds, with his features hardening with disbelief. Of all people, Jynxson knows I would never be bested by an untrained civilian.

"If you're protecting her—"

"Amethyst might be the key to finding not just my father but all the children he's grooming to become assassins," I say. "And she's out there somewhere, frightened, alone, or maybe in the clutches of X-Cite Media. The last thing she needs is to be hunted by assassins."

Jynxson stares into his phone and frowns. "All evidence points to Amethyst killing Nocturne because he was connected to X-Cite Media and her mother because she's Dolly."

"It's looking that way," I mutter.

"Why would she take out our best lead to find Delta?"

I shift on the cot, my lips tightening. "You haven't met Melonie Greaves. She's aggravating. Amethyst might have finally snapped."

"And the EMP blast?" He shakes his head. "It doesn't add up."

He's right, but I refuse to believe Amethyst disabled all the electric systems just to murder her mother.

Jynxson scowls and is about to say something else when Tyler interrupts. "This is a long shot, but the same truck with a different registration entered Mannez Airport."

My head snaps up. "Is it still there?"

"It was towed three hours ago," he mutters. "It might be a coincidence or another criminal group, but I'm checking the airport's security feed."

With a nod, I turn my attention back to the video of Amethyst fighting off Reverend Thomas.

"Why, little ghost?" I whisper under my breath.

"Found her!" Tyler yells.

"Show me."

An alert pops up on my laptop, and I double-click a video containing footage from the private jet airport ramp. A white truck pulls in, and a blond man emerges from the front passenger side. Jynxson and I lean closer as Amethyst slips out, clad in a black leather corset and short skirt.

I grind my teeth. Since when did she have male friends?

My blood boils as she links arms with the blond and saunters toward the jet's steps as if she didn't just try to burn me alive before committing a string of murders. The driver's side door opens, letting out an athletic-looking dark-haired man, who walks to the back of the truck.

All my attention is on the man with Amethyst, who wraps an arm around her waist and pulls her in for a kiss as they approach the steps of the jet.

Then the footage skips to take off.

"Is it spliced?" I hiss.

"Very badly," Jynxson mutters.

"Let me see if any other cameras caught another angle," Tyler says.

I forward the clip to Tyler's assistant with a request to look up all flights from Mannez Airport, and she messages back with:

Xero. I was investigating the cause of the fire and checked the browser history of your office computer. I saw the first few seconds and scrubbed forward, wanting to find out who filmed you and Amethyst together, and I found something that might explain the cause of the fire.

A second later, she sends a link to a video of Amethyst running through the cemetery. Recognizing it as the clip her mother played the day she barreled into 13 Parisii Drive like a disgruntled banshee, I skip forward.

What happens after the cloaked figure chloroforms Amethyst sends me throwing the laptop across the room.

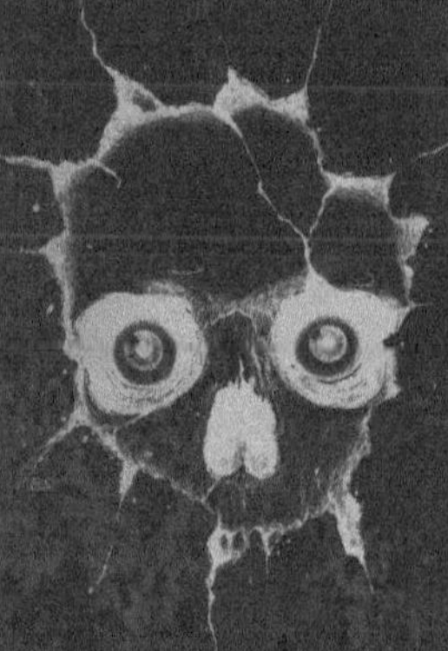

FIVE

AMETHYST

The bus advances toward the derelict hospital, over the uneven driveway, passing weeds taller than its windows. Every instinct beats against the cushiony haze of drugs to scream the same warning:

Do not enter that building.

I have no memory of ever having been there, yet the sight of its crumbling brick facade and tall, blackened windows awaken primal terrors that make my skin break out in a cold sweat. I duck beneath my seat, trying to sink through the floor, hoping it's a way to exit this dream.

Locke and Dolly laugh at my futile attempt to escape, but I'm too sickened with dread to care. If I allow these people to take me inside, it will be horrific.

The bus stops, its doors opening with a familiar pneumatic hiss. The straitjacket I'm encased in becomes too heavy, too tight, too scratchy. Its neckline constricts around my throat like a noose, making me choke.

"Fen," Dolly snaps. "Bring her outside."

I close my eyes, clench my jaw, quicken my breath and focus. Focus on breaking out of this nightmare or coma induced hallucination. Focus on working out how the hell I'm going to escape.

Two sets of footsteps retreat, only for a heavier set to

approach. I wriggle beneath the seat, pressing my head to the floor in a futile attempt to hide.

"Hey," Fen says, his voice tight. "Get out of there."

I'm going nowhere. They'll need to cut me out of this bus.

The large man paws at my body, trying to pry me out of my hiding spot, but I've already tucked my ankles close to my belly. If he wants me off the bus, he'll have to drag me out by my ass.

With a grunt, he lumbers around to the front, trying to approach me from another angle, but I've already scooted out of range.

"Come on, Amy. We can't stay here all night," he says, his calloused hand reaching for my arm.

I twist and turn, writhing across the floor in my straitjacket. He walks around to the seats behind where I've wriggled, trying to grab me by the straps around the back, but I've already scooted forward.

Nausea clogs my throat, and my heart pounds desperately against my rib cage, trying to escape. Each breath is a dry gasp that scrapes against my lungs like sandpaper. I can do this all night, stay in this decrepit bus until they tire of coaxing me out and leave.

Fen drops down to his hands and knees, placing his head on the bus's floor. "Amy," he says, his voice soft. "Don't anger her."

"Leave me alone," I rasp, the words muffled by the head harness.

"What's taking so long?" Dolly screeches from outside.

Another set of footsteps approach, followed by a low, masculine chuckle. "Having trouble?"

"Why don't you shut the fuck up and help?" Fen snarls.

Locke crouches down and clears his throat. "I'm going to give you two choices. One, you can crawl out like a good girl and meet our producer."

Gulping, I wait for him to continue, but I'm only met with silence.

"What's the second choice?" I whisper, the words coming out like a strangled whimper.

"Or I can dose you with enough ketamine to knock out an elephant," he says, his voice hardening. "Then you'll wake up hours later with all four holes aching and filled with half a dozen different varieties of cum."

Revulsion shudders through my insides, making me gag, and my mind dredges up the memory of seeing myself on video, being gang-raped in the graveyard.

"What's the fourth hole?" Fen asks.

"Stab wound, which is something you're about to get if you keep standing so close, you oaf," Locke replies, his voice cold.

My stomach plummets. These people are monsters, and I have no doubt they'll carry out their threats.

"I-I'll come out," I reply, my voice muffled.

Locke's self-congratulatory chuckle grates on my nerves, but I force my legs to uncurl, letting Fen drag me out by the ankle.

Outside, the air is so heavy with pollen that my skin itches. I hold my breath and squeeze my eyes shut, not wanting to complicate this nightmare with hay fever. A familiar sense of unease overwhelms my senses as Fen carries me through the asylum's open doors. The air is thick with the scent of damp, and a musty odor clings to my nostrils, making the fine hairs lining them tremble.

Ivy crawls across the hallway's vaulted ceilings, and moss blankets one side of its crumbling walls. We pass doors hanging off their hinges, revealing rooms littered with rusty equipment and overturned bed frames, giving the impression that the hospital was overrun by a riot.

Dolly and Locke stride ahead, filling the empty space with their excited chatter. They're discussing production plans, lighting arrangements, and the recruitment of extras for their shoot.

My breath shallows, and everything I remember learning about X-Cite Media rises to the surface like a slap. I'm about to end up tortured and raped and murdered for a snuff movie.

Despair washes through my insides like acid. I dip my head onto Fen's shoulder, unable to bear the thought of my impending death. His grip tightens around my middle, almost as if he's offering me his strength.

It's wishful thinking, and I'm projecting his non-existent

compassion. If Fen felt an ounce of empathy for my plight, he would have taken back the wheel and driven me to freedom.

At the end of the hallway, we pass another door that opens into a wing in much better condition. Dolly and Locke disappear into a set of double doors marked STUDIO.

Fen follows them, carrying me into a large hall with lightweight scaffolding around its perimeter and across the ceiling. Lighting equipment lines the room's edges, along with cables snaking across the wooden floor, leading to cameras mounted on tripods.

My brow furrows. I'm almost certain this used to be a dining room.

Locke walks to the left corner, where a black-haired man with a ponytail adjusts lighting fixtures under the direction of a muscular brunet in a leather jacket.

Dolly walks to the opposite corner, where an older man sits behind a desk with a fake office background. He leans forward, his eyes widening as he sees me in Fen's arms.

"Uncanny," he says, his cultured filled with awe. "Bring her here."

I shudder, my heart pounding so hard it's on the verge of rupturing. This has to be the producer.

Fen carries me toward the desk, his grip around my waist tightening. The man sitting behind it is stunning, with a strong build, ice-blue eyes, high cheekbones, and a regal nose. My gut twists as I recognize his face, even through the trim beard, tanned skin, and tawny brown hair. His features are a perfect blend of Camila and Xero.

This is Delta.

And Dolly is his wife.

Delta rises from his seat like a gentleman, revealing a three-piece tweed suit tailored to his athletic frame. "Amy Bishop," he says, his voice breathy. "I've been waiting to be reunited with you for years."

Bishop? Reunited? I glance at Dolly, making sure to avoid her eyes, to find her smirking with an unsettling mix of hunger and pride.

"Told you I'd find her," she says.

"Remove her clothes. Let me take a better look," Delta says with a warm smile.

My hackles rise, and my mind dredges up everything Xero told me about his father. He murdered Xero's adoptive mother, impregnated the housekeeper, made Xero endure years of bullying, only to prepare him for nearly a decade of training to be an assassin.

Fen sets me on my feet and places heavy hands on my shoulders so I can't run. Dolly reaches between our bodies to unfasten the buckles of my head harness, letting the fabric fall to the floor.

Delta steps forward and reaches out to cup my cheek. His hand is large and warm and soft, as though he's spent his entire adult life delegating all his dirty work. I shrink backward, recoiling from his touch.

His eyes narrow, and his smile fades into something more sinister. "Keep pulling faces like that and you'll age before your time."

Gulping, I drop my gaze to the floor.

"Turn on the cameras and take her over to the waterproof backdrop," he says.

Fen marches me to a corner where a green screen is set up on a stand, covering both the wall and a large portion of the floor. The three younger men move around, arranging cameras and softboxes, as if preparing for a movie scene.

A scream lodges in the back of my throat, and my breath comes in short, panicked gasps. This is it. The moment they gang-rape me and snuff out my life. I drag my heels, and struggle against Fen's grip, but he positions me atop the screen.

"Take off the straitjacket," Delta says.

Fen fumbles at the straps around the back of the restrictive garment, but Dolly strides forward.

"Don't touch her," she snaps, her voice laced with venom.

Fen's grip on my shoulders releases, and I stumble forward. Dolly grabs my arm, but her touch is like a jolt of electricity. I bolt toward the exit to a chorus of male laughter.

"You're so fucking useless," Dolly screeches. "Get her!"

Before I can even reach the door, strong arms encircle my waist and yank me off my feet. I kick and scream, my voice echoing around the cavernous room as Fen hauls me back to the green screen.

Panic tightens around my throat like a noose as the trio of younger men stare at me with mocking smiles. Delta scowls, his arms folded across his chest, his features etched with impatience. I can't bring myself to meet Dolly's eyes. If I look the monster in the mirror full in the face, something inside me will crack.

"Get undressed," Delta snaps. "Both of you. Locke, administer a mild sedative. Barrett, Seth, get the steel cables and suspend her from the rigging grid."

"No!" I scream.

The three men disappear in different directions. Delta works the ties on Dolly's corset. Fen's fingers dig into my shoulders as though conveying a silent message to stay calm or things might get worse.

"Please," I say, my vision going blurry with tears. "Don't."

Delta releases Dolly's corset, revealing a back criss-crossed with scars. Shock hits me in the gut and I hiss through my teeth.

She steps out of her skirt and bends over to unzip her boots. Cuts mar the backs of her legs, making me wonder if it was her who was in that car accident and not me.

Delta reaches into his jacket and pulls out a knife. "Dolly, get a ring gag. I don't want her ruining the shot while we carve identical patterns into her skin."

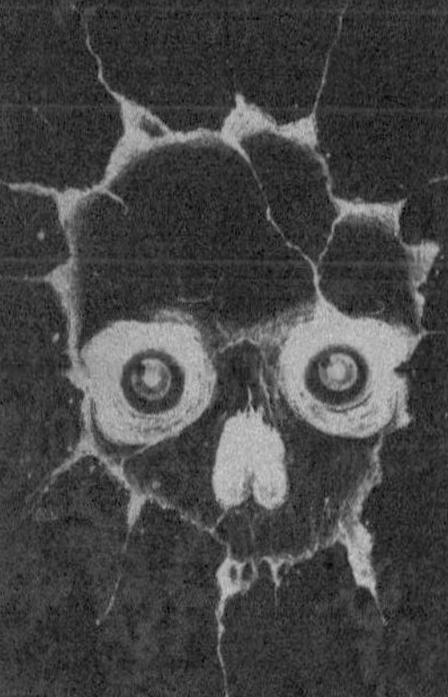

SIX

XERO

The laptop crashes against the wall along with the foul video, the pieces rebounding on Tyler's shoulder. I throw off my oxygen mask just as Jynxson rises from his seat.

"What are you doing?" He places a hand on my shoulder, trying to push me back on my bed, but I knock him into the wall.

Before I know it, the IV has slipped out of my arm, and I'm barreling toward the exit.

The man in that video wasn't me. I would never allow any man to touch Amethyst, let alone four. I would never release footage of the woman I love onto the internet.

Jynxson lands on my back, sending me sprawling onto the hallway floor. I roll us to the side, driving an elbow into his midsection before scrambling to my feet. Jynxson grabs my ankles like an asshole, yanking hard to stop me from leaving the infirmary. I kick back, aiming for his face. My foot connects, and he grunts, loosening his grip just enough for me to pull away and race down the corridor.

"What the hell happened?" Tyler catches up with me and grabs my arm.

"Isabel!" Jynxson roars.

My sister emerges from a door on the left, her eyes widening as she spots me trying to escape. Jynxson springs to his feet and wraps both arms around my torso.

Pivoting, I run the other way, dragging Tyler and Jynxson, not wanting to hurl Isabel into the wall.

"Dixon!" she yells.

Shit.

A door on the right opens. Dr. Dixon steps out with a tranq gun. He's one of the few men in our group taller and bulkier than me, and the only Moirai-trained doctor who defected. And he isn't afraid to overmedicate. If he hits me with that tranquilizer, there's no telling how long I'll spend here sedated and unable to explain myself to Amethyst.

I raise both hands in surrender. "Alright."

The doctor flicks his head back toward the hallway. "Return to your room, operative."

My jaw clenches. Dr. Dixon is our Chief Medical Officer. He outranks me across all our infirmaries, but being ordered around by him in my own organization is still irksome.

A needle slips into my arm. I turn around and lock gazes with Isabel, who scowls.

"I told you to stay in bed," she says, her voice laced with disapproval.

"What did you..."

My knees buckle, and the hallway spins as the sedative takes hold. I want to explain, but my tongue thickens and settles to the back of my throat.

Jynxson catches me around the waist before I fall, and he drags me back to my room. As darkness closes in, I try to make sense of who the hell would make a deep fake of Amethyst being violated in that graveyard.

The next time I wake up, I'm strapped to the cot in a mockery of my last day in prison, with thick bands around my shoulders, chest and waist. Moonlight streams through the vertical blinds, illuminating the infirmary room.

Instead of a hated half-brother in the bed next to me, Jynxson's head rests on my mattress. I knew he'd be here, watching over me. He's the brother I always wanted. The only man I'd trust with my life... Maybe even with my little sister.

"Hey," I rasp.

He raises his head and gazes up at me through bleary gray eyes. "What the hell is going on, Xero? And don't bullshit me this time."

My throat tightens, and I swallow. "Sometime this morning, Amethyst attacked me with a bottle of chloroform. By the time I woke up, she was gone, and the entire crawl space was on fire."

"So, she tried to kill you," he says.

"She had her reasons," I reply.

"You know what you sound like?"

"I don't give a fuck."

"A battered boyfriend."

I scoff.

He shakes his head. "And I know what triggered your rampage."

My nostrils flare. "Did you watch it?"

"I wouldn't invade your privacy like that. Camila told me. She thinks Amethyst is working with X-Cite Media."

Even though I still cling to the idea of a deep fake, betrayal still sinks its claws into my chest, filling my veins with cold venom. I can't stomach the possibility of Amethyst being connected with the likes of Father and his deadly pornographers.

"And what do you think?" I rasp.

Jynxson falls silent the way he always does when the answer is obvious. From his point of view, it looks like Amethyst's connection to Father goes deeper than the mere coincidence of her mother being his wife. Without that sprinkler system—the one neither I nor Amethyst knew existed—I would have been dispatched to hell in flames.

"I know Amethyst," I mutter. "She wouldn't sign up for anything so Machiavellian."

"But her alternate personality might," Jynxson replies.

"She doesn't have Dissociative Identity Disorder. I would have met her alters by now."

"Then she's a sleeper agent, programmed to act when triggered."

Something her uncle told me before we released him hits me like a truck. Shortly after he was imprisoned, Amethyst's mother visited him at the penitentiary, wanting information on her missing daughter. She thought Clive would know because he had a working relationship with Father through his failing membership site.

Meaning, she believed Father had Amethyst. Could Father have programmed Amethyst to kill me?

No. I refuse to accept that.

I huff a laugh, wanting to blow off the suggestion, but the sound is hollow. "This isn't science fiction."

"Your father performed experiments on us all. What's to say he didn't go deeper with the Lolitas? There's a reason the girls were taken away from us, and it wasn't because we found their crying off-putting."

My jaw clenches. Jynxson makes some excellent points, but the markers in Amethyst's history indicate that she grew up with her mother—at least after the age of ten. By eleven, she enrolled in Tourgis Academy with Myra Mancini. By thirteen, she pushed her music teacher off the roof garden, after which she went through the court system, where she was deemed not guilty by reason of insanity.

I have records of her time at the Greenbridge Academy for Behaviorally Challenged Girls, followed by her enrollment at Alderney State University. Tyler and his team found articles about the disappearance of Sparrow and Wilder Reed, who were last photographed gyrating against Amethyst at a party.

"Admit it," Jynxson says.

"Someone might have gotten to her while she was at the Greenbridge Academy. Something could have happened then. But if Father wanted me dead, he would have sent an assassin to Death Row."

"What if he wanted your secrets?" Jynxson asks. "You have a firm that rivals the Moirai. Connections among its existing support staff. The means for him to claw back everything that was taken when you made him fall from grace."

He makes several excellent points. Excellent, but wrong. I shake my head, not wanting to believe Amethyst would work with Father, even against her will.

"Come on. It's not that much of a stretch," he says. "Out of the hundreds of women sending you letters, how many of them came from your father or his agents? They could have split test over time, and refined their approaches until they honed the perfect candidate to slip past your defenses."

Heat courses through my veins, fanning the flames of my denial. I turn to him and scowl. If I wasn't strapped down like Hannibal Lecter, I would slam my fist into his face.

"Do you think I'd be so easily manipulated?"

"No, not easily. But how many years of data did he have on you? Field reports, observation, psych evaluations, medical records, surveillance footage. Amethyst's persona would have been irresistible. A civilian who made her first kill at the age of thirteen, imprisoned by heavy-handed parents, crying out for a hero to set her free."

"Did you read our letters?" I snap.

"It's my job to watch your back."

"I'm not on death row anymore," I snarl. "If you're so concerned about my welfare, then help me out of this bed."

He frowns. "What for?"

"Because your theory has more holes than a practice target at a firing range. You forgot the part where I saw Amethyst stabbing a man in self-defense, and the part where four assholes broke into her house and tried to rape her over the kitchen table."

He flinches, his face paling, but he shakes off the image. "Then how do you explain that video or the clip of her boarding a private jet?"

"I can't. But I know a man who might."

He frowns. "Who?"

"Reverend Thomas Dinsdale. Let me out and come with me to Simon's Memorial Hospital. We'll be gone for two hours."

Jynxson's eyes dart to the door. He rubs his jaw with the pad of his thumb. He's wondering if he really can sneak me out without alerting the medics. It's the same expression he used to make whenever I suggested sneaking out of bed to rob the pantry. He's tempted but doesn't want to anger Isabel or Camila.

"Amethyst doesn't want to be there," I say. "No matter what you think of her, she doesn't deserve to end up in the clutches of a man like my father."

His expression melts, and he sighs. "Fine, but if you don't return, I'll shoot your kneecaps and drag you back to face your sisters."

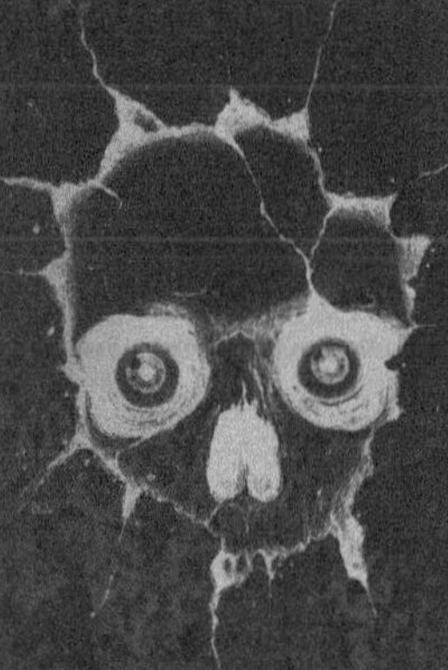

SEVEN

AMETHYST

Dolly's body is identical to mine, except for the scars. The deep ones Mom told me came from the car crash also run along her torso, but they're bisected by multiple smaller slashes.

They're the kind of marks I'd expect on a hardened warrior, not a woman of twenty-four, and I can't tell if they're self-inflicted or if someone has used her for target practice.

The topography of her skin is the least of my problems. After Locke stuck another needle into my neck, Dolly sent Fen away, leaving me slumped on the green screen floor.

Locke didn't even administer a sedative. A sedative would have rendered me unconscious or at least dulled the terror and humiliation of being stripped naked by my own doppelgänger.

Every touch made my skin crawl and my stomach churn to the point that I thought I'd choke on bile. She laid me bare for those men's eyes, exposed me to their lewd comments. I wanted to withdraw into the deepest recesses of my mind, blank out the horror of being on display, but the paralyzing drug wouldn't even allow me the dignity of closing my eyes.

What the hell do these people plan for me before I die? It's obvious I'm about to star in one of their snuff movies, but will it be as bad as Lizzie's ordeal? I think I would rather die now.

"Pull her up. I want her standing." Delta's voice cuts through my thoughts.

Dolly steps back, and the black-haired man named Seth draws forward. He's the second tallest of the younger men after Fen, with olive skin a shade deeper than Camila's. His eyes are so dark and penetrating that it's impossible to distinguish the pupil from their irises.

As he hauls me to my feet, the fourth man attaches handcuffs to each wrist. He has a mop of messy brown hair and cinnamon-colored eyes set within features sharper than a hawk. I think his name is Barrett.

With Locke's help, they attach cuffs to my wrists and clip them to steel cables, suspending me off the metal scaffolding running parallel to the ceiling. Throughout this, Delta and Dolly stare at me like I'm a prized lamb about to be skinned and slaughtered for their entertainment.

Once I'm standing in position with my arms stretched above my head, Locke injects me with something else to restore control of my muscles. My throat burns with fury, frustration, and fright. They didn't even allow me the dignity of fighting back.

"Dolly, raise your arms," Delta says.

She mirrors my pose, even mimicking my frantic breaths. I stare straight ahead, my jaw clenching, my heart pounding hard enough to rattle my bones.

Delta finally approaches, his large body looming over me like a specter of my painful demise. I inhale the mingled scents of sandalwood, peppermint, and sage, which scratch at a part of my brain that begs to stay untouched.

He reaches into his jacket pocket and pulls out something that resembles a craft knife with a tapered blade. With his free hand, he grabs my chin, forcing me to meet his cold, blue eyes.

My throat dries, and my body goes rigid. I can't move, can't breathe, can't do anything but stay locked in his malevolent gaze.

"Shall we begin?" he asks.

"No," I try to say, but the word is obscured by the gag.

He glances at Dolly, who turns her body to the left, exposing a long cut running from a few inches below her armpit to her hip.

"Stay still, Amy," Delta says, his fingers pressing into my flesh. "I want to avoid excess bloodshed."

Chills race across my skin and seep into my bones, but it's not enough to numb the sting of the craft knife piercing my flesh. I jerk away, every nerve ending screaming as the blade glides through my tissue like he's cutting through butter.

Warm blood trickles down my side, replacing the scent of Delta's cologne with copper. I want to grit my teeth, but the ring gag forces my jaw open. Instead, I breathe hard and fast, trying to process the pain.

"Good girl," Delta says, his deep voice curling around my senses like a serpent.

"Get the one on the underside of her tit," Barrett says, his words quickening with excitement.

"This one?" Dolly chuckles.

Out of the corner of my eye, I see her raising her left breast, drawing Locke to her side. He wraps an arm around her waist and nuzzles her neck, making her groan.

Delta glances over at them, the fingers holding my waist tightening. If I wasn't so preoccupied with my survival, I might wonder about the dynamics of Delta's relationship with Dolly. Despite being the leader, he allows other men to touch his wife. The micro expressions he tries to hide each time she cozies up with Locke tell me he finds the sight unsettling.

He grabs my breast, forcing a gasp from my lungs.

"Look at me, Amy," Delta growls.

I shut my eyes.

He leans in close, his breath hot against my cheek. "You'd be wise to obey the man in control of the depth of your cuts."

My eyes snap open, and I stare into his irises. They're nothing like Xero's. Xero's were pale blue with white striations, yet Delta's have faint starbursts of orange that remind me of flames.

"I know he survived the execution," he says, his voice low. "But did he survive your pyromania?"

Pain lances through my heart, burning brighter than the sensation of the craft knife slicing through my breast. I swallow back a sob, replacing sorrow with the metal taste of fear.

All this time Xero searched for his father, when the man was several steps ahead. How else would he know about the fire or that I would leave Parisii Drive in search of Mom?

"Do the cross on her back," Dolly says, making Delta draw away.

He turns me around, his touch gentle once again. Barrett and Seth stand at my sides, seeming more interested in watching me bleed than observing Locke and Dolly's exchange.

Delta's large hands land on my back, his fingers tracing the lines of an invisible X before positioning the blade on my skin.

I shiver as he makes the first precise cut, my body tensing under the shock of pain.

"Relax, Amy," Delta murmurs, his lips grazing my ear. "Your sister finds this pleasurable."

Anguish wraps around my chest like a constrictor, making each breath a battle against unseen restraints. My throat burns with the urge to scream, yet I can't form a word through the gag. I have no sister. Even if I did, she wouldn't be as malicious or as twisted as Dolly.

Barrett chuckles. "She's crying."

"Let me see," replies Seth.

I've never felt so powerless. Never felt so overwhelmed with confusion. Prickly heat builds behind my eyes, which threaten to well up with tears. My lungs work like bellows, trying to hold back the well of emotions, but I refuse to let them see me cry. I won't give these sick bastards the satisfaction of seeing me break.

The knife makes another slice across my back, and my mind goes numb. It's like a switch has been flipped, and now I'm watching everything unfold from a distance. Maybe it's finally registered that I'm in a dream. Maybe something inside me has cracked. But whatever it is, I'm no longer fully present in my own body.

My limbs feel heavy and distant, as if they belong to someone else. The pain should be overwhelming, but it's muted, like it's happening to an avatar. My surroundings fade into a blur, the voices and scents and unwelcome touches blending into a jumble of muted sensations.

Strangely, this new state of being is peaceful. It's like I'm floating above it all, observing the chaos below with a sense of detached curiosity. Right now, the world feels distant. For the first time since I stopped taking my meds, I feel a glimmer of peace.

As the cuts continue, I can even appreciate Delta's determination to match every major line on Dolly's skin. He works with the precision of an artist, making me wonder if he was responsible for Dolly's tapestry of scars.

It's surreal to become a human canvas. Even more surreal to not use any of Xero's methods to escape.

Dr. Saint would call this process dissociation. By the time I return to my senses, I'm lying alone on the backdrop and all the lights are off. I wait for the pain to register, but my body remains numb.

A huge man dressed in the white pants and matching shirt of an orderly kneels at my side and stares down at me through the dark. I can't see his face because it's obscured by a white mask.

As he lifts me off the floor, I suck in a sharp breath, expecting a flood of pain. Instead, there's an odd pressure against my skin, like I'm wrapped in compression bandages.

The man carries me through a dim, cold hallway. The echoes of clomping steps fill the air with black shockwaves, making me realize I'm still drugged.

Stopping at a metal door, he pushes it open to reveal a white room illuminated by spotlights. The floor and four walls are padded, save for the patch where a TV screen hangs close to the ceiling.

As the man drops me to the cushioned floor, the TV screen flickers to life.

It's the tail end of that video of Xero inviting men to defile my body in the graveyard. I'm lying unconscious and naked, covered in urine and semen, and surrounded by men.

"Cut," says a voice off camera.

On screen, I open my eyes and hold up my hand in a silent gesture for someone to help me up.

The camera pans up as one of the men pulls me to my feet and wraps his arms around my shoulders. As we part, he stares into the camera and smirks.

It's Locke, which must mean the woman is Dolly.

I stop breathing for the seconds it takes me to realize the truth about the video. It wasn't me being gang-raped. It was my doppelgänger.

And she was performing for the camera.

My heart lurches.

What the hell have I done?

I killed Xero by mistake.

The video plays over and over until realization sinks in, becoming as tangible as my mounting grief. I don't know how long I remain watching Dolly impersonate me with her men, but guilt mounts until it becomes a physical entity haunting the edge of my vision.

"Well, well, well," a familiar voice says from the corner of the room. "Look who's realized she stabbed the wrong guy in the back."

I turn my head toward the voice. It's Xero, and he looks pissed.

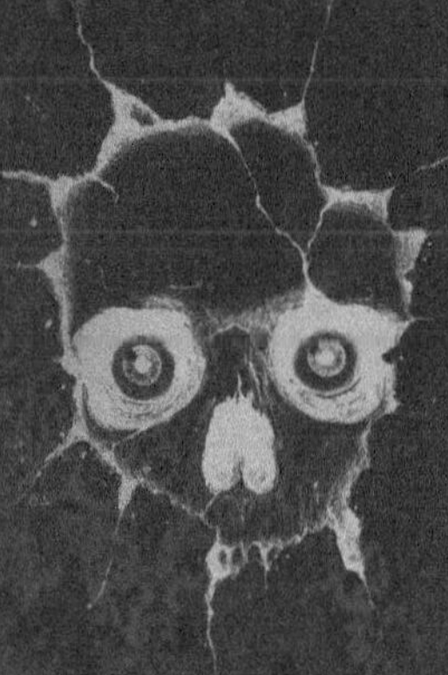

EIGHT

XERO

The burning in my lungs intensifies as I walk through the hospital's utility exit carrying my prey. Jynxson distracted the night nurse as I extracted Reverend Thomas from his bed.

I throw his unconscious body into the back of a van, where he lands with a thud. Bandages encase his neck and one side of his face where Amethyst knifed him in the eye.

The mystery behind her peculiar behavior unravels, making my jaw tighten. She thought it was me. That I was the one who orchestrated that nightmare. No wonder she snapped.

Rage sears through my chest, but beneath the fury is an instinct that burns brighter. I want to protect Amethyst, even now. I haven't told my people the full truth, because deep in my heart, I still believe she needs my help.

What I can't work out is when the hell it happened.

The video is a near replica of how I chased her through the cemetery and fucked her on my grave. After that, I only left her unattended to investigate X-Cite Media. It was never for more than a few hours, and I would have noticed bruises on her body if she'd been assaulted by multiple men.

Then there's the circumstances of our correspondence. No matter what Jynxson says, I still think she was a lonely woman reaching out to me for excitement after my mugshot went viral on social media. Even Father couldn't manufacture a connection as profound as the one I share with Amethyst.

A pained groan pulls me out of my musings, and I turn to where I left the priest sprawled across the van's interior.

I stamp on his chest, making sure to crack a few ribs. "Open your eyes."

He cries out. "Who's there?"

"What's your connection to Amethyst Crowley?" I crouch at his side.

"Who?" he wheezes.

"Wrong answer." I press my thumb into his bandaged eye, earning a shriek that gets absorbed by the truck's sound-proof walls. "Tell me exactly why you attacked Amethyst."

He groans, his breath coming in shallow gasps, the undamaged eye streaming with tears. "Please... I'll tell you. Just stop."

I ease off the pressure and take hold of his bandaged hand. In the videos my people retrieved from the vicarage, Amethyst stabbed a knife through his palm before she escaped.

The truck's driver-side door opens, and Jynxson steps in just in time to witness the priest's confession. He fires up the engine and pulls out of the parking space.

"I don't know her as Amethyst," Reverend Thomas says. "I only know her stage name was Little Doll or Dolly."

"What are you talking about?" I snarl.

"She's a porn star... Sort of." He grimaces.

"Meaning?"

"Dolly started out with X-Cite Media the same as all the others. A few hot sex scenes, followed by the finale."

Fury and disgust battle within my gut for dominance. He talks like the victims consented to being murdered and mutilated for his viewing pleasure. I clench my teeth and snarl, "By hot sex, you mean gang-rape, and finale means getting killed on camera?"

Reverend Thomas gulps. "Yes, but something went wrong. In the last scene, the man who was supposed to make the kill choked her out, but Dolly grabbed the knife and slit his throat."

"And you know this because...?"

"I was watching the live stream. Everyone went wild to see

her win. She scrambled off the bed, covered in his blood, and started slashing everyone who came close."

My throat tightens. "What happened next?"

"The screen went black. All of us at home were going wild, wanting more of her. No one had ever seen anything like it."

"When?" I rasp.

"I don't know... Ten years ago?"

"A child?" I snarl.

"Hey, I had nothing to do with it. I was just a viewer."

The last shreds of self-control snap. Vision narrowing, I punch him in the face, feeling the satisfying crunch of his nose breaking under my fist. His screams echo in my ears, intensifying my fury.

"Easy," Jynxson yells from the driver's seat. "We need him conscious."

I pull back my fist, my molars grinding. Jynxson is right. We still haven't gathered enough information. I glance over my shoulder to the windshield to find him already racing down the highway.

Turning back, I ask, "Then what happened?"

Reverend Thomas cowers, his body curling into a tight ball. I repeat my question with a sharp kick into his ribs.

"Weeks passed," he replies with a groan. "Everyone on the forums was asking what happened to that girl. Eventually, Delta said she was still alive and set up a poll on how we wanted her to die. By then, we were all calling her the little doll."

Reverend Thomas describes the next video on a gladiator set, where Dolly fought against three actors who took turns assaulting her in front of a crowd of men dressed as Romans.

Revulsion tightens my chest, aggravating my damaged lungs. I don't believe this Dolly is my Amethyst—I can't believe it—but every instinct screams at me to tear this man apart for contributing to the torture of an innocent girl. I hold back, my hands clenched into fists. He's too useful. I need to keep him alive. At least until I've found my little ghost.

My mind makes rapid calculations across everything I know about Amethyst's timeline. She joined the Greenbridge Academy for Behaviorally Challenged Girls ten years ago, just before turning fourteen.

Given that Melonie Crowley kept Amethyst at arm's length, anything could have happened to her during that time. It's not unusual for criminal enterprises like the Moirai to haunt boarding schools, looking to recruit children estranged from their parents.

"She killed the gladiator guy, and maimed the others," the reverend says. "And stabbed the next one in a dystopian-themed movie. After that, Delta must have decided to keep her alive because they stopped trying to kill her."

"What the hell does that mean?" I ask.

"She got cut, but that was it."

A sickening wave of heat rolls through my gut. He's talking about Dolly, but every instinct tells me he's describing my Amethyst. All of it—the mutilations, the fights, the blood. They did that to her. A girl who was barely more than a child. My chest tightens until I can't breathe.

Oh, my darling girl... what did they do to you?

Sorrow hits like a knife to the heart, sharp and devastating. I can see her now, young, covered in blood, fighting for her life. How could she even survive? How could anyone? And then—just as fast—the sorrow gives way to rage. Hot and pulsing and so blinding I could burn the world to ease her pain.

They did this to her, and I wasn't there to stop it. Every fiber in my being screams for vengeance. For her.

My brow pinches as I force down the emotion, trying to hold on to reason. Amethyst wrote about having to stay in school during most vacations, but she never mentioned any traumatic experiences outside that music teacher.

"Fuck," Jynxson says.

"When did she stop appearing in these videos?" I ask, my voice brimming with rage.

He coughs. "I don't know... Three or four years ago? They say she became a director."

I shake my head, not believing a single word, even though the priest shows no sign of deception. But could there be another side to Amethyst—someone hidden, like Jynxson suggested? Is there a part of her I haven't seen?

"Why can't we find her videos advertised on the site?" I ask.

"Old content gets pulled, so new members don't get to join for a month, stream the entire archive and leave," he replies. "But if you want to see them, I made screen recordings on my phone. They're in my study at the vicarage."

"Jynxson?" I ask.

He makes a right. "Already on my way."

"Why did you attack her on camera?" I ask.

"It wasn't like that. I didn't target her. I thought she'd retired, so I wanted to give her privacy."

"Answer the fucking question," I growl.

"They were calling for auditions for the next movie. When she appeared in the vicarage, I thought she'd come to check my worth."

I slam another fist into his face. This time, Jynxson doesn't object. Over the drive across town, Father Thomas reveals that X-Cite Media is a private members' club that offers subscriptions for thousands of dollars a month.

Members access months of content that's streamed to the public for nearly a hundred dollars an hour. Piracy is expressly forbidden, and Lizzie Bath's use of my execution video—which she'd screen-recorded to use as a background on her video—was what led to her abduction. Her fate was a public punishment for daring to pirate X-Cite Media content.

I shake my head, my fists trembling with the force of my rage. Rage at the members for buying into such wanton depravity. Rage at Delta for a catalog of atrocities that would take a lifetime to list. Rage at myself for wasting time punishing Amethyst, when I should have been keeping her safe.

But under that rage, there's something worse—sorrow. My chest tightens at the thought of her as a broken girl, the things they made her endure.

If what the reverend says is true, then Amethyst must have escaped Delta and returned to her mother, only to spend the next few years in a drug-induced haze. Perhaps Dr. Saint suppressed those traumatic memories with medication and even more rounds of electroconvulsive therapy.

But that doesn't explain the lack of scars. The thick ones

across her belly are consistent with a car accident… or a single attack.

Amethyst exposed herself across social media with my fan club, not realizing Delta wanted her back. Father must have arranged that disgusting gang-rape to trigger her into a murderous rage.

It partially explains why she murdered her mother and uncle. But I don't understand the scene at the airport. Was Amethyst deciding to rejoin the devil she knew?

Reverend Thomas wheezes. "Please… I've told you everything I know. Just take me back to the hospital."

"We didn't find a membership link on the site," I say.

"That's because it's invite-only. Anyone who rents enough videos gets vetted before getting a chance to join the inner circle."

My throat clenches. Thank fuck I kept the recruiter alive. I make a mental note to have Harlan Still re-interrogated.

"You're still a member, right?" I ask.

"That's right," he replies.

"And you said auditions were running for the next video?"

He nods.

"Then you're going to send a message to Delta and tell him you want to be his next star."

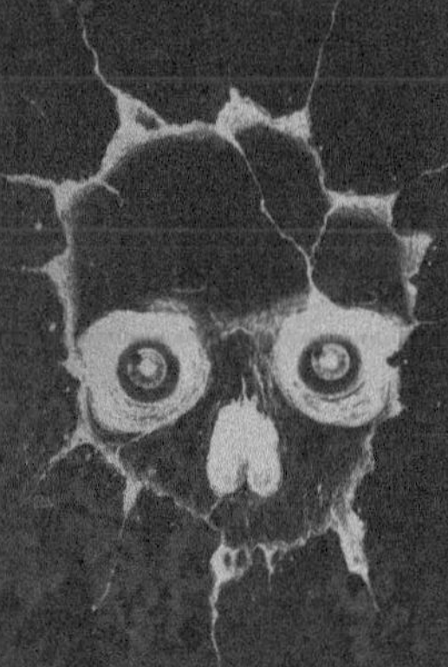

NINE

AMETHYST

I roll onto my back, my eyes widening at the sight of Xero. He wears the tuxedo from last night at the Ministry of Mayhem, or was that the night before? I have no idea how long the drug at the airport rendered me unconscious. They could have trafficked me as far as Australia.

"Xero?" I whisper. "What are you doing here?"

He leans against the padded wall, tall, and strong, and alive. "Why don't you tell me, little ghost?"

I bite down on my bottom lip, but it's numb. I'm not even sure how I'm moving my mouth. "You're dead."

He nods. "Keep going."

"And you're haunting me for revenge?"

"Is that what you think?"

My throat tightens. There's no such thing as ghosts. "You're a hallucination. Just like Mr. Lawson and the others."

His brow rises. "Which others?"

"Sparrow and Wilder?"

"Anybody else?"

"I don't know if I hallucinated Jake. You were always trolling me with his corpse."

He grins, his eyes sparkling.

"Why would you even do something like that?"

"Amethyst."

I flinch. He hardly ever addresses me by name. At least not since escaping death row. "Yes?"

"You're in the worst trouble of your life."

I nod, my breath quickening.

"Do you understand what's happening?"

I stiffen. "Um... Yes? No? I don't know."

Xero crosses the room and crouches in front of where I'm lying. His pale eyes bore into mine with the same level of intensity as the times he disguised himself as a wraith. I swallow hard, my pulse quickening.

"This isn't a dream. Dolly isn't a monster or a doppelgänger, but an identical twin."

"I don't have a—"

"Listen to me," he snarls. "You have a twin."

"How?"

He taps the side of his head. "You'll have to work that out for yourself. Dolly knows you. She thinks you stole from her, and she's brought you here to die. Just like Lizzie Bath."

"And you're here to help me escape?" I whisper.

His eyes soften, and the look he gives me is so pitying that I squirm within my straitjacket and bandages.

"I'm dead, remember? You broke a bottle of somnochloride over my head and set the crawlspace on fire."

A sob catches in my throat, and my eyes sting with tears. "Xero, I'm so sorry. I thought—"

"Save your apologies for later. You need to focus on escaping."

I give him a shaky nod. "Do you know where we are?"

"Anywhere within the United States. Based on the amount of time you were on the plane, we could even have made it to Canada."

"Okay."

"The surroundings are familiar. This is certainly where they took the polaroids. Are you getting stronger feelings of déjà vu?" he asks.

My breath shallows. "I think so."

"Listen, Amethyst. The time for hiding behind excuses is

gone. You're about to face unimaginable torture and pain, but you might have a chance of escaping this ordeal with your life."

I scoot forward, my heart pounding so hard that every inch of my body throbs. "What do you mean?"

The door opens, and the large man in white from earlier steps into the room. I want to shrink away from his touch, but my body still feels numb. He lowers a double dog bowl on the floor, with one side containing water and the other some form of mush.

Even though his face is partially obscured by a white surgical mask, I still recognize his gray eyes.

"Fen?" I whisper.

He pauses, his gaze meeting mine. "It's Grunt," he replies, his voice muffled. "Eat."

Straightening, Grunt turns on his heel and exits the room. I stare at his broad back, wondering if Dolly relegated Fen to being my caretaker. Xero and I remain silent as his footsteps disappear down the hallway.

"Don't trust him," Xero says.

I nod. Everyone who associates themselves with the likes of Dolly and Delta is automatically deemed as evil.

"Xero, why can't I move properly?"

His face tightens. "You don't remember?"

"Remember what?"

"Kicking Delta in the balls," Xero replies with a chuckle. "Locke had to administer a neuromuscular-blocking agent to stop you from tearing down the rigging."

"You saw me do that?" I ask.

"What does Dr. Saint say about the brain's ability to absorb information?"

"As long as our senses are still working, we take in more sensory data than our brains know how to process," I reply.

Xero nods. "You're more capable and intelligent than you give yourself credit for. I'll help you process everything around you that you can't handle."

"Thanks," I rasp, my chest tightening with gratitude, and also regret, knowing I don't deserve kindness from the ghost of the man I betrayed. "What do you think is happening with Grunt?"

His face tightens. "There are only five men in this abandoned asylum: Delta, Locke, Barrett, Seth, and Fen, who was sent away after they strung you up. They want you to believe that Fen has either fallen out of favor with Dolly or has become the group's scapegoat."

"So, it's a trick?" I whisper.

"This is the same group of people who sent photos of you as a child with threatening letters. They also created that graveyard scene to fuck with your mind. Grunt is a persona designed to be your caretaker or even a confidant."

"Why do you think it was me in that photo and not Dolly? She has the same major scars as me."

"Which of you has no memory of the other?" Xero pauses, his pale eyes boring into mine, challenging me to engage my brain. "Which of you holds an unreasonable amount of resentment towards the other, and which of you has a brick wall around their childhood memories?"

I shift uncomfortably on the padded floor. "It's obvious when you put it like that."

The screen mounted on the wall still plays, this time with body cam footage from the point of view of someone walking through Mom's driveway. The sound of multiple footsteps echoes through the speakers, accompanied by excited breaths.

Based on the dim sunlight, I can tell it's morning. The point of view character walks around the hedge maze, lifts one of the stones at the foot of its shrubs, and picks up a key. The hand is identical to mine, save for a scar running from the wrist to the space between the thumb and forefinger.

My heart sinks into my stomach as she continues toward the back door, unlocks it, and strides through the mud room, into the kitchen, pausing at the counter to extract a knife from the block.

"I can't watch Dolly kill Mom," I whisper, my eyes squeezing shut.

"What the hell did I tell you about hiding behind excuses?" Xero growls. "Open your fucking eyes so I can see what's happening."

Unease churns through my gut, and I force my gaze back to the screen, where Dolly walks across the flagstone steps, through the house's wood-paneled hallways, and up the stairs.

"Mom had her faults, but she didn't deserve to be murdered by her own daughter," I murmur.

Xero grunts, considerate enough not to mention that I drove to Alderney Hill to do the same, but my hypocrisy hangs over my head like a cloud.

I fall silent as Dolly reaches the upstairs landing and heads straight to Mom's room. The morning sun drenches the space with light, illuminating the mahogany four-poster bed and its rumpled sheets. Scoffing, she turns toward the fireplace, continues toward the ensuite, and knocks on the door.

The sound of running water stops. "Clive?" Mom's voice drifts through the closed door, sounding completely at ease. "Is that you?"

"Mom?" Dolly says, her voice broken.

Mom sighs. "Amethyst Crowley. What the hell did I tell you about turning up at my house?"

"I don't remember."

"Yes, you do." Mom flings the door open. She's wearing a cream silk dressing gown, with her hair hanging loose at her shoulders. Her eyes are hard, but there's no trace of fear.

"Because she thinks that's you," Xero adds, seeming to be in tune with my thoughts.

Before I can remind myself that he's a figment of my imagination, Dolly raises the knife.

Mom's eyes widen. "What's this?"

"I've thought about how our conversation would go if we ever met again," Dolly says. "How could someone be naïve enough to believe the word of one child while condemning another to a painful death?"

"What are you talking about, Amethyst?"

"Amethyst," Dolly says, her voice hardening. "Guess again."

Mom pauses for a beat before her eyes widen and her face turns slack. "It's you."

"It's you," Dolly mimics.

"Dahlia?" Mom's whisper rises an octave.

"Is that all you have to say after fourteen years?"

For the next several heartbeats, Mom's gaze darts to a point beyond the camera, as if she's calculating her method of escape.

I've never seen her look so unsettled. She was always distant with me, but her expressions were always tinged with impatience and irritation. Never terror.

If Mom treated me like a dog making messes, she looks at Dolly like she's a wolf.

"How did you find me?" Mom asks.

"When your golden child went viral on social media with her Xero Greaves fan club, she left several clues, including a New Alderney mailing address."

Mom's face twists with a mix of fury and disgust. "Amethyst."

"Say her real name," Dolly says through clenched teeth.

"You have to understand that we looked for you," Mom says, her voice rough. "By the time I realized the truth, you'd disappeared. It was like you'd never existed."

"None of this would have happened if you hadn't thrown me away like trash," Dolly says.

"Dolly... Dahlia." Mom's voice breaks. "I'm so, so sorry."

"What's this?" Dolly asks with a harsh laugh. "The slow realization that you sent away the wrong killer?"

"Please—"

"I'll count to ten. If you can escape me, then I'll put aside the knife and listen to your side of the story, but if I catch you, I will cut out your vocal cords."

"Dahli—"

"One."

Mom's eyes widen, and she bolts out of screen, her heavy footsteps disappearing. Chuckling, Dolly pivots, and the camera pans to the bedroom door.

"Two."

My gaze darts to Xero, who turns from the screen to shoot me an annoyed scowl. It finally registers that he can't see what's happening if I'm too busy looking at the patch of empty space my brain imagines he inhabits.

"Sorry," I mutter, and force myself to watch.

Dolly jogs back through the house, her breath quickening, seeming so excited by the hunt that she's forgotten to finish counting. When she reaches the kitchen, Uncle Clive is entering through the mud room, clad in a white shirt and cummerbund.

"Amethyst?" he says.

"Don't call me that!"

The man's eyes widen. "Amaryllis?"

"Wrong answer!" She hurls the knife across the room, lodging it in his gut.

Eyes bulging, he stumbles back through the mud room and out into the garden. "Dahlia."

Dolly strides across the kitchen, snatching up another knife from the counter before reaching the mud room. As she steps outside into the garden, Uncle Clive staggers backward, only to trip head over heels into the hedge maze.

A scream has Dolly turning away from my fallen uncle and toward the side of the house. At the second scream, she breaks into another jog, her feet crunching over the gravel path.

If I wasn't so numb with drugs, the fine hairs on the back of my neck would rise. "What the hell happened in our past to make Dolly so murderous?"

"Same reason why you went there this morning to kill Melonie," Xero mutters.

"I thought Mom was Dolly."

"How the hell do you think a girl your age ended up marrying a man like my father?" he replies.

Xero is right. From the way Dolly speaks, she makes it sound like Mom handed her over to Delta. And nobody gets that amount of knife wounds without suffering something heinous.

Back on screen, Dolly rounds the corner to find Mom wriggling within the grip of Locke and Fen dressed as guards.

"What should we do with the MILF?" Fen asks with a grin, his fingers in Mom's mouth.

Dolly stops moving. "You want to fuck my mom?"

Fen's features fall. "No, it's just a figure of speech—

"Don't gaslight me with mansplaining," Dolly snarls. "You distinctly called her a Mom I'd Like to Fuck."

"I didn't—"

"Fuck, Fen. Dolly is a goddess, not some bitch you can disrespect," Locke says. "Apologize to her and stop wasting precious time. One of our members just live streamed his altercation with Amethyst Crowley."

"He'd better not hurt her," Dolly says.

"She defeated him and escaped."

"Good. Let's get moving."

My stomach churns. I don't want to watch, but I also don't want to miss any vital clues. Dolly trails after the men as they drag Mom back around the house and back into the kitchen.

"I wish there was more time to carve you into strips," she says, "But Amy keeps messing up my schedules. Men always disappear when I send them to her house, and now she's found herself a protector."

The two men release Mom's arms, just as Dolly reaches out and slashes the knife across her neck. A red line of blood appears on her skin, and Mom clutches her throat before crumpling down to the floor.

"Leave," Dolly says and crouches to get Mom in the shot.

Blood roars through my ears, muffling what Dolly says next. My vision blurs as I try to focus on the screen.

"Blink, little ghost," Xero says, his voice soft.

I obey, loosening two fat tears that roll down my cheeks. When I open them, Dolly's hand is grabbing Mom's chin.

"Thank me, Mother, because I showed you mercy. You were just a stupid bitch who believed the word of a sniveling psychopath. Amy won't be so lucky. I plan on keeping her alive long enough to know what it feels like to be me."

My stomach plummets, and my mind fills with memories of Lizzie Bath's snuff movie.

I can't let her punish me for something I don't even remember.

TEN

XERO

Jynxson and I stand over Reverend Thomas, recording the steps he takes to access X-Cite Media's membership forum. It's on a separate URL from the pay-per-view site and has multiple levels of security.

I grip the back of his seat, resisting the urge to gouge out his remaining eye. We're in a quaint little study within the new vicarage, overlooking the courtyard it shares with St. Anne's Church.

The clergy paid for this sick bastard's little office space with solid wood floors, lace curtains, and a cushioned office chair, so he could jerk off watching the rape and murder of innocent women and children.

I would have taken the username and passwords from this asshole already, but the system has a record of the IP address, device, and browser the member used during registration. Access is denied if a single one of these variables changes.

It's been thirteen hours since Amethyst left, thinking I'd subjected her to the worst possible betrayal. I didn't understand when she asked me if I'd ever rendered her unconscious with chloroform. It was a fantasy we'd discussed on the phone, by letter, and agreed to in our sex contract.

If I had known there was a video floating about where a man

impersonating me invited others to violate her body, I would have helped her track them down and handed her the knife she'd use to slice off their balls.

"There," the reverend says, his voice breaking me out of my thoughts. "This is the main forum, where we chat with other members. Do you want me to show you the videos?"

"Is Amethyst..." I shake my head, not allowing myself to believe they're the same person. Not until I have concrete proof. "Is Dolly in any of them?"

"No."

"Then show me the thread where they're discussing the next production."

Reverend Thomas navigates a labyrinth of members-only threads, each title more disturbing than the last. I grind my teeth, seething at the glimpses of depravity lurking among the members. I want a list of their names, addresses, careers—every piece of information I can use to expose these monsters to the world.

There's a difference between me and these men. I don't gain sexual gratification from the suffering of women, unless they're Amethyst and I'm making her orgasm.

"Project March Lily," he says, and clicks on the thread. "This is where they were asking for auditions."

"What does March Lily mean?" Jynxson asks.

"It's usually a nickname for the victims," the reverend explains, his voice trembling. "The last one was Jersey Lily, who was really Joanna Mazek."

It takes a second to register that as Lizzie Bath's real name.

Jynxson snatches the mouse and scrolls down the screen to a post where one of the members asks about auditioning. Underneath, Delta responds that he'll select from a pool of candidates who have uploaded their auditions to the video page.

"What's required for these auditions?" I snarl.

Reverend Thomas shivers. "Anything, really," he replies, his voice choked. He clears his throat, then adds, "As long as it's in line with the members' tastes."

I grab the back of his neck, making him flinch. "Elaborate."

"It can be violent... She can be unconscious... Underage—"

"Enough," I snap, already regretting having asked. "How about murder?"

"That will earn you a speaking part," he replies. "And the chance to fuck the actress."

I punch him in the back of the head, the impact crashing his face into the monitor. "Victims, not actresses."

"Any other ways to get a front row seat at the shoot?" Jynxson asks through clenched teeth, sounding already impatient that I'm breaking all the rules to terrorize a willing subject.

Reverend Thomas slumps back in his seat and groans. "Some members have too much to lose and don't want to risk filming themselves doing anything illegal. Others don't have the guts. Anyone willing to pay two hundred and fifty thousand to help fund the production can watch from the sidelines."

My heart skips, and my breath hitches. Jynxson and I exchange glances. We can take advantage of this opening.

"Is that all you get for that money?" I ask, my voice quickening.

"There's usually some kind of drinks reception before the shoot, followed by an afterparty."

"Are plus ones allowed?" Jynxson asks.

"No."

The corner of my mouth lifts. A lack of invitation doesn't matter. This won't be the first time we've forced our way into a clandestine operation. All we need is the date, time, and location.

"Tell Delta you want to invest," I say, my breath coming out a painful rasp.

The reverend whimpers. "But I don't have that kind of money."

"We'll make sure it's in your account." Jynxson gives him a playful shove. "Now, write a request in your own words."

He wipes a trembling hand over the parts of his face not concealed by bandages and starts typing.

"If you use any hidden messages or codes to even suggest you're being coerced, I'll remove more than just your good eye," I snarl.

"How will you tell?" he whispers.

"You don't want to find out," I wheeze.

Jynxson and I close in around him as he taps out a message to Delta. Sweat slides down his face, splattering onto the keyboard. I grip the back of his neck, putting on the pressure until I'm satisfied with the wording, and he clicks send.

"What now?" he asks, his voice still trembling.

I ease my grip, feeling my own body starting to weaken. "Now, we wait."

"Time for you to return to your hospital bed," Jynxson says.

"Oh, thank God." The reverend slumps forward with a sigh.

Jynxson slaps him upside the head. "Not you, padre."

I grind my teeth. We finally have a concrete lead, and Jynxson wants me to return to the infirmary. I know better than to bicker with an ally in front of a hostage, but his devotion to following my sister's instructions grates on my nerves.

"Let's take him down to a holding cell first," I say through clenched teeth.

"Wait," Thomas says. "I did everything you asked. You have no reason to keep me here any longer, and I'm still injured. Please, let me return to the hospital."

I haul him to his feet, the effort making me gasp for air. "That wasn't part of the arrangement."

The smaller man looks to Jynxson for a trace of mercy, but all he finds is cold indifference.

"But I've served my purpose," he cries. "Somebody, help—"

A fist to the back of his skull cuts him off, and he slumps onto the floor.

"What's the plan?" Jynxson asks. "Impersonate him online until we get the address of the shoot?"

"I want to keep him alive until we know for sure he's given us everything," I rasp, forcing back the sensation of flames burning my respiratory system to ash. "A man like Delta won't be so easy to track."

Jynxson grunts. "He might make a good Trojan horse for the drinks mixer."

"Or an explosive one."

He snickers.

We remain in place until someone from Tyler's team comes

in to take control of the computer, and another operative drags the reverend to a holding cell in the catacombs.

By the time we're done, my lungs are screaming, each breath a painful rasp. Tight bands of defeat close in around my chest, forcing me to sway on my feet.

I don't put up a fight when Jynxson bundles me into the back of the van. This side-quest may have set back my recovery, but Reverend Pervert gave me a better understanding—however horrifying—of my girl and why she did what she did. And now I finally have a lead on finding my way back to my Amethyst.

ELEVEN

AMETHYST

I stare up at the screen, where there's now a slow-motion replay of Mom's death. My chest burns, and the pulse between my ears pounds to the beat of my broken heart.

If Dolly hadn't gotten to Mom first, I would be the one slashing her throat. Dolly manipulated me into thinking Mom was behind the attacks and those threatening notes. Dolly made me think Xero arranged for me to be gang-raped, just so I would turn on my protector, eliminate the one person who cared for me, and run into her trap.

"What are you going to do now, little ghost?" Xero asks.

I swallow hard, my head dipping toward my shoulders to wipe away the tears. "Xero, I'm so sorry. If I'd known—"

"Don't apologize to a figment of your imagination," he snaps.

"Right." I gulp. "Sorry." I cringe at the words.

He snaps his fingers, bringing my attention back to his pale eyes. "Amethyst. This isn't the time to zone out. You can't keep thinking you're stuck in a nightmare. You're alone, surrounded by enemies. You need to stay alert."

"Right," I say, my voice breathy, my mind still whirring with these revelations. "So, that photo of me with the electrodes... Is that her?"

His eyes soften, and the pity in his expression makes my

throat tighten. Maybe it's because I'm asking questions where the answer is already obvious. Breathing hard, I force myself to stay calm, but my eyes still burn with fresh tears.

"It's good that you're acknowledging she's real, but you need to open your eyes to think about what I told you earlier?"

Nodding, I remember Xero's assessment of my blank memories. They're consistent with suffering from medical abuse. My insides roil as I think back to the intensity of Dolly's resentment. She remembers everything, while I hadn't even known I had a sister. "That was me."

He nods.

"So, I must have been at an institution like this when I was young, while Dolly got sent somewhere worse?"

"That's how it seems," Xero replies.

"Why would my mom do something so cruel?"

"Dolly hinted at the reasons when she called you a sniveling psychopath."

"Mom believed me over her," I whisper. "But she hasn't explained what even happened. Now she's going to make me die slowly for something I don't even remember."

"I'll protect you," Xero says.

Dipping my head, I force myself not to say the obvious in case he disappears. Figments of the imagination can't break through locks. Nor can they fight off attackers. I'm trapped, all alone, and far away from home. The only person strong enough to break me out of this asylum is dead.

Because I killed him.

"I know what you're thinking, but I can protect your mind," he says.

"How?"

"Because, no matter what they do or say to you, no matter how they break your spirit, I'll be here to piece you back together. Even when you don't believe in yourself, you'll believe in me."

I shudder, the truth of that settling deep into my soul. Despite my bone-deep terror, despite everything that's happened between Xero and me, his spirit is keeping me grounded. Even if he's no more than a trick of my damaged mind.

"Okay," I whisper, breathing hard to stave off the waves of guilt and grief and overwhelming dread.

He settles beside me on the cushioned floor and wraps an arm around my shoulders, pulling me into his strong chest.

"You feel so real," I murmur.

"Locke injected you with ketamine and DMT," he says. "Now, you really are having a compound hallucination."

All those times I thought my hallucinations were a mix of visual, auditory, tactile, and olfactory, it was Xero terrorizing me from the shadows. And I was so angry with him. I'd give anything for that to be true now.

"What's DMT?" I ask.

"Sorry, little ghost," he replies with a soft chuckle. "My knowledge is limited to what you know. You heard him say DMT, but you don't know what it means, so I also don't know."

"Did he at least explain why?"

"Dolly asked him to dose you with something to give you a bad trip."

Footsteps echo outside the room, growing louder as they reach the door. Freezing, I grip Xero's arm. He tightens his hold around my waist.

"Whatever happens, remember that I'm here," he says.

"What do I do?"

"Keep your eyes open, focus on survival, and don't let them know you have me."

The door creaks open, and the huge orderly from before steps inside. My gaze darts into the darkened hallway, and I calculate my odds of escaping.

"Don't do it," Xero says, his voice low.

"You haven't eaten," the man says.

I glance at the dog bowl across the floor, and my stomach roils at the prospect of consuming that gray, unidentifiable mush.

"It's nausea," I say, feigning a gag. "My stomach won't stop heaving."

He crouches down at my side, his gray eyes unable to meet mine. "Dolly will be displeased."

"I'll eat it later, when my insides have settled."

The man's gaze finally locks with mine, his eyes flickering

with understanding. Beneath the mask obscuring the lower half of his face is the same strong jaw as Fen's.

That comment he made about Mom being a MILF rushes back, as does Dolly's disgusted reaction. At least that explains why she's treated him like a scapegoat the entire day. If Fen has lost Dolly's favor, then maybe I can take advantage.

"Don't do it," Xero murmurs.

"I don't want to throw up all over this nice floor, knowing you'll have to clean up the mess," I say, trying to sound contrite.

Fen's gaze flickers between me and the bowl before he exhales a long sigh. Nodding, he rises and lumbers out of the room, pulling the doors shut.

"I don't like this plan," Xero says.

Fen's footsteps fade down the hallway, but I wait for them to disappear before muttering under my breath, "Can you think of anything better?"

"Not until we gather more information," he replies.

I nod. "Then this guy is our only shot."

"Close your eyes and get some rest. You're going to need all your strength tomorrow morning."

The screen has stopped replaying footage of Mom's death, leaving only a slideshow of the images like those I found on Xero's crime board. When I glance up to find a picture of a ten-year-old version of me sitting in an ice bath, I drop my gaze to my lap and shudder.

His large hand brushes through my curls. "Go on. I'll keep watch."

"How?"

"Don't worry about it. I'll wake you up if anyone approaches."

Reluctantly, I lie on my side, curl up into a ball, and close my eyes, even if it's to lose myself in the inky blackness of my mind. Anything is better than facing reality.

Xero's larger body spoons around mine, warming my back through the straitjacket. His steady breath tickles the nape of my neck, the rise and fall of his chest a comforting rhythm against my spine.

It almost reminds me of that peaceful lull we had when he

was stalking me from the crawlspace and used to climb into bed with me as I slept.

During the day, I would write, and at night, I'd sleep in the arms of what I thought was his ghost. It wasn't so bad, especially since he'd started to allow me to come. But then everything turned to shit the moment Dolly's men broke in through the front door and shattered the illusion.

I drift into a light sleep, my consciousness lingering close to the surface, ready to snap awake if Xero calls my name. His arms tighten around my waist, reminding me of his presence.

Hours later, as I'm slipping into a deeper slumber, Xero says, "Wake up."

The click-clack of heels echoes through the hallway, accompanied by heavier footsteps. Adrenaline surges through my veins, and my heart slams against its cage. Eyes flying open, I scramble to my feet.

Xero rises, pressing a finger to his lips, his pale eyes burning with hatred.

I nod.

The door creaks open, and Dolly steps inside with Locke. She's dressed in a lace camisole and silk shorts, with a sleep mask pushed against her hairline. Her curls are piled on top of her head. Despite the disdain twisting her expression, she appears well-rested and radiant.

The part of me that recoils at mirrors shrinks in her presence. No amount of drugs or electric shock therapy could erase the primal fear I have of Dolly. She might call me a psychopath, but my psyche screams that she's evil.

Seeing her again is even more harrowing than the gruesome slideshow playing on the screen. Subconsciously, I always knew she existed. I thought of her as the creature that lurked behind every reflective surface, biding her time until she was ready to strike.

I glance at the space where Xero was standing, only to find it empty.

"Still refusing food?" Dolly points a taser toward the untouched dog bowl, her lips twisting with distaste.

"What do you want from me?" I ask. "Why am I even here?"

"Don't you remember anything?" She cocks her head to the side.

"No."

"You have three days to regain your memory before the extras arrive for the gang bangs. After that, it won't matter what you remember."

The words hit like a punch to the chest, my heart stuttering. Blood drains from my face, replaced by ice water. I expected only Delta and four others. The thought of more strangers arriving sends the room spinning.

"Would you like me to administer something to help her suppressed memories resurface?" Locke asks.

He's wearing a white coat atop a navy, three-piece suit, with his golden curls styled into subtle waves. In his hand is an old-fashioned doctor's bag.

Dolly turns toward the door. "Grunt. Take her to the gyno chair. We may as well use this for B-roll footage."

The man from the night before ambles through the door, still dressed like an orderly with the lower half of his face still obscured by the surgical mask. As he approaches, Locke reaches into his bag and extracts a syringe large enough to overdose an elephant.

Gasping, I step backward toward the wall, my stomach twisting into painful knots. "What are you doing? Don't touch me."

"You told Grunt you were nauseous, so I wanted to make sure you keep down your medicine," Dolly says. "Locke will shove a pessary into your cunt, so you don't throw up anything to help your memory recovery."

My heart lurches. "What the hell is a pessary?"

"Just another way to deliver a drug," she replies with a smirk. "We'd stick a suppository up your ass, but where's the fun in that?"

I skitter to the other side of the room. "Don't do this."

"Take her."

Grunt closes the distance, but I duck beneath his arm and dart toward the door. The wounds Delta gouged into my skin split open, and I'm sure blood is seeping through the bandages. None of that matters. I can't let them stick drugs in my vagina.

As I'm seconds from the doorway, a white-hot pain sears through my back, delivering several agonizing shocks. Breath flees my lungs as I crumple onto the padded floor, my muscles convulsing. I try to rise, but my limbs refuse to obey. I look around, frantic to find Xero, but he's gone.

Grunt looms over me, his large hands reaching for my shoulders. Despair crushes my lungs, and I'm struggling for air as he gathers me in his arms.

Have I lost Xero forever?

I don't think I'll be able to survive what happens next without him at my side.

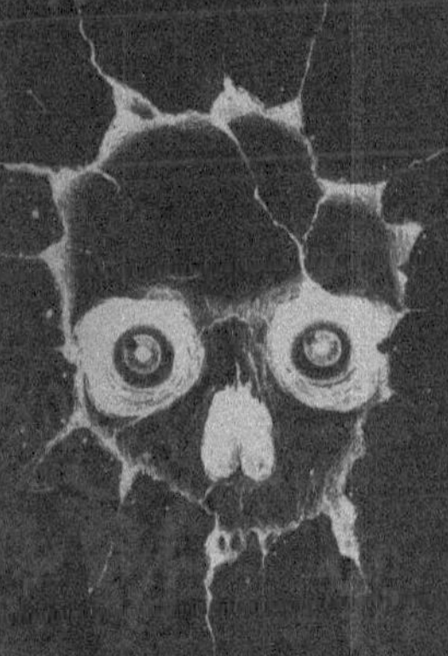

TWELVE

XERO

By the time I return to the infirmary, I'm gasping for the oxygen mask. The adrenaline sustaining me through interrogating Reverend Thomas has wrung dry, leaving me trembling and weak.

Each breath is like inhaling fire and my lungs have reduced to the size of my fists. I allow Jynxson to strap me to the cot without complaint, because fighting him is beyond my capacity. He fastens the mask over my mouth and nose, and I suck in the fresh air with hungry gulps.

I succumb to sleep within seconds and remain unconscious for what feels like only moments before the door slams open with a resounding bang. Sunlight streams through my closed eyelids, forcing me awake. Isabel's sharp voice slices through the haze.

"Did you enjoy your nighttime jaunt?" she asks, her voice cutting through the beeps of the machines.

"It was worth it," I mutter, my eyes still closed.

When my sister rattles off my test results, nothing at all is a surprise. Decreased blood oxygen, elevated carbon monoxide levels, not to mention inflammation. The ECG results show signs of increased cardiac stress, brought on by the night's escapade.

She continues with her chastisements, but I'm not listening. I finally have a lead. Amethyst's blond companion was one of the actors in X-Cite Media's graveyard video. If we can get Father to invite Reverend Thomas to the video shoot, then I'll capture them both.

A cough explodes through my chest. I still can't puzzle through Amethyst's connection with Father. Was she brought back to him against her will, or did she return to him out of a sick sense of Stockholm syndrome?

"Are you listening to me?" Isabel snaps.

I crack open an eye and wince at her fierce gaze.

"Keep this up and you risk permanent lung damage. We need to monitor you for complications like pneumonia."

"Okay," I rasp.

She reinserts the IV needle and checks the line. I follow it to a set of IV bags on a stand.

"What are those?" I ask.

"Saline and medications to help with the inflammation and pain."

She rattles off a long list of drugs, along with their intended purposes, which raises my suspicions. Isabel isn't usually this talkative unless she has an ulterior motive.

"You're stalling for time," I say, piecing together her intentions.

Her features harden. "I told you to stay in bed, but you convinced Jynxson to help you gallivant around the city, endangering your life. So now you're going to rest."

"Izzy." I jerk within the restraints binding me to the bed, my chest erupting in a fresh cough. "There's no time for this."

Her gaze softens. "I won't let you burn yourself out. Rest. By the time you wake up, we'll have collected all the information we need to track him."

And Amethyst, I want to say, but my words are cut off by another bout of wracking coughs. I struggle against the sedatives coursing through my veins and fight to keep my eyes open, but each blink feels heavier than the last.

The room blurs around me, and I cling to consciousness, desperate to stay alert despite the overwhelming pull of drowsiness. I grasp at my scattering thoughts, trying to anchor myself into consciousness, but it's like trying to hold on to smoke.

Isabel retreats, her shoes squeaking on the polished floor. The beeping of the monitors becomes a soft drumbeat that lulls me toward sleep. Amethyst's face is the last thing I see before I succumb to oblivion.

THIRTEEN

AMETHYST

My stomach lurches as Grunt pulls me into his broad chest. I wriggle in his grip, trying to break free, but his arms tighten.

As he carries me out of the cell and into the derelict hallway, I cry out, "This is sick. You can't just inject drugs into people's vaginas."

Locke sidles up to me, his blue eyes glimmering with amusement. "Not people, just yours."

Dolly's tinkling laughter follows me through the hospital's arched corridor, making every fine hair on my body stand on end. Will she be there while Locke violates my body?

Panic surges, hot and thick and stifling. My cries echo off the stone walls as I thrash back and forth, my breath coming in desperate gasps, but Grunt's grip is ironclad.

We pass open doors, revealing rooms containing contraptions I've only ever seen in my nightmares. Tarnished metal tables with leather straps, rusted cages, bathtubs filled to the brim with mossy water.

Ice fills my veins, and my imagination spins through a carousel of torturous scenarios. What if I get cut? What if I get infected? I choke on a sob, my mind racing desperately for answers.

"I'll take the pills," I scream. "I'll eat from the dog bowl. Just don't do this."

Grunt carries me through a set of double doors and back into the large hall from the night before, which is now arranged into multiple sets to resemble some of the rooms we passed. Four new men in overalls who weren't there last night carry pieces of old equipment into the compartments, adding touches of authenticity.

My stomach roils. I don't know if I should be revolted that the strangers don't give a shit that a woman is being brought here against her will or relieved that I'll be tortured with new props.

Grunt walks to a set lined with browning paper that mimics the hospital's crumbling walls. In its center is a gynecological examination chair with stirrups.

Adrenaline surges through my veins as he tries to place me on the apparatus. I ball my hands into tight fists, my nails digging into my palms.

"Please," I whisper, my voice already hoarse from screaming.

Locke chuckles. "She likes you."

With a disgruntled noise, Grunt grabs my hands and squeezes, forcing me to release his shoulders. I drop onto the cracked leather chair with a thud.

The two other men from last night crowd around, blocking out the light. Seth, with the black hair and penetrating eyes, grabs my arms, while Barrett, with the hawkish face and messy brown hair, wrestles my ankles into stirrups.

I thrash like my life depends on it because it does. As the men place my limbs in restraints, I glance at Locke, who's turned his back to speak into Dolly's camera. It looks like he's explaining the impending procedure, but I can't hear him through my screams.

"Cut," Dolly yells. "Someone put a gag on this bitch."

Grunt lumbers forward, holding a ring gag. With his free hand, he cups the side of my face and eases open my jaws. His touch is gentle, almost apologetic, but that doesn't stop him from placing the hard silicone circle in my mouth and buckling it around my head.

The men back away, leaving me tied to the chair. I stare up into the harsh studio lights hanging from the rigging above, not knowing if my heart will burst. It's beating so furiously against its cage that it muffles Locke's speech.

Xero steps out from behind the false wall, his eyes frantic. A sob catches in the back of my throat. Where did he go?

"I'm here, little ghost," he says, his fingers curling around mine. "Look at me. Can you do that?"

With a shaky nod, I focus on his pale blue eyes. Up close, they're whiter than usual, with flecks of varying shades of silver.

"Action!" Dolly yells.

Xero flickers around the edges. "Focus on me, Amethyst."

I whimper.

Locke drifts into my line of sight, wearing a white mask and a scrub cap. "Grunt tells me you're being a very naughty girl and not taking your meds. That won't do, Dolly."

"I'm not Dolly," I scream, but the gag distorts my words.

He wags a gloved finger. "Enough excuses. You've given me no choice."

"Look at me," Xero says.

My gaze snaps back to his pale eyes.

Xero gives me an encouraging nod. "That's right. Don't play their game. They want to see you fighting."

Harsh fingers unbuckle the crotch of my straitjacket, making me flinch. Xero's words of support fade into nothingness when Locke fondles my labia and rubs a circle around my clit.

"Grunt also tells me you've been a very dirty girl. Now I'll have to cleanse your filthy cunt with a sterile solution before inserting the pessary."

The large man enters the scene, holding a colonic irrigation bag filled with clear liquid. At its base is a plastic tube, which he passes to Locke. The cylindrical object pushes into my opening, making me shudder. Before I can even adjust to the intrusion, Locke turns a valve and cold liquid enters my vagina.

I squirm, try to push away, but the straps restraining my limbs are too tight. The muscles of my vagina clench, expelling the fluid.

Locke taps on my clit. "Pay attention, Dolly. The more water you push out, the more times we'll have to repeat this cleansing."

"Stay with me," Xero says, his voice a beacon of sanity. His fingers tighten around mine with a pressure hard enough to crush the bones. "Breathe and relax."

My breath deepens, and I focus on Xero. His arched brow. His regally straight nose. The way his cheekbones curve, creating a dip that leads down to his strong jaw. He's the personification of masculine perfection and was all mine until I ruined everything by setting him alight.

"Don't think about that," he snarls.

I focus on how handsome he looks in that tuxedo, and how he entered the Ministry of Mayhem with the swagger of a king. I think about how he sat on that leather throne and commanded the man from the club to get us drinks. Everyone wanted him, but he only had eyes for me.

"That's right, baby," he says. "Only you."

Somewhere on the edge of my awareness, cold water fills my vagina, but I imagine myself in a stone bath with moonlight streaming in through stained-glass windows. Xero hugs me from behind, his strong arms wrapped around my waist.

A gloved hand slaps my thigh, and a voice orders me to release the liquid. I push it out, my head turned to the side so my gaze is still locked with Xero's.

When something rubbery and thick enters my vagina, I picture myself lying in Relaney's spare bedroom with Xero between my spread legs, inserting the toy.

"You know I strung you up to a light fitting because I knew it would break," he says.

At the time, I thought I was going to die. Especially after I stepped out and found Chappy hanging from the ceiling hatch.

"Don't think about that guy," Xero says.

My mind skips to the red envelope containing Chappy's tongue, complete with the ball piercing. His punishment for daring to offer me pleasure.

"Cut!" Dolly says.

Xero vanishes, leaving me alone again. There's a camera in my face, another standing behind where Locke sits between my open legs, and another behind my head. All three men back away, giving Locke the space to rise.

He pulls off his gloves, making a show of disdain as he tosses them between my legs. That only makes Dolly giggle. When he removes his mask, he turns to Dolly.

"How was she?" she asks.

"A cheap imitation," he replies with a grimace.

Laughter and applause fill the studio, and the few onlookers who had gathered to watch the scene walk away to finish working on their sets.

Revulsion trickles down my spine. Both at my inability to maintain Xero's hallucination in Dolly's presence and at Locke's pathetic attempt to gain favor with his boss's wife.

As the pair saunter toward another part of the set, Seth removes my gag, unfastens my restraints, and marches me across the hall and through another set of doors, into an unlit corridor.

His grip tightens on my arm. "I won't carry you around like Grunt does. If you run, I'll just tackle you to the ground and fuck your ass."

The threat hangs in the air like a noose. I glance into his black eyes and nod, knowing full well he's begging for an excuse to assert his dominance.

He stops at a door with light seeping through its edges, raps on it twice, and waits. I shuffle on my feet, my breath ragged, my insides on fire, and my head spinning from not having eaten in nearly thirty-six hours.

A draft meanders through the walls, chilling my legs, which are still wet from the water dripping from my vagina and gathering at my bare feet.

I bow my head, focusing every ounce of effort on removing the object lodged deep in my body, but it's as useless as trying to push out a tampon.

"So, did you come?" Seth asks.

I flinch away. "What?"

"Dolly says she comes during every shoot. Are you the same?"

My jaw clenches. "Is this your idea of small talk?"

He leans into me, the tip of his long nose grazing my cheek. "Only Dolly gets away with that kind of attitude here. Cheap imitations like you get used up and discarded."

I swallow hard, forcing down a surge of fear. He isn't anyone powerful—just a lackey trying to flex his muscles, now that Dolly isn't here to tell him to keep his hands off.

"Thanks for the tip," I murmur, low enough not to be heard by whoever's making us wait. "I'll make sure to be myself."

Seth draws back, his brow furrowing. Before he can respond, the door swings open to reveal a room filled with white fabric arranged around a structure of metal stands to form an open tent. Studio lights surround it, creating a giant lightbox.

Inside is a backless couch upholstered in brown leather to look cozy, but the metal structures behind it remind me of the type of furniture available for sale in the Wonderland Fetish Store.

Seth shoves me in the back, and I stumble inside. The door behind me swings shut with a click. I whirl around, finding it devoid of handles, and gasp.

What the hell kind of room is this?

Footsteps sound from behind, and I pivot to find a large figure moving around the back of the tent. Delta steps out, clad in a tweed waistcoat and his shirt sleeves, tailored to accentuate his broad shoulders and muscular physique. He's styled like a 1940s gentleman, making him look even more sinister.

His smile is more like Camila's than Xero's but there's no mistaking the coldness of his blue eyes. This is a master manipulator. The kind of man who destroys young lives while he sits back to reap the spoils.

And somehow, he's convinced Dolly to be his wife.

"Amethyst," he says, his gaze raking down my unbuckled straitjacket and settling between my legs. "You and I need to get better acquainted, since we're family."

I would say no thanks, but I have a feeling he might invite Seth back inside to teach me a lesson.

His stare infuses my spine with ice, and I try not to shiver. When he sweeps his arm toward the tent, I force myself not to flinch. Seeing him alone in this room makes me feel young and vulnerable in a way that's familiar, although I can't remember why.

With a soft smile, he asks, "Why don't you lie on the couch?"

FOURTEEN

XERO

I spend the next twenty-four hours under mild sedation, barely able to focus on watching recorded interrogations conducted by my team on my behalf. My eyes droop as Jynxson grills Dr. Saint about Amethyst's past, and I snooze through her answers. When I'm lucid, I stare into the mirror of Reverend Thomas's computer.

Another day has passed, and I'm no closer to locating my little ghost.

Tyler has a person stationed at the vicarage, ready to transfer funds to Father the moment he replies to the reverend's request to pay for a place as an investor.

A small team is monitoring X-Cite Media's downtown house where I met their content manager and recruiter, Harlan Stills.

Jynxson conducted another interrogation of the man, which confirmed what we learned about the membership site being invite-only. Stills also told us where we'd find a database of everybody who joined X-Cite Media's inner circle, as well as those who rented its movies.

We're making progress, but not quickly enough. Nobody knows the location of the next shoot. According to Stills, Amethyst and Father could be anywhere within the continent of North or South America.

I run through my last twenty-four hours with Amethyst, still unsure whether she attacked out of a sense of betrayal or loyalty to Father.

The next morning, Father replies on the forum, the message containing an acceptance of Reverend Thomas's offer to fund the shoot along with the payment details. Using the credentials we took from our newest prisoner, Tyler transfers two hundred and fifty thousand dollars to Father from the centralized bank account shared by all the churches in the denomination within Beaumont City.

He's also packed away the Reverend's clothes, passport, and suitcases, leaving behind traces of a man addicted to pornography and gambling. When the bishop comes searching for the missing priest, he'll assume Reverend Thomas has absconded with the church funds.

Hours later, Isabel walks in. "Your vital signs are stable, your respiratory symptoms have improved, and your lung function is normal."

"Then you'll turn off the sedation," I say.

She nods. "I'll taper it off. You'll be fully alert within an hour."

"And the restraints?" I ask.

"They stay in place until you're cleared by Dr. Dixon."

The only thing keeping me from tearing through the restraints is the need to maintain the appearance of cooperating. Isabel can and will increase the sedatives if she thinks I plan on escaping.

When she leaves, Jynxson walks in. "What do you want to deal with first, the new lead I squeezed from Dr. Saint or the raid on X-Cite Media's HQ?"

"What did she say?" I ask.

"After I showed her the crime scene photos, she finally admitted Amethyst was referred to her by the Salentino twins who run the Newton Crematorium. Apparently, she's their niece."

"Why do I know that name?"

"They're the second cousins of your fellow inmate, Roman

Montesano. That explains how her house on Alderney Hill was purchased from Enzo Montesano's real estate company."

"All very interesting, but what else did the psychiatrist say?"

"Dr. Saint still can't remember the name of Amethyst's institution, but she said Amethyst arrived already addicted to a cocktail of anti-anxiety medication and antipsychotics, which had caused her to hallucinate. Her mother wanted her well enough to attend boarding school."

I stare at Jynxson for several seconds, my mind reeling. "That's it?"

"That's all she could tell me about Amethyst's background, but she confirmed increasing the doses after Amethyst killed the teacher, and again after she killed the Reed brothers at her college dorm."

"Can she account for Amethyst's time at the Greenbridge Academy?"

He nods. "There were bi-weekly visits and no talk of her being forced to appear in videos. I've sent someone to Dr. Saint's office to pour through her records, but I don't think Reverend Thomas is lying about the little doll."

I squeeze my eyes shut, trying to fit together these contradictory stories. It's the same level of frustration I get when I consider the impossibility of that graveyard video. Nobody, however well trained or steeped in delusions, could shrug off the physical effects of multiple assaults.

"What if there are two of them?" I crack open an eye.

His brow pinches. "Come again?"

"One woman can't be in two different places at the same time," I snarl. "They also can't live two parallel lives. Dolly is the twin who married my father. Amethyst is the twin whose memory was altered—for whatever reasons—and kept under a regimen of drugs and partial house arrest by a neurotic mother."

Jynxson rubs his chin. "Say I believe they're twins. Which one tried to burn you alive?"

My jaw clenches hard enough to crack my molars. I have my suspicions it was Amethyst, infuriated at seeing a video of me inviting other men to violate her while she was unconscious, but that line of thinking leads me to a harsh truth.

Amethyst didn't trust me enough to believe I wouldn't do something so heinous. All the months we spent together meant nothing, and my love for her was unrequited. I was nothing more than a threat to be neutralized.

"We'll find out when I catch up with them at the shoot," I reply.

"One more thing," he adds.

"What?"

"If Dolly was at the airport with the blond, where was Amethyst?"

My phone buzzes with a message from Tyler. It's a link to a video on the social media platform where Amethyst used to post content.

Title: XERO SIMP CAUGHT BY COPS FLEEING THE COUNTRY

A woman with Amethyst's hair is at an airport ramp, running toward the camera, her features hidden beneath a mask. Her arms are encased in a straitjacket, and she's fleeing from a burly man in a flat cap and navy-blue uniform.

He tackles her to the tarmac and wrestles her onto her back before picking her off the ground and slinging her on his shoulder like a rucksack. Then he charges the camera, and the video ends with a thud.

There's no way Amethyst was the woman willingly boarding a plane with a blond man and also the bound woman at the airport, desperately trying to escape.

I shove my phone in Jynxson's face, knowing even my devil's advocate has to admit this truth. "Tell me again why you think my twins theory is bullshit?"

His eyes widen. "Fuck."

"Twins separated around the age of ten. One goes to school, while the other survives multiple snuff movies. Don't you think there'll be some resentment?"

Jynxson gulps, finally seeming to agree with my theory. "What do you want me to do?"

I send a message to Tyler, demanding the flight information for all the private jets that left the airport at the time of takeoff.

"Help me out of this bed. Then ask Isabel for my meds while I'm out of shooting range. It's time to get Amethyst back."

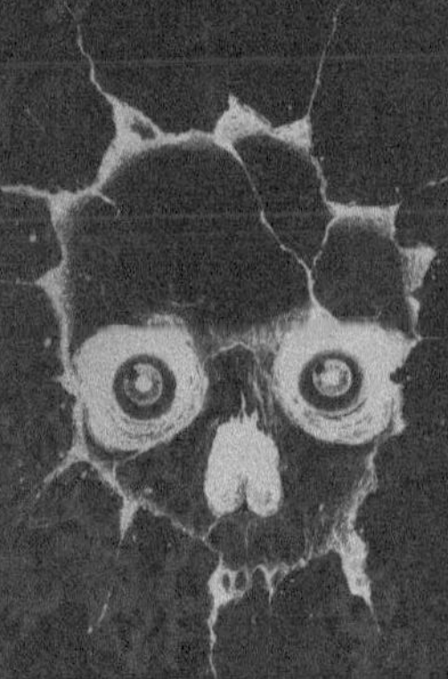

FIFTEEN

AMETHYST

I stand on trembling legs, staring into the cold blue eyes of Xero's dad. The tent lights make my vision go strange, but I blink away the glare.

"What do you like to be called?" he asks.

My lips part, but I can't make a sound. Delta's presence is so intimidating that he swallows up my words and makes my tongue feel like lead.

He chuckles, but it's a hollow, heartless sound that makes my skin erupt into goosebumps. Did he laugh like that when his sons beat Xero half to death? Or when he relegated Xero to a windowless box and made him eat scraps?

How about the children he groomed into becoming assassins? Did he laugh like that when the little girls returned from missions traumatized?

"Amethyst, is it?" he asks.

I manage a feeble nod. His gaze is so piercing, it feels like being trapped in the coils of a snake that hypnotizes its prey.

"Then let me give you a choice, Amethyst. I can make this experience pleasant or add to the trauma you're likely suffering from having been exposed and humiliated in front of your twin sister and half a dozen men."

I flinch at the reminder, my eyes squeezing shut.

"Now, lie on the couch like a good girl, and we'll talk," he says in a voice so smooth that it slips through my defenses.

Swallowing hard, I walk across the swept floor toward the peculiar looking tent and lower myself onto the bondage furniture upholstered to look like a psychiatrist's couch. A voice in my head is screaming at me to do anything else, but it's dull and far away.

Delta points a remote toward a camera mounted on a tripod on the other side of the room. It whirs to life with a small red light indicating it's recording.

Shivers travel across my skin at the thought of appearing in yet another movie clip. I glance back to Delta as he activates smaller cameras hidden within the tent's metallic structure. Their tiny lights remind me of spiders' eyes.

He pulls up a director's chair and positions it at the foot of my couch. "Lie back. Locke gave you a powerful herbal extract from the nightshade family to help make you more obedient and to reduce your inhibitions."

My stomach lurches at the realization of just why I feel so out of control. Is this where I'm raped and killed, like Lizzie Bath? Or does Delta have something else in mind?

"Why?" I whisper. "Don't you make snuff videos?"

His breathy laughter makes my skin crawl. "This session is for me, not the movie. I plan on taking you deeper into your subconscious than you've ever gone before, so I would prefer if you would recline before your body collapses."

A rapid beat echoes through my ears, and the blood racing through my veins heats. Sweat breaks out across my brow, and my head swims. I don't want to know what's buried in my mind, and I sure as hell don't want to be vulnerable to this monster.

The words from earlier trickle into my skull, and I blurt, "Locke gave me deadly nightshade?"

"Devil's trumpet," he says with a fatherly chuckle. "I can see from the flush across your skin that it's already taking effect."

I drop back on the couch, my breaths turning shallow and erratic. My limbs are so heavy, it feels like I'm sinking into the upholstery. The lights tilt and spin, creating a monochromic haze. Every shade of white, from ivory to alabaster, transforms the world into a maelstrom of colorless hues.

"Good girl. Now, I want you to relax and answer a few questions."

When I blink, my lashes flutter like butterfly wings, cracking through the room like a whip. They slice into the echo of my pulse and the roar of blood rushing in my ears. Delta's serpentine voice slithers through the confusion.

"Tell me about your relationship with Xero Greaves."

The truth surfaces, breaking my defenses. A single word spills from my lips. "Xero."

"Yes?"

Alarm bells ring in my head. He can't know about all the people Xero worked so hard to protect.

"Tell me about him."

I blurt truths that were recorded across social media, harmless pieces of information in the public domain. I tell him about the murders, how he was caught by the police holding his stepmother's heart. How they called him the angel of death because of his masculine beauty.

"Enough," he says, his words sharp. "What did he tell you in his letters?"

"He doesn't like fava beans or chianti."

Delta scoots his seat forward, frustration radiating off his shoulders in silver waves. "Regarding his plans," he says, his voice a low rumble that shakes my eardrums like thunder. "What did he tell you about his organization?"

I picture Camila and Jynxson and all the people who worked so hard to protect me from X-Cite Media, and how I betrayed them by setting their boss on fire. I can't let them fall into Delta's clutches, so I dredge up information about the fan club.

"There were two organizations," I murmur. "One official. The other is unofficial."

"Tell me more," he says, his voice slipping past my guard.

"We made the warden increase their recreation time, and we raised funds to buy things for their book club—"

The director's chair topples back, sending shockwaves through the room. Delta looms, his large hand crushing my throat.

"What did Xero tell you?"

"About what?"

"People, plans, places. I want to know it all!"

"Death row?"

"What was in his letters?" he hisses.

My eyelids droop. "He told me about his piercings. The pervy prison guard... He wanted me to send nudes."

"That's it?"

"He wanted a conjugal visit."

Delta chuckles. "I can hardly blame him. You are quite the beauty."

His fingers travel down my collarbone and over the swell of my breast. "It's like having two wives. One who's battle-forged and the other a blank slate."

"I belong to Xero," I whisper.

"How did he survive the execution?" Delta asks.

The question knocks me sideways. "We called his spirit from another realm."

His hand slips down to my breast, his fingers closing in around my nipple. Revulsion ripples through my chest, making my stomach lurch.

"Are you telling me the truth, girl?"

"I don't know," I reply. "Sometimes, it's hard to tell what's real."

"Who were you talking to in your cell?"

"Xero."

His fingers squeezing my nipple loosen. "Do you hallucinate him often?"

"Yes."

He sighs. "Your mother damaged you more than I anticipated. Tell me what happened to the men we sent to your house."

"I think they're dead," I murmur. "It's hard to tell. Men keep popping up at the worst times."

"More hallucinations?"

I nod.

"And you killed them?"

"I didn't mean to. Not really. It was self-defense."

He laughs, a maniacal sound that penetrates the marrow of my bones. "Maybe you aren't so useless after all. Dolly wants you to remember her, so cast your mind back to the last time you saw your sister."

"She was holding the camera," I say, my breath hitching. "Filming me while Locke did all those horrible things."

He slaps my cheek so hard that my vision bursts into white-hot sparks, my head snapping to the side with a sickening crack. "Can one person really be so stupid? You're like a child, stumbling into dangers you're too feeble-minded to comprehend."

The words would sting if I gave a shit about what he thought, but I remain silent.

He pulls out a pair of scissors and snips through the neckline of my straitjacket, exposing my collarbone and the tops of my breasts. "Melonie did a marvelous job, keeping you hidden from the outside world. We couldn't find either of you, anywhere, until you went viral with your Xero fanclub."

A riot breaks out across my brain, but my senses are too muffled to react. I concentrate on his words, trying to commit them to memory.

The scissors glide down my skin, the cold metal making me squirm.

"Melonie coddled you so much that you have no function in the world. I researched your past extensively, hoping to find something of value, but there was nothing but a string of failures."

My breath quickens as his fingers slide over my bandaged belly and toward my crotch. Alarm snakes through my veins, freezing me from the inside. I throw every ounce of energy into my limbs, but they refuse to move.

"Tell me something. Has any man touched you since that teacher?"

"Mr. Lawson," I whisper.

"That's right. Have you taken any cocks since then?" He parts my legs, his thick fingers rubbing over my genitals. Everything down there is numb.

"No." My voice catches. "I can't. Don't."

"Isn't that precious," he says. "Such innocence. No man who ever touched you is still alive."

When he pulls away his hand, the tightness in my chest unravels, and I release a shuddering breath.

"Shall we try again? Next time you fail to give me a satisfactory answer, I won't hold back."

I want to scream that this is sick, but the words die in my throat. The world dissolves into a storm of swirling whites. Delta's shadowy figure looms closer, the point of the scissors tracing a cold, cruel line up and down my folds.

Panic mounts. I try to fight back again, but the drug won't let me move.

"Cast your mind back to when you were ten." His voice snakes into my thoughts. "What was the last thing you remember before the asylum?"

"I don't know."

"Close your eyes."

My eyes flutter shut.

"Good girl. Now, picture yourself with Lyle. He was taking you somewhere, yes?"

I want to ask how he knows Dad's name, but the words remain stuck in the back of my throat. All I can choke out is, "Yes."

"Where did he take you? What happened that day?"

My mind rolls back to the blank wall encasing my earliest memories. It's made of gray bricks, covered in the same photos Mom placed all over my bedroom. Among them are sticky notes, reminding me that I lost my memories in a car crash brought on by unbuckling my seatbelt.

I try to tell Delta what I see, but he tells me it's a construction of lies. I float around it and find a tiny crack.

"Good girl. Look harder. Squeeze through. What's on the other side?"

Images explode through my consciousness in glorious technicolor. My nostrils fill with the mingled scents of burnt metal, gasoline, and motor oil. Looks like the car accident was real.

"I'm lying on a stretcher, surrounded by paramedics," I reply.

"Look around. Where are you?"

"I don't know. There's an ambulance. Its lights are still flashing. A truck. Lots of bystanders in a circle behind tape. And the police."

"What else? Can you see anyone familiar?"

I turn my head to find a gray car, crumpled beyond recognition. Firemen just extracted a man from the wreckage, but his body is limp. I relay all this information to Delta until I catch a glimpse of the man's face.

Heart clenching, I choke out, "It's Dad. He's dead."

"Good girl." Delta says. "What else?"

The girl I was then and the woman I am now are swamped by the pain and horror of that day. My throat closes, and I force out the words, "They're putting him in a body bag."

My stretcher gets wheeled backward and lifted into the interior of an ambulance. I reach out with my mind, wanting to stay with Dad, but the paramedics close the doors.

"What happens next?" he asks. "Focus."

Darkness overwhelms my vision, and my ears fill with the sound of beeping machines. My mind gets pulled under until even the grating sound of Delta's voice fades into the echoing drone of my pulse.

I did it. I finally broke through the wall of false memories and found a sliver of truth. Dad died all those years ago, yet I remember him so vividly during key points in my later childhood and adolescence.

While I was recovering from the accident at home, the father who came to my room and kept me company must have been a hallucination. All those words of comfort he offered when I got into trouble at school were figments of my imagination.

Somewhere on the edge of my consciousness, I'm aware of probing fingers, scissoring and twisting, and of Delta's voice comparing the state of my vagina to my sister's. I summon every ounce of energy into my legs, desperate to kick him in the balls, the face, to launch myself off the couch, but the drugs keep my limbs paralyzed.

A whimper lodges in my throat. My tongue is so heavy, I can't scream at him to stop.

"If you want this to end, you'll answer some questions about Xero and his organization."

As I slip into unconsciousness, my last thoughts are to protect Xero's people from Delta.

He must never know their location.

SIXTEEN

XERO

Less than an hour after the sedative wears off, I exit my car and step into the sun-drenched parking lot of Newton Crematorium. It's a simple brick building that backs onto the Parisii Cemetery flower gardens. The only thing that stops it from looking like a church are its tinted windows and the tall chimneys rising from its roof.

I left Jynxson in the infirmary to distract Isabel, who's likely to stop me from entering what could be enemy territory. The only people in the world who can shed further light on my twin theory are the Salentino twins, since they knew of Amethyst before she even visited Dr. Saint.

The disguise I'm wearing is enough to make me look different from the mugshot that went viral, but not so drastic that I arouse suspicion. Dark blond hair tint, a light covering of bronzing lotion, and iris-darkening contact lenses to alter the pale blue to something less memorable.

Footsteps hurry after me as I reach its entrance. I turn around and lock gazes with a furious-looking Camila.

"Don't tell me Isabel sent you here to drag me back to the infirmary," I say.

"She just wants to make sure you take your meds," Camila snaps.

Nodding, I let her accompany me through the entrance into a white reception area where two bouquets of lilies sit in elegant vases on a mahogany desk.

A door opens to the right of the desk, and a hard-faced woman in black steps out. Her gaze skips over Camila and settles on me.

"I'm here to see Aria and Elania Salentino," I say, meeting her stare.

"What's it regarding?"

"It's about their dead sister-in-law and missing niece."

I could have phrased it better, but I've lost days in my search for Amethyst. Everyone thinks she's some kind of sleeper agent who tried to kill me before taking out her mother and boarding a plane to join Father.

They're overlooking the footage of her trying to escape in a straitjacket because her face is obscured by a mask. While we're waiting for Father to give Reverend Thomas an address, I plan on proving she's a victim who needs our help.

The door on the left opens, and a dark-haired man steps out holding a gun. He wears the somber suit of a mortician, but his face, marred by a broken nose and jagged scars, has the look of a gangster's hired thug. He's supposed to be menacing, but that shit on his face is a sign of slow reflexes.

"Who the fuck are you?" he growls, pointing the gun at my chest.

I raise my palms. "Easy now. I'm here because my girlfriend was abducted."

He snorts. "The bosses don't have any niece, and I don't know any girlfriend. Now, I suggest you leave."

My jaw clenches. Any other day, I would spend time entertaining this low-level grunt, but my entire strategy depends on speaking to Amethyst's aunts.

"Take me to the Salentino sisters, and I'll overlook your confession of being a forty-year-old virgin."

He swaggers toward me, his lip curling. "Watch who you're talking to, pretty boy, or I'll—"

My fist lands on his nose, making him stagger backward, but not before he tries to land a kick to my crotch. I sidestep, delivering another punch to his gut. He doubles over, and I snatch the gun.

A bulldog of a man charges out from the same doorway, brandishing a pistol. Camila rushes to his side, her foot connecting with his kneecap. As he stumbles forward, she disarms him and points his weapon at his head.

"Do I need to search every room in this building to find the Salentino sisters, or is one of you going to take us to them?" I ask.

Bulldog's lip curls, his beady eyes darting to the forty-year-old virgin still clutching his gut. "Neither of them are here, but you can leave a message."

"Tell them Dolly is back in town, and she's dangerous." I fold my arms across my chest.

The door on the right opens, revealing Aria Salentino, a woman in her mid-thirties with cropped black hair, wearing a man's black suit with a matching shirt buttoned up to the throat. Despite the cuts she's etched into her brow, nothing can detract from her delicate bone structure.

She motions for both men to stand down. "And who the fuck is Dolly?"

"The missing girl whose twin sister you helped fourteen years ago," I reply.

Aria glares up at me for several seconds, her gaze never leaving mine. My pulse quickens. She knows. Knows that Amethyst isn't an only child. Knows there's a chance the sister who was either taken or sent away has returned for revenge.

"Put down the guns and come inside." She disappears behind the door.

Camila and I exchange glances. I flick my head, motioning at her to watch my back. While I don't think the sisters are dangerous, they're connected to the oldest crime family in New Alderney. Elania could be inside, calling for backup.

After placing the weapons on the desk, we step past Aria into a tasteful office of black walls and hardwood floors covered in a charcoal rug. A black desk takes center stage, along with two leather chairs. The decor reminds me so much of Amethyst's little study that my heart aches.

If I had protected her the night the first man from X-Cite

Media came after her, instead of tormenting her from the shadows, she would have known the contents of that video would be impossible. Now, I'll do everything I can to make things right.

The woman standing behind the desk is Elania Salentino. She's identical to her sister, but with features softened by layered brown hair with highlights. She wears light makeup, with a figure similar to Amethyst in her body-hugging black dress, convincing me of the family connection.

"What's this about twins?" Elania asks.

Aria stands beside the door, keeping a hand hidden inside her jacket, ready to draw her concealed weapon. I position myself by the wall between the windows, where I can keep an eye on both sisters. Camila stands by the corner wall, out of sniper range.

"I know Amethyst didn't kill her mother, and I have footage of two identical-looking women at the airport."

The Salentino twins lock gazes.

"Who are you?" Aria asks.

"Amethyst and I have been in a relationship for months."

Elania snorts. "My niece is practically a shut-in. Besides, she's too wrapped up in that prisoner to make time for men."

"I never said we went out on dates," I mutter.

"What do you want from us?" Aria asks.

"Anything that can lead us to Dolly."

"We haven't seen that one since she was a baby," Aria says with a sigh. "Melonie was married to our brother, Giorgi, who was an abusive piece of shit. She skipped out on him a year after she had the twins and disappeared on us for nearly a decade."

My heart skips. "Did he track her down?"

"Giorgi met with an unfortunate accident before he got the chance," Elania says with a smirk.

"Melonie returned to us ten years later, looking for help," Aria says. "She told us her new husband was dead, Dahlia had been trafficked, and Amy was abused so badly that she needed to be institutionalized. We sent private investigators looking for Dahlia, but she'd disappeared."

"Which institution?" I ask.

She shakes her head. "It was such a long time ago. Most of the men my uncle sent to raid the asylum are dead. I don't even remember the name."

"What happened to the husband?" I ask.

Their eyes meet again before Elania says, "He died in a car crash."

"Was Amethyst with him?"

"How did you know?" Aria asks.

"She mentioned losing her memories in a car accident, but she never said a word about having a sister."

Elania walks around her desk and approaches me, her gaze sharpening. "Tell me about the footage at the airport?"

"Can I show you?"

She nods.

I pull out my phone and play both clips from the same day. One of a woman looking exactly like Amethyst boarding a private jet. The other of Amethyst running toward the camera in a straitjacket.

"How do you know it's not the same girl in both clips?" Elania asks.

"I know Amethyst," I reply. "She's quiet, she's introverted, she only has one real-life friend. She's too sensitive about her mental health to stage herself as a lunatic being tackled by a guard." My voice falters. "She's terrified."

Silence descends on the room, and the twins share another glance.

Aria stares me full in the face and asks, "Are you really her boyfriend?"

"Yes," I say, my voice hoarse.

"If you're not a cop, tell us your name," Elania says.

I swallow hard, determination steeling my resolve. I can't afford to blow my cover, but if telling them the truth will help Amethyst, then I have no choice. My heart pounds, and I clench my fists to keep steady.

"It's Xero. Xero Greaves." The words burn as they leave my throat, each one a calculated risk.

She nods as if she already guessed it. "Then you'll know Roman."

"Montesano was in the cell opposite mine," I rasp. "Our exercise times overlapped, and we spoke a little in the death row book club. He shared some of his housekeeper's home cooking."

They exchange glances again before Aria asks, "Why do you think Amy is in danger?"

I tell her about X-Cite Media's attempts to capture Amethyst, along with Reverend Thomas's account of Dolly being forced to participate in snuff movies and surviving. I replay clips from where I interrogated Harlan Stills, the employee we lured out of X-Cite Media's stronghold.

With each word, the Salentino twins' disgust deepens. Aria snarls, her fury palpable, while Elania curls her lip in disdain. I can hardly blame them. Interrogating Stills the first time was infuriating enough.

"Why didn't Melonie tell us Amy was in trouble again?" Aria asks. "We could have helped."

"I think Melonie grew tired of covering up Amethyst's kills," I mutter.

Neither of them speak, not wanting to implicate themselves in covering up murders, but I'm almost certain they helped dispose of the brothers who went missing from her college.

"Give it to him," Aria says.

I straighten, my gaze darting to Elania, who returns to her desk and pulls out a red, leather-bound book.

"What is it?" I ask.

"When Melonie returned from her disappearance, begging us for help, my mom wanted to put a bullet through her skull for losing one granddaughter and traumatizing the other, but Melonie handed over this diary, explaining how it happened."

She presses the book into my hand. "The information there is fourteen-years old and might lead to nothing, but when I heard Melonie had been killed and Amy went on the run, I picked it up, looking for answers."

"We wanted to be involved in her life, but her mother didn't want her connected with our side of the family," Aria says.

Elania's features tighten with annoyance. "Judges tend to dole out harsher punishments for people connected to the Montesano family tree."

I nod, already aware of how Roman Montesano was framed for the murder of a woman he hadn't even met. "Thank you."

Throat tightening, I turn to the door, gripping the diary, determined to show it to Amethyst once I've rescued her from the clutches of Father and her sister.

"Hey."

I turn around and lock eyes with Elania. "When you find her, let us know. Our cousins have a small army of men who will march into hell to get her out."

Nodding, I shelve her offer as potential back up.

As I step out into the hallway, my phone buzzes with a message from Tyler's assistant. It's a list of four locations the private jets went to around the time Dolly boarded.

Martha's Vineyard Airport in Massachusetts, Helsing Island Airport in New York, Jackson Hole Airport in Wyoming, and Hilton Head Island Airport in South Carolina. Four far-flung cities, each one a potential rabbit hole leading to a dead end.

I walk out into the parking lot with Camila, clutching the little red diary. Her gaze burns the side of my face, and I turn to meet her eyes. The conversation with the Salentino twins has just confirmed my suspicions that Amethyst isn't any kind of sleeper agent working for Father, but a woman in the clutches of psychopaths.

"What's next?" she asks.

"If Father doesn't reply to Reverend Thomas with the location of the shoot, we'll have to scour the locations, one by one."

"That's going to take forever." She unlocks her vehicle and picks up a paper bag from the pharmacy. "How are your lungs?"

Burning with frustration. Time isn't on our side. Anything can be happening to Amethyst, and all we can do is gather information. I take the bag and mutter something about being fine. No amount of smoke damage can compare to what she's suffering. Or even to what my heart endures with each passing moment of my desperate search.

SEVENTEEN

Sunday July 4, 2010

Dr. Forster says I should write my thoughts in a diary to work through the stress of becoming a mother again. The psychiatrist thinks my worsening health is linked to my heightened state of anxiety, and he could be right. I went through pregnancy once already, but this feels like uncharted territory.

Last time, I lived in the Salentino mansion with Giorgi, his mother, his sisters, and a small army of staff. The housekeeper, maids, and cook, took care of all my needs. All I needed to do was to stay pretty, go to my appointments, and avoid his fists.

Living there was like stepping into a gilded cage, not realizing it would be lined with barbed wire. I didn't know a thing until it was too late. While we were dating, Giorgi told me the crematorium was his family business.

I was already married when I discovered it was a front for the mafia, and I tried to run. That first time, Giorgi beat me unconscious. The second time, he ripped out my birth control, locked me in a room for months, and didn't let me out until I was visibly pregnant.

The third time I left was with Lyle's help. I'll never forget how he risked everything to save me and my baby girls. He loved being in the FBI and was so close to taking down both the Salentino and Montesano families. He'd worked so hard to establish his cover, yet he engineered our escape.

When they fired him for breaking protocol, we fled to New York, changed the twins' names from Dahlia and Amaryllis to Dolly and Amy, and started a new life together. Then, shortly afterward, Giorgi ended up in one of his own ovens at the crematorium.

I should be happy to have left such an abusive marriage. Even happier to have a husband who treats my girls as his own. Lyle never raises his voice, let alone a hand. I should be grateful to have him, but I'm overwhelmed.

Dolly has inherited Giorgi's cruelty and his ability to mask it under a veneer of charm. She's only ten, but she already has the makings of a psychopath.

When I stopped bringing pets to the house, she turned her sadistic attention to Amy. I've had to stop Dolly from attacking her multiple times, even with weapons. It's a horrible thing to admit, but at times, I'm afraid of my own daughter.

Amy isn't so innocent. Instead of reporting Dolly, she retaliates. Sometimes, she even instigates with her spiteful pranks. Buckets of water in Dolly's bed, thumbtacks in Dolly's shoes. She even destroyed Dolly's favorite figurine, leaving fragments scattered across her bedroom floor.

Every day, the violence reminds me of Giorgi so much that it feels like a knife twisting in my gut. Lyle says they're mirror images of me, but all I see is their father.

The house has become a battleground. Lyle works late at the adoption agency to avoid the chaos, leaving me to referee their disputes. When the girls were expelled from school for the incident with the knife, Lyle showed me a pamphlet for a program designed to help troubled girls.

It's the Three Fates Therapeutic Boarding School. A peculiar name, but the prospectus showed a countryside location, and a quaint brick mansion converted into a school. They offer counseling to address behavioral issues, emotional difficulties, and even academic challenges.

The photos showed girls their age playing in meadows,

studying in cozy libraries, and even horseback riding. It's the kind of idyllic environment I've always wanted for my daughters. Lyle assures me that the counselors have dealt with troubled twins and will separate them so they can be free to express their individuality.

They've been gone for two months, and I don't miss them.

Not one bit.

There. I said it.

But they're returning tomorrow, and all I feel is an overwhelming sense of dread.

Lyle and Dr. Forster say Amy and Dolly will put aside their animosity toward each other for the sake of the baby. But I'm worried he'll get hurt.

Maybe I should have left them behind when I escaped Giorgi, but I had no way of knowing they would inherit their father's worst traits. Sometimes, I feel that the Salentino family might have been a better environment for my girls.

It's too late now. I'm stuck with the twins. Even with Giorgi dead, his mother is likely to throw me into one of their incinerators for daring to run. And his sisters would be corrupted by now. They were only ten when I left. I imagine Mother Salentino has poured enough poison in their ears to turn them into her loyal, ruthless enforcers.

I've just read through this entry. I'm ashamed of expressing such blistering resentment toward two innocent children. I'll do better. I'll get help. Lyle suggests a live-in nanny to lighten the load. Someone young enough to handle the girls, because this pregnancy is kicking my ass.

Even thinking about the future makes my blood pressure skyrocket.

Maybe Lyle is right about getting extra help. I like the idea of a British supernanny, who comes in and whips us all into shape with a firm hand and a warm heart. A Mary Poppins-style woman with a knack for taming wild girls.

I'll ask him in the morning to reach out and see if this mythical woman exists.

EIGHTEEN

AMETHYST

My eyes snap open, and I find myself back in the padded cell. My chest burns for air, and I convulse against the tight restraints of the straitjacket. The pain between my legs is as unmistakable as it is unbearable. I've been violated. Contaminated. Was Delta the rapist, the man who transported me back to this prison of white, or both? Either way, the hatred boiling through my veins turns to despair.

Tears sting my eyes. I just want to curl up and die.

"Amethyst?" Xero says, his voice soft.

"Do you know what happened to me?" I ask.

He hesitates. "Yes."

"How many of them?"

"Delta, when he removed the pessary."

He doesn't elaborate. I don't ask how many times or what else he might have done to me on that couch. What's the point, when my sanity is already frayed? My breath shallows, and my heart thuds a sluggish beat. I've never felt so powerless, so unclean.

A lump forms in my throat, and I swallow hard, fighting back burning tears. "It's no wonder you're going to such lengths to track him down. He's diabolical."

He grunts.

"Did I say anything incriminating?" I ask.

"He knows you're hallucinating me, but that's the extent of the information you shared." His warm hand lands on my shoulder. "You were trying to protect us."

I roll onto my back and gaze into his pale blue eyes. "It's the least I can do after what I did."

Xero winces. I'm surprised he's being so understanding. This entire situation with Dolly, Delta, and the others is a mess of my own making. If I had questioned him further that morning—not flown into a murderous rage—I would still be safe in the crawlspace.

"Don't think like that," he says.

I squeeze my eyes shut, unable to control my thoughts any more than I can control my hallucinations. My mind is still a jumbled mess. Even if I regained my memories for Delta, there's no stopping me from dying horribly.

"Amethyst," Xero snaps.

"What else do you want me to think?" I open my eyes, loosening tears, and rise up to sit. "My situation is futile. I'm going to die."

When he flinches, my heart plummets. I didn't mean to lash out at Xero. He's the real victim here, even if he is a figment of my imagination. It's bad enough that I killed him for nothing. Now he has to watch me suffer.

Before I can spiral into a maelstrom of despair, my thoughts are interrupted by the thud of approaching footsteps.

Cold sweat breaks out across my brow. My breath quickens. Thick bands of tension wind around my chest, making the edges of Xero's form flicker. I skitter to the farthest corner of my cell. I can't let him drag me to another part of the set, where I'll be tortured or violated.

"Stay calm, little ghost. You're hyperventilating," he says.

I force in a deep breath, but it barely registers, leaving me suffocating. Something's wrong. I'm having a panic attack. At this rate, I'll die before I even reach the cameras.

The footsteps echoing through my ears become so loud that every bone in my body trembles. Spots dance before my eyes, and the edges of my vision turn dark. The pressure around my chest increases until Xero's form flickers in and out of existence.

He moves his lips, but I can't hear anything through the roar of blood between my ears. Something's going wrong. I'm having a bad reaction to one of the drugs.

By the time the door swings open, my vision goes black, and I land on the padded floor with a thud.

Everything goes still for several heartbeats until water splashes on my face. As I return to the painful present, large hands roll me onto my back. My eyes snap open, and I inhale a noisy gasp.

Grunt stares down at me through wide eyes, his face hidden by that surgical mask. "Amy," he says, his voice panicked. "Are you alright?"

The question tickles something inside me I didn't know existed, a bizarre kernel of black humor. A laugh traps in my chest, cutting off my air. My entire life has already gone to shit. I've been sliced open, violated with pseudo-medical equipment, drugged and raped. How the hell does Grunt think I'm feeling?

"Can't breathe," I reply. "The straitjacket is too tight."

His brow furrows. "I brought your food."

"Can't eat. Jacket's too tight."

He rolls me onto my front and loosens the buckle holding my sleeves together. My arms fall free, and I suck in lungfuls of air.

"Better?" he asks and helps me sit up.

I blink away the spots. Shake my head from side to side, dislodging the brain fog. Xero has disappeared again, which could mean anything. Since he isn't around to discourage me from trusting Grunt, I take a chance to establish some communication.

"Eat," he says.

My gaze lands on the dog bowl containing the same mush as before, now hardened with a brown crust.

"If I eat that, I'll throw up."

Grunt glances toward the door. "Dolly says you must eat."

"Then I'd better have something solid, because that isn't even fit for a dog."

The large man's shoulders sag. "She won't be happy."

"I'm going to die, right?" I ask.

When he drops his gaze, I add, "That's what I thought. Why would I add to my suffering by eating that slop?"

Silence stretches between us for several heartbeats. Grunt continues to crouch in front of me, his gaze softening to something close to pity or even regret.

I want to say something else to humanize myself, but my mind goes blank. He works for an organization that makes snuff. I wouldn't be surprised if he was one of the men in that graveyard movie. Nobody stumbles into this line of work by mistake. If he's feeling empathy, it's only temporary. He's upset Dolly, and the others treat him like shit.

Rising to stand, he retreats toward the door, reaches into his pocket and extracts a cereal bar. I straighten, my gaze darting up to meet his masked face.

Before I can even ask what he wants in return, he tosses the bar across the floor. It skips past the dog bowl and lands by my bare feet.

The door swings shut, and his footsteps disappear down the hallway, leaving me alone with the bar. It's covered in transparent wrapping, which will be difficult to remove since I'm in a straitjacket, but at least he freed my arms.

I pick up the cereal bar with fingers encased in thick cotton and examine its wrapper for punctures. So far, it's untouched.

"Good idea," Xero says. "In case they injected it with something."

Some of the tightness around my chest eases at his return, and I exhale a breath of relief. Holding the bar between my teeth, I twist and pull at the wrapper until the plastic gives way, releasing the mouth-watering scents of honey, nuts, and oats.

I take a bite, filling my mouth with enough crunchy, sweet goodness to chase away the taste of chemicals. I chew slowly, savoring each bite, allowing the flavors to spread across my dry tongue.

My stomach growls at the reminder that it's been days since I last ate or drank. Tears spring to my eyes, and I shuffle toward the dog bowl and examine the liquid. It's clear enough to look like water, but how do I know it's not laced with drugs?

I shuffle forward to take a sniff, but all I smell is the mush.

"Don't risk it," Xero says.

I draw away from the fluid with a frown.

A metallic clink has me flinching back toward the corner of my cell. It's coming from a square hatch in the door that slides open to reveal a pair of dark eyes.

It's Seth. The man who escorted me to Delta's room and threatened me with anal rape.

"Hey. Looking for this?" He draws back and pushes a plastic water bottle through the hatch.

My heart skips, and I wait for him to let the drink fall to the floor, but he only moves it from side to side.

"Go on, take it," he says, sounding gruff.

I glance at Xero, who shakes his head.

My throat constricts, escalating my thirst. Bits of cereal bar cling to the inside of my mouth. I need something to wash it down before I choke.

Seth pulls back the bottle. "Alright. Suit yourself."

"Wait." I rush forward toward the hatch, already reaching out for the disappearing water, but it's replaced by a long, skinny erection, already dripping with precum.

"Suck on this!"

Bile rises to the back of my throat as I recoil from the hatch, my pulse quickening. Blood pounds through my veins, sending up a surge of adrenaline. I should have fucking known.

"Come on, baby." Seth strokes himself, his voice breathy with excitement. "It's only a mouthful."

"Don't give him the satisfaction of an audience," Xero snarls.

I turn my gaze toward the wall.

"Look at me," Seth growls. "If you want that fucking drink, you're going to watch me come."

I grind my teeth, not wanting to give him a second of acknowledgment. It dawns on me then that I'm the only available woman on the set. Dolly is married to Delta and has gained some sort of power in X-Cite Media. Everyone else here is a man with a taste for extreme pornography. There's only one door separating me from a gang of predators.

Seth groans. "Look at me when I'm coming, you worthless cunt."

He can go straight to hell.

After a skin-crawling eternity, he grunts his release, and the hatch slams shut. Seth leaves, his laughter echoing through the hallway.

I turn back toward the dog bowl, but the water is now cloudy with semen. Ropes of cum trail from the hatch and spread across the floor toward the bowl. That bastard, Seth, sabotaged my water on purpose.

Xero places a hand on my shoulder. "Don't even think about it."

I scoff. "Is this your idea of a joke? I'd rather die."

Hours later, Grunt returns to take me back to the studio room and stops at a set of artificial green tiles featuring a pair of steaming bathtubs. Locke stands between them, dressed in a white coat and a surgical mask, holding a clipboard.

My throat, which is already parched from not drinking, tightens. Grunt deposits me between the tubs and steps back as the crew point their cameras.

"No need to clutch your pearls," Locke says. "We're only shooting B-roll footage."

When I give him a blank look, he adds, "Background footage, so our patrons get the look and feel of an abandoned asylum. These days, it's not enough to gang-rape a bitch and leave her to bleed out on a dirty mattress. People want atmosphere, drama, artistry."

"You're going to all this trouble so a bunch of sick fucks can jerk off?" I rasp.

He tuts. "Dolly always said you didn't appreciate the arts."

Someone turns on the dry ice, filling the set with fog, which mingles with the stifling heat emanating from the tub. Chills crawl over my skin, and my head swims. I sway on my feet, panting like a dog while the entire set spins in a kaleidoscope of whites and greens and stainless steel.

"Amethyst?" Xero's voice echoes through my skull.

Someone else repeats my name, but I collapse, hitting the floor with a thud.

"What the fuck is this?" Dolly's voice rips through my brain fog. "What's wrong with her?"

Locke crouches at my side. "She's fainted. How unprofessional."

"Get her up!"

Rough hands haul me to my feet. I sway from side to side before my legs collapse, and my knees hit the painted floor.

"Grunt, I gave you one job," Dolly says, her voice turning to ice. "Keep her fed and watered. How the hell is she supposed to perform if she can't stand?"

"Last time I checked on her, she hadn't touched her food or water," Seth adds.

"When did she last eat?" Dolly screeches.

I remain on the floor, breathing hard, while the set whirls and spins into chaos. Men surround us, pointing fingers at Grunt who they blame for my weakened state, with Grunt arguing back that it wasn't his choice to feed me gruel.

As the men break out into a scuffle, I crawl to the set's farthest corner and crouch beside a rusty table. The dry ice gets turned off, with the only source of steam rolling off the bathtubs. Barrett, Locke, and Seth crowd around Grunt like a pack of bullies, with Dolly at their backs, dressed as Florence Nightingale. The stagehands stop working to gather around the edge of the set and watch the spectacle. This is chaos, with Grunt as the target for all the hate.

"Teach him a lesson," Dolly screams.

Grunt shoves Barrett aside and tries to run, but the other men grab his arms. Barrett springs to his feet and punches Grunt in the throat. The others join the attack, punching, kicking, and shoving Grunt until he falls backward into one of the baths.

Hot fluid splashes out in a wave, hitting us all. My skin tingles and burns from the boiling water. The crew scatters, abandoning their equipment, but I'm frozen in place. I can't tear my eyes away from Grunt, thrashing and screaming. My heart pounds, my breath catching, paralyzed by the horror.

His screams ring across the set, mingled with Dolly's shrill laughter. Guilt claws at my chest and burrows its way into my heart with the savagery of a beast. I did this. Grunt was punished because I wouldn't eat the gruel.

Dolly turns to me, her eyes glinting with malice, her lips curling into a cruel smirk. Stomach clenching, I swallow back a wave of nausea and force my gaze to the painted floor.

"See what we can salvage from the shot. We still need more B-roll footage. Someone grab that stupid bitch and prepare her for force feeding."

NINETEEN

Sunday July 11, 2010

The girls returned on Monday morning with one of their counselors, who has agreed to stay with us until we find a suitable candidate for their care.

Her name is Charlotte. She's twenty-two, blonde, five-ten, and looks like she just walked off a runway. She has a degree in child psychology and a soft spot for Dolly.

Amy has returned withdrawn, barely able to leave her room. She reads the same book of fairy tales over and over. The girls no longer fight, but the silence between them is unsettling.

No matter how much I ask, Amy won't tell me what's wrong. I asked if Dolly bullied her, and she shook her head. I asked if she was happy to be home, and she shrugged.

Dolly, on the other hand, is blossoming under Charlotte's care. The pair of them spend hours playing in the park. They were both enthusiastic when I suggested Amy join them, but Amy simply recoiled.

I spoke to Lyle about the changes, but he's confused. Isn't this what I wanted? An end to the warfare, and someone to help with the twins so I wouldn't be overwhelmed? It is, but not like this.

Dr. Forster recommends therapy for Amy and has referred

her to a professional who specializes in children. He thinks the silence is a symptom of a much deeper issue. She could be envious of Dolly's connection with Charlotte or worried about the baby. It could be anything.

Meanwhile, the pregnancy continues to take its toll. My blood pressure is constantly high. Some nights, I wake up in a panic, gasping for air. Other nights, I dream that I'm back with Giorgi. Then memories of the violence return with vivid clarity until Lyle wakes me up, reminding me that I'm safe.

Dr. Forster says nightmares like this are normal due to past trauma and suggests meditation. I plan on including Amy in these sessions to bring her out of her shell.

My ob-gyn has put me on new medications and complete bed rest. I need to avoid strenuous physical activity, prolonged standing, and sex.

If my blood pressure continues to stay high, I'll have to spend the rest of my pregnancy in the hospital or even have the baby early.

I can't let that happen. I'm only thirty weeks along. I had the twins at thirty-five weeks and they turned out fine. Physically, anyway. If I can hang on for another month, then I can give my son the best chance.

Lyle is being supportive as always and has cut down his hours to spend more time at home. He and Charlotte have stepped up with managing the twins and household chores.

They're a dream team, and I'm grateful they're picking up the slack. I couldn't manage without their help. But after the twins go to bed, Lyle spends time with Charlotte downstairs in the lounge.

I can't hear them talking from our bedroom upstairs with the TV blaring, but I can feel they're bonding over this shared responsibility. It almost reminds me of how Giorgi flaunted his mistress throughout my pregnancy. Men have urges, he would say, and I'm not doing anything for him when I'm looking like a pot-bellied whale.

Any mention that Giorgi impregnated me against my will would earn me a slap across my face or even a kick to my stomach. I was trapped within the mansion. Trapped in my marriage. Trapped in a maternity hell.

Lyle isn't Giorgi. He would never hurt me, but I can't have sex without risking the pregnancy. Men have needs, and Charlotte agreed a little too readily to move in with us at short notice.

I'm being paranoid. Ungrateful. Looking for ways to make my life miserable. But those were the things I'd tell myself when I was Giorgi's prisoner.

Is history repeating itself or is it all in my head?

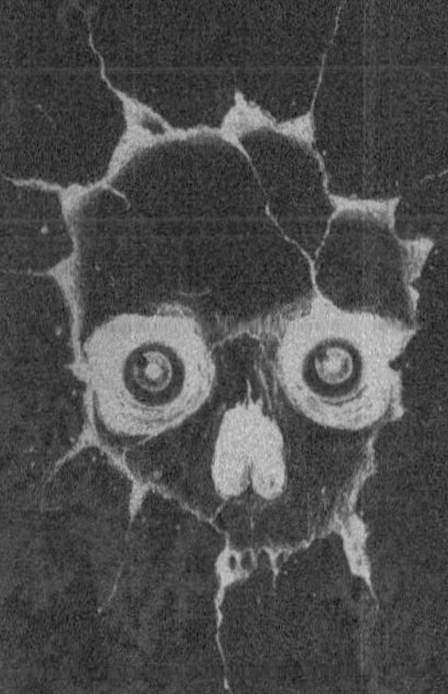

TWENTY

XERO

I'm back at the infirmary, with Isabel glaring at me over the writhing reverend. She's fitting him with a series of subcutaneous devices we can activate via remote control, so he can perform as our Trojan horse.

Tyler messaged me while I was reading through the first entries of Melonie's diary, which charts the woman's gradual descent from indifference to her children to hatred. I barely reached the part that hinted at the origin of Amethyst's trauma when I received some good news.

The money from Reverend Thomas's church account has cleared, and Father has sent over details of a pre-shoot reception at the Hotel Royale in Helsing Island, New York. It's one of the destinations we identified from the private jets that departed the airport around the time we found footage of Dolly and Amethyst.

As one of the investors, the reverend will get a meet and greet with Delta and Dolly at the hotel's function room, before joining them the next morning for two exciting days of filming.

Father's words, not mine.

Two days of rape and torture for entertainment and profit. I plan on reaching Amethyst before Father and his film crew even get the chance to say, *Action*.

The reception is tomorrow afternoon at four, followed by a

viewing of exclusive footage. There's no mention of the shoot's exact location, as transportation there will be provided the following morning at eight.

Jynxson has boarded a high-speed catamaran to the island with a small team of operatives and a large cache of weapons. Tyler and his team are scouring all 150 square miles of the land mass for production studios, abandoned warehouses, and other venues large and isolated enough to stage an illicit shoot.

Reverend Thomas rears up, his movements barely contained by the restraints pinning him to the cot. "For the love of God, please stop this!"

"That's it," Isabel snaps. "I can't operate under these conditions. He's going under sedation."

She turns toward one of the cupboards at the edge of the room, but I place a hand on her shoulder.

"He never showed an ounce of mercy for any of the victims in the snuff movies, so he gets to feel every slice of your scalpel," I say.

My sister's features harden. "In that case, you won't object to a muscle relaxant so I can work in peace?"

I smirk. "Go ahead."

She pulls away to a trolley and draws a clear liquid into a syringe. I turn back to the trembling reverend, staring into his stricken features. His face is pale, covered in a film of sweat. He's no longer the charming asshole who tried to impress my little ghost by turning budget groceries into holy water.

"How does it feel to be the one at another's mercy?" I sneer, my lip curling at his naked cowardice.

"Not too different from the last time," he replies through panting breaths. "Why are you doing this? I've cooperated. Done everything you asked. Isn't it time to show me some forgiveness?"

Laughter bubbles up in my chest, and I let it spill out, grinning with a savage delight.

His eyes widen. "What did I say?"

"Absolution isn't given. It's earned. You're the one who will lead us to Delta and all his supporters."

Alarm flashes across his features as it finally sinks in that I plan on making him betray his fellow snuff-loving subscribers. He stares up at me, his jaw falling slack. "You don't understand. Delta doesn't take treachery lightly."

I clap him on the cheek. "Cheer up. You'll get to see Dolly before you die."

Isabel approaches with the syringe, making him thrash. His unbandaged eye, bulging with terror, remains on mine, silently begging for my nonexistent mercy. He mouths 'please' as she slides the needle into his vein and presses the plunger.

As the drug takes effect, his whimpers and gasps slow into pained groans, but I continue staring into his eyes.

"Better." Isabel picks up her scalpel and makes an incision near his collarbone. "Make yourself useful and get me the leads."

Smirking, I pick up the wires for the reverend's pacemaker and hand them to my sister.

She takes her time, threading them through a vein into his heart. As she makes minor adjustments, I pick up the lightweight pacemaker.

"Anything you can do to accelerate the healing of his injuries? I can't send him to the meeting point looking like this."

"I'm a medic, not a miracle worker," she mutters and slides the device into a pocket of skin in his chest. "Testing."

I tap a few buttons on the pacemaker, watching the monitor for changes in his heart's rhythm. When it stabilizes, I grin with triumph.

"It's in everyone's interest if he doesn't shuffle in looking fresh from the torture table," I add, prompting her for a solution.

She closes his incision with sutures, her brow furrowing. "The best I can do at such short notice is cauterize the wounds and combine that with a course of anti-inflammatories and antibiotics. You'll have to make up the difference with cosmetics."

I grunt. "That will do for now."

Reverend Thomas won't live a second once he's served his purpose.

After Isabel inserts enough tech into his body to track him to an accuracy of a millimeter, we test the app that controls our pain distributing devices and the beating of his heart.

Once the muscle relaxant wears off, he trembles openly at the violation, glaring up at me like I'm the monster.

I cup the bandaged side of his face. “Good boy. You took that pacemaker so well. If you screw us over in any way in Helsing Island, we’ll keep you suspended in agony long before you beg us to stop your heart.”

Isabel sets down her instruments and whirls around, her eyes hardening. “Now that we’ve prepped the Trojan horse, it’s time to finish your course of treatment.”

TWENTY-ONE

Sunday July 18, 2010

This pregnancy was supposed to be a healing process—a new start to get me over the wreckage of my past with Giorgi. I wanted to have a water birth at home, with a qualified midwife and Lyle holding my hand. In the end, my body betrayed those plans.

Once I noticed how close Charlotte was getting to Lyle, my stress skyrocketed. Meditation failed to distract me from the unsettling parallels between this pregnancy and my last.

Dr. Forster made a home visit since I was confined to my bed. He suggested I open up to Lyle about my insecurities. My stomach churned at the thought of being so vulnerable. I told him Lyle had been nothing but supportive, tender, and loving. He'd already sacrificed so much to give the girls and me a good life. I couldn't drag him into my cesspool of worries and trauma.

Later that afternoon, I was reading Rapunzel to Amy. She's too old for fairytales, I know, but it's the only way I can connect to my youngest. Charlotte came in with an early dinner of tomato soup and grilled cheese. She called Amy over to eat with her and Dolly.

Amy was reluctant to leave and asked if she could eat with me, but Charlotte insisted, saying that I needed my rest. I didn't contradict her, wanting Amy to socialize with the rest of her family instead of keeping to herself.

The soup was nice enough with a rich umami flavor that I didn't recognize until my throat closed up with an all-too-familiar reaction. Even the smallest amount of shrimp can trigger my allergy, and there was enough in a few mouthfuls to send me into anaphylaxis.

I screamed for help through a swollen throat, and crawled out of bed, looking for the EpiPen I was sure I'd left in the nightstand drawer. It was a mess. I couldn't breathe, couldn't balance, and collapsed on my hands and knees with shooting pain.

It's been ages since I've had such a strong reaction. During my captivity with Giorgi, he once fed me pasta laced with shrimp as a punishment. I reacted so badly that he had to call his family physician to administer an emergency shot. I looked monstrous—my body was a mess of swelling, blisters, and hives. For once in his miserable life, he looked shaken. After that, he stopped fucking with my food.

This time, I was on my own with my EpiPen missing. I groped around for my phone to call 911, but all I found was my charger. I was choking, half-blinded by the swelling around my eyes, and feeling like I was going to die, when Lyle appeared in the doorway.

He took one look at me and knew exactly what was happening. Lyle pulled out his phone, dialed 911, and laid me in the recovery position. Everything else happened in a blur. He found an EpiPen in his home office and gave me a shot in the thigh. By the time the ambulance arrived, I was stable, but they loaded me inside anyway. When I asked about the girls, Lyle told me Charlotte had taken them both to the park.

He came with me in the ambulance and was horrified when I suggested that Charlotte could have tampered with my soup. To his credit, he didn't deny anything, and I felt comfortable enough to broach the subject of their closeness. Lyle assured me that both he and Charlotte only spent so much time together because they were worried about Amy's mental state. He agreed to spend more time with me in the evening.

The doctors kept me in for observation, saying they needed to monitor the baby for fetal distress. So, for the next several days, they put me through endless tests and observations. Lyle came to visit as much as he could, juggling work and care of the girls, but my suspicions continued to mount.

I didn't pull that allergic reaction out of my ass. Charlotte poisoned my soup. Probably because she overheard me expressing my concerns with Dr. Forster. She wants my husband. She's getting her claws into my family.

When I asked the ob-gyn to return home and continue my bed rest there, he said I needed to prioritize the baby. Lyle agrees. He wants to give his son the best start. So, I'm confined to a hospital bed, wondering where I went wrong and mourning the loss of that idyllic home birth.

Meanwhile, I'm going to ask Lyle to find another nanny.

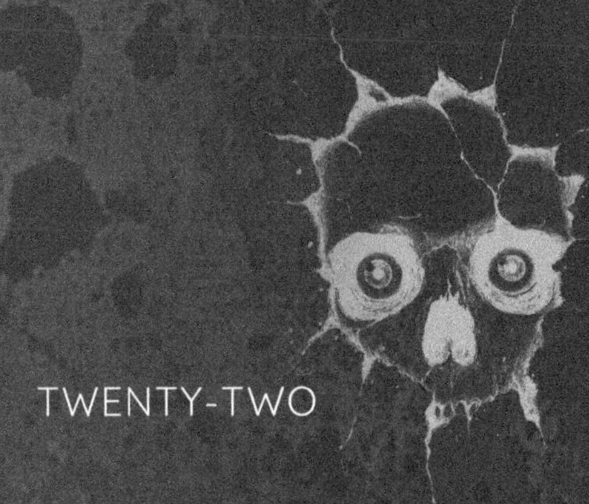

TWENTY-TWO

AMETHYST

My jaw aches from being wedged open. I double over, my stomach muscles contracting with painful spasms. Wave upon wave of nausea have me crashing to my knees. I can't see, can't breathe, can't hear Xero's words of comfort through a pandemonium of panic.

They could have used a ring gag to wedge my mouth open, but Dolly insisted on something Locke described as a mouth distractor. It looks like a pair of scissors, but with curved hooks instead of blades and a hinge that reminded me of a protractor.

Dolly strapped me to a dentist's chair while Locke, Seth, and Barrett jerked off into my open mouth. When only one of them managed to come on my tongue, she invited the crew to participate.

After that, they force-fed me the disgusting gruel.

I wish they'd thrown me into that hot bath. The scalding water might have burned away this festering disgust, this nauseating sense of contamination and filth.

"Amethyst."

Xero's voice finally breaks through the haze. I draw back, sitting on my heels, letting the padded room return to focus.

What the hell could I have done to Dolly to have earned this insane amount of cruelty? She's too blinded by her hatred of me to notice that every man in the building also holds her in contempt. If they didn't, they wouldn't mistreat her identical twin.

Xero places a cool hand on my cheek, helping me clear my thoughts. "Correct. You're just her proxy."

"What am I going to do?"

"It's time to use Grunt," Xero says.

"I thought you said he couldn't be trusted."

"We've run out of choices. While you were dissociating, one of the crew mentioned that the extras are arriving tonight. Delta and Dolly will fly to another island to meet some investors tomorrow at a cocktail reception. They're shooting the movie in less than thirty-six hours."

My breath catches, and my mind returns to full alertness. I can't talk about this out loud. Delta once asked who I was speaking to in the cell. They're monitoring what I'm saying. But what could the drinks reception even mean for me?

"There might be a chance of escaping the asylum," Xero replies.

Xero fills me in on everything he overheard while Dolly was filming, including glimpses he caught of Grunt rising from the other set with the bath.

One of the crew members suggested that Delta would fire him for keeping me in a weakened position, while another guessed they were setting him up to be murdered on screen.

That's the opening I need to get Grunt on my side.

Hours pass in the cell. The screen has turned white, trapping me in a monochromatic hell. The only source of color comes from a stray curl. Even the vomit I left in the corner is pale. Locke comes in to inject me with something that makes my body go limp, and Grunt carries me through the hallway for another round with Delta. I give him the same bullshit answers before my mind turns to mush.

At some point, I'm strapped to a gurney and injected with

thick needles before a man in a white coat presses electrodes into my temple.

The sight of him triggers long-forgotten memories of being a child at the mercy of a mad doctor. At least, I don't think he's part of the here-and-now. None of Delta's men have such bright red hair. But I'm not sure if it's a dream or my mind trying to shield information about Xero's people from Delta.

The electric current jerks me awake, and I stare into the padded walls.

Xero sits at my side, staring down at me with a frown. His cool fingers slide through my hair, reminding me of how Dad comforted me after the accident.

"You're alright," he says. "Stay with me, okay?"

I give him a shaky nod. My head throbs, but it's nothing compared to the pain in my anus. Delta must have torn me up pretty badly. I blink, trying to focus on Xero's face through the haze of pain and drugs. His features swim in and out of focus, but his touch anchors me to reality.

Xero doesn't tell me what happened. I don't ask, because the answer is obvious. We stay locked in each other's gazes as my body metabolizes the drugs. I don't think I'll be able to survive another round with Delta. I'd rather die.

Eventually, the door opens, and Grunt walks in with a pair of large dog bowls. His exposed skin outside his mask is still reddened from yesterday's contact with the hot water.

He stiffens at the sight of dried vomit in the corner and sets down the bowls containing water and a substance that smells like oatmeal.

I clear my throat. "Sorry."

He flinches. "What?"

"It was my fault you got punished."

He disappears through the door, only to return with a bucket and mop.

"Eat. Don't apologize," he replies in a monotone, not bothering to look in my direction.

"Could you free my hands again, please?" I ask.

With a huff, he lumbers behind me and releases the fastenings around my back that keep my arms folded at my chest. They drop forward, and I sigh with relief.

"How did you end up working for X-Cite Media?" I ask.

Ignoring me, he continues toward the vomit in the corner.

"I can clean that up."

He huffs a bitter laugh. "If you want to help me, then eat."

I stare at his broad back, my lips parting with protest, but Xero steps between us and shakes his head.

"Show him you're cooperating and take a mouthful of that oatmeal," he says.

With a shaky nod, I shuffle across the floor. Any strength I might have gathered from being force-fed semen and gruel vanished a long time ago when I ejected the contents of my stomach.

I crouch on all fours in front of the water bowl, sipping mouthfuls of cold liquid. It's unexpectedly refreshing, as I imagined it would taste metallic and stale.

After swallowing enough to quench my thirst, I move onto the second bowl and lower my head into the oatmeal. It's warm, as though prepared not too long ago, and sweet. Since my fingers are still encased within the jacket's sleeves, I eat the creamy substance like a dog.

My tastebuds welcome the flavor, and I continue alternating between water and oatmeal until my stomach is full.

"Amethyst," Xero hisses.

I sit up to find Grunt staring down at me, still holding the mop and bucket.

"Better?" he asks.

"Throw him off-balance," Xero says.

"Um... I think so," I slur, trying to sound drowsier than I feel. "Thank you for taking such good care of me, and I'm sorry again for causing you so much trouble."

After setting the mop and bucket into the hallway, he returns to kneel at my side. "They're not usually like this, with all the bullying. Things changed here since she took creative control."

Nodding, I pretend to give a damn. Grunt is only upset because some of the animosity falling on me is now being targeted at him. Regardless of his shitty working conditions, it still amounts to women getting tortured, raped, and killed for entertainment.

"Focus," Xero snaps.

He's right. I can judge him later. Preferably from miles away and in a police precinct.

"Have you told your boss about them?" I ask.

His face twists into a scowl beneath the mask, and his neck muscles expand like a cobra. "Delta's the one who gave her all the power."

Grunt rants about the good old days, when Delta took more interest in producing the movies and used to care about his members. I listen for an opening I can exploit, but all I hear are veiled complaints that Dolly has ruined what was once a brotherhood of men with eclectic tastes.

"He was one of the men in the graveyard video," Xero says.

I nod, still trying to get a word in edgewise, but Grunt continues his torrent of frustration.

"They used to pay us a percentage of earnings. Now we work for protection," he mumbles.

My gaze darts from Xero back to Grunt. "What does that mean?"

"Someone leaked footage of us without our masks. We're now wanted by the cops."

"Who would arrange something like that to force you to work for X-Cite Media for free?" I ask.

The hint sails over his head as he continues to wallow in self-pity. I grind my teeth. Surely, he could make a deal with the police to bring down the operation from the inside.

"Change tactics," Xero says.

"Hey, I overheard two of the crew members talking about you earlier. It sounded like they were joking, but..." I shake my head. "It was probably just banter."

He frowns. "What did you overhear?"

"I don't want to get between you and your friends."

"Tell me."

My gaze darts to Xero, who helps me paraphrase what the men were saying while Grunt was in the scalding water. Grunt's eyes widen as I reference events and information that only other people in X-Cite Media would know. I end with something else Xero overheard about a crew member using Grunt's real name to hire items for the shoot.

He rears back. "You must have heard it wrong."

Shit.

Xero scoffs. "He's in denial. Try something else."

I place a hand on his bicep, making his breath catch. "Grunt, has anyone taken a look at the burns on your skin?"

His gaze drops to my hand, then he looks me full in the face. When his breath quickens, and his broad chest heaves, my stomach plummets. He's misinterpreting my concern as a come-on.

"What do you mean?" he says, his voice lowering several octaves.

"Amethyst," Xero snarls.

Fuck. I didn't mean to flirt.

My tongue darts to lick my lips, and Grunt's eyes track the movement. If I don't think of something else to distract this sexual predator, I could lose what's left of my mind.

"Those burns look very—"

Stopping mid-sentence, I hurl myself to the padded floor, making myself spasm and jerk.

"Amy, what's wrong?" he asks.

"Allergic to—"

I let my eyes roll to the back of my head and make my body tremble and convulse. My breath comes in noisy gasps, and I foam at the mouth.

"Amy?" Grunt's hands close in around my shoulders.

Flailing my limbs, I arch my back, contorting my body into unnatural positions. Grunt yells through his mask, but I drown out his shouts with so much guttural choking that I bring up a mouthful of oatmeal. It trickles down the side of my face, adding to the performance. When Xero places a hand on my shoulder, I force my body to go limp.

"Shit!" Grunt bellows.

I hold my breath and play dead. Grunt places trembling fingers beneath my nostrils. After a few seconds of sensing nothing, he presses his fingers into the side of my neck, missing the pulse point by inches.

"No, no, no, no..." he wails, his voice rising with panic.

"Keep it up," Xero says.

Grunt scrambles off his knees, his heavy footsteps thundering to the door. Exhaling, I wait for a count of five after he exits before I'm on my feet.

I have to time my next move perfectly. Screwing this up will mean getting a more diligent babysitter, like Seth.

TWENTY-THREE

Sunday July 25, 2010

Things have gone from bad to worse. Yesterday, Lyle came to visit with the girls and a tray of hot chocolates. The baby was doing well, and we were talking about being discharged. When I asked to speak to Lyle alone about finding a new nanny, he sent the girls to the waiting room to sit with Charlotte.

Knowing he'd brought her along was like a punch to the gut. We still haven't gotten to the bottom of how I ended up with anaphylactic shock, yet he's allowing that woman around my children?

I told him my fears about Charlotte and that I wanted her out of my house. Lyle looked at me like I hadn't changed from the battered wife who was still in denial and needed saving from Giorgi.

It hurt so badly to be dismissed like that and for Lyle to interpret my distrust for delusion. I ALWAYS knew I needed to leave Giorgi, from the moment I discovered he was in the mafia. The trouble was that I had no one to trust. It took so long for me to accept Lyle's help because I was convinced he would betray me to my psycho husband.

No amount of platitudes can convince me that Charlotte isn't a threat, but Lyle refuses to see it. What kind of nanny cozies up to the husband? One who wants him for herself. I was becoming so stressed that Lyle didn't understand the threat she posed that I told him to leave—him and his poisoned hot chocolate. He looked so wounded when he left that I spent the night tossing and turning.

The next morning, my urine test showed elevated protein levels. My BP also rose. Now I have preeclampsia. I don't know if it's due to stress or if there was something in the hot chocolate, but this is the second time Charlotte has been around something I've consumed that's messed with my health.

I can kiss goodbye to going home. This diagnosis means new medication, more tests, and I won't be discharged until after a c-section. I asked if I could at least have a natural birth, but the ob-gyn explained that this is the safest option for me and the baby.

Lyle isn't answering his cell. Or the landline. Charlotte is probably pouring poison into his ear and doing God knows what to my girls. I can't remember the last time I was so isolated, trapped, or frightened.

I worry, both for myself and the baby.

If I had a mother, brother, or siblings, I would call them for help and damn the consequences, but I didn't stay at a foster home long enough to make any connections. I only have Lyle. Giorgi might be dead, but I can't contact his mother because I still stabbed the Salentino family in the back.

I keep calling Dr. Forster, but the number keeps going to voicemail. Even my shrink is tired of my paranoia. The only thing I can do is practice meditation, calm my thoughts, and focus on staying healthy for my children.

And of course, accept food or beverages from only the hospital staff.

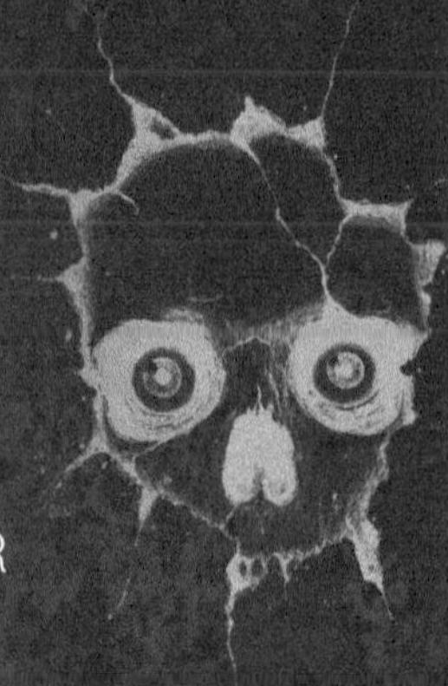

TWENTY-FOUR

XERO

I arrive at Helsing Island airport later that evening in full disguise. Even though the investors' reception is tomorrow evening, I need to be in the Hotel Royale, ready to capture Father the moment he arrives with Dolly for the meet and greet.

Depending on whether he intends to share his companion with the investors, he might even bring Amethyst. I'll need to be careful with capturing her to make sure I have the right twin. Both are his victims, but one has devolved into a creature so twisted and hateful that she would wish trauma on her own sister.

Reverend Thomas will arrive at Helsing Island tomorrow, as instructed, with Camila watching his back. By the time he steps into the drinks reception, he'll have enough tech in his orifices to qualify him as a cyborg.

Helsing is an island nestled within an archipelago off the coast of New York, bordered by the Atlantic Ocean to the south and the Long Island Sound to the north. It's renowned for its status as a nature preserve and the site of a prestigious private academy.

The Hotel Royale is located at its southernmost point, twelve miles from the airport. It's a three-story colonial-style building in a prime spot overlooking the ocean. According to the website, there are three hospitality rooms available for private events, as well as a single penthouse suite with panoramic views.

Father would definitely choose this kind of location for its privacy, not just for the luxury of a private helicopter pad. Hotel employees might enter a hospitality room unannounced, but not a penthouse.

I upgrade to the penthouse for tonight, since it's already booked for tomorrow. The receptionist reminds me to check out by 10 am, but I plan on leaving before then.

Once I take the key, I make my way up. The penthouse is a white space with a king-sized bed, two banks of sofas, a fully stocked wet bar, and plenty of room for entertaining guests.

I step out through the floor-to-ceiling windows overlooking the marina and walk across a wraparound balcony leading to the private helipad.

Noting it as a possible hiding spot, I return to the suite to explore its closets, when Jynxson calls my phone. "We're docked at the marina," he says through the sound of crashing waves. "Ready to storm the hotel whenever you are."

"Any word from the Spring brothers?" I ask, remembering we left them to infiltrate X-Cite Media's out-of-town studio.

"No one from their other shoot can tell them the location of Delta's snuff production. It looks like he only shares that information with his inner circle."

After telling Jynxson to stand by, I check in with Tyler's team for updates on possible shooting locations within the vicinity of the Hotel Royale.

"We've run through all the venues for hire on the island," he replies. "Everything's either set up for tourism or connected to the academy and located within four highly trafficked areas."

"How about houses and cottages for hire?" I ask. "Warehouses, industrial buildings? There has to be something."

"Still running through possible locations, but this island has limited potential. A group of eight or more men torturing a screaming woman on an island as small as this will attract attention."

"Then where?" I snarl.

"We're already looking at the other islands in the archipelago.

Some of them are completely uninhabited. Plenty of space to shoot where no one can hear you scream."

My gut churns. We're so close to where they're keeping Amethyst. She could be under our noses, suffering unimaginable horrors, yet we're running around blind.

"Send me your findings."

"Just remember, Delta is arriving in less than twenty-four hours. You can extract the information you need when you capture him."

I pinch the bridge of my nose. Tyler may have gone through four years of academy training, but he didn't qualify to be an assassin. I poached him from the Moirai's IT department, where he specialized in surveillance and research. He can't put himself in the mind of a man like Father.

"How much torture do you think Delta will withstand before he gives us the information we need?" I ask.

He hesitates, sighs, and mutters, "Point taken."

I hang up. Delta won't just be resistant to torture. If he doesn't send us into a trap, then he'll feed us enough misinformation so we're chasing false leads while Amethyst might already be wishing for death.

My search around the penthouse suite continues. I can only hope when he arrives tomorrow, it's with Amethyst and at least one lackey who will cave in to pressure.

TWENTY-FIVE

Sunday August 1, 2010

I had the c-section. My test results were getting so bad that my ob-gyn decided not to delay the procedure. I now have a beautiful baby boy with soft brown hair, just like Lyle's.

He was there when I woke up, already holding our son. The love in his eyes erased weeks of paranoia. Now he spends every day at my bedside, telling me everything he sacrificed to save me and the girls is worthwhile, because our family is complete.

I broke down, apologizing for all those crazy accusations. Lyle just smiled and said it was normal. Paranoia is a woman's survival instinct to protect her baby from danger. When he explained it like that, I didn't feel quite so stupid.

He visited every day with flowers and cards from our girls, along with photos of them helping him to set up the nursery. I can't remember the last time I felt so loved. Amy wrote a darling little story that filled my heart with warmth. It's about a princess who fought a monster to save the queen and the newborn prince.

She's finally coming out of her shell and trying to connect. Dolly wants to name the baby Delta, after the principal of her summer school, who sent her a certificate for her outstanding achievement. Lyle wants to name him after his father, Heath.

We were discharged four days after Heath's birth and returned home on Friday evening. When I found the house was empty, I asked about the girls. Lyle drove them to Three Fates in the morning, so I could settle back home without distractions.

I wanted to speak to them right away. Lyle said I should relax and let him make dinner, but I insisted on calling Three Fates. The line was busy, but I kept calling, even though Lyle looked at me like I was crazy. Maybe it was my leftover paranoia, but I burst into tears, needing to see my daughters.

When he asked for permission to call Charlotte's number, I felt like the world's biggest bitch. Charlotte answered and brought the phone over to the girls' dorms. We had a video chat. Amy burst into tears at the sight of her baby brother. Dolly sat back and smiled.

I asked if they were getting along, and Dolly said she was taking care of Amy. My girls sat together, like sisters, with no traces of animosity. Looks like Lyle was right. The baby really brought us closer together.

The girls wanted to know everything, including when they could come home. It was too late in the day to send Lyle out to get them, so I said tomorrow morning.

Lyle didn't like me wasting the money he'd invested on a quiet weekend break, but I needed my family under one roof. He apologized, remembering I'd spent so long in the hospital and at home under bedrest. It's natural that I would want my family to be together.

That night, I had my best sleep in months. Maybe I was no longer resistant to my medication. I wasn't about to question why. I woke up the next morning, drowsy and relaxed, seeing Lyle standing over me, feeding the baby.

He didn't want to wake me. Isn't that sweet? He let me cuddle with Heath before taking him back to his crib. Over breakfast in bed, he told me that the girls were just an hour away and would arrive by the time I showered and dressed.

I fell asleep again, relieved that all was finally well. Later, I woke up to the sound of chatter. My girls were in the room with Lyle, taking turns holding Heath.

And standing at the doorway with a serene smile was Charlotte.

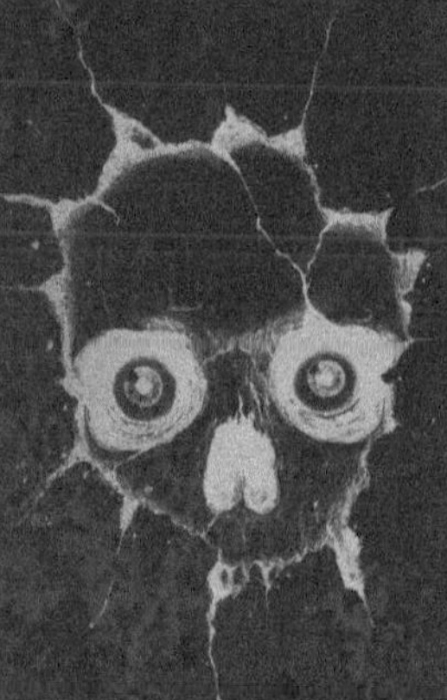

TWENTY-SIX

AMETHYST

Xero reaches the exit before me and sticks his head through its metal surface. I flinch backward, my stomach tightening at the peculiar sight.

Seeming to sense my distress, he turns back to me with wide eyes. "What's wrong?"

"You just..." I point at his head, then drop my hand, realizing that hallucinations can do whatever they want. "Never mind."

I reach the door, a solid metal barrier with no handles. Finding a tiny gap where it meets its frame, I wedge my fingers into the slit and try to pull. My nails are too thick, since they're encased in the straitjacket's sleeves.

"What are you going to do?" Xero asks, his gaze trailing down my form. "Take it off?"

Shaking my head, I pull my arms out of the sleeves, leaving them trailing down my side, and fumble with the fastening around my crotch. Now that it's no longer so restrictive, I twist the entire garment, so I'm wearing it almost back to front.

Finally, I slip a hand through the jacket's opening at the back and reach for the gap in the door. This time, my nails slip into the tiny slit, and I pry it open with a gentle creak.

I peek out into the hallway, finding it empty. On the far right, the heavy door leading to the filming room swings shut. I probably have less than thirty seconds before Grunt alerts someone of my supposed reaction to the oatmeal.

That doesn't give me much of a head start.

"There's no time to think about risks," Xero growls.

Sucking in a deep breath, I dart into the hallway and run in the opposite direction. Ignoring the bite of fallen plaster beneath my bare feet, I head to the fire exit straight ahead.

Sunlight filters through windows blackened by years of grime, casting an eerie glow on the neglected hallway. The air is thick with dust and the smell of stale water.

Xero jogs at my side, his steps matching the slap of my sleeves against my bandaged legs. "Keep going. You're doing so well."

I reach the fire exit and yank open its heavy door, fully expecting to trigger a fire alarm. When nothing happens, I slip into a darkened stairwell that descends into shadows.

"Keep going," he growls as I charge down the steps, clutching the handrail. "There'll be a door at the bottom of the stairs. Wedge it open."

Sure enough, when I reach the ground floor, sunlight streams in through gaps in a heavy metal fire exit at the base of the stairwell. Triumph surges through my veins. I press my shoulder against it, straining to compensate for its rusted hinges.

"That's right. Throw your weight against it."

"I am," I say through clenched teeth.

With a screech, the door grates open, letting in a gust of meadow-scented air. I'm about to step out onto a walkway overrun with ivy and weeds, when Xero places a hand on my shoulder.

"Good work, but we're going in the opposite direction."

"What?"

Footsteps thunder overhead, making me stiffen. Panic seizes my chest in a grip so punishing that I wince.

"There's an autopsy room through that door." Xero flicks his head to the side. "That's where you'll find sharp objects."

We should be going out toward the exit, not venturing deeper into this derelict nightmare. Before I can even protest, Xero grabs my arm and drags me down the corridor, away from my last chance of freedom.

I would scream, but that would only alert the people upstairs.

"What do you think you're doing?" I hiss.

"You're half-naked, barefoot, and unarmed. If you go out there, it's only a matter of minutes before you get caught. A weapon will increase your chances of survival."

"How do you know we're even going in the right direction?" I whisper.

"What do you think?"

I can consider the implications of his knowledge of the hospital's layout another time. At the end of the hallway, we reach another heavy door. I push it open, emerging into another vacant corridor that runs the entire length of the building.

It's darker here, the natural light too feeble to penetrate the thicker layers of grime on these lower-level windows. The air is chillier, carrying with it a dampness that seeps through the straitjacket and into my bones.

Shivers seize my skeleton. I want to duck back into the safety of the stairwell, but footsteps echo from beyond the doors. Either it's another hallucination or they've already found out I've escaped.

Up ahead and to my left stands another set of double doors leading into a room with tiled floors. How do I know that? Every instinct screams at me not to enter. That's where people go in and never return.

"Move." Xero jogs straight ahead and disappears into the room.

Terror claws at my chest, rooting me to the spot. I follow him, terrified of the rumbling noises and the prospect of being left alone.

Swallowing a lump of dread, I step into a room with red-tiled floors and steel furniture. The once-white walls, now green with water damage and moss, resemble one of the upstairs sets.

Xero stands at a set of drawers, his features held in a hard mask. "This is where they keep the instruments. See if you can find a scalpel."

I walk toward him on trembling legs, my gaze darting toward an autopsy table covered in watermarks and rust. Flashbacks slam through my consciousness all at once—a body sprawled on the table, a man in a white coat and mask, that red-haired doctor telling me this is what happens to girls who don't behave.

Then there's the blood.

"Amethyst, look at me," Xero barks.

His voice snaps me back to the present. Blinking away the images, I rush across the tiled floor toward him, ignoring the way my heart wants to crawl out of my throat.

"Find a scalpel. Now," he commands.

I grab the nearest drawer, which opens with a rusty creak. In one are strange-looking saws arranged like kitchen utensils. Another contains hammers, chisels, and something that resembles a pick.

My insides roil, and what's left of the oatmeal in my stomach turns to stone. When I finally find the drawer containing knives and scalpels, I grab a handful.

"What now?" I ask.

"We take another exit," Xero says, "But first, we hide."

I whirl around, finding him jogging toward another doorway. Not wanting to be left behind, I sprint after him, clutching the scalpels.

The next room is even wider than the first, lined with stainless steel compartments resembling supermarket freezers. In its center stands a tilted table with two sets of overhead surgical lights descending from the ceiling. Beneath the table, the floor is marred by dried blood.

This is insane. This is gruesome. This is a hospital of horrors. My mind conjures memories of bodies dissected and discarded. Shaking off those visions, I follow Xero into a long corridor lined with gurneys.

"This way," he says.

My throat dries, and I try not to consider how I know each of these metal contraptions used to contain corpses. Instead, I focus on the exit up ahead, where they used to transport the bodies outside for burial.

Xero takes a right turn through a door left ajar. Inside, it's completely dark. I don't ask myself how I can see him when there's no light, but I take his hand and let him position me behind the door.

"Is this where we're hiding?" I whisper.

"Yes. But don't speak out loud. I can read your thoughts," he replies.

I nod, certain I hid here before when I was a resident. Xero must be able to access my memories, but I still don't understand why I only get tiny snippets.

"You can't handle it right now," he says.

I want to ask him if it could really be that bad, but then I remember all those polaroids on his crime board. Does Xero know how I ended up in this institution?

"That part is foggy," he replies, "But I think it happened after the accident."

My throat tightens. It's no wonder memories of my childhood are so inaccessible. I can't imagine losing my father to a car crash and then getting thrown into an asylum to suffer abuse.

Xero wraps his arms around my waist and pulls me into a hug. We both lean against the wall, listening out for footsteps.

By now, the help Grunt called for would have noticed I've gone and tried to follow my trail. They probably expected me to take the fire exit, because hiding in a creepy abandoned asylum is counter-intuitive.

He nods behind me, his grip around my waist tightening. "They'll waste time checking the grounds, expecting you to run toward the gate."

I smile. With any luck, they'll make Dolly take my place.

"At least we've bought ourselves some breathing space. While we're waiting for the right time to exit, you should turn those sleeves into a pair of socks."

"What for?"

He chuckles, the sound harsh and low. "You're going to need something comfortable on your feet to hunt these bastards."

TWENTY-SEVEN

Monday August 2, 2010

We had our first argument yesterday, after I discovered that Lyle hadn't fired Charlotte. He said I'd feel less paranoid after the baby and realize I would need her help.

Something inside me snapped, bringing up years of suppressed fury. When Lyle convinced me to leave the Salentinos, he said we would be together as a family. Instead, he left me alone in a small apartment with two babies. I spent the first few years alone, without help, without a means to communicate with the outside world.

It was like I'd entered another prison, with Lyle visiting sporadically to drain his balls. When he finally moved us to a real home, he would leave for weeks on end. By then, I had Dr. Forster to pick up the slack, but there were limits to how much I could share.

Lyle spent more time working on his adoption agency than on his new family. He worked long hours and was always stressed. He even lost interest in sex. So, I let loose a tirade of accusations, accusing her of seducing him and trying to usurp my position in this household.

For the first time since we got married, Lyle yelled back.

What hurt the most wasn't the fact that he raised his voice, but that he defended Charlotte. He told me she was doing a better job keeping my daughters from tearing out each other's throats than I ever did. The house was spotless, the meals were on time, and she created the kind of home he'd imagined we'd have when he discarded an illustrious career in the FBI.

The words stung. He's never thrown that in my face. My hormones were everywhere, and I burst into tears. Lyle watched me cry for several minutes before walking out. Out of the room, out of the house, and out of our lives.

He didn't return to bed last night, and his car has left the driveway. I'm now alone with Charlotte and the girls. I don't know what to do. I don't know where he's gone. He won't answer his cell phone or his office number.

I stayed in my room with Heath, expecting Charlotte to take Lyle's absence as a chance to finish the job she started. She sent Amy in with food, but I refused to fall for that trick again.

In the evening, when I turned down dinner, Charlotte barged into the room without permission. Well, she knocked, but I told her to go away. She wanted to know why I wasn't eating when I needed all the nutrition I could get to nurse the baby.

The girls stood at her sides, staring at me like I'd gone crazy. I wanted to scream at her to get out and take away her poison, but I didn't want to frighten my daughters.

All I could think of to say was that I'd order something online. Her gentle smile, her contrived compassion, the way she wrapped her arms around my twins made me sick. It was all an act to groom my girls into thinking I was an unfit mother.

She's already slithered into my husband's pants—I know she fucked him with that tight, nubile body while I was hospitalized. That's why Lyle is being so intolerant. Why, in Giorgi's words, would he need me when he can have Miss Perfect?

I didn't say any of this out loud. That's what she wants. She even made a show of looking disappointed that I didn't appreciate the special, nutrient-rich meals she and the girls had lovingly prepared to nourish me and baby Heath.

My fists clenched under the comforter. I wanted to laugh in her face, but it would come out as a deranged cackle. Instead, I said her services were no longer required, and she had until tomorrow morning to leave.

Dolly howled, clinging to Charlotte like she was the one who had carried her for thirty-six weeks. Amy stared, not knowing what to think. Charlotte explained in that sugary voice that she was employed by Lyle to help me during this difficult time. I snapped back, telling her that she was a conniving cunt.

All three of them stared at me like I'd turned into Medusa. Then Charlotte pulled the girls out of the room and comforted them outside the door with soft, soothing words.

FUCK HER! And fuck me for playing into her hands. Now, my daughters think I'm a psycho.

If this bitch doesn't leave my house voluntarily, then she'll be leaving in a hearse.

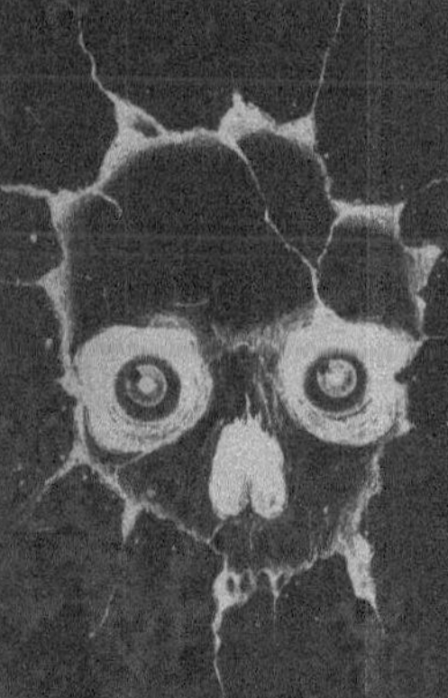

TWENTY-EIGHT

AMETHYST

By the time I've cut down the sleeves of my straitjacket and slipped them onto my feet, both sides of the hallway echo with distant noises. It sounds like they're having a full-scale search party.

I try to remember how many men I saw the last few times they took me out for filming, but Xero interrupts my thoughts.

"Eight. Delta, Locke, Seth, Barrett. Plus the other four from the forced feeding." He pauses. "Ten if you count Dolly, Fen and Grunt."

Because the last two are the same person. I shake my head, wondering if Grunt left the door unlocked on purpose.

"Don't look too deeply into his motives," Xero snarls. "Thinking of him as an ally, even subconsciously, might make you drop your guard."

He's right. No matter how much they're making Grunt a scapegoat, I should never forget the reason he joined X-Cite Media.

Noisy footsteps echo through the hallway, cutting our conversation short. We both stiffen, pressing our bodies into the cold wall. The door we're standing behind is ajar, with the barest of light streaming in where its hinges meet the frame.

The steps coming toward us are heavy, deliberate, and

growing louder. Dread pools in my gut at the prospect of being caught.

"You have the advantage," Xero hisses in my ear. "Lure him in and take him out."

My breath quickens. My heart pounds so hard that its vibrations reach my fingers, making them tremble. Sweat breaks out across my brow and trickles down my temple.

I'm no longer the woman who hid in the corner, trembling as Xero tortured the men who broke into my house. The cruelty I suffered has ground my human decency to dust. I need to get out of this hellscape alive, even if it means carving through every man with my scalpels.

"That's right, little ghost." Xero's large hands land on my shoulders, infusing my body with the strength and determination of a trained assassin.

But where should I stab him? The neck might be a good spot, but I don't know the exact location of the jugular vein.

"Remember the day after you read my letter about Officer McMurphy?" Xero asks. "Where did I say I'd stab her before fucking you in a pool of her blood?"

My lips twitch at the reminder of that heated morning. It was the base of her skull.

"That's my girl."

I tighten my grip on both scalpels, my veins filling with cold adrenaline. Every man involved in the production of these videos needs to die. Not just to save myself, but to protect others.

"Focus on your fear. Let it sharpen your senses. Let your survival instincts turn these predators into prey."

A beam of light fills the hallway. It's weak compared to a flashlight and has to come from his phone. I shrink against the wall, slowing my breaths to lower the volume of my heartbeat.

The footsteps get louder. I fix my gaze on the gap in the doorway where a dark figure ambles past. He pauses for a second to fill my room with illumination before continuing toward the exit.

"Amethyst," Xero whispers, "Now."

I slip out from behind the door, my footfalls muffled by my newly-fashioned socks. The man in front of me is five-ten, stocky, wearing a black sweater and a baseball cap. He's still facing the double doors, giving me his broad back and the perfect target.

Leaping onto him, I wrap an arm around his neck. He lets out a choked gasp and drops his phone. A second later, he regains his composure and charges backward, slamming me into the wall.

Pain explodes across my spine, dulled by a surge of adrenaline. He grabs my arm, trying to tear off my grip, but I shift the scalpel and slash his neck. Warm blood sprays across my fingers, making me shiver. I drop to the floor, heart pounding, and scramble to my feet, narrowly dodging his wild punch.

He stumbles toward me like a wounded animal, clutching his throat, gurgling and choking on his blood.

"Finish him," Xero snarls.

Determination powers my steps. I jog around him and position myself at his back. This time, I won't fail. Using the strap of his baseball cap as a guideline, I drive the scalpel deep into the flesh beneath his cranium.

It sinks in with a wet sound that makes my stomach roil. He stumbles forward before dropping to the floor in spasms.

Xero wraps an arm around my shoulder. "Well done."

My blood roars with triumph. I stand above the fallen man, breathing hard, waiting for his body to stop twitching and convulsing.

An alert sounds from further down the hallway, turning my attention back to his phone, which now lies face-down in an expanding puddle of blood.

I pick up the device. There's an alert from a group chat, labeled ASYLUM SHOOT. Delta has divided the grounds and building into sections, assigning each crew member to search a specific area.

It looks like the man at my feet was given the ground floor, west wing and its surrounding courtyard.

What the hell do I do next? If they don't hear from him, they won't just know something has gone wrong, they'll concentrate their efforts on my hiding place.

"They'll know something's wrong the moment he doesn't return," Xero mutters. "Wait for the first person to report and then write something similar. We'll decide what to do next when Delta responds."

I glance down at the corpse, wondering if I should bother to hide it under one of the gurneys.

"No point when there's nothing to clean up the blood."

Nodding, I walk around the expanding pool, making sure not to create bloody footprints, and return to my hiding spot.

My adrenaline is still high as I lean against the wall, breathing hard. I clutch the phone with trembling hands and stare at the group chat, waiting for the next update.

What the hell am I doing? I should use this chance to call the police.

"Don't forget that Delta doesn't technically exist, and you're probably a person of interest in relation to at least four murders," he says.

I gulp. JakeRake69, who I killed, Chappy, who was found hanging outside the room where I was staying, the first two men in the basement who formed the human caterpillar. Big Dick Johnson and the Well Hung Man took care of themselves.

"Then there's your mother and your Uncle Clive," Xero adds.

My chest aches at the reminder. I didn't kill Mom. Dolly did, while dressed like me. Even if I pleaded insanity again, I might still end up in an institution, just like she'd always threatened. Right. And now this guy, who I stabbed even when he was down.

"With your track record, you'll probably get the electric chair."

I swallow hard. A third option would be to use the arrival of the police as a distraction and slip away unnoticed. That would make me a fugitive, but it's better than falling into the hands of murderous predators.

Xero stays silent. He knows I'm screwed. My choices are to risk dying with dignity or remaining here to guarantee a painful and humiliating death.

My fingers tremble as I call 911. I don't dare speak in case my voice carries across the hospital, but I leave the line open.

"911," the dispatcher says. "What's your emergency?

I breathe hard into the receiver, remaining silent. Blood

pounds through my veins, and my heart beats so hard that I feel sick.

"Caller, can you speak? What's your emergency?"

My throat tightens. I should at least tell her I need the police.

She pauses for several seconds before asking, "If you can't speak, press any key."

I press 5, hoping to hell they can track my location.

"Alright. Officers are on their way. Stay hidden and keep the line open. Help is coming."

Another alert pops up on the screen from the ASYLUM SHOOT group chat.

Upstairs east wing cleared. No sign of anything unusual.

I make a slow count to ten before typing my own response:

West wing clear.

Delta replies with: *Grounds?*

I type out: *Still searching.*

Xero hugs me from behind. "How do you feel?"

My stomach roils with a mix of bubbling emotions—desperation, dread, and a determination to survive. If I get taken by the police, there will be a public trial. I'll go viral on social media again, this time as a cautionary tale for simping over murders. Xero's people might infiltrate my prison cell. They'll probably torture me for killing their boss.

Xero doesn't reply because everything I've speculated is true. I turn around to meet his eyes, wondering if calling the police was a mistake.

TWENTY-NINE

Tuesday August 3, 2010

Charlotte made a single phone call and Lyle rushed in like a white knight to her rescue. I heard her whispering outside my door, telling him how much I upset the girls with a supposedly unhinged rant. She even added in a little twist that I'd made Heath cry.

I didn't even raise my voice, so unless Heath's English comprehension skills expand to veiled insults, then she's being manipulative. Again.

The absurdity of her claims don't matter, because Lyle will believe her without question. The mere fact that she's still here after poisoning me twice is proof that I'm not paranoid.

On cue, he entered the room, his gaze flicking to the crib as if he thought Heath's life might be in danger from his deranged wife. Then he shot me a look of pity and fear that made my blood boil.

Lyle sat on the edge of my bed and sighed, his handsome face creased with worry. I waited for him to start a rehearsed speech, telling me my mental issues are getting out of hand. Instead, he looked into my eyes and asked what would make me happy.

I told him to get rid of Charlotte. If we can't find a nanny, we can hire a housekeeper. He held my gaze, his expression unwavering, like he was trying to look into my soul.

Finally, he nodded, asking me to give him until the end of the week to find a suitable replacement. Every instinct screamed at me to demand that he send her packing immediately, but I held my tongue. The last thing I wanted was to appear unhinged.

My stomach rumbled, and he asked when I'd last eaten. I looked away, unable to meet his gaze. If I told him I was too frightened about being poisoned again, he would definitely think I'd lost my mind.

I muttered something about losing my appetite, and he walked out of the room. If I hadn't been post-operative and weak with hunger, I would have followed him out into the hallway and down the stairs. Instead, I waited.

The girls tiptoed into the room, their faces pale and drawn. Dolly stepped in first, clutching Amy's hand. Dolly asked if I was mad at her for loving Charlotte. The confirmation that she was under that bitch's influence was like a blade to the heart.

Swallowing hard, I forced a smile, but I couldn't hold back the tears. Pulling her into a hug, I whispered a string of reassurances. Amy stood a few feet away, her eyes wide with fear.

I beckoned her to come closer, and she hesitated for several seconds before shuffling forward. It was heartbreaking to see her look so insecure. I wrapped an arm around her shoulders and whispered that everything was going to be alright.

Lyle came in shortly after with a bag of chips and a bowl of chili, swearing to God that he'd warmed it up himself straight from the can. Laughing, I let him place the tray on my lap, and the three of us picked from it like it was a feast.

When he picked Heath out of the crib and sat at the bedside, it was like a family picnic. Five of us together... without that blonde interloper.

Just when I thought my marriage had gone to shit, he brought us all together with a simple bowl of chili. That's why I love him so fucking much.

We stayed together all night like it was a sleepover.

The next morning, Dolly found Charlotte in her bedroom, dead.

THIRTY

XERO

The next morning, after checking out, I return to the penthouse and remove a panel at the back of a closet, which separates it from the rest of the roof space. Jynxson sits inside with a laptop, its screen providing several viewpoints around the suite.

I spent the rest of yesterday evening working through the islands within the archipelago. There are thirty in total, eight of them currently occupied. We started with those first, with Tyler and his team identifying every possible shooting venue.

Our goal is to disable Father and his entourage, leaving as many of them as possible alive to help us dismantle X-Cite Media and locate the facility of child assassins. I refuse to believe Father just abandoned the boys to concentrate on making snuff. Somehow, the two ventures are connected. It's only a matter of time before I discover how.

"Any updates?" I ask Jynxson.

He yawns, his gaze still fixed on the screen. "Camila's flight just landed. She's in a rental car, tailing the padre's taxi."

"Give me a visual."

He swivels the computer, bringing up her dashboard camera feed. On screen, a yellow cab navigates a winding highway set between rolling hills.

"Camila, report," I say.

"He threw up once on the flight and already burst into tears twice. He's going to need some help walking into this evening's mixer."

"How about a miniature C4 charge in the rectum?" Jynxson asks.

She scoffs. "Dr. Dixon already administered that explosive so he wouldn't fuck up at the airport."

"Give him a shot of Lorazepam before the event. Any word from Father?"

"Yeah, he's set up a group chat. Nine people, including him and Thomas."

Jynxson whistles. "So, he's already made one and a half million just from selling front-row seats."

I grind my teeth. Eight people at a quarter million investment each. That's more than our entire operation earns from a single assassination. "Not to mention the amount he'll rake in from memberships and from renting the content for a hundred dollars an hour. All without getting his hands dirty."

As the hotel's cleaning staff comes in to turn over the penthouse, I patch into a mirror of the reverend's phone and find the group chat. At the top is a message from Delta, welcoming them to a glimpse into his inner circle. It's already filled with eager replies about the nature of the shoot, along with commentary on the previous movie starring Lizzie Bath.

Each man asks if they'll meet Dolly and gushes when they discover she'll star in the next movie. Their excitement is sickening, yet I force myself to scour through each comment for clues on where Dolly and Delta are keeping Amethyst. It's crowded by requests for them to be the first to fuck her corpse.

Rage roils in my gut. Father isn't planning on murdering his wife. He's using Amethyst as a stand-in for Dolly.

Jynxson reads over my shoulder. "This is some twisted shit."

Someone in the chat, with the codename of Nemesis, asks how many have already arrived at the Royale. Two other men mention that they're having brunch and invite the others to join them at the hotel's restaurant. From the way they chat, I can tell this isn't their first time observing an X-Cite Media shoot.

I send a message to Tyler and his team to gather the names

and addresses of everyone checking into the Royale. After Amethyst is safely back in my possession, I want to hunt down Father's most ardent supporters.

We spend the rest of the day coordinating operatives waiting at the marina and place small explosives in discrete locations around the penthouse. Our aim is to create the maximum amount of chaos to make it easier to capture Father.

Later, Reverend Thomas checks in, and Camila installs herself in the room next door.

"Something's gone wrong," Jynxson says as I'm testing the last explosive.

I straighten. "What?"

He passes me the phone. "There's a message from Delta, informing the investors that he's running late due to technical errors on set. Dolly will meet them for an early dinner, and he'll join as soon as possible."

"What kind of problems?" I wait for someone to raise the question, but the members are too distracted by the chance to meet Dolly without her usual chaperone.

"So, we're going to be stuck in that roof space for longer?" Jynxson mutters.

"We can't risk Dolly or the investors warning Delta that we're coming," I reply.

At three thirty, the sound of an approaching helicopter makes us both startle. I expected them to arrive in a limousine, but this method of transport makes me wonder if they're shooting on one of the other islands within the archipelago.

"Camila," I say into the headset. "Dose him up."

Jynxson switches his laptop screen to a display of all the monitors we set up around the penthouse. I check the group chat to find that Dolly has entered, telling the investors to join her upstairs at the penthouse at four.

I stare at the screen for the first glimpse of Dolly. A blond man, with hair identical to her companion at the airport, steps through the balcony door.

Fury heats my blood at the reminder that he and his friends put my Amethyst in a straitjacket and trafficked her across the country. I enlarge the image, recognizing him from that graveyard video.

Behind him is a woman who looks identical to my little ghost, from the striking green eyes to the two-toned hair. My heart lurches. The only difference is the taste in clothes. Amethyst would never wear white.

"That's your girl," Jynxson mutters.

"That's Dolly," I growl.

"I can't tell the difference."

She steps into the penthouse and spins around in a circle. The blond follows close behind and wraps his arms around her waist.

"This is gorgeous," she says and kisses him on the mouth.

"There," I say. "Amethyst wears black. She likes black decors."

"She also likes blonds," Jynxson says.

I flash my teeth.

A black-haired man in his late twenties steps in through the balcony and pauses to take in the penthouse with a low whistle. From the bulge in his leather jacket and the way his beady eyes check out all the exits, I can tell he's here as security.

The blond man leads Dolly straight toward the wet bar and fills a bucket with ice. She extracts a bottle of champagne from the cooler and places it in the bucket.

"Amethyst recently had a bad experience with champagne," I mutter, remembering the time I had to save her from that book fair bastard's limo. "And she prefers vodka."

"We won't be able to make any moves until Delta arrives anyway," Jynxson replies, still not sounding convinced that Dolly is Amethyst's twin. "Once we capture him, we can sort out who's who."

There's a knock on the door, and the black-haired man crosses the space to let in a stream of room service staff pushing in trolleys of food. They park the buffet at the side of the room, along with several bottles of wine and an assortment of drinks.

The black-haired man hands the staff tips before escorting them to the door. As soon as it shuts, Dolly strides up to him with two glasses.

"Seth, I want you watching my back. Intervene if any of those assholes get too close."

The black-haired man turns to Dolly and frowns. "But Delta said—"

"Delta isn't coming," she snaps.

Eyes widening, I lock gazes with Jynxson.

"I'm his wife, which means I own fifty percent of X-Cite Media, which means I get to choose who I fuck."

The blond wraps an arm around her shoulder. "That's right. This evening is just a meet and greet. We'll stay for an hour or two and then take the chopper back to the asylum."

Asylum?

I jerk forward, this new information hitting like a fist to the gut. We thought they were keeping Amethyst in a studio or a rented house converted for filming.

Jynxson grabs my arm. "This is big."

"Tyler," I say into the headset. "Are you listening?"

"Already searching for psychiatric hospitals within Helsing and its surrounding islands," he replies. "Give me a minute."

Heart pounding, I listen to their discussion, and piece together that Amethyst escaped her cell and is hiding in a four-story asylum set within acres of grounds. Dolly is tense because Father will use her for tomorrow's shoot if Amethyst remains uncaptured.

"We need to get out of here," I say.

Jynxson gives me a tense nod. "Tyler, have you found anything?"

"There's three," he replies with a sigh. "Two on Helsing Island. A third on Ravencliff."

"Which of them is abandoned?"

"One second... Saint Christina was shut down nearly a decade ago. Let me pull up satellite pictures. Yeah. Here it is. A massive Victorian-style property, surrounded by woodland. Very isolated, with a single road leading to its gates."

I close the laptop and rise. "Let's go."

"Should we steal that chopper?" Jynxson asks.

"Delta will get suspicious and know something's wrong." I

walk around the roof's perimeter, toward the back of a storage closet that opens into the public hallway.

"Wait. Don't you at least want to take Dolly as a hostage?" Tyler asks.

That would be the sensible thing to do, but the investors will be the first to complain on their group chat if their starlet is missing. Plus, Father isn't the type of man to give a shit when his wife is in peril.

That bastard watched me murder his entire family, never once telling me to stop. If I take Dolly, that will only endanger Amethyst.

As I pull on the door, the elevator opens, revealing a quartet of middle-aged men in suits. I draw back, letting them stream out into the hallway toward the penthouse's entrance.

If we find Amethyst before the end of their soirée, I'm going to detonate those bombs.

"What about Thomas?" Jynxson whispers at my back.

"Camila," I say into my headset. "Stay back to handle the reverend. He's going in as planned. If we need any extra information from him, we'll ask."

The penthouse doors open, letting in the investors. I slip out into the hallway with Jynxson and take the fire exit.

"Tyler, do you have the asylum's exact coordinates?" I ask as I charge down the stairs.

There's no reply.

"Tyler?"

"We've lost connection," Jynxson says.

My heart sinks. Without Tyler and his drones helping to pinpoint Amethyst's location, our chances of finding her before the shoot are looking bleak.

THIRTY-ONE

Wednesday August 4, 2010

I'm still reeling. We had the most perfect night together as a family. After we ate the chili, Lyle took Dolly down to the kitchen, and they returned with the most ridiculous chocolate fudge brownie sundae.

They put an entire tub of ice cream in a bowl and layered it with chunks of brownies, whipped cream, hot fudge, and sprinkles.

Amy stared at the sundae, her eyes rounding with disbelief. Dolly handed her a spoon, and seconds later, the pair of them descended on the dessert like wolves. Lyle gave me a spoon, and I joined in on what was the sweetest moment I've had since the girls were young.

We locked gazes and shared a nostalgic smile. I glanced down at the girls, wondering if this was the start of a perfect new era.

I know I'm talking around Charlotte's death, but I need to give what happened next a bit of context. Dolly and Amy were getting along, bonding over Lyle's extravagant dessert.

Maybe it was the baby. Maybe it was the summer school. Maybe it was the absence of Charlotte. I can't tell what triggered this moment of togetherness, but for those few hours, we were a family for the first time in ages.

It finally registered what Lyle sees in them: miniature versions of myself with similar curly brown hair, green eyes, and wide smiles. There wasn't a hint of Giorgi in their faces, words, or actions. We were a unit. One family, oblivious to the impending shit storm.

After we finished the sundae, the girls left to get changed into their pajamas, leaving Lyle to undress. I fed Heath, put him back in the crib and returned to bed. Lyle spooned behind me and nuzzled my neck, murmuring how much he enjoyed spending time with us tonight.

Then the door opened, and two identical faces popped in, both dressed in identical pajamas. They wanted to sleep in our bed.

Lyle scooted us both backward, giving the girls space to crawl in. They both squirmed into my side, giggling and whispering until I had to tell them to settle down. It was dark, and I couldn't tell which girl was cuddled into my front and which one slept at the end. I was just so happy that I didn't care. For once, everything felt as it should.

I woke up twice last night to feed Heath. The first time, both girls were cuddled together like baby koalas. The second one had gone, presumably to the bathroom. It's hard to tell them apart at the best of times. Impossible when they're asleep and in the dark.

So, when I woke up the next morning hearing screams coming from the other side of the house, I nearly burst my stitches jolting out of bed. Lyle rushed out, long before my feet had even reached the carpet.

I picked up Heath, cradling him to my chest as I ventured out to investigate. Amy grabbed my hand, telling me to hide in the closet. She had a point. If there were intruders, the last thing I needed to do was confront them holding a newborn.

After walking her into the bathroom with a cellphone, I handed her the baby and ordered her to lock the door. With a nod, she did as she was told, and I ventured toward the source of the screams.

It was Dolly. She was standing in Charlotte's room, holding a knife. The front of her pajamas was covered in blood. Lyle crouched in front of my girl, trying to coax her into releasing the weapon, but she was too far gone to listen.

Behind her, Charlotte lay on the bed, her neck sliced open with multiple stab wounds through her white nightgown. I didn't need to be an FBI agent to know what had happened to the nanny or even why.

It was last night's outburst. Words carry in this house and travel into little ears. All those accusations I made of Charlotte trying to steal my husband's love and my daughters' affections had ignited a spark within Dolly that had set off this horrifying chain of events.

Maybe Dolly read my diary. Maybe she pieced together Charlotte's machinations. Dolly, in a fit of guilt at having been duped, killed the nanny to protect our family. This isn't the first time she's attacked someone with a knife. The whole reason she ended up at Three Fates was because of what she did to poor Amy.

We need to cover this up. My little girl won't end up in an institution.

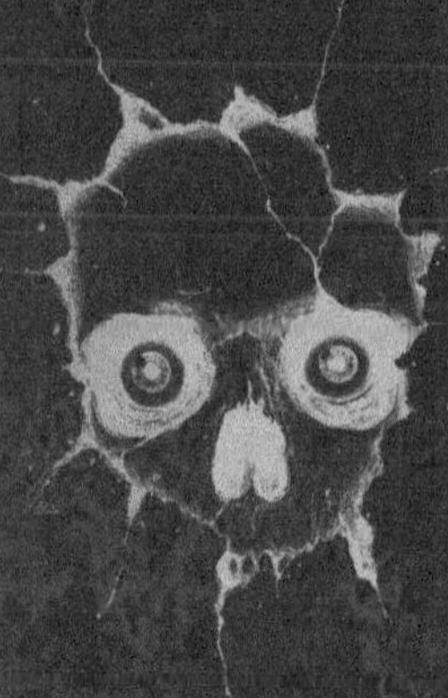

THIRTY-TWO

AMETHYST

I can't hide in this closet all day. When they realize the man I killed is missing, the first place they'll check is the west wing. Then they'll find his corpse and concentrate their search around the pool of blood. Then my punishment will make the forced feeding ordeal feel like a friendly tea party.

"You make a good point," Xero says, sounding gruff. "What do you suggest?"

I should go outside and meet the police halfway. Maybe if I sneak through the weeds, I'll have a chance of slipping out unnoticed.

He nods. "And if you bump into one of Delta's men?"

Gulping, I glance down at my scalpels and decide not to leave without an additional backup weapon.

Xero kneads my shoulders like he's my trainer and I'm a boxer about to step back into a fight. "Are you ready?"

I breathe hard, needing a minute to gather my courage.

Thirty seconds later, I'm crouching in a pool of blood, rolling the corpse onto its front. My fingers grip the scalpel sticking out from the base of his skull, and I pull it out with a sickening squelch. Nausea clogs my throat, and I force myself not to gag.

After wiping its blade and handle on the man's shirt, I twist my curls into a high bun and secure it with two scalpels.

"Good thinking." Xero nods at the scalpel remaining in my hand. "Let's go."

Any other time, I would preen at his praise, but there's no room for anything but survival. Xero moves to the fire door and points at the horizontal bar running across its middle.

"Don't panic if this triggers an alarm. You'll still have a head start over the men searching the grounds."

I nod, even though my stomach roils and my heart wants to explode. Xero's features are grim, looking like he's also forcing down a surge of panic.

Walking toward him on numb legs, I reach for the bar, press down, and push. The door opens with a groan, letting in the harsh sunlight. A blast of warm pollen hits my sinuses, making my nose itch. Just as I'm about to step out into the blinding light, an alarm rings.

My muscles stiffen. It's a dull sound, like it's on its last batteries. Not loud enough to carry upstairs, but insistent enough to attract any of Delta's men on the grounds.

I glance around, my eyes still adjusting to the intense daylight, and find a courtyard where baby trees sprout through pavement cracks. Beyond them, shrubs loom almost six feet tall, overrun by climbing plants. Fifty feet into the jungle of weeds, a gnarled tree stands with outstretched branches entangled in a struggle against plants trying to smother its existence.

"Go," Xero barks, snapping me out of my stupor.

My heart races. I glance around again, looking for a means of escape—the gate, the road, the truck—but there's nothing but foliage.

"I'll guide you. Just run toward the tree." Xero sprints away, leaving me gaping at his broad back.

I dart through the courtyard, my wet feet slapping on the concrete. It's too late to consider that I've created a blood trail for the men to trace.

"Don't worry about that." Xero calls over his shoulder, already disappearing through a narrow gap between two shrubs. "We'll use these weeds as cover. The next man who lays a hand on you is as good as dead."

The alarm keeps ringing through the empty courtyard as I

dart into the overgrown plants. Then the air shifts, becoming heavier–thick with the scent of damp earth and decomposing foliage.

I continue onwards, with branches whipping my face and arms, leaving stinging cuts. Thorns tear at my makeshift socks, making me wince with each step.

Climbing plants form a thick canopy that blocks out most of the light. I stumble over tangled roots, not knowing if the ground beneath me will give way and send me tumbling into some animal's underground lair.

Xero doubles back, offering me his hand. "Come. It's straight on."

He pulls me forward, his grip my only source of comfort. I want to think his body is a protective barrier between me and the unknown, but he's just a figment of my imagination.

"Focus, little ghost," he snaps, jolting me back to reality.

I place a hand over my mouth and nose, trying to filter the pollen and blink through watering eyes.

Male voices echo in the distance, accompanied by approaching footsteps. As Xero guides me to the right, I picture myself running through a manicured garden bordered by shrubs. Attendants in crisp white uniforms stand at the perimeter, ready to intervene at the first sign of misbehavior.

My nose tickles, and I stifle a sneeze. What the hell was that?

"A suppressed memory," he says. "This used to be the hospital's garden. There's an exit on the other side of the old oak, but you need to focus on the present, alright?"

Sending Xero a silent word of thanks for holding onto my repressed memories, I keep moving.

"Step where I step."

As I follow Xero through the dense foliage, the ground trembles with thundering footfalls. It's so exaggerated that I can't help but wonder if I'm hallucinating.

"Assume it's real." He pulls me into a hollow within a thicket of thorny bushes.

I set the phone down on the ground and crouch with the scalpel pointed outward.

"She has to be here somewhere," a male voice says from a distance.

"Shhh!" hisses another.

My heart pounds so hard that every inch of my body quakes. I'm sure the shrub I'm hiding in is trembling in sync with my panic.

"Deep breaths." Xero hugs me from behind, cocooning me in his strong arms. "Just stay quiet."

My nose itches again. I hold my breath for what feels like an eternity, listening for signs of movement. Beneath the chirping of the crickets and the rustling leaves, I catch the sinister sound of male whispering.

They're creeping closer, closing in on us from behind.

"You don't know that," Xero whispers and tightens his embrace.

I grasp onto his every word, desperate for any hint of reassurance. Breathing through my sleeve, I will my heart to slow and beg my sinuses to ignore the incessant urge to sneeze.

Just as I stifle another release of air, the phone at my feet rings.

"Over there," someone roars.

I shrink into my hiding spot, but it's too late. Rough hands haul me out of the shrubbery and into a broad chest.

He snickers. "Got you."

"Stab him," Xero yells.

The hand holding the scalpel swings up into his midsection, and I slice a path between his ribs. He screams, his grip slackening long enough for me to wriggle free.

"Run," Xero shouts.

I leave the man to drop to his knees, all notions of picking up the phone forgotten as survival instincts push me forward. Adrenaline pounds through my system, numbing the pain of brambles piercing my soles and branches whipping across my face.

My lungs burn. Every inhale tastes like fear. Every exhale leaves me wanting to expel the contents of my stomach.

"Stop running or I'll shoot," someone yells.

"He won't," Xero snarls.

I round a shrub, seeking cover. This part of the weed jungle is even thicker, its canopy only allowing in a trickle of light. The air grows heavy with pollen once again, battering my sinuses. I struggle onward, eyes streaming, breaths wheezing.

Plant particles cling to my lungs like wet cement. Each step tightens my chest, making every breath a struggle. Tears blur my vision, obscuring my path as I'm forced to navigate with my arms outstretched.

A gunshot pierces the air with a deafening boom. Heart lurching, I trip over a root and tumble forward.

"Keep moving," Xero shouts in my ear like a drill sergeant.

He's right. I'd rather die from a bullet than allow myself to get caught. Digging my fingers into the moist soil, I haul myself upright and continue stumbling. Another shot misses me by several feet, making me flinch.

"It's a bluff," Xero yells.

"Stupid bitch, I told you to stop!" A man charges forward, knocking me face-first into a tree.

The scalpel I'm holding drops from my fingers, disappearing into the undergrowth. I push against the trunk's rough surface, trying to shove him off, but he's too heavy.

He twists my arm behind my back. "You killed Vance and stabbed Bill. Delta's going to punish us all."

"You know how to get out of armlocks," Xero shouts through my panic, reminding me of my training. "Move."

Muscle memory kicks me in the solar plexus. I swing my free arm backward and strike him in the groin. Roaring, he doubles over and staggers back with a hand over his crotch.

Sirens sound in the distance. My heart leaps. I need to reach the police.

"Don't run," Xero says, his voice tense. "Take him out. Now."

He's right. This bastard will recover in a few seconds, then he'll be after me again.

I reach into my hair and pull out one of the scalpels I hid in my bun. As I thrust it at his throat, he catches my wrist and lands a fist in my face.

His punch connects with an explosion of pain across my cheekbone, filling my vision with white. I stumble backward, trying to right myself, but the man shoves me back into the tree.

"Dolly was right," he snarls, his large hand closing around mine and squeezing so tightly that the second scalpel slips through my fingers. "You really are a worthless cunt."

He grabs me by the back of the neck and lifts me off my feet, holding me at arm's length. I kick and flail within his grip, trying to reach some part of his body, but he only draws back.

My vision is so blurry that I barely make out his figure when Xero appears at my side. "Calm down. He'll slip up in a minute. When he does, be ready with your last scalpel."

I scratch the hand around my neck, drawing blood. Snarling, he drops me to the ground. I land on my knees, only for him to punch me in the temple, making me spin to the side.

My vision darkens, and he approaches me with his teeth bared. He pulls back his fist, ready to deliver another punch, but his head explodes with a shot of gunfire.

The man falls into a nearby shrub, revealing Grunt approaching me with a gun, his face still hidden behind that surgical mask.

THIRTY-THREE

Wednesday August 4, 2010

I didn't know what the hell to do. The situation was beyond my comprehension. I didn't know how on earth to make a murder disappear. More importantly, I had no idea how to protect my child from the consequences of actions I instigated.

Lyle stared at me, looking like he'd finally had enough. He knew. Knew that this was down to Giorgi's tainted genes. Knew that Dolly wasn't entirely at fault. Knew that Charlotte would still be alive if I had kept MY MOUTH SHUT.

What if those allergic reactions really were psychosomatic? Anything is possible in the realm of pregnancy-induced psychosis. I want to talk to Dr. Forster about it, but he's still avoiding my calls. Besides, I don't want to tell him too much and endanger Dolly.

Lyle wanted to call the police. I think it was a knee-jerk reaction due to the years he spent in law enforcement. Dolly wailed the house down, and I screamed at him to stop.

No child of mine would be stuck in an institution. I suffered years of abuse in the foster system. I would burn down the entire street before Dolly endured the same.

When Amy came out with the baby to investigate, it took

every ounce of willpower not to scream. She was supposed to be hiding.

Dolly charged across the room with the murder weapon, screeching that this was all Amy's fault. If Lyle's reflexes weren't so fast, Dolly would have stabbed through the baby to get at her sister.

Amy, to her credit, ran back to the master bedroom, slamming two sets of doors for protection. Lyle managed to twist the weapon out of Dolly's hands and tossed it across the room.

I can't believe the thoughts that rushed through my head: Lyle's fingerprints were all over the knife. If he called the police, they would see him as the prime suspect. I could tell the officer he was having an affair with the nanny. That *he* had poisoned me with allergens so he could fuck a younger woman in the house he shared with his pregnant wife. Men have needs, right?

While waiting for the police, I would order Dolly to stick to the story that she found her beloved nanny dead and woke us up with a scream. I wouldn't even need to place blood on Lyle's pajamas—they transferred when he grabbed Dolly.

Without voicing these plans, I asked Lyle to get rid of Charlotte's corpse. Channeling every bitch I encountered from the mafia, I nod at his bloody hand and let my gaze linger over the blood on his chest. It's something I picked up from Giorgi, that worthless bastard. He never needed to speak his threats out loud. He'd point out the obvious with his eyes, and everyone would fall in line.

I think I broke my husband that morning. The murder of a relatively innocent woman is hard to bear. Even harder is knowing it was committed by an innocent child. Worst of all is being responsible for its cover-up. What the hell could I do in my condition? I just had major surgery. Technically, I should be on bedrest.

Without touching Dolly, I got her into the family bathroom and told her to scrub herself clean in the shower. The moment I assured her she wasn't in trouble, the tears stopped. While she was getting clean, I checked up on Lyle, who was in Charlotte's room, soaking up the blood with my postpartum sanitary pads.

Whatever. We bought them in bulk. I still have enough to last the next few days.

I had to return to the bedroom to feed Heath, who hadn't stopped crying since Dolly lunged at Amy with the knife. When it took Amy ten solid minutes of persuasion to open the bathroom door, I realized this was the beginning of the end of our family.

The twins won't get past this. They've lost all the progress they made in summer camp and will be back to accusations and tearing each other apart.

That overwhelming feeling of dread returned. I'm surprised my milk didn't sour at the prospect, but Heath continued to nurse, oblivious to my inner turmoil.

Amy cuddled at my side, trembling, knowing without being told that what happened today would be our ruin.

Fuck it. I need to stop writing for a minute. Lyle is calling for my help.

THIRTY-FOUR

AMETHYST

Xero's voice filters through a barrier of nothingness. He's screaming at me to wake up, but that would mean plunging myself back into the nightmare. The nightmare where I'm hunted by predators with guns.

My body is encased in strong arms that carry me through the darkness. Each step aggravates the pain that pounds through my skull. The world returns to me in a slow, painful haze, punctuated by heavy, frantic breaths, and the whip of branches against my back.

I crack open an eye to find my face pressed into the white expanse of Grunt's chest.

"Finally," Xero mutters.

When I try to move my head, the hand cradling the back of my skull presses harder. What the hell is happening?

"All I can see is what you see, but it looks like Grunt killed that man so he can be the one to return you to Delta," Xero says.

He's right. I'm not naïve enough to believe Grunt saved me for his own redemption. I need to break free. Every muscle in my body struggles against his hold, but he simply adjusts his grip, pressing me into a wall of muscle.

"Grunt," I say out loud. "Let go of me."

"Stay quiet," he says. "I'm going to get you out of here."

I stiffen. "Why?"

"It's just like you said. They're setting me up to take the fall for your death. I'll be fucked if I let that happen."

Some of the tightness around my chest loosens at the prospect of having an ally.

"Don't trust him," Xero snarls.

A temporary ally, whose motives are dubious. I relax in his hold, trying to focus on staying conscious. My eyes sting, my nose streams, my throat itches, and each inhale is labored and shallow.

Grunt continues through the foliage, his pace never wavering.

"Where are we going?" I wheeze.

"Remember that old school bus?" He doesn't wait for me to answer. "That's how we're going to escape."

"I thought this was an island," I ask.

Male shouts pierce the air, cutting short our conversation. Footsteps echo through the undergrowth, seeming to grow near with each passing second. The anxiety in their voices is palpable. They know that at least one of their friends is dead.

"Three incapacitated or dead. One defected, leaving five men plus Dolly," Xero says.

My brows pinch. I could have sworn she and Delta left for some kind of event, but it's better to overestimate the threat than to be overconfident.

"Hang on and be quiet," Grunt whispers into his mask, breaking my train of thought.

I give him a tense nod. He readjusts his grip around my body and creeps through the dense growth, still managing to crack twigs underfoot.

Sunlight shines through the canopy, warming my skin. I blink through streaming eyes, trying to see where we're going, but everything is a blur of greens and grays.

When he stops abruptly, I startle.

"What's happening?" I whisper.

"We're at the edge of the courtyard," he replies, his hot breath falling across my cheek. "We need to cross it to get to the bus."

Xero strokes my hair. "Stay small. That courtyard is a sniper's paradise. If Delta and the others plan on shooting, you're going to be the smaller target."

Shuddering at the prospect of being shot at, I dip my head and tuck my legs closer into Grunt's body. I also grip the front of Grunt's shirt. Xero might sound ruthless, but he's right.

"Good girl," Xero says.

Grunt's heart thrashes against my side, reflecting my own rising anxiety. He shifts me in his hold once more before whispering, "Ready?"

I nod against his chest, not daring to speak, and suck in a noisy breath to ready myself for the impending run.

Grunt's muscles tense, and his breathing quickens. With a low growl, he bursts from the undergrowth and sprints through the courtyard.

Sunlight drenches my vision. My hay fever is so bad that I couldn't break free even if I wanted. Grunt's heavy boots pound against the hard, uneven surface. My heart races in double-time to his footfalls. Xero runs at our side, his large hand on my shoulder.

Someone shouts, ordering him to stop, but he only quickens his pace. A gunshot rings out. Grunt flinches, his hold on me tightening as he stumbles.

My heart lurches. I squeeze my eyes shut and clutch his shirt tighter.

Grunt rounds a sharp corner, his footsteps skidding. Then, with a metallic screech, the bus door lurches open. He stumbles inside and drops me to the sun-warmed floor with a hard thud.

Before I can even get my bearings, the doors hiss closed, and he starts the engine.

Outside, the air fills with shouts and gunshots. Bullets hit the vehicle's sides like hailstones. I lie on the aisle, not wanting to rise even an inch above seat level in case I get shot.

The diesel engine rumbles to life, and the bus lurches forward, making me skid across the floor and collide with a bolted seat.

"Hold tight," Xero yells.

I reach out with trembling hands, wrapping my fingers around the seat's steel posts.

The engine roars louder, and the bus picks up speed. My body thrums like a raw nerve, both from the bus's vibrations and the adrenaline surging through my veins. I listen out for gunshots or the sound of chasing vehicles, but all I hear is the engine and the rush of wind.

I raise my head and stare out to the front. Through my blurry vision, I can make out Grunt sitting in the driver's seat with the sleeve of one arm soaked in blood. Up ahead are the asylum's open metal gates.

As soon as we pass them, I collapse on the floor, overwhelmed with relief. The bus roars down a seemingly endless road. I'm not sure whether to laugh or cry, so I settle for wheezing.

"Stay alert, little ghost," Xero growls.

My attention snaps back to the present, and I hear the wailing of sirens growing louder and then fading into the distance. My heart sinks. Did we just drive past the police?

A fresh set of tears fills my eyes, washing away the pollen. I sniffle, forcing down a wave of despair. After all that shit I went through trying to escape, I'm still not safe.

Warm hands thread through my hair, making me crack open an eye. Xero lies beneath one of the seats, his outline a blur of platinum and white.

"A man like Delta would have bribed the police anyway. You might have a better chance of escaping Grunt."

My gaze flicks to the large man driving the bus. I blink away the tears, my vision sharpening. Grunt is no Delta, but he also isn't someone to take lightly. It's hard to tell if he views me as a prisoner, a plaything, or a replacement for Dolly. None of these prospects sound appealing.

I sneeze once, twice, three times, clearing my sinuses, my determination hardening. Grunt is not a savior. Once the danger clears, he'll realize I'm a witness to his involvement in snuff movies. He'll make sure I never get a chance to report him to the police.

"Or use you as leverage against Dolly and Delta," Xero adds.

Shuddering, I pull myself up onto my elbows.

"How's the hay fever?" Xero asks.

"Still there, but at least I can breathe." I release my grip on a metal post, resisting the urge to rub my eyes.

If I had the mental bandwidth right now, I would scream, but

I need to keep it together. It's only a matter of time before Delta assures the police he's making an innocent documentary on abandoned asylums, and they drive back to their precinct, leaving us swarmed by attackers.

Grunt might not even have a plan for leaving the island. If I don't want to end up the victim of another perilous situation, then I'd better work out a strategy to escape Grunt.

"What are you thinking?" Xero asks.

"At my second school, some girl escaped the bus on a trip."

He gives me an approving nod. "A bus is a large target. It's going to take the others much longer to spot a lone woman running through the wilderness."

First, I need to get close enough to the emergency exit handle without Grunt noticing. Second, I need to wear something other than a white straitjacket. Releasing the metal post, I crawl on my belly toward the driver's seat. On the floor beside it is a jacket, which might contain a gun, a phone, or both.

"Are you alright?" I ask Grunt.

He tilts his head in my direction before turning his attention back to the road. "Just a flesh wound."

I rise to my knees to get a better look through the windshield. We're on a long highway, surrounded by woodland. In between the trees on the left are snatches of the sea, shimmering in the sunlight. If I can exit somewhere here, I could hide in the woods until I hear the police returning from the asylum.

"What's our next move?" I shuffle toward him, so I'm kneeling on his jacket.

"What do you mean?" Grunt snarls, that infernal mask still stuck to his face.

"Told you. Men like him are followers," Xero says.

Ignoring him, I ask, "This is an island, right? How do we leave it?"

Grunt's shoulders rise to his ears. "Don't worry about that. I have a plan."

"He doesn't," Xero says.

Then it's a good thing I do. Moving forward, I tuck the jacket toward my feet, so it's completely hidden from his view.

"Can I take a seat, please?" I ask.

"Sure," Grunt mutters, not taking his eyes off the road.

I turn around and rise to my feet, clutching Grunt's jacket to my chest. One glance over my shoulder tells me he's already dismissed me as harmless. I turn back, my gaze fixed on the emergency handle in the middle of the bus and just a few seats within my grasp.

Outside, the scenery on the left changes from woodland to sparse trees surrounding a rugged coastline. The ocean stretches out as far as I can see, with a boat gliding on the water. It's sleek, sporty, and slicing through the waves in our direction.

My heart thrashes. If I could stow away or even get close, this might be my ticket off the island.

Xero nudges my shoulder. "Go."

I slip into the seat adjacent to the emergency exit, shrug on the jacket, and zip it up to my chin. Grunt is still driving, seeming oblivious of my plans.

With trembling fingers, I reach for the emergency handle and pull. The door releases with a pneumatic hiss, letting in a rush of sea air. Time slows as I hesitate to take a deep breath before taking my leap to freedom.

Just as I'm about to jump, Grunt swerves the bus, making me tumble backward. The doors snap shut with a metallic clang, the brakes screech, and the bus comes to a halt.

"Amethyst!" Xero yells.

My gaze snaps to the side. Grunt rises from the driver's seat and charges toward me, his features twisting with fury behind his mask.

THIRTY-FIVE

Wednesday August 4, 2010

Dolly just ran down to the kitchen, brandishing another knife, screaming no one will believe her that Amy killed Charlotte.

As for Charlotte, her body is no longer in the house. I don't know if Lyle put her in the basement, the garage, or the trunk of his car. She's gone.

Dolly sliced through Lyle's hand when he tried to take the knife. The blood splattered on the floor tiles made me double over and heave. Amy was safely locked in an upstairs bathroom with Heath, probably fretting for both of their lives.

My little girl has regressed since the last time she lost control. Before the summer camp, Dolly used to injure Amy, often breaking her skin. When Amy reported it to me, I would confront Dolly, only to find her with the identical injury. She claimed Amy did it, of course.

Back then, I didn't know who to believe. Every time Amy would come to me with an injury, I'd rush to Dolly, only to find her in the exact same condition, adamant that Amy was the perpetrator. It was a cycle of accusations, injuries, bandages, and tears. And it never made any sense until the incident at the school.

It was a leather carving class, which required the use of specialized tools to cut patterns into the hide. Some snide comments were exchanged—the details are irrelevant. At the end of the class, as the kids were pouring out, Dolly carved a horizontal line into Amy's stomach.

Amy's scream alerted the teacher, who took her straight to the school infirmary. By the time she returned to deal with Dolly, Dolly had an identical gash on her own stomach. By then it was too late for her to create the illusion that Amy was the one causing harm.

The principal called us in for an urgent meeting and wasted no time in expressing her outrage at the horrific incident. I suggested taking them to a child psychologist, but the counselor recounted every incident involving the girls. They were inspiring their classmates to violence and needed to be expelled for the safety of the other students.

I was pregnant and already stressed with morning sickness. There was no way I could cope with the screaming, sabotage, and sadistic violence at home. That's when Lyle suggested the Three Fates Therapeutic Boarding School, which came with therapists, psychologists, and everything we thought was needed to help Dolly.

We know people who have sent children there. Lyle has a colleague named Dalton who he invited over for dinner. During the meal, Dalton revealed that he recently discovered he had a son from a previous relationship with a woman who passed away from cancer.

The son was a little older than the twins, but so disturbed by his mother's death that he struck out at another of Dalton's sons, smashing his head over and over into a urinal! Dalton sent him to Three Fates, and the transformation was nothing short of miraculous.

The story gave me hope. Maybe this was what Dolly needed. A place where someone could get to the root of her issues and help her overcome this troubling behavior.

The morning of the tour, I was so crippled with morning sickness that I could barely get out of bed. Lyle had to take care of

ately and use the more compliant Dolly for tomorrow's shoot. A shudder runs down my spine as I force myself not to contemplate the horrors he'd inflict on a woman identical to the one he subjected to years of degradation and near death.

"Anyone there?" A voice crackles over the speaker, pulling me out of my thoughts.

"Tyler?" I ask.

"I'm back," he replies, the relief in his voice palpable. "And I might have spotted her." Tyler launches into an explanation of how he hacked into the maritime surveillance satellite system and located a bus moving at high speed along the coastline.

"How do you know it's her?" I ask.

"The system only captures still images at five-minute intervals," he says. "I tracked the bus's route back to the asylum, where someone was firing shots at its rear end."

My heart picks up speed. "Where is it now?"

Tyler rattles off coordinates, and the helmswoman punches them into the navigation system. The vessel adjusts course, and I glare out into the endless expanse of sea.

"We're heading to intercept," I say.

"Are you sure?" Jynxson asks. "Amethyst might still be in the asylum."

I shake my head. He didn't see her kill an attacker and hide his corpse, all while thinking she was hallucinating the man she murdered. Amethyst is resourceful.

"The moment we're in range, I want you to send out drones in both directions. If she isn't on that bus, I want a team storming the asylum and shooting everyone in sight."

The next several minutes are tense as Tyler helps us intercept the vehicle. I'm holding on to the chance that Amethyst's encounter with Dolly and Father has unlocked her survival instincts, and she's escaped alone. Alternatively, she might have left the asylum with another captive. Anything is possible, but my gut tells me she's on that bus.

I turn to Jynxson. "What's the update from the penthouse?"

He shakes his head. "Just Dolly talking about coming out of retirement to star in one last movie. The investors are lapping it up, not knowing she's set up her twin to die."

"We're seven miles away," says the helmswoman. "Drones are ready to deploy."

My breath hitches. "Launch them."

Moments later, the drones take off into the sky, spreading out in a fan formation, racing toward both the asylum and the bus.

"Call me when you get a visual." I rise off my seat and walk out onto the open deck. Wind assaults my senses, and I squint against the glare of the sun and the relentless spray of the sea.

I grip the railing, watching the drones disappear into the horizon. They're military grade with gun capabilities, but will take at least seven minutes to reach their targets. Seven minutes of waiting before all hell breaks loose.

My heart pounds a staccato beat, drowning out the roar of the sea. This is the closest I've gotten to Father in at least five years, yet all I can think of is Amethyst. What will I find when I reach my little ghost? Have they shattered her already fragile mind?

They were working on her long before my execution, with constant death threats disguised as online trolling. I don't know if that first man she killed that night was sent to capture her or to test her skills, but they never stopped trying to torment her.

When they couldn't get to her through the pictures and poison pen letters, they remade the graveyard scene and sent it to Melonie Crowley.

Her mother would have watched the entire thing, thinking Amethyst had branched into violent porn. After all these years, Melonie probably assumed Dolly was long dead. It was unfortunate that Melonie didn't tell Amethyst she'd been gang-raped while unconscious. We would have watched through the footage and pieced together the truth.

When they couldn't use Melonie to tear us apart, they sent a link to the video, making Amethyst think she was the victim, and I was a predatory ringmaster. That everything that happened between us was part of some kind of revenge against her for trying to make money from her relationship with me. If I hadn't completely forgiven her for that yet, I have now.

"Xero," someone says from behind. "Over here."

I hurry back to the bridge, where Jynxson and a few others

are gathered around a quartet of laptops displaying the drones' feeds.

On one screen, officers stand beside a police patrol car parked at the asylum's entrance, exchanging tense words with a pair of young men. I turn my attention to another screen, where a yellow school bus races down a lonely stretch of road.

The drone slows to peer through its windows, and I hold my breath to find a small figure crouched between the seats. She's instantly recognizable from the blond curls on one side of her hair.

My heart lurches. It's Amethyst.

She's wearing a straitjacket with bandages covering her legs. Her head turns, looking like she's in conversation with someone beneath the seat.

"Zoom in on that image," I say.

The feed sharpens, bringing into focus the bus's interior. Amethyst's face is swollen and encrusted with a mix of blood and dirt. What the hell did they do to her?

"She's hurt," Jynxson says.

Rage sears through my chest, burning the back of my throat. "Who's taken her?"

A second drone flies over the bus, capturing the driver's face. He's a large, dark-haired man, dressed in white. With half his face obscured by a white mask, it's difficult to tell if that's Father or one of his lackeys.

"She's on the move," Jynxson says.

I switch back to the first drone, where Amethyst crawls between the seats toward the driver. My brow furrows as she occasionally glances to the empty space at her side. Is she seeing things or communicating with another captive?

"Did she stow away?" Jynxson asks. "Looks like she's trying to sneak up on the driver."

I grunt. "That, or he told her to keep low so as not to get shot. How many minutes until we intercept the bus?"

"Five, sir," replies the helmswoman.

Shit.

On-screen, Amethyst continues moving toward the man until

she pauses on top of his jacket. As she exchanges words with the driver, she moves the garment behind her back.

My jaw clenches. She must see him as a threat.

I watch helplessly as she clutches the jacket, dragging it to the center of the bus. Dread settles in my gut as she slips it on and fastens the zip, all the while glancing at an invisible spot to the side. What the hell is she planning?

As if in answer to my question, she reaches for the red exit handle.

Someone mentions that another car has left the asylum's back gate, but I'm too engrossed in what's happening with Amethyst for the words to fully register.

"Is she going to pull the emergency stop?" Jynxson asks.

She yanks the lever, and the bus's side door swings open. The vehicle lurches to a stop, jolting Amethyst backward in her seat.

My gaze switches to the second screen, where the driver jumps out from behind the wheel and races down the aisle. Alarm hits me in the gut. I should be there, snapping that bastard's neck.

"Damn," Jynxson says, his eyes fixed on the images.

Amethyst tries the lever again, opens the door, and leaps off the bus just as the driver lunges to grab her shoulder. She hits the ground rolling before finding her feet and sprinting across the road into the trees.

My heart pounds as the driver charges after her, his large strides swallowing the distance between them with sickening speed.

"Close in on them, now!" I snarl.

The drone tracks their movements. It's impossible to shoot the driver without risking Amethyst's safety. She's barely ahead of the driver, darting from side to side to evade his grasp.

She weaves in and out of the trees, using the evasive movements we practiced, but the man is determined to get her back on that bus.

"Three minutes, sir," the helmswoman says.

Every second with Amethyst in the line of fire is excruciating. We can't get a lock on the persistent bastard. Rounding a tree, she pauses to reach into her pocket. When she extracts a gun, my heart roars with triumph. I grit my teeth, waiting for her to fill him with bullets.

But nothing happens.

She glances at the gun, her eyes widening with panic. It's either out of ammunition or jammed.

"Two minutes," says the helmswoman.

I rise off my seat.

"Try again," I snarl at the screen.

She charges at the driver.

"What are you doing?" I yell.

The man spreads out his arms in anticipation of her attack. I hold my breath, wondering if there's a method to this madness. At the last minute, she ducks low and veers off toward the bus.

"She's trying to steal it now?" I ask.

"Looks like it," Jynxson mutters.

The driver jogs after her, seeming pleased with this change of events. Perhaps he thinks he intimidated her back into compliance.

"As soon as she's out of range, take the shot," I snarl.

"Sixty seconds, sir," says the helmswoman.

I clench my teeth, wanting to stay long enough to watch the drone shoot him down in a rain of gunfire. We're about to arrive a hundred feet from where the bus has stopped. I have mere seconds to intercept Amethyst before she drives away.

Just as I race across the deck, the air fills with the roar of a helicopter. I glance up at the sky, wondering why the hell Camila didn't inform us that Dolly had left the penthouse. Alarm punches through my chest. In my haste to chase after Amethyst, I left my sister alone, without backup, in a hotel filled with predators.

THIRTY-SEVEN

Thursday August 5, 2010

I hugged Dolly goodbye, telling her that no young girl her age can see such a brutal death without psychological damage. The psychologist at Three Fates would help her process the trauma.

Speaking the truth—that she killed a woman in cold blood and blamed the murder on her sister—would have resulted in another outpouring of denials. Independent witnesses at school have already confirmed what I know: Dolly has inherited her father's psychopathic tendencies. This needs to be suppressed before she kills again.

Dolly didn't respond to my explanation of why she has to go back to Three Fates. She kept her eyes glued to the floor and her fists clenched so tightly that her knuckles turned white. I'll have to endure her resentment for a short time, but it's better than being in denial and enabling a potential killer.

Lyle took her, promising to stop for ice cream and fudge brownies. I wanted to accompany her on the drive to Three Fates, but I didn't have a babysitter for Amy, who still hasn't left the bathroom since Dolly's violent outburst.

Hours later, he returned from the long drive, drawn. He said Dolly had another murderous episode in the car that nearly had him driving off the road. He managed to pull over and talk her down by promising she would return as soon as the psychologists deemed her well enough.

Mr. Delta was away on business, but his assistant assured us we'd have daily updates on her status. I asked if we could call her, but Lyle explained that situations as extreme as Dolly's require a period of no contact during the initial stages of treatment.

If I'm honest with myself, I was a little relieved. I'm still coming to grips with the thought of Dolly being a murderer.

Amy, meanwhile, has reverted to her withdrawn state from when she first returned from Three Fates. She spends hours in the bathroom, and won't eat unless she's forced.

I called Dr. Forster's home and begged his wife to put him on the line. He was furious at me for crossing a boundary, but that's what he gets for ignoring my calls. I told him we were having a family crisis, but I couldn't bring myself to reveal the entire truth. He knows about the twins' violence and the incident that got them both expelled, but I had to keep quiet about the murder.

After warning me never to call him at home again, he asked about Charlotte. She had been the topic of conversation for several sessions. I tried to brush him off, saying that I finally opened my heart to Lyle and spelled out my insecurities of being usurped by a younger woman, but the blasted therapist wanted to know what made the difference.

What does it matter? I asked. Charlotte was fired. Dr. Forster explained that understanding how I convinced Lyle to get rid of Charlotte could help me approach future conflict with my husband.

I told him things between Lyle and me were back to being perfect. He asked how I was coping as a mother, but I had nothing to say. A new baby is a walk in the park compared to my traumatic twins.

The conversation felt more like a game of chess than therapy, so that's probably the last time I'll speak with him until Dolly returns. I can't risk anyone finding out the truth. Even if the authorities won't punish a mentally ill ten-year-old too severely for killing Charlotte, Lyle won't get off lightly for concealing a murder.

What does that make him? An accessory? That makes me one, too, for insisting that we didn't call the police.

Later, I took Heath to the nursery for a change. When I opened his laundry basket, all his little clothes were cut up with scissors. This act of sabotage was the kind of thing Amy would do in retaliation for Dolly's violence, but I wasn't about to be fooled.

I couldn't even muster up the usual anger. Instead, I felt an overwhelming sense of dread.

What kind of girl murders a woman in cold blood, blames her innocent sister, nearly stabs a baby to attack said sister for existing and, when that fails, frames her for slashing the baby's clothing?

Do I even want her back?

It's a terrible thing to admit, but I need to think about the well-being and continued survival of my other children. The ones who don't express their anger with sharp objects.

I showed the basket to Lyle, and he stared at it, speechless. All the color drained from his face, and his features fell into an expression I'd never seen on him before—fear. Fear for our children, fear for us, and fear that Dolly has become a monster.

That night, he worked late in his study. I expect he's still reeling from the enormity of our daughter's atrocities. I went to sleep, fully expecting to wake up finding his side of the bed to be empty save for a handwritten note, telling me he can't cope.

But the next morning, he lay beside me, fast asleep. But when I picked Heath up from his crib, there was a spot of blood on his onesie.

THIRTY-EIGHT

AMETHYST

I stand between the trees, pressing on the stuck trigger. My heart pounds so hard I'm sure Grunt can hear the cadence of my fear.

He freezes twenty feet away, raising his palms. His chest heaves like a bellows, but the panic won't last. In a minute, he'll work out that the weapon is useless. Then he'll tackle me to the ground like he did at the airport and carry me back to the bus.

I could run, but the past few days with X-Cite Media have sapped my strength. Either way, I'm screwed.

Pressure coils around my chest, threatening to crush my lungs. The forest is silent, save for our labored breathing. Grunt's gaze flickers to the gun, then back to my eyes, his jaw moving behind the white mask.

Xero places a hand on my shoulder, but it does nothing to ease the tension. "Take your finger off the trigger. Time to switch up tactics."

Grunt takes a tentative step forward. "Put down the gun, Amy."

My throat tightens. He knows. Knows the gun is useless. Knows I'm powerless. Knows it's only a matter of time before he bundles me back onto that bus.

Leaves rustle overhead, mingling with the whir of tiny helicopter blades. Imagining them as a hallucination, Ignore the sound and focus on the immediate threat.

"I told you to stay back," I snarl.

"What are you doing?" he asks. "Delta is on his way. We have to get out of here. Now."

My stomach plummets like a lead weight to the forest floor, hitting it with a painful thud. The mere thought of spending another minute in Delta's company makes my spine stiffen with dread. Every nerve ignites, sparking with the idea that I might be able to steal the bus.

Gathering lungfuls of courage, I charge at Grunt, still pointing the gun at his chest.

"Don't do this, Amy." He steps back, widening his stance, bracing himself for impact.

I pick up speed on a collision course, powered by adrenaline and fear. He twitches, ready to scoop me off my feet. At the last minute, I duck beneath his arm and sprint through the trees, back toward the road.

"Follow me and I really will shoot," I scream over my shoulder.

Trees whizz past in a blur. The bus is only seconds away, its door left open. If I can get to the driver's seat before Grunt, then I'll finally have a chance to escape.

My breath comes in ragged gasps, my muscles screaming with each painful step. I keep pushing forward, fueled by a heady cocktail of desperation and terror.

Grunt's heavy footsteps rumble after me as I reach the road, making every hair on the back of my neck stand on end. I'm going to fail. This detour will have meant nothing. Then Delta will catch up with the bus and kill us both.

Gunshots ring out from above, making my steps falter. I glance back to see Grunt falling to the ground in a rain of bullets.

My jaw drops, and my heart tumbles into my stomach. What the hell? How did Delta send that drone so quickly? It's hovering above the treetops, its cameras turning on me.

"You're next," Xero snarls. "Run!"

I whirl around, finding a black car racing toward us from the direction of the asylum. Panic kicks me in the heart. It's probably Delta, come to drag me back to die.

Pouring every ounce of energy into my legs, I charge at the bus. Its faded yellow exterior glints in the sun like a last glimmer of hope. The drone follows me, raining gunfire. I'm so numbed by fear and cortisol that my body doesn't even feel the bullets. I clamber up into the bus and jump into the driver's seat.

But when I grab the steering wheel, its ignition key is gone.

"No!" I cry out loud.

Grunt must have pulled it out when he stopped the engine. It's probably in his pocket.

"What am I going to do now?"

"You know what to do," Xero growls and nods toward the tree.

He's right. There's a gun battle outside, but something's off. The drone and the man in the car—both sent by Delta—are shooting at each other. Why? I pause, trying to make sense of what I'm seeing. Could they be working against each other now? Fighting over who gets to take me down? Or is my brain malfunctioning again and conjuring up a savior? It's possible. I killed Xero, yet he's at my side, helping me escape.

Either way, I need to prepare myself to fight whoever's left standing.

I slide off the driver's seat and stay low, crawling toward the vehicle's rear. Every nerve flares on red alert, making me super sensitive to the gunfight. The drone's firing is relentless, with bullets hitting metal, but the person in the car fires back with precise shots.

Xero moves at my side, his face as pale as mine feels.

"Do you have another scalpel?" he asks, his voice low.

I reach up to the back of my head. The bun I twisted earlier has gone, along with my final weapon.

"No," I rasp, my voice still breathy with exertion.

"Then you'll have to fall back on hand-to-hand combat," he whispers.

Stomach churning, I shuffle to the back door and yank on the emergency lever. It opens with a creak, letting in the cacophony of gunfire. Leaving the door ajar, I scuttle backward and slide beneath a seat.

"Good thinking," Xero says. "Anyone boarding the bus will see the open doors and assume you escaped into the woods."

I nod. It worked at the asylum. When Delta finds me gone and goes searching through the trees, I can sneak out, check Grunt's pockets, and take control of the bus. My plan beyond that is fuzzy. I have no idea how to leave the island, but maybe if Grunt has a phone, I can call the police again.

My ears ring, muffling the sounds of gunfire. I turn to where Xero lies beneath the seats opposite, wondering why the drone would even attack Delta.

"You're assuming that's him in the car," he replies.

Who else would be in it?

"Seth, Locke. One of the investors. A newly arrived crew member. A rival pornographer. Or one of Delta's many enemies."

He could be right. I picture Delta back at the asylum, operating the drone from his desk, while his lackeys stand outside, convincing the police that the 911 call was just a pocket dial. That's one possible scenario. The other is Delta being the man in the black car.

"You're about to find out, because the shooting just stopped," Xero says.

Footsteps charge up the bus. They're as heavy as Grunt's, yet graceful. I hold my breath as the man's shadow stretches across the aisle.

As he approaches, I inhale the scent of gunpowder and faint cologne, reminding me vaguely of Delta.

"He's here," Xero says, his face a tight mask.

I swallow hard, wishing he was lying here beside me, instead of across the aisle. Maybe then he could infuse me with the strength to continue, because I'm spent. The footsteps grow louder, closer. I swallow hard, ready to strike.

"Amethyst," Xero's voice says from another direction. "It's me.

My eyes widen. I stare at Xero, who shakes his head. If that wasn't him, then it has to be Delta. None of the other lackeys know Xero well enough to imitate the way he speaks.

Delta pauses every few steps to check beneath the seats. His progress down the aisle is a slow and relentless march to my inevitable death.

As his boots draw closer, every ounce of blood drains from my face and pools in my pounding chest. My heart thrashes within its cage, desperate to escape.

"Get ready to fight," Xero growls.

My muscles go rigid.

I can't freeze. Freezing won't just mean death. Delta will return me to the studio and every man there will take turns with me until there's nothing left. And when my spirit is broken, they'll do it all over again until my life is snuffed out like a used candle. Before my body goes into rigor mortis, they'll defile my corpse.

If I'm going to die, it'll be right here. Right now. With some motherfucking dignity. If I can kill him along the way, even better.

Gritting my teeth, I steel myself for the inevitable confrontation. Xero stares at me from across the aisle like this is the last time I'll see him before my mind shatters.

My heart bleeds at the thought of facing the last moments of my life without him, but he gives me a firm, reassuring nod. In that gesture, he conveys respect, determination, fear, and love. He believes in me, even when I feel like all is lost.

Delta's footsteps halt inches from my hiding spot. My pulse quickens to a drumroll, and my lungs burn from holding my breath. Letting out a trembling exhale, I shrink into the shadows, hoping he'll think I've escaped through the back.

He crouches, his gloved hand running over the seat where I'm hiding. I press my back against the wall and stay small.

"Amethyst," Delta says in a voice that's heartbreakingly familiar. "Are you there, little ghost?"

Little ghost.

He could have gotten that nickname during one of the interrogations or from overhearing me with Xero in that cell. It's just a trick to lull me into a false sense of security. He wants my drug-addled mind to superimpose Xero's features onto his face, so I'll drop my guard.

His hand inches toward my chest, his fingers brushing over

the front of my borrowed jacket. Without thinking, I flinch, making him pull back. My heart shatters. He has to know I'm here.

In a minute, he'll replace that hand with a tranquilizer dart and shoot me down like an animal, leaving me completely at his mercy.

I can't allow that to happen. Not again. Not without a fight. He won't bring me back to that asylum alive. I'll go down in a blaze of violence and tear out his jugular with my teeth.

Tightening my jaw, I snarl, "Alright, I'll come out."

He steps back, seeming pleased with my submission.

But inside, my adrenaline surges, transforming every ounce of fear into incandescent rage. Rage at being manipulated into killing Xero, the man I loved. Rage at the abduction. Rage at getting tied up and sliced by him to mirror Dolly's scars. Rage at being drugged and degraded and raped.

As I crawl out from my hiding spot, I lock gazes with Delta. He's shaved off his beard in a pathetic attempt to look like his son. Well, I won't fall for his cheap cosmetic tricks. I'm no longer that helpless prey. I'm a feral animal, ready to fight and kill and maim for my freedom.

THIRTY-NINE

Tuesday August 10, 2010

It's been a few days since I last wrote. My head hasn't been right since I saw that blood on my baby. Lyle says it was probably Charlotte's. According to him, murder scenes aren't just restricted to the room where the victim died. A perpetrator can carry traces of their crime around the house, leaving them in the most unlikely spots.

I wasn't convinced, but then, I didn't stand over Dolly when she showered or track her movements after she left the bathroom. She could have left the blood there when she sliced apart the contents of Heath's laundry basket.

Lyle had the nerve to stare at me like I was being unreasonable for doubting his forensic expertise. I get that he's a former FBI agent and therefore all-knowing, but sometimes I hate the way he dismisses my concerns as if I'm a paranoid over-thinker with an overactive imagination.

Our nanny is dead. Murdered by a little girl who tried to knife her twin sister, not caring that she was holding an infant. Yes, I know I'm spiraling but THAT ISN'T THE KIND OF THING TO TAKE LIGHTLY!!!!

Amy is having bad dreams. She screams in the middle of the

night, claiming to see the ghost of Charlotte. According to her, Charlotte appears at the foot of the bed, asking why she did it.

I've told Amy she's innocent. Dolly killed Charlotte. If anyone is to blame, it's me. I noticed Dolly went missing in the middle of the night and just went back to sleep, assuming she'd gone to the bathroom. This entire mess could have been prevented if I'd gone out to investigate.

No amount of assurances will soothe Amy. She's sensitive. Highly strung. Jumpy because she's been stuck in a house with a psychopath who's systematically hurt her and then covered it up by marking her own skin.

Amy doesn't leave her room, even though that's where she claims Charlotte haunts her at night. She barely communicates except for stammered apologies to an imaginary ghost. I would call a professional, but I'm trying to cover up a murder.

Lyle tells me to give Amy some time. She's processing a major trauma, and hallucinating Charlotte is her way of making sense of the tragedy. Everything he says sounds reasonable, but he gets to leave the house for work. I'm stuck with a newborn and a little girl going the way of Lady Macbeth.

Two nights ago, Lyle got an urgent phone call from Three Fates, saying that Dolly had knifed another child. They wanted him to drive over there and pick her up. This triggered a blazing argument. If Dolly is attacking strangers as proxies for Amy, then bringing her back is insanity.

When he asked if I wanted someone else's daughter to die, I wanted to slap him for treating Amy like a sacrificial lamb. Three Fates has medications, equipment, and qualified personnel. Mr. Delta was supposed to make things better for our family, yet Dolly has gotten worse.

I told Lyle to do whatever he could—say anything to convince the headmaster to fix my daughter. To keep her at Three Fates or transfer her to another facility that can handle her violent episodes.

We're in this together, I said, not needing to elaborate. Lyle and I both know it was HIM who cleaned up a crime scene, HIM who disposed of a body, HIM who's responsible for creating the circumstances that led Dolly to kill.

He read the accusation in my eyes and flinched, but I no longer give a fuck. If Lyle had listened to me the first time I complained about Charlotte, then we'd all be happy with a gray-haired old nanny who brought the family together and not tore it apart.

That night, he left for Three Fates, leaving me alone with Amy and Heath. I dragged the crib to my bedside and ordered Amy into my bed. If she woke up in the middle of the night, screaming about Charlotte's ghost, I'd shoot footage of the empty space on my phone and play it back.

As we shared a leftover bowl of coconut rice pudding in bed, I told Amy that the nightmares were a side effect of the twin connection. She didn't kill Charlotte, so she shouldn't shoulder Dolly's guilt. That seemed to lift her spirits. As we cuddled up together, she thanked me for finally believing her about Dolly.

My chest tightened with guilt. Denial was the reason I'd let Dolly get so out of control. That, and an over-reliance on a therapist who acted like everything wrong in my life was a manifestation of inner shortcomings only he could resolve.

Dr. Forster wanted me dependent on him as a permanent source of income. I worshiped him like a god and placed him above Lyle. With my husband absent or working late, the doctor was my only source of affirmation. If he'd referred the girls to a specialist when I'd asked, he would have lost his cash cow. I should have seen it sooner.

Amy fell asleep first, and I congratulated myself for calming my little girl.

But the next morning, I woke up to my phone ringing. When I opened my eyes, Heath's head was trapped between the bars of his crib.

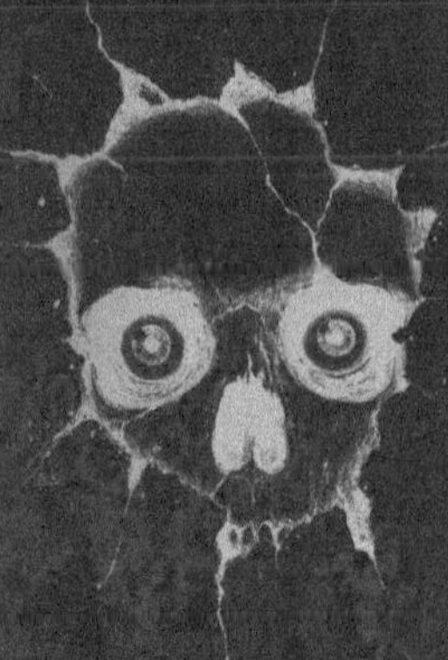

FORTY

XERO

I charge out of the catamaran, flanked by operatives. Motorcycles at the rear roar to life, preparing Jynxson and his crew to storm the asylum.

Trees whip past as I sprint toward the road where I last saw her. She's only a hundred feet away, but it may as well be a thousand. Everything blurs into the background. My entire being concentrates on finding Amethyst. My colleagues, the gunshots firing ahead, the forest, until I reach the car barring the way between me and the bus where she's hiding.

Emerging from the trees, I aim my gun at the car window's integrated firing slot, squeeze the trigger and release a bullet.

It's a direct hit. The figure behind the tinted window slumps out of sight. A bullet grazes my shoulder. Hissing, I retreat behind a tree.

The drone attacking the tires flies off toward where the helicopter landed, while the other fires at the driver, stopping him from opening his door. Seconds later, the car races away from the bus, its tires squealing against the asphalt. The drone we left follows closely, trailing the vehicle as it speeds down the road.

There's no time for me to contemplate whether Father was inside, because I need to reach Amethyst.

I board the bus, scanning the rows of sun-bleached seats. I call out her name, my heart racing, but all I hear is the roar of blood between my ears. I walk down the aisle, checking the spaces between the seats, pausing every few rows to see if she's curled beneath them in a tiny ball.

She's hiding somewhere, terrified of getting caught and taken back to that hellish place. My gaze darts to another emergency exit. Could she have snuck out through that door and closed it without the notice of the drones? It's possible.

"Amethyst," I say, my voice hoarse. "Are you there, little ghost?"

She shifts, giving me a glimpse of a bandaged limb. My heart lurches, anger mixing with fear. What the hell did they do to her? Crouching, I feel beneath the seat at the back.

Her sweet voice reaches me from the rear of the deserted bus, making my knees buckle under a wave of relief. The tight bands of anxiety constricting my chest dissolve with an exhale, and my muscles finally relax.

She's alive.

I step back, giving her space to crawl out from her hiding spot. She's pale, her eyes bloodshot. Her hair is a tangled mess of leaves and twigs and curls. Plant particles cling to the bandages encasing her legs, making me wonder once again what the hell they did to her at the asylum.

"She's in there?" an operative asks from outside.

"Affirmative," I reply, my heart swelling so much it's about to burst.

I move towards Amethyst, my steps hesitant. On instinct, my arms reach to pull her close, but the look in her eyes makes me pause. Her gaze is empty, unseeing, seemingly lost in terror.

"Amethyst?" I pull back my arms.

Will the touch of a man dredge up her trauma? I don't want to make her condition worse. My breath hitches when her eyes flicker with recognition, then stills as her pretty features twist with hatred.

She charges like a wild animal, her eyes crazed, her fingers curling into claws. I step forward, my hands reaching for her wrists as she releases a primal scream.

"Amethyst!" I yell. "It's me. It's Xero."

She's so immersed in the nightmare that she can't see that I'm not her enemy. Sobs tear from her chest, loud and guttural, each one ripping my heartstrings.

Her punches barely register, but the intention behind them stings. Is this temporary, or have I lost my little ghost to insanity?

Fingers closing around her wrists, I turn her around and pull her into my chest. She struggles against the bear hug, her movements becoming more frantic. With a sudden burst of strength, she throws back her head, hitting my nose with a sharp jerk.

Pain explodes through my skull as she kicks and thrashes to break free. I tighten my grip, blinking away a wave of dizziness.

Growling, she bites at my arms like a rabid animal. Blood trickles down my nose, but I shake it off and hold on tight, refusing to let her go. No matter what happens, I will never allow her out of my sight.

"Fuck, little ghost. You're safe!" I yell over her shrieks.

But it's no use. The last time she switched to berserker mode, I had to restrain her to the bed. This time, tying her up might shatter her mind beyond repair.

Her body convulses against mine as if my touch burns. The screams magnify, becoming more panicked and desperate. Her heart thrashes against my chest like a trapped animal, erratic and violent.

"Xero?" the operative at the back door yells over her screams. "Need help?"

"Stand back," I grit out and carry her kicking, screaming, and thrashing body out of the bus and onto the road.

Cold fear flushes through my veins, and my mind dredges up everything Jynxson said about her being a sleeper agent. As I stumble into the trees with her, I can't help but wonder if this is why her mother kept her drugged.

The Lolitas from our facility were never so volatile, but we only saw them for a short time. Whatever drugs they dosed her with must have changed her temperament, making her a possible time bomb.

I trudge through the forest, her wailing making the birds take flight. We reach the edge of the bank, and her screams drown out the crashing waves. I carry her across the ramp leading to our catamaran.

Her gut-wrenching screeches startle the skeleton crew, who stare at her through wide eyes as I take her into the vessel's interior, where her cries echo through the hallways.

"It's me, Amethyst." My voice breaks. "You're safe."

A door bursts open, and Isabel rushes out with a syringe. "Bring her here."

I hesitate, my arms still wrapped around her struggling form. "What's in that?"

"A sedative." Her face hardens the way it does when she's ready for a fight.

My mind races. "Won't it react with whatever they gave her at the asylum?"

Before my sister can even reply, urgent footsteps charge behind us and an operative bursts into view. "Explosion at the asylum. Two men down!"

My stomach drops like an anchor.

Jynxson.

FORTY-ONE

Wednesday August 12, 2010

We've just returned from the ER, where I spent hours with Heath. I managed to free his head from the crib without causing major damage, but they're keeping him overnight for observation.

Amy hasn't spoken a word since I woke up screaming. The shock of seeing her baby brother on the brink of death shook her to the core. She clung to me while I dialed 911 and quaked at the doorway when I let in the paramedics.

The ride to the hospital was excruciating. Heath's wails echoed in the ambulance, every cry a sharp dagger to my heart. I tried to be strong for Amy, but I couldn't hold back my tears. My hands shook so much I could barely sign Heath's admittance papers.

Amy continues to be haunted by the specter of Charlotte. Every time a blonde nurse came close, she would squeeze my hand so tightly that her fingernails almost drew blood.

I tried calling Lyle, but he's in a spot with poor reception. He left a message, saying he's consulting an attorney to stop Three Fates' from sending Dolly home while she's still a danger to others.

He's staying at a nearby bed-and-breakfast, refusing to sign any paperwork with the institution until he's satisfied Dolly will be in safe hands. All these sacrifices he's making for the family squeeze my heart. He's been like this from the beginning.

Neither Amy nor I could sleep that night, with Heath's health hanging in the balance. I clung to my little girl, staring into the empty cot, wondering how an entire baby's head could slip through such a narrow space.

As if Amy was reading my mind, she told me that Charlotte's ghost did this to Heath because she wants retribution. A life for a life. As much as I wanted to dismiss Amy's words as the imaginings of a traumatized child, I couldn't help the chill that ran down my spine.

I told her it was nonsense. There's no such thing as ghosts, but Amy insists she saw what she saw.

As the sun rose, I drifted in and out of sleep, thinking about how to help Amy without incriminating the family for Charlotte's murder. I looked it up online. Doctor-patient confidentiality only applies when the patient isn't a threat to themselves and others.

A little girl talking about sacrificing a baby to appease the woman her twin sister killed and whose murder her father covered up, will attract a horde of police. They won't just throw Amy in an institution. They'll imprison Lyle and me, then Heath will be left alone, a ward of the state.

Foster care is a fate I wouldn't wish on anyone, especially not my own flesh and blood. He'll grow up among a succession of strangers, not knowing he once had a loving family.

With those bleak thoughts, I decided to buy some books on trauma and work through the exercises with Amy. I will be her therapist and help her sift through the nightmares. I will mend her fragile heart.

The next morning, Lyle arrived from his legal wrangling with Three Fates, looking like he hadn't slept. He crashed on the sofa while Amy and I picked up Heath from the hospital.

Amy was in better spirits, seeming relieved that Heath was given a clean bill of health. I ordered a crib with wider slats, placed an inch apart, making the spaces barely large enough to fit a baby's hand. It's still a mystery how this could happen to a newborn, but I wasn't about to tempt fate again.

I was so wrung out from all the stress that I trudged past the living room, not bothering to wake Lyle, and took Heath upstairs. After feeding him, I fell into a deep sleep.

When I woke up, I found Amy carrying Heath out of the room.

FORTY-TWO

XERO

It took every ounce of willpower to tear myself away from Amethyst and leave her in Isabel's care. Our attention was already divided enough with the explosion at the asylum and the driver trying to escape via helicopter.

I rush back to the bridge, where the four operatives I left in charge of the drones are glued to their laptop screens.

"Jynxson," I say through my Bluetooth headset. "Report."

"Looks like the asylum had a gas leak," he replies. "Major casualties on their side. Minor injuries on ours."

"What do you need?" I ask.

"It's already settled. Dennis is currently en route to transport the injured hostages."

"Good." I turn to one of the operatives at the laptop. "Status on the helicopter?"

"Its passengers are armed with machine guns. This drone has taken damage to its targeting system."

"Can you stabilize it?" I ask.

He shakes his head. "Impossible. And the other drone's weapon mount is toast. We've lost tracking and fire control."

I clench my teeth. In other words, we're flying blind and defenseless. "And the drones we sent to the asylum?"

"Already en route to the helicopter. Should be there in three minutes."

Time is against us. I sent a team to pursue the car, but they're ill equipped to handle an aerial assault, let alone take down a helicopter. At best, they can shoot at the driver when he finally emerges.

"Hey, Xero," Tyler says in the Bluetooth. "Just re-established contact with Camila. She's asking what you want to do about the men left behind in the penthouse."

"Stay clear until further notice."

I have a hunch that the helicopter personnel are attacking the drones instead of flying to safety because they're protecting Father. Why else would they leave the investors' meet and greet to help out a simple driver? Father is in the front seat, within killing range. Any other time, I would rush to assist in his capture or to kill him outright, but my priority is Amethyst.

"Keep me updated," I say as I leave the bridge.

When I return to where I left Amethyst, Isabel has her laid out on a cot, covered in blankets, and is cutting through the bandage on her leg. The skin beneath the fabric is marred with red and inflamed cuts.

My feet root to the floor, the sight hitting me like a punch to the chest. "What the hell did they do to her?"

"These are incisions." She runs a pad of gauze over each laceration. "They're too precise and shallow to be anything else but torture."

"How was she able to escape in this condition?"

She sighs, the sound carrying a weight of sorrow. "They would have injected her with painkillers, and antifibrinolytics to stop her from bleeding out, and any manner of stimulants to keep her functional but capable of suffering."

My mind conjures up a vivid image of Amethyst, helpless and trapped in that straitjacket, drugged against her will and forced to endure relentless torture and pain. Hot fury charges through my veins, pulsing with each beat of my heart.

Nostrils flaring, I demand, "What else have you discovered?"

"It's going to take a while to tend to all these wounds, to see which need stitching. I've already drawn blood to be sent to the lab for analysis, but from what I can tell, she's been starved, dehydrated, and drugged."

I clench my fist, my knuckles tightening as I suppress the urge to tear the infirmary apart. The question I shouldn't ask fills my chest with flames, and I can't hold back. I have to know. My throat is raw, but the words feel like sandpaper as I force out, "And what about the sexual trauma?"

She raises her head, her eyes glassy. "That's next on my list to check. I want to stabilize her before gathering DNA and checking for injuries, but you'll need to leave."

"No." My voice comes out cracked. "I'm not leaving her side."

Her expression hardens. "Then stay on the other side of the curtain. She's endured hell and doesn't need an audience."

Isabel sets down her forceps and gauze, bustles across the room, and picks up a surgical drape pack. After unfolding it with an annoyed snap, she sets it up, creating a thin barrier between myself and Amethyst's broken body.

Sighing, I comb my fingers through the foliage tangled in her curls, while Isabel resumes her work on the other side of the curtain. The amount of debris caught in her hair tells me how much it took to escape the asylum.

I pluck out the leaves and twigs and feathers, each item telling its own story. As I brush off orange pollen scattered into her blonde strands, I loosen flakes of dried blood. The black side of her hair hides a layer of dirt that cakes my fingertips.

What could have motivated such cruelty to my beautiful little house-bound ghost, and from her own twin sister?

Grief weighs my steps as I walk to the sink and wash my hands before returning with the items I need to clean her face.

I snap on a pair of sterile gloves, my fingers trembling with a mix of fear and fury. Fury that Father has once again hurt a woman I love and fear that she might never be the same.

My heart aches as I tend to what's caked on her beautiful face, revealing a network of fine cuts. What did they do to her? How many men? Will she ever recover? With each swipe of the antiseptic-soaked gauze, I want to wash away all her pain and suffering.

It's futile. Amethyst was already fragile. She won't easily recover from such horrific abuse. Not without my help.

The vengeance I'll unleash will be so unfathomable that no one will dare lay a finger on her again. Those who harmed her will cower at the mere mention of her name because my revenge will know no bounds.

I will line up those men, bind them like an offering, and serve them to my little goddess as a mark of my undying devotion. And if she wants to kill them herself, I will hand her the instruments of torture and make her my queen of retribution.

Dolly might once have been a victim, but the way she targeted Amethyst is unforgivable. My little ghost needs to punish her twin, just as I plan on punishing Father.

Finally, Isabel emerges from behind the curtain. I can't remember the last time I saw my sister looking so grim or unable to meet my gaze.

"What is it?" I ask.

"We've done all we can for now," she murmurs. "The rest depends on the results of the toxicology report... And on Amethyst."

My throat becomes too tight to form words. Nodding my thanks, I remain silent, swallowing hard when Isabel squeezes my arm before leaving.

The door clicks shut, and I turn back to Amethyst. She looks so angelic in her forced slumber, but it's only a matter of time before she awakens and those pretty features contort with pain.

"We'll get through this," I murmur, more to myself than anyone else.

Saving Amethyst is only the first step in what's going to be a long journey. The ordeal she suffered might have opened wounds her mother tried to seal with electroshock therapy and drugs.

We'll work through her trauma together, step by painful step. I will never give up on my little ghost, no matter her mental state.

FORTY-THREE

Thursday August 13, 2010

Seeing Amy carry my baby into the hallway was the bucket of cold water I needed to snap me into alertness. I chased after her, demanding what the hell she was doing with Heath.

She told me that Charlotte had come to the bedroom, threatening to smother him while I slept. Amy was trying to protect the baby from a ghost. My heart sank. She'd escalated from seeing dead women to taking actions on imagined threats.

I took Heath back and rushed down the stairs to shake Lyle awake. He stared up at me from the living room sofa, looking through dead eyes as I explained what had just happened. Then he closed his eyes for several minutes.

He's had enough, and I don't blame him. Our entire lives are spiraling out of control, and I have no idea how to fix it.

I yelled his name over and over until he yelled back to keep quiet because he was trying to think. I told him Amy needs professional help and asked if we could take her to an out-of-town child psychiatrist. We could tell them Charlotte never even existed. She's an imaginary friend Amy thinks she's murdered.

Lyle told me I was being ridiculous. His younger brother has mental problems. That's not how it works. All that talk of sacrificing a baby would have the professionals calling the police. They'd interrogate Amy a hundred different ways until they uncovered the truth.

I waited for Lyle to use his big FBI brain to come up with a solution. All he did was clasp his hands over his face and take deep breaths, looking like a man on the verge of a breakdown.

Heath started fussing, so I sat at the other end of the sofa to feed him, while waiting for Lyle to break out of his fugue.

He didn't.

When Amy started wailing upstairs, I shook Lyle, asking if he was in a fit state to hold the baby. His only response was a tired nod, so I handed Heath over and raced to the source of the sound.

Her bedroom was a mess. The sheets hung over the window and all her clothes lay scattered across the floor. I searched for her in the chaos, only to find soft whimpers echoing from behind the closet door.

I knew better than to fling it open in case she was hiding there with a knife. Instead, I knocked on the wooden panel and asked if she was alright.

She cried, saying she was only trying to help, which broke my heart. I thought back, wondering how the hell we got into this situation. We were such a happy family until I announced the pregnancy.

That's when the problems started, I'm certain. That was the week Amy first came to me complaining that Dolly had cut a chunk of her hair while she slept. When I confronted Dolly, her hair was missing in exactly the same place. The next night, Dolly complained her mattress was wet.

Dr. Forster dismissed their antics as sibling rivalry, saying that Amy was threatened by a potential baby. Then his theory changed to the twins working together to stop me from having another child. He told me to speak with them and explain how the baby would complete our family.

I was a fool to have listened to him. Everything he suggested was like putting a Band-Aid on a festering wound.

It took every effort to push aside my resentment for Dr. Forster and focus on Amy. When I finally coaxed her out from the closet, she crawled out, holding a doll and a pair of shears. I asked what those were for, and she told me Charlotte wanted a lock of Heath's hair.

Charlotte wants to turn the doll into a body she can inhabit to avenge her murder. For reasons Amy couldn't explain, Charlotte also needed a few drops of the baby's blood to complete a ritual.

I asked a lot of questions to get to the bottom of the request. Amy said she convinced Charlotte that the true murderer was back at Three Fates. Charlotte wanted Amy to transfer her soul into a doll that she can mail to the facility, to punish Dolly.

Amy has the makings of a master storyteller. I have to admit that it's an imaginative plot, but I'll be damned if I hand over parts of my baby to appease a figment of her imagination.

I held out my hand and ordered Amy to give me the shears. She did, but only after stabbing me in the palm and drawing blood. When I screamed, Lyle didn't come charging up the stairs to see what was wrong.

For the next several seconds, I froze, watching Amy spread the blood on the doll. She believed she was doing this to save the family. I wondered if I'd dispatched the wrong twin. Maybe I failed to notice they're both disturbed because of Dolly's flair for the dramatic.

One more incident like that, and I might have to send Amy away, too.

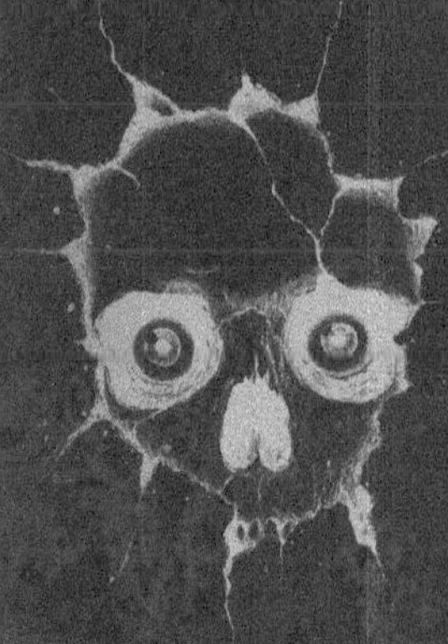

FORTY-FOUR

AMETHYST

My consciousness floats from the confines of a heavy sedative, bringing with it the sound of gentle beeping. Every muscle aches like I've run a marathon, my skin burns, and my insides are wrung dry. It's as if someone took out my batteries and left me out in the desert to die.

Memories float back to my awareness like pollen. The autopsy room, the weed jungle, the bus... And Delta. I tried to fight him, but he was too strong.

My heart splinters. He brought me back.

I wait for Xero to wrap his arms around my waist and give me a summary of what I missed, but all I hear is the rapid beat of my pulse. If he isn't here, helping me sift through my jumbled thoughts, then they must have drugged me with an anti-hallucinogenic to keep us apart. My chest squeezes. I can't endure Delta's punishment alone.

Xero?

When there's still no answer, I crack open an eye. I'm in an infirmary. It's mostly dark, with moonlight streaming in through its windows.

The walls are white and sterile, but at least they're not padded. And I'm lying on a hospital bed instead of the floor.

Thick straps secure my body to the hard mattress, but I couldn't move right now even if the room was on fire.

I glance at an array of machines with bright LED displays that make my eyes sting. Whatever happened between being captured at the bus and now has to be traumatic enough for me to need life support.

Delta must have moved me to another location because I compromised the shoot by calling the police. He must have punished me because my body feels like hell.

I wait for Xero to fill in the details, but he's silent.

Pain lances through my chest, and tears sting my eyes. Losing him is like being naked in the face of a storm. Xero was my buffer from reality. The part of me that was strong enough to witness the abuse, while I drifted away to where it was safe.

Footsteps approach from the other side of the door. My stomach churns with dread, and my heart tries to crawl through the bars of its cage. Cold adrenaline floods my system, powering my muscles, which tense in anticipation of an attack.

The door swings open, and I close my eyes, not wanting to lock gazes with Dolly or Delta or whoever's come to drag me to my fate.

"Are you awake, little ghost?" I hear Xero ask.

My heart skips. Did he return? I wait for him to read my mind and answer, but he remains silent. When warm fingers brush over my forehead to tuck away a stray curl, my breath quickens.

It's Xero.

Why isn't he updating me on what's happening? By now, he'll have worked out a strategy or at least asked what I want to do next. He's just hovering at the side of my bed, breathing hard.

"Open your eyes," he says, his voice so gentle that I could cry.

I peep through my lashes and stare up at Delta. He's shaved off his beard, but it's unmistakably him.

Alarm rips through my chest, making the machines beeping around me shriek. Dread crushes my lungs until I force out the air with a scream. Eyes widening, Delta steps back, presumably for a syringe.

I thrash within my restraints, powered by the last vestiges of my strength. I can't let it happen again. Not while I'm still conscious. Not while I still draw breath.

The door slams open. A dark-haired woman in a white coat charges in, looking nothing like Dolly. She's short, like me, yet she places her hands on Delta's chest and manages to shove him out of the room.

As soon as the door shuts behind him, the pressure on my chest lightens, and I draw in a noisy breath. Shudders run through my frame and settle in my trembling fingertips. Before I can even process what just happened, she returns to my side.

"Amethyst?" the woman says.

She's pretty, with a heart-shaped face, soft features, and loose waves that cascade down to her shoulders. Something about her is familiar, but I don't have the mental bandwidth to pinpoint what. Even though her features are sympathetic, I can't help but recoil at her touch.

What if Dolly has disguised herself as a medic? When I stare into her deep brown eyes, I don't get the usual terror response. She's someone else. Maybe another of Delta's employees?

"My name is Isabel," she says. "And you're in a safe house on the outskirts of Beaumont City. I'm here to help with your recovery. Can you tell me how you're feeling?"

My brow furrows. How can I be safe if I'm with Delta?

Her eyes soften. "Amethyst, you're back in New Alderney."

I swallow hard, not believing a single word. Delta is a murderer, a trafficker, a corruptor of children, a rapist, and a thousand other things that don't equate to safety.

As the machines continue to beep and whirr, she checks the monitors, her soft hands loosening the straps around my chest.

"We had to restrain and sedate you earlier because you could have hurt yourself and others," she murmurs. "We did this for your protection."

"I'm feeling better now," I lie through clenched teeth. "Could you release the straps? Please."

She stares into my eyes for a heartbeat longer than needed and searches my face as if trying to work out whether I'm sane. I stare back, doing everything I can to convey that I'm not a threat.

Finally, she says, "I need to make sure it's safe to release you. Can you tell me more about how you're feeling right now?"

My jaw tightens. "Is this a new form of psychological torture? What the hell does Delta want from me now?"

"Delta?" she asks, her features falling.

"You're working for him, right? Is this a new way for him to crack my skull?"

Her eyes widen, and she shakes her head. "No, no! Amethyst, you're far away from him. Xero brought you back."

Hearing his name is a knife to the chest. It pierces my heart, making it bleed streams of guilt. I squeeze my eyes shut, trying to block out the unbearable truth, and loosen streams of tears. He's gone.

All that remains of him is what weighs on my conscience.

"Xero is dead," I choke out through a sob, my body shaking with grief.

"He was just in the room a minute ago," she says.

"Do you think I don't know that was Delta without his beard? And you're one of his lackeys. Is this another film shoot?"

Sighing, she places a hand on my arm. "I'll be back in a minute."

Isabel's footsteps retreat across the room, then the door swings open. As soon as it shuts, I crack open an eye. It's time to escape before she changes tactics. Delta still needs me alive so I can spill Xero's secrets. The moment he discovers their base in the catacombs, he'll record my grisly death on camera.

Straining against the newly loosened straps, I pull one hand free. I reach down the side of the cot, my fingers brushing against the cool metal frame as I fumble for something—anything—that might give me an edge.

My fingers find the buckle on the strap securing my chest. With trembling hands, I fiddle with the metal fastenings, finally managing to slip my second hand free. Liberating my shoulders takes seconds. Once they're released, I work on the strap around my waist.

I sit up, my vision blurring as blood rushes from my head. As I'm freeing my legs, the door swings open again, and Xero walks in with his wet, platinum hair sticking to his face.

FORTY-FIVE

Friday August 14, 2010

Why am I writing this? Nothing could ever shift the weight of this grief. I've lost everything, and it's all my fault for being blind.

The madness continued after Amy stabbed my hand. She was still haunted by Charlotte, who demanded either a lock of Heath's hair or his life. I should have gathered up a few wisps to satisfy her, but at the time, I thought she would demand more, like blood.

That night, I slept with the door locked to protect the baby from my daughter's psychosis. Lyle looked at me like I was being ridiculous, but he didn't interfere. Everything went fine until Amy woke us with a blood-curdling scream.

Lyle and I both charged out of the room to see what was wrong. My little girl was crouched in the corner of the room, bleeding and begging Charlotte over and over for forgiveness.

I cleaned the wounds, changed her nightgown, and hugged Amy to sleep, assuring her that everything was going to be alright. Charlotte wasn't real. We'd get her some medicine in the morning to chase away the visions. I was half dead by the time I crawled into bed and passed out.

When I woke up the next morning, Heath wasn't breathing.

Lyle performed CPR on the baby while I called the ambulance. After that, my mind went numb. There were sirens, medics, the police, and a tiny body bag.

Lyle was inconsolable. He blamed himself for not acting sooner, for not seeing Amy as a danger to Heath. I asked what he meant. One of my biggest concerns about giving birth too early was the increased risk of Sudden Infant Death Syndrome. If Charlotte hadn't poisoned me twice, I might have carried Heath to term.

He grabbed my hand, dragged me up the stairs, and threw me into Amy's room. I've never seen him so angry.

Amy rocked back and forth on her bed, her face puffy and red from crying, her curls standing on end. She mumbled the same words over and over again, "I didn't mean to. Charlotte did it."

I said it had nothing to do with her. No one could have entered the bedroom. It was locked.

Then I realized it wasn't. I'd spent so much time calming Amy that I'd forgotten to lock the door. Nausea rose in my throat as I asked what happened.

Amy told me Charlotte had shaken her awake, brought her into our bedroom with a pillow and smothered Heath while we slept. Afterward, she shoved her back into her bedroom, saying they were even, and walked down the stairs.

My stomach heaved at Amy's confession. Ghosts don't murder babies. That's the realm of disturbed children.

Lyle barreled in, saying it was time to tell the police everything. That the daughters of Giorgi Salentino were both deranged psychopaths. I stared at Amy, my mind still numb from the shock of losing Heath, and reminded Lyle what would happen if our faces appeared on the news.

The authorities would be the least of our problems. If Mother Salentino and her twins didn't kill us, then they'd pass on the job to their more powerful cousins from the Montesano family.

Lyle broke down in Amy's bedroom, clutching at his hair, saying he'd sacrificed everything for nothing. I glanced from my daughter to my husband, not knowing what the hell to do next, then I found myself asking him to call Mr. Delta at the Three Fates.

I convinced Lyle that Amy made up the story about smothering Heath. She still thought she killed Charlotte, remember? Lyle gazed up at me, a broken man. I repeated this story over and over, adding more details until he turned to Amy and sobbed.

Lyle called Mr. Delta, who reluctantly accepted Amy. My husband wasn't in any condition to drive, so I made Amy's favorite meal of arancini stuffed with caciocavallo, and we spent the whole day cuddled together as a family. I stayed awake, watching over them, as if my vigilance could somehow protect us from the demons of our past.

Later, I packed Amy's things, including a cell phone so she could text me when she reached Three Fates. It's one of the things I regretted when Dolly left. Apart from the incident where she harmed another child, they haven't called us since she was admitted.

The next morning, Lyle left so early that I was still sleeping when the phone rang. It must have been a pocket dial, because Amy didn't speak. All I heard was Lyle ranting to my little girl. And I couldn't believe what he was saying.

FORTY-SIX

XERO

Isabel told me Amethyst thinks I could be Father, which explains her distress. I washed the brown wax from my hair and wiped off the tint I used to darken my skin, so that I look more like myself.

When I step into the room, she's already sitting up in her bed, having escaped most of her restraints. My chest swells with pride that she's used everything I taught her to survive. I pause in the doorway, marveling at my determined little ghost.

We kept her sedated for the journey back to Beaumont City, where a triage truck waited to transport her to this out-of-town safe house. We're providing everything she needs to recover from her ordeal, but she needs to understand that she's free.

Amethyst turns her head, and her pretty green eyes flicker with recognition. All the tension in her features melts to relief, and my heart soars.

She isn't lost to insanity.

Without speaking, she communicates with a wide-eyed expression and a tilt of her head that beckons me closer.

"Amethyst?" I ask.

"I said where did you go?" she whispers.

My brow furrows, and I make a tentative step to her bedside. "What do you mean?"

She stares at me as if I'm a puzzle she desperately needs to solve. "You vanished," she whispers, her voice barely audible over the machinery. "I couldn't reach you after Delta boarded the bus."

I inhale a sharp breath, disturbed she could ever mistake me for a bastard like Father. Amethyst once told me she only hallucinated men she murdered. She probably thinks I died in that fire.

Isabel warned me not to argue with her if she's hallucinating, saying it would distress her further. I need to guide her back to reality without dismissing her perception.

"Where do you think we are now?" I ask.

"You don't know?" she asks back with a frown.

I shrug. "I have an idea, but I want to hear your opinion first."

She turns her attention back to the straps encasing her legs, removing them with trembling fingers. "Delta must have taken me to one of his hideouts after I messed up his filming schedule."

My chest tightens at the thought of her fighting her way to freedom.

"He's cut off the painkillers as a punishment and left me here until he can rebuild his sets," she continues.

"I see," I reply, a lump forming in my throat at the thought that she's distressed. "What if I told you Delta wasn't here?"

She pauses, her gaze darting toward mine. Tears cling to her long lashes. She's paler than usual, with dark circles ringing her eyes. I've never seen her look so heartbreakingly vulnerable.

"Did you overhear something while I was dissociating?" she asks.

The question hits like a punch to the throat. I school my expression, wondering if her experience at the asylum created more damage than I originally feared.

Does she think I'm one of her alters?

Not wanting to trigger any confusion, I shake my head.

After freeing her legs, she removes the electrodes from her temples and chest, leaving her skin sticky with residue. She slides out the needle from her vein with a wince and tosses it aside.

It takes every effort to hold back a warning. Intervening might shatter her mind, but allowing her to discover she's free could start the healing process.

Wiping the blood on her gown, she swings her legs off the bed and stands on shaky feet.

My hands twitch out to steady her, but I force my arms to remain at my sides. This isn't the first time she's mistaken me for a hallucination. I'm only glad that she thinks I'm a trusted one.

Staring up at me with fierce determination, she says, "Let's go."

Without another word, she strides to the door. I step backward, not wanting to get in her way.

"Amethyst," I say.

Her hand pauses at the door handle. "What?"

"Put on some slippers and a heavier robe."

She turns around, her gaze following where I'm pointing toward a pair of thick-soled slippers and a plush robe hanging on a hook by the wall. Her eyes widen, as if she's seeing them for the first time.

Nodding, she rushes over to the garments and slips them on. "Thanks," she murmurs. "I can always rely on you to notice the little things. Are these hallways guarded?"

"No. You're safe." Her eyes narrow, so I add, "The guards are all outside, and I heard Isabel's footsteps disappear down the hallway and through a door."

The suspicion on her features melts into relief. Nodding to herself, she grips the robe's neckline and heads toward the door. "Come on, then."

I follow her out into the dimly lit hallway, our footsteps creaking on the hardwood floors. This safe house is a two-story residence nestled within a seven-acre lot on the outskirts of Beaumont City.

We've evacuated our underground hideouts until I can assess how much information Delta forced out of Amethyst. My operatives are scattered across the city, with only my sisters, Jynxson, and a small retinue of guards on the grounds.

Amethyst strides down the hallway, her head swiveling from side to side in a state of heightened vigilance. She descends the stairs and pauses at the oak front door.

"That's probably alarmed," she mutters, her gaze flicking to a security panel.

"Good call," I murmur. "What should we do next?"

She points toward the kitchen. "We'll need weapons in case we bump into our enemies."

Amethyst moves through the kitchen, her fingers sliding over the quartz worktops. She searches through its oak drawers and cabinets until she finds one containing a collection of knives. After tucking several small ones into her robe pocket, she selects the largest weapon with the heaviest blade.

I watch in awe, wondering what the hell her time at the asylum has unlocked.

She opens the refrigerator, sucking in a sharp breath at the sight of all the food. After cracking open a protein shake and draining it in a few hearty gulps, she grabs several small items and stuffs them into her pockets.

A creak coming from upstairs has her head snapping up. "What's that?"

"The medic," I whisper, hoping Isabel is still in her quarters. "She's harmless."

She closes the refrigerator door, scuttles across the room, and ducks behind the kitchen island.

My brows pinch, and I wonder if she's hallucinating something new. I crouch at her side and whisper, "What's happening?"

"This is a trick," she hisses.

"Explain."

"The drugs are wearing off. Everything hurts and you're glitching." She turns to me, her eyes watering. "Delta would never leave me alone in a house. What if this is another movie set?"

A knot twists in my gut, tightening with each trembling word. I want to hold her close and promise she's safe, but this supposed hallucination of me is the only thing she trusts. Her confusion slices through my chest, leaving me raw and helpless, knowing it will take more than the truth to break through the barriers in her broken mind.

"You asked me earlier if I noticed anything while you were dissociating," I whisper. "Do you remember being carried onto a boat and drugged?"

She nods, her breath quickening.

"You were sedated for hours, and the medic cleaned your wounds." I flick my head toward the ceiling. "She took blood samples and swabs."

Her eyes go round. "Swabs?"

"To track the DNA of any man who touched you," I snarl. "They're going to die."

Suppressing a shudder, she nods again.

"They moved you to this out-of-town hideout. I noticed acres of land with outbuildings."

"Studio sets?" she asks, her voice rising with alarm.

I wince, the weight of her fear tightening my gut. Injecting a note of reassurance into my voice, I add, "The point is that you're alone in the house with Isabel, who's here to monitor your vitals."

"Maybe Delta no longer trusts the male guards," she mutters.

My jaw tightens, and I grind my molars. I clench my fists so tightly that my nails dig into my palms. Every instinct screams at me to ask what happened with the man who stole her away on the bus, but I force back the question. Her Xero alter would know everything she suffered because he was with her the entire way.

"Can you eat something before we find an exit?" I ask.

She shakes her head and grimaces. "It's hard enough to keep down that shake. Everything I eat reminds me of the force feeding."

My chest burns, and I clench my teeth, swallowing down a burst of rage. The thought of them forcing her to do anything makes me want to tear Father and his cohorts into shreds.

Footsteps echo down the stairs, making us both freeze. Isabel was supposed to stay in her room, leaving me to handle Amethyst. My heart races, my insides twisting with dread. Not for my sister, the fully trained assassin, but for Amethyst.

"What do you want to do?" I ask, my voice soft.

She glances toward the stairs, her gaze sharpening. "Anyone who associates with Delta knows what they're doing."

I swallow, wanting to avoid a confrontation. Knowing Isabel, she's armed with both a tranq gun and a syringe.

"Or we can find a way out without setting off any alarms," I whisper.

"Or I can just kill her," she whispers back.

A chill runs down my spine. Amethyst is no longer in denial about her murderous instincts. I wanted to unlock her cold, ruthless determination, but not at the cost of her sanity. Or my family.

"Don't risk it." I raise a hand, ready to drop the pretense of being a hallucination and grab her if she springs out at my sister. "Isabel might raise the alarm."

Her eyes dart around the kitchen, and her body tenses as if she's on the verge of bolting. My pulse quickens, every muscle in my body primed to react. The tension mounts, thickening with every heartbeat. Perhaps it was a bad idea to let her take so many knives.

Finally, she nods. "Let's find another way out."

I rock forward, my chest deflating with relief. "If she comes in, we'll round the island and slip out through the hatch I noticed earlier in the utility room."

Isabel's footsteps grow louder, and I motion for Amethyst to move. The last way I want my oldest sister and the woman I love to be better acquainted is through a fight to the death.

FORTY-SEVEN

Saturday August 15, 2010

I need to write this down before I forget, because what I overheard on the phone was too twisted to be believed.

Amy asked where they were going, and Lyle said they would meet their mutual friend, Dalton. That didn't make sense. The only Dalton I know is Lyle's former colleague, who recommended Three Fates. He came for dinner a few times, but that was past the girls' bedtime.

Lyle explained that Dalton was Mr. Delta. And he had a job for her that required twins. My brows pinched as I tried to pick through his ramblings over the sound of Amy's crying. She said a jumble of words, mostly about not wanting to return to Three Fates, but I managed to piece together that the summer she spent there was terrible and involved getting hurt.

I wanted to hang up and call Lyle, but something compelled me to stay on the line. I slid out of bed and rushed to call him on the landline. It rang and rang, finally switching to voicemail. I left it and listened to the rest of their conversation.

Lyle chuckled, telling her that Charlotte would explain it all to her at Three Fates. Amy gasped. My jaw dropped. Then Lyle gloated that he had hired Charlotte to help extract her and Dolly from the family and assassinate the baby.

I went numb with shock, unable to process the betrayal until Lyle boasted about including allergens in my meals, trying to make me miscarry. When that didn't work, Charlotte upped the dose. She and Lyle faked her death and he let her smother the baby.

I slid down the wall, my mind going blank, not quite believing my devoted husband would arrange something so horrific.

Amy kept asking what he meant, and Lyle explained in gleeful detail how he had set me up to look like a lunatic, estranging me from my daughters. He needed to extract Dolly and Amy with my consent, and his plan worked.

My girl begged to go home. She didn't like Delta. She didn't want to do those terrible things. I listened, my eyes widening, my mind whirring. Had I just handed over my daughter to a sex trafficker?

Lyle said it wasn't personal. That he needed something in return for throwing away his entire life for a woman who turned out to be a cheating cunt. Amy didn't know what he was talking about—how could she?

He raised his voice, screaming that he knew I was listening. He called me a deluded bitch for thinking that a man with a nil sperm count could suddenly father a son.

I dropped the phone, my fingers shaking, so I missed what he said next. By the time I picked it up again to catch the tail end of his rant, all I heard were some chilling words about his plan to kill Dr. Forster.

Somehow, Lyle worked out that Dr. Forster was the one who helped with our fertility problems.

Alarm kicked me into gear. I hung up on the landline and called 911, but froze when Amy yelled that it was his fault her baby brother was dead. Then chaos erupted from the other end of the line. Glass broke. Tires screeched. Metal crunched. In between was a cacophony of screams and horns. And then there were sirens, confirming a car accident.

In a panic, I dropped everything, jumped in the SUV, and took to the streets. Three Fates was somewhere in Carmel, New

Jersey, and there was only one highway linking it to our suburb. Driving like a madwoman, I tore through red lights and stop signs until I reached the scene of a pileup.

The crowd was too dense to break through, but I caught glimpses of paramedics pulling Amy out of the wreckage and loading her onto a stretcher. At the same time, police officers were extracting Lyle from the driver's seat. Something was poking out from his neck. At first, I thought it was a piece of debris from the accident, but someone in the crowd shouted that it was a pair of scissors.

I don't want to think about how they got there.

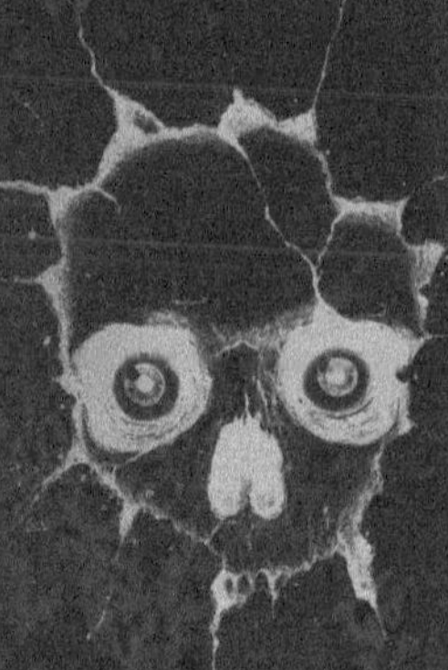

FORTY-EIGHT

AMETHYST

Xero leads me through a dimly lit utility room and points to a small hatch hidden behind a laundry basket. I crawl through the cramped space and emerge onto a patio, taking deep breaths of the cool night air.

It's too early to celebrate. Delta, Dolly, and the surviving henchmen are still out there, throwing together a brand-new set to replace the one they had to abandon. Straightening, I stare into a moon-lit lawn that stretches out toward a thick of trees.

Xero crawls after me, his features etched in shadow, and his pale eyes never leave mine. When he stands, I turn my gaze across the darkened landscape, so he can help me scan the tree line for signs of movement.

"What next, little ghost?" he asks.

"We'll walk around the house and see if there's a driveway," I whisper.

With a nod, he gestures for me to lead the way. We stick close to the building's perimeter, trying to avoid the notice of cameras. Throughout this, Xero stares at me as if I'm the figment of his imagination.

"What?" I ask, shooting a glance over my shoulder.

"How are you feeling?"

"Like this is too easy. Like they're using this escape attempt to shoot new B-roll footage." At his silence, I add, "Like the bathtubs, the pessary, the feeding?"

He gives me a hesitant nod. Something is off about Xero. The version of him I hallucinated at the asylum often vanished under extreme stress, but he always returned looking exactly the same.

I glance at his black hoodie, dark jeans, and boots. "Where's the tuxedo? And why is your hair wet?"

"You need to work that out for yourself," he mutters.

Shaking off his cryptic answer, I continue around the house. Another thing that's off about him is his inability to read my mind. Maybe it's my brain trying to distract me from the horror of my situation... I don't know. But what I do know are the consequences of wasting time. As we tiptoe around the corner of the house, I spot a long driveway leading into the distance toward a dimly lit gate.

All thoughts of Xero's peculiarities vanish at the sign of an exit.

"Which way?" he asks.

"We keep to the dark side of the lawn, not stopping until I either climb or burrow my way to freedom. Once we're out of here, I'm sure we can stick to the trees until I can hitch a ride back to town."

He nods. "Let's go."

Gathering all my courage into a deep breath, I dash for the expanse of grass, making sure to stick to the shadows. Terror grips my throat, silencing the whimpers that try to break free. With Xero at my side, the pain from the cuts they made into my skin becomes more bearable.

Wind roars through my ears, drowning out my pulse's rapid drumroll. Every distant rustle of leaves sends my heart climbing up my chest until it lodges in my throat. I don't dare glance over my shoulder. My focus is on that gate.

Up ahead, two figures emerge from behind the trees, and my steps falter. One is tall and broad, the other petite.

"Why have you stopped?" Xero asks.

I point straight ahead. "It's Dolly and Delta."

He shakes his head. "The woman has straight black hair, and she looks familiar."

When she waves, my heart skips a beat. "She almost looks like..."

"Camila?" Xero whispers.

"Wait—you think your people were looking for me? Because I..." The words stick in my throat. "They're going to kill me for what I did to you."

Xero shakes his head. "They won't know unless you tell them. Don't wait around, or Delta's people will get to you."

He's right. My priority is getting away from those snuff-making psychopaths. Picking up my pace, I sprint toward the trees, my gaze fixed on Xero's sister.

"Keep going," he says, his warm hand pressing on the small of my back.

The heat from his palm seeps through the thick fabric of my robes, burning like a brand against my skin. The comfort is almost overwhelming, a stark contrast to the cold sterility of the infirmary. I steal a glance at Xero, who looks at me with an intensity that sets my nerves aflame.

My breath hitches. Whatever drugs they injected into me this time have heightened my senses, because he almost feels real.

"Amethyst?" Camila beckons me over.

"Camila?" I run, even though she might be a figment of my imagination. Because the next best thing to seeing Xero alive and well would be his ass-kicking sister and best friend.

"Come on," she says, her voice breaking. "You can do it."

Next to her, Jynxson gives me an encouraging nod. I want to know why they aren't running to meet me halfway until I notice they're on the other side of the gate.

"Keep going, little ghost," Xero says, his voice choked with emotion.

Tears sting my eyes, and I blink them free. What if this is real? It's the moment I've both been anticipating and dreading. Xero's people will kill me for what I did, but they might make it painless if I lead them to Delta.

I continue running toward them, my steps plagued with a tumultuous mix of doubt and hope. Uncertainty gnaws at my resolve, threatening to trip me up. I stumble once, then again, but each time Xero's hand remains on my back, his touch propelling me forward. His unwavering support fuels my determination, and I push through the fear, driven by the desperate need to reach the gate.

Glancing up for another glimpse of those pale blue eyes, my heart lurches. They're so alive, so intense. Despite the physical impossibility of it all, the love and determination blazing through them feels heartbreakingly real.

My breath comes in shallow gasps. The tall iron gate is just ahead, and beyond it, Camila's beautiful, smiling face.

"Nearly there," she says. "Amethyst. Hurry."

I pick up my pace, not stopping until I reach Camila's outstretched fingers. She clutches my hands, pulling me against the bars into a hug.

Jynxson keeps his distance, but his presence is just as comforting. Xero stands so close that his body heat radiates into my skin, wrapping me in a cocoon of reassurance. His unwavering presence is a constant reminder that I am not alone. Every breath he takes, every subtle movement, fills my spirit with a profound sense of safety and peace.

"You're real," I say, my voice choking with a sob.

She stares back, her eyes misting with tears. "Can you climb over?"

I glance up the length of the gate, finding no curls or crossbars or convenient footholds. Releasing Camila's hands, I reach up and grab the bars. They're too smooth, too straight, and I don't have the upper body strength to haul myself up.

When I lift a foot to scale, my slippers find little purchase. It's even worse than crawling out of an open grave.

Jynxson steps forward, but Camila elbows him in the gut and flicks her head to a point behind my shoulder. The gesture is so exaggerated that I'm forced to turn around, and I meet Xero's unwavering gaze.

His hand lands on my shoulder, warm and strong and solid. As his fingers tighten with gentle reassurance, the rusty gears in my mind start turning, bringing me closer to a dawning realization.

My gaze darts to the side to find Jynxson and Camila both staring at what's standing at my back. Hope flickers in my chest, igniting a spark of possibility. I turn again, my breath catching in my throat, heart hammering hard enough to crack my ribs. My eyes widen with disbelief, and the world narrows to a single figure.

It's Xero, standing tall and majestic.

Moonlight filters through his platinum hair, casting a soft glow over his chiseled features. His high cheekbones and strong jawline are thrown into sharp relief, while his eyes, illuminated in the pale light, seem to burn with blue flames. The sight of him, almost otherworldly in the night, jolts me back to razor-sharp awareness.

If they can see him, that means...

"Xero?" My voice is a fragile whisper.

He nods, his eyes filled with a gentle sadness. "It's me, little ghost."

My eyes well up with tears. "But... You're dead. I saw you. I saw the fire."

Xero takes my hands, his grip firm and reassuring, grounding me to this newfound reality. "I survived," he whispers, his voice thick with emotion. "And I haven't stopped trying to get you back."

I shake my head, loosening tears that stream down my cheeks. "No... How? Don't you want me dead?"

His gaze softens, and he brushes away the tears with a tenderness that breaks me further. "I saw that video. They wanted to break you, but you survived."

My sobs intensify, my body wracked with pain and guilt. "Oh, my God. I'm so sorry."

He pulls me into his arms, holding me in a hug so tight that I could melt into his strong chest. "It's not your fault," he murmurs into my curls, his breath warm and comforting against my scalp. "You were manipulated, mentally tortured for longer than you even realize. But you're free now. We're free."

The words only make me sob harder. All the pent-up emotions rise from the pit of my stomach like a tsunami, threatening to consume what's left of my mind. I cling onto Xero's waist like he's the only lifeline in this tidal wave of self-recrimination and regret.

I stared down at my daughter, coming to grips with the burgeoning horror. Lyle set out to destroy me, and he succeeded.

My baby was dead. My twins were bitter enemies. Amy was seeing things that didn't exist. Dolly... I had no idea what the hell they were doing to her at Three Fates.

I asked Amy how to find the facility, but she was too distracted by an apparition to answer. She trembled and sobbed, repeating over and over that Charlotte was telling her to kill me to make up for her failure with Heath.

When we reached the hospital, I stood in her room, rooting through my phone for the number I'd saved for the Three Fates Therapeutic Boarding School. It kept going through to voicemail. I kept leaving messages for an address, so I could pick up Dolly.

I returned home to search through Lyle's study for the number he had for Dalton, who turned out to be Mr. Delta. Why the hell would a former FBI agent run a boarding school? All I found were dossier upon dossier of children. Children with price tags.

Some came from overseas, others were marked as runaways whose backgrounds Lyle had carefully researched. Three Fates wasn't a school and Lyle wasn't arranging adoptions—he was running a child trafficking ring.

I called the police. They "escalated the case" to a high-ranking officer who exchanged all the evidence for a business card—one with a fake number. I hired a private detective, who took a cash deposit and then demanded an exorbitant daily rate. By the time I tried to withdraw more money, I found our bank accounts were depleted to their limit.

My world was crumbling, with my only anchor being Amy. She was still in the hospital, tormented by hallucinations of Charlotte. Then the hospital called about problems with payments, saying that our health insurance had expired.

I drove straight to Dr. Forster's house to find him stuffing suitcases into the trunk of his car. Blocking his drive, I told him everything. That Lyle found out he'd impregnated me and then orchestrated a convoluted revenge plan to steal my daughters and kill our baby.

Forster tried to gaslight me about the affair, until I revealed I'd recorded our sessions, including the ones where he crossed the lines of professional conduct, using my vulnerability to obtain easy sex.

When he asked what it would take to get me to move my car, I was ready with a list: Help finding Dolly, help with Amy's mental state, and help with Amy's medical bills.

He called his colleague at a prestigious mental hospital to arrange a transfer and gave me a check for twenty thousand dollars. I asked for more, but he mumbled something about all his money being used up to fight another accusation of misconduct.

Despite my resentment, I took the check. The only other choice I had was to throw myself at the mercy of the Salentino family, who were more likely to put a bullet through my skull than help.

That evening, when I drove home, a man stood at the door, and a procession of people were carrying away our furniture. The man introduced himself as our landlord and said that Lyle had canceled our lease months ago. He had agreed to vacate the house by today.

Then the foreman in charge of the removal crew told me that all our furniture had been purchased on credit, and Lyle hadn't paid.

My heart sank. Everything made sense. Lyle had insisted on a ridiculously extravagant shopping spree the moment I announced I was pregnant. Everything he'd done had been an elaborate scheme to strip me of everything I loved and leave me destitute. All I had left was one damaged little girl.

And by the time I returned to the hospital, Amy had already been transferred.

FIFTY

XERO

When Isabel and I planned the charade to ease Amethyst back to reality, I expected tears and even an outpouring of emotion. I didn't expect her to make another escape attempt after we'd put her to bed.

We had to restrain and sedate her again. Part of her psyche still believes she's in danger, although she won't explain why.

I watched over her last night while she slept, noticing when the drugs wore off and her nightmares crawled to the surface. She thrashed within her restraints, whimpering and crying the same cryptic phrases over and over: *It's all my fault. I killed her.*

"Xero?" Camila's voice breaks me out of my musings. I jerk in my seat and glance around the study at three faces staring at me as if I've zoned out for hours.

My sister leans forward in her seat and frowns. "Are you still with us?"

I rub the back of my head and blink away the fog. "Run that past me again."

All eyes turn back to Jynxson, who repeats his status report. The six men we captured at the asylum are in stable condition, tied up in holding cells in a bunker within the grounds of this safe house. All claim to be members who won the opportunity to become extras, with little more information to add about where Delta might be hiding.

Reverend Thomas is begging for a chance at redemption after helping Camila capture the other investors at the penthouse. After Dolly and her companions left in the helicopter to rescue Delta, the men tired of waiting around and started to leave. Camila hid in a doorway and hit each of them with tranquilizer darts.

The reverend helped her drag the bodies to the stairwell, where our operatives returned later to transport them to holding cells. We're interrogating them for information about Father, but only one of them seems to know anything—a high-ranking officer in New Alderney State law enforcement. The rest were kept in the dark.

My suspicions about the driver in the bullet-proof car were correct. After the helicopter passengers took out our drones' weapons systems, we captured footage of Father exiting the vehicle. The men I stationed took shots at him, but he was wearing bullet proof armor.

The man he left bleeding on the front passenger seat wasn't quite so fortunate.

"Adrian Tanner." Jynxson pulls up an image of a dark-haired man on the computer screen. "You might recognize him from the Lizzie Bath video, where he had a non-speaking part as the mortician. He, along with other men we identified, are wanted in connection with several murders."

"What's his condition?" I ask.

"Not good," Isabel replies. "He's lost a lot of blood because a bullet hit an artery while it lodged in his skull. The doctors are worried it might have also hurt his brain. Dr. Dixon has him stable for now, but it's still touch and go."

"Delta must have tried to shoot him in the head before he left for the helicopter," Jynxson mutters.

Camila leans forward. "Tyler ID'd him in every major X-Cite Media production currently on their member's site. He always has a key part."

"Which is all the more reason why we need him conscious," I

snarl. "Adrian Tanner could lead us straight to that bastard's location."

"Did anyone ID the man in the bus?" Isabel asks.

"Tyler says he's Fenrick Greer," Camila replies. "He performed on six X-Cite Media videos but can be seen as an extra in four."

"His name was used to book the penthouse and some of the specialized production equipment abandoned at the site," Jynxson says.

"Also wanted for murder," Camila adds.

I nod, remembering everything Reverend Thomas and Harland Stills, the recruiter, told me about the firm's inner workings. Father won't allow anyone off the street to act in his snuff movies.

It's a slow process of climbing the ranks, beginning with submitting incriminating footage of yourself as part of an audition, followed by working as an extra. Only then are candidates elevated to performing atrocities on camera. By that time, Father will have gathered enough evidence on the men to ensure they have no way out.

Silence hangs in the room for several moments as I digest the information, and all eyes turn in my direction. They're waiting for me to give a command, but my thoughts are consumed by my little ghost.

"Has Amethyst shared anything yet?" Jynxson finally asks.

Isabel answers before I can muster a reply. "She's in no condition for questioning and is still heavily medicated."

That's an understatement. Amethyst is still working through a cocktail of drugs. At some point this morning, the coagulants wore off and blood seeped through her bandages. Isabel had to redress the wounds again. She's been asleep ever since.

"Her mental health comes first. Give her time." I rise from my seat.

Jynxson frowns. "Can we get her to journal her experience?"

I raise a palm. "Assume she knows nothing until she says otherwise. Our focus now is interrogating the men we captured and identifying the pair who rode in the helicopter with Dolly."

He falls silent. It goes against our training for me to delay a debriefing, but Amethyst isn't part of our organization. Even if she is a former Lolita assassin, the last thing I want is to dredge up her suppressed memories to worsen her trauma.

I walk out of the study, leaving Camila and Jynxson firing up a video chat with Tyler. Isabel follows me through the hallway and up the stairs, her gaze burning the side of my face. The house is silent, save for our synchronized footsteps and the distant chatter filtering from below.

"What?" I ask.

"You really care about this woman."

I cast my sister a sidelong glance. "Is that a problem?"

"Are you sure you have the right twin?"

"What does that mean?"

"One of them left you in a burning basement to die."

I grind my teeth. "Get to the point."

She grabs my arm. "I have nothing against her, but you need to consider that Delta had her under his control for days. Days where he could have brainwashed or manipulated her against us."

The weight of her words sinks into my gut like lead. That possibility has plagued me in varying amounts since I woke up surrounded by flames. I look her dead in the eye, conveying my unwavering commitment to Amethyst.

"He got to all of us at some point during our lives, and we all want him dead," I say. "If I see any signs of manipulation or betrayal, I'll handle it. Until then, we'll treat her with respect and care."

She releases my arm. "I hope you know what you're doing."

I stare after her as she continues down the hallway and into the room next to the infirmary. Every instinct says Amethyst isn't a Trojan horse, but I won't discount the risk.

We're finally hitting Father where it counts—his wallet. That's not something he will take lightly. The chance he will use Amethyst to strike at me again is dangerously close to inevitable.

Forcing aside the nagging doubts, I continue down the hallway toward the infirmary. Amethyst's drowsy voice floats through the crack in the door, making my heart stir.

It reminds me of the early mornings I spent in the prison's

blind spot, waking her from a slumber with phone sex. When she giggles, the sound makes my chest inflate with hope.

I push open the door and step inside to find her strapped to the cot, which is set at an incline. She's still dressed in yesterday's hospital gown, with the blankets pulled up to her chest. The morning sun filters through the blonde side of her curls, making them shine like spun gold.

She stops mid-sentence, her eyes going round.

"Who are you talking to, little ghost?" I ask.

Her gaze darts to the side for a second, then she meets my eyes, her face falling with what looks like disappointment. "I was dreaming."

"You dream with your eyes open?" I ask.

"I thought I was back in my room before any of this happened," she replies with a shudder. "Looks like my mind won't stop playing tricks."

"What was happening in this dream?" I ask.

"Xero was..." She shakes off that sentence. "You were in my room, telling me you'd escaped prison for the night."

Smiling, I step forward and reach her bedside. Amethyst shrinks into the mattress and swallows, her breath quickening. The monitors measuring her vital signs beep faster, and her gaze darts around the room, seeming to search for an escape.

A lead weight sinks into my stomach. She still sees me as a threat.

"Easy," I murmur and step back to create a little distance. "It's okay. No one's here to harm you."

Her eyes search mine, scanning for any traces of deceit. I hold her stare, conveying the depth of my commitment and love. Her gaze wavers, then steadies with a flicker of trust. The connection between us deepens, filling the silence with an unspoken understanding.

"Do you need anything?" I ask.

"You can remove these oven mitts from around my hands."

"Mittens," I reply with a sigh. "After we put you back in your bed, you pulled out your IV and tried to escape. Twice."

She raises her chin, her eyes hardening. "Am I your prisoner?"

My heart clenches, and my arms ache to pull her into my chest, to offer a measure of solace. But I resist, despite my mind being in turmoil with conflicting emotions of caution, compassion, and guilt. It's gut-wrenching to keep her in captivity, but she's a danger to herself.

"You're dehydrated, malnourished, and still under the influence of drugs," I say.

The door behind me swings open and Isabel strides in. "I gave the order to secure you, not Xero. Your toxicology report came in earlier. We identified three types of hallucinogenic drugs in your system, along with traces of painkillers, antifibrinolytics, sedatives, and two substances we still can't identify."

"What?" Amethyst whispers, her lips trembling.

"We're doing our best to flush them out of your system, but it's impossible to tell what kind of reactions they might cause. We're not trying to hold you hostage, Amethyst. The restraints are for your protection."

My little ghost deflates, her gaze dropping down to her restrained hands.

"Am I dangerous?" she asks, her voice breaking.

My chest aches. She looks so small, so defeated. She spent years being drugged and controlled by her mother, only to end up still shackled. This is the opposite of the life she deserves.

I move closer and reach for one of her mitten-clad hands. When she flinches, my heart shatters.

"You're not dangerous," I say. "Just fragile. The cuts they made all over your body have reopened. We won't be able to heal the damage until those drugs are out of your system."

She bows her head, her shoulders shaking with sobs.

"We'll get through this together," I say, my voice cracking.

When she finally raises her head, it's to gaze at me through red-rimmed eyes. "How the hell am I supposed to know if I should believe you, or if you're only keeping me alive until you pump me for information?"

FIFTY-ONE

Tuesday August 24, 2010

I'm back where I started: On my knees, begging the Salentino family for mercy.

Dr. Forster's secretary told me he'd left town and couldn't be reached. The professional conduct situation he mentioned was an understatement. Six women accused him of crimes far worse than getting them pregnant.

Lyle's brother, Clive, got arrested for making snuff movies. His trial was fast-tracked due to the overwhelming evidence, and he ended up with a life sentence. I managed to visit him in jail to ask where Dalton had taken my daughter, but he kept raging about being framed.

You know what? I believe him.

If Lyle can orchestrate such devastating revenge over the course of six months, then Dalton can set up the owner of a BDSM nightclub for a crime as heinous as filming the murder and rape of women. Maybe Dalton and Lyle weren't really expelled from the FBI solely for protecting their targets' victims.

The Salentino twins have confined me to a room while they conduct their searches. By the time I reached their mansion, I'd forgotten the name of the hospital Dr. Forster had transferred Amy to, and its location. I'm furious with myself.

Giorgi's sisters have read this diary. It's the only thing keeping me alive. Apparently, they knew Lyle was working for the FBI. He was their inside man, feeding them information to keep the authorities at bay. He told me we were "in hiding" from the Salentinos when, in fact, he'd continued working for them for years after I'd escaped, making everyone think I'd been abducted by a gang in New Jersey.

My disappearance from the family aggravated an already tense truce, and that led to the deaths of Giorgi, his father—head of the family, Don Salentino himself—and one of the Montesano cousins. Relations between the families are stable now, but the Salentino sisters say the only thing keeping me alive is that my girls will need their mother when they return.

The investigator they hired took a week to locate Amy. An entire army of men moved in on her location and extracted her from an asylum. She's now staying in the infirmary at the Montesano mansion, under the care of the doctor they have on retainer.

While she was comatose, the twins debated whether to kill me and raise Amy as a Salentino. They were nice enough to stand outside my room so I could hear them discussing whether I lived or died.

I would call them cruel bitches, but they're my only means of survival. Besides, I'm in no position to judge.

When Amy woke up, hallucinating Lyle, their plans to steal her from me turned to shit. Not wanting to be saddled with a mentally deranged girl, they arranged a house for her on the same stretch of road as their mansion and told me to give her a good life. Or they'd burn me in their incinerator.

They're still looking for Dolly, but their detectives say the trail has gone cold. Dalton Grey doesn't exist. Not in the FBI. Not in any criminal database, and the pictures I have of him don't match anyone they can find.

He's vanished into thin air with Dolly. The idea that my daughter might be lost to me forever is unbearable. She's probably dead. Or trafficked. Or indoctrinated by that evil bitch, Charlotte.

Every time I look at Amy's face, all I see is my failure. That, and her identical twin, who I handed to the wolves, and the beautiful baby whose life was cut short. I can't help but wonder if we'd still be a happy family if I had been satisfied with my two daughters.

Sometimes, I wish I'd never met Lyle at all. If Giorgi had killed me, then my daughters would still be together, living with their aunts and grandmother. Maybe they'd be spoiled brats, but they'd be alive. And sane.

They've already chosen a psychiatrist to help Amy. Dr. Saint is the kind of professional who doesn't keep records of her underworld patients and won't run to the police at the first sign of criminal activity.

I'm supposed to spill all my secrets to her, but it's obvious she'll report back to my Salentino overlords. They all think I'm a fuck-up. Maybe I am, but I'll do my best to help Amy and create a welcoming home when the detectives find Dolly.

Amy has a place at the Tourgis Academy, where she'll be safely out of the way while I repay the Salentino family for their generosity. Mother Salentino said that a two-timing whore like me is only good for entertaining men.

As soon as Amy is in school, my job is to 'seduce the president of the New Alderney Cemetery Board and gather enough evidence to make him stop harassing the Salentino's fine crematorium for a bunch of violations he's fabricated out of thin air.'

Once he's blackmailed, I must 'sink my slutty claws into the assistant mayor and get hold of a list of classified documents.'

So, that's my life. I escaped the Salentino family as an abused wife and returned as an indebted courtesan. That's my karma. One day, Amy's memories will return, and I'll have to explain why I allowed her to be abused and her sister to disappear.

I have no idea how I'll reply. Sometimes, I wish Giorgi had carried out his threats against my life, because existing like this is a living hell.

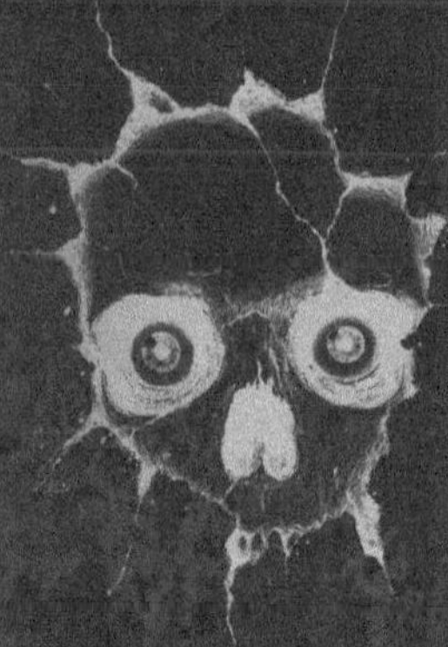

FIFTY-TWO

AMETHYST

Isabel puts me through a detox that takes twice the amount of time that I spent as Dolly and Delta's prisoner. Every morning, she draws blood to check my system's levels of foreign substances. She connects me to an IV filled with fluids and nutrition because my stomach keeps rioting. I alternate between vivid nightmares and daytime hallucinations as my mind tries to work out what's real.

When I'm not hallucinating, I dream about being admitted to the asylum as a little girl, under the care of a red-haired doctor with piercing gray eyes.

He would loom too close as orderlies in white strapped me down to a metal bed, and then he'd inject me with a drug to make the room dissolve into a kaleidoscope of colors and shapes.

The doctor's voice would drone on, repeating the same words until they seeped into my consciousness. Those words built a brick wall around my memories until I didn't even know my name.

They kept the lights on in my room and kept me awake with hot and cold baths. If I screamed for Mom and Dad, then he moved me to a room and attached electrodes to my temples. The pain was unbearable, and I would return from those sessions blank. The moment I begged to go home, the torture would start all over again.

Xero gave me a phone so I could dictate my memories and work out what's imagined, recent, and old. They're easy to tell apart, based on who's in them and what they want. The present-day Delta wants me to remember, while the red-haired doctor wants me to forget. In between are fractured scenes with nurses, orderlies, and patients staring into nothingness through dead eyes.

Throughout this, Xero watches over me like a sentinel. Sometimes he's clad in the tuxedo, other times wearing black. Both versions of him offer silent support as the drugs leave my system and memories trickle back to me like sludge.

One afternoon, I wake up to the absence of pressure. The bands keeping me tethered to the hospital bed are gone.

Xero stands over me, the sunlight streaming through his platinum hair, casting a halo that makes me think I'm hallucinating an angel. His black shirt and leather jacket break the illusion, but there's a rugged beauty to him that makes my heart race.

I glance down at his hand, where intricate tattoos peek out from under his sleeve, dark ink against pale skin. He's reaching for my hand, his fingers tentative and hesitant, as if afraid of my reaction to his touch.

My pulse quickens, and my fingers curl into fists. It's strange how I draw comfort from the version of him I hallucinate, yet the real Xero makes me jumpy. The sunlight catches on his pale eyes, ringed with shadows, as though he's been trapped in nightmares as dark as mine. His features flicker with pain when I don't immediately respond to his touch. The expression is fleeting, but even I can see he's upset.

"Isabel says your toxicology report is clear. Are you up for a walk in the garden?" His voice is a low rumble, laced with concern.

My chest lifts with hope at the prospect of going outside. "Yes..." I rasp, my voice barely a whisper. "I think I can manage that."

As I sit up, swinging my legs off the edge of the mattress, Xero drops to his knees. His hands are gentle as he helps me slide my feet into the same slippers as before. The brush of his fingers sends shivers up my spine. I place a hand on his broad shoulder to steady myself as I stand. The room rocks sideways, and my knees buckle.

Xero catches me instantly, his strong arms wrapping around my waist, pulling me close. His eyes lock onto mine with an intensity that makes my insides tremble, a storm brewing in those pale depths. His scent, a mix of leather and something uniquely him, fills my senses.

For a moment, I can't help but notice how he looks a lot like how I imagine Delta might appear if he bleached his hair blond, shaved off his beard, and smothered his face in my collagen cream.

A memory bubbles up of the time Xero scooped handfuls of my expensive face serum and stuck it up my ass. The absurdity of the thought makes me bark out a laugh.

"Are you alright?" His voice softens, concern etching his handsome face with a frown.

"Yes," I manage to say, a smile tugging at the corner of my mouth. "I mean... thank you." I flick my gaze down to the slippers, trying to hide the warmth flooding my cheeks.

Cracking a tiny smile, he releases his hold around my waist. There's a reluctant loss in his eyes as he steps back and holds up the robe like a gentleman. The simple gesture, combined with his intense presence, makes my heart flutter in ways I can't explain.

"Put this on. It's chilly outside," he says, his voice so gentle that my throat thickens with emotion.

I slide my arms into the plush robe, the heavy fabric barely brushing against my dressings. When Xero's fingers brush against mine, heat rises to my cheeks and creeps up my neck. I dip my head, hoping to disguise the flush.

My first steps are shaky, my legs weak from days of being confined to the bed. Isabel told me I tried to run away the first time she released my restraints to let me into the bathroom. I'd even torn some stitches on the back of my legs. Since then, she's restricted me to a bed pan.

I shuffle out of the room with Xero at my side. His presence is steadying, his gaze never leaving me. Each time I stumble, his hands hover close, ready to catch me if I fall. I can't remember the last time anyone cared so deeply for my wellbeing or even showed me this level of concern.

"Give me your arm," I say.

He hesitates for a heartbeat before offering me his elbow. I grip his biceps, feeling secure in the strength beneath his leather jacket.

The walk through the house is silent, the air thick with unspoken words. I barely remember running through this hallway, thinking the Xero running beside me was a hallucination.

My most intense memory is the overwhelming surge of euphoria at discovering Xero was still alive. It even overshadowed the relief I felt at being free. As much as I hated being Delta's captive, thinking that I had murdered Xero was far worse.

We descend the stairs at a gentle pace, with Xero taking care to support me with each downward step. My heart flutters at the attention, my chest filling with warmth. He's treating me like I'm fragile, even precious. Each touch, each glance, feels like what I've missed for a lifeline.

After passing through a short corridor to a side door, Xero pushes it open to reveal a vast garden bathed in the golden afternoon light. The sight steals my breath. We step out onto a lawn resembling a green carpet, edged by vibrant flower beds and low shrubs.

Sunlight warms my skin, and I inhale, savoring the freedom and the beauty. The air is filled with the scent of fresh grass and blooming flowers, a welcome change from the sterile infirmary.

A shudder runs down my spine at the thought of how this garden would look after a decade of neglect.

"Are you alright?" he asks, his voice edged with worry.

"It reminds me of the asylum."

He turns to me with a frown. "That forest of weeds?"

"It wasn't always like that," I murmur, struck by the irony that my hallucinated Xero reminded me of what the asylum gardens looked like when I was little. "Its lawn and flowerbeds were well maintained once, just like this."

"You remember that much of the time you spent there?" he asks, his voice softening.

"Enough of it," I reply with a shiver, the memories flitting through my mind like dark shadows. "I'm almost grateful for the memory loss."

"Want to talk about it?" His concern wraps around me like a warm blanket.

"Not yet."

"Just know if you need a sounding board, I'm here. Or a shoulder to cry on, I'm here. If you need a valet to hold your weapons while you tear through the city on a violent rampage, I'm here," he says, his voice lightening with amusement.

I turn to meet his eyes. Eyes that gaze down at me like I'm the only woman in the world. Eyes that belong to the man who captured my heart with his letters, phone calls, and unwavering devotion. Eyes that never stopped searching for me, even when I thought all was lost.

Tension builds between us, the air thick with unspoken words. I forget about the garden, and the entire world narrows down to Xero. I don't know if I'm ready to talk about what happened at the asylum, or even share my feelings. I'm certainly not ready to lash out at my attackers.

"Thank you," I whisper, my voice barely audible.

Eyes softening, he steers me back toward the house. We walk around its perimeter, passing flower beds that fill the air with their sweet scent. The house's brick facade gives way to a large patio with a fire pit at its center, surrounded by comfortable seating.

My legs tremble, and I point at a bench that curves around the pit in a semicircle. Xero guides me to sit on its cushioned seat, his touch lingering on my arm. I gaze out onto the grounds, the lush greenery calming my racing heart.

The garden is not as regimented as the one Mom kept at the house in Alderney Hill. This one blends into small trees and larger shrubs carpeted with wildflowers. Taller trees frame the background, their canopies forming the beginnings of a forest. The tranquil surroundings, the distant bird calls mingling with the rustle of leaves, form a sanctuary that makes the asylum feel like a distant dream.

"We bought this safe house before I went to prison." His posture straightens, his gaze sweeps across the grounds. "It's going to be one of many halfway homes for children we rescue from the academy and the underground facility."

"You wouldn't take the older ones to the catacombs?" I ask.

He shakes his head, a lock of platinum hair falling across his brow. "Everyone who defects from the Moirai gets a choice on whether they want to join us or have a normal life."

"Is there such a thing as normal if you've spent years training to be an assassin?" I murmur.

When he doesn't answer, I turn to stare at his profile. His eyes are focused on the distant trees, seeming lost in the implications of my question. I take in the sharp angles of his cheekbones, the strength in his jaw, and the tension around his eyes and mouth. His Adam's apple bobs as he swallows.

"Some have been through so much, we don't even remember normal," he replies, his voice heavy with the weight of his words. "Most stay with us for protection, because defying the Moirai means constantly looking over your shoulder."

My brows pinch in concern. I was expecting him to lead with something more optimistic.

"That's why we plan on taking out its leadership, starting with him," he snarls.

Delta.

The name hangs between us like a specter.

Xero turns to meet my gaze, his eyes blazing with barely restrained fury. "He'll pay for what he did. Him and his accomplices."

I fidget on my seat, looking everywhere but at him. Twin worms of guilt and shame wrestle in my belly, making me squirm under the spotlight of his attention. No matter how much I try, I can't shake off the unease.

This version of Xero is more like the one I've known—ruthless, vengeful, never letting a slight go unpunished. No one has betrayed him recently except me. It's unsettling that he's being so nice when I don't deserve this care. Yet there's a part of me that will die if it ever goes away.

The silence stretches until it squeezes my lungs. I fight against the suffocating urge to speak, wanting to stay in this peculiar bubble of peace where Xero is too preoccupied with finding

Delta to confront me about trying to burn him alive. Clenching my teeth, I try to force my mouth to stay closed, but the words spill from my lips.

"When are you going to bring up the fire?" I clap a hand over my mouth, wanting to stuff that question down my throat.

My breath stills as I wait for his response. If he haunted and tormented me for leaving him at the altar and writing a book about our relationship, then what I did to him before I ran away should earn me a death sentence.

"Look at me," he commands.

I shake my head, fixing my gaze on my lap. Unease squeezes my chest, tightening its grip on my heart.

"Amethyst," he growls, his voice a mix of frustration and something deeper.

Dipping my neck, I peer up at him through my lashes. The intensity in his eyes is almost too much to bear, but I can't look away. Breathing hard, my heart thrashes against its cage like a trapped bird. His gaze holds mine, as if he can see into the very depths of my soul.

"I watched that video." He pauses, his features flickering with emotions I can't pin down. There's frustration, rage, sorrow, and even pride. His lips tighten as if he's choosing his next words with the utmost precision. "If I thought something like that had happened to my sisters, I would also set the man responsible on fire."

"That wasn't me," I murmur, my voice barely audible.

"I know it was Dolly."

My head snaps up, and I finally look him full in the face. "How do you know about her?"

"We abducted nearly everyone connected to your disappearance and uncovered a few secrets about your past. I know you have a twin who went missing when you were nine or ten. I know you were sent to that asylum to erase your memories."

My breath shallows, each revelation hitting me like a blow. I stare at him, my eyes widening with disbelief and a flicker of hope.

"What else did you discover?" I whisper, my voice trembling.

"Your mother left a diary that can fill in the gaps. Would you like to read it?"

My throat thickens, and the grief I suppressed rises to the surface. There was a window of time when I thought Mom was the monster behind the polaroids. She was a lot of things, but she didn't deserve to be hunted and killed.

"I didn't kill her. Or my uncle," I say, my voice cracking.

"I know," he responds, his eyes never leaving mine.

"How?"

"From the start, I knew whoever did it had connections. They took out two operatives I sent to watch over your mother's house."

My throat tightens, and I swallow hard. "I'm sorry."

"Don't apologize for their actions."

We sit in silence, and I sag under the weight of our unspoken words. Tears spring to my eyes, and I wipe them away with the back of my hand. Xero turns toward me, his eyes softening with compassion, but I shrink to the other side of the bench, creating some distance.

"Sorry," I mutter, trying not to sound so small and fragile. "Sometimes I can't believe it's really you."

He nods, his shoulders sagging, making my heart squeeze with guilt at having caused him even more pain.

His phone buzzes, breaking the heavy silence. "Are you ready for a surprise?" he asks with a hint of a smile.

"What kind?"

"Myra just arrived at the gate."

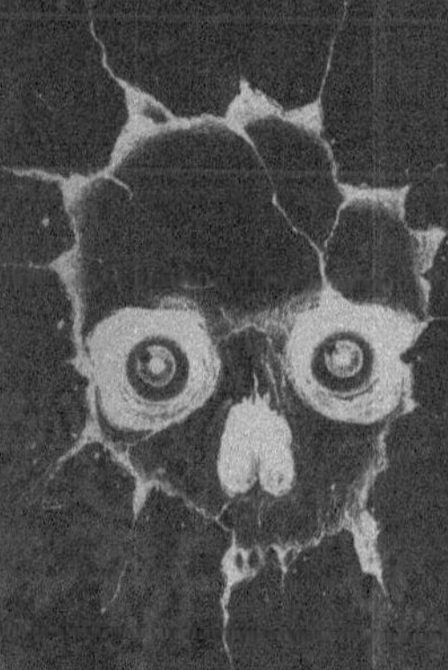

FIFTY-THREE

XERO

As Camila rounds the corner of the house with Myra Mancini, the air fills with the sound of feminine squeals. I rise off the bench and retreat into the kitchen, leaving the women to reconnect. Myra might be just what Amethyst needs to feel like she's finally safe.

I walk past a wall of oak cabinets and enter a pantry filled with shelves of canned food. Stretching my hand up to the highest shelf, I pull the lever that releases the hidden door leading down to the basement. It springs open, revealing a darkened stairwell. As I descend, Myra's voice grows faint, replaced by the gentle hum of our backup generators.

Fury powers my steps. Knowing that Amethyst is afraid of me is a dagger to the heart. I hate myself for making her suffer after I escaped prison. She should be recovering from her ordeal, not dreading my retribution.

Better still, she shouldn't have ended up in Father's clutches at all. I need to find that bastard. Kill him slowly for every torment he and his underlings inflicted on Amethyst. And for all the other women and children he corrupted and killed.

And for me.

I break into a jog, my footsteps echoing off the concrete walls.

I don't stop until I reach the passageway leading to the bunker where we're holding our most promising of Father's investors.

Its steel door grinds open under my fingertips, releasing damp air drenched with the mingled scents of blood and sweat. A fluorescent lightbulb swings from the ceiling, casting moving shadows across a dimly lit room equipped with chains hanging on the walls, and a metal table lined with tools.

Its single occupant slumps, blindfolded, bruised, and bound to a chair welded to the concrete floor with metal plates. Four IVs lead from his arms: sodium pentothal to lower his defenses, an amphetamine to keep him alert, scopolamine for compliance, and a saline solution to keep him alive long enough to talk.

He's a middle-aged man who works out but still piles on the carbs, making him look more bulky than buff. His head is shaved in that defeated way of men losing to male pattern baldness, yet a thick ring of hair on his chin extends up his sideburns and around the back of his head. Nothing says 'holding on to youth' like a balding man clinging to his last scraps of dignity.

I press a button on the wall that sends a burst of electricity through the chair. He jerks awake with a scream, the restraints digging into his bloated flesh.

Inhaling a deep breath, I savor the scent of his fear.

"Good afternoon, Carl," I say. "You and I are going to have a little chat."

"Who's there," he slurs. "Do you know who I am?"

He's a resistant fucker. Either he's been trained to resist truth serums or he's belligerent to the core. By now, the cocktail of drugs should have him broken and drooling. I cross the room and tear off his blindfold.

"Deputy Chief Carl Hunter," I sneer. "Second-in-command to the Chief of Police of New Alderney."

Hunter blinks over and over, his eyes adjusting to the sudden influx of light. He squints, closes his eyes then, forces them open. Recognition melts his battered face into a mask of shock. His pupils dilate, and his ruddy skin drains of all color.

"X-Xero? Xero Greaves?" he stammers. "You're supposed to be dead."

I flash my teeth at the memory of my piece-of-shit half-brother who I left to fry on the electric chair. "I'm not that easy to kill. Now, let's talk about Delta."

Hunter's face tightens, the shock giving way to defeat, even dread. He swallows hard, his lips pressed into a grim line. No matter how much he tries to maintain his composure, his stoic mask is riddled with cracks.

"My colleagues will have launched a manhunt. They're probably already on their way."

I let out a short, humorless laugh. "That's doubtful, unless they know you flew to Helsing Island for a front-row seat to a snuff movie."

His gaze darts around the room, his restrained hands clenching and unclenching. "Let me go," he spits out, his voice rough. "Delta will kill you."

"Delta abandoned you long before we hauled your carcass onto our catamaran. Do you know what he did when I updated your group chat with photos of the investors' unconscious bodies?"

He stiffens.

I lean in close, my voice barely above a whisper. "Absolutely nothing."

Hunter's eyes flicker with a mix of doubt and fury. He struggles against his restraints, his face flushing red. The veins on his forehead stand out like bolts of lightning.

He draws a harsh breath, his barrel chest heaving to match the rhythm of his rising panic. "You're lying. Delta wouldn't. He has an entire team of operatives—"

"If you mean the Moirai, you're out of luck. They cast him out years ago."

I walk to the table of torture instruments and select Hunter's phone. After unlocking it with his face, I select the group chat and turn the phone so that Hunter can see the screen.

He draws in a sharp breath, his face contorting with disbelief, taking in the truth displayed on the app. The last message reads: 'Delta has left the group.'

"Now, are you ready to talk?" I ask.

Hunter swallows hard, his features falling into a mask of

resignation. "I can't tell you much. Delta is a secretive man who keeps all his members at arm's length."

"I would believe that from any of the other investors we captured, but you're the only one who never sent any funds. Why would that be?"

We both know the answer. Hunter's high-ranking position in the police force gives Father the freedom to operate his illicit movie network without fear of being caught. It's probably how he got Nocturne implicated when X-Cite Media switched from femdom content to snuff.

Bending his neck, Hunter closes his eyes, tightens his lips, and swallows. "You'd better kill me, because I don't have any information."

"I hoped you'd say that." I slip on a pair of gloves, not wanting to contaminate my hands with his filth.

His head snaps up. "What?"

The first punch lands with a satisfying crunch against his cheekbone. He grunts, his head lurching to one side from the impact. I lean in, my teeth bared.

"I need to work out a fuckload of frustration, and you just volunteered your bloated carcass as my toy."

His eyes widen for a fraction of a second before reverting to the stoic mask. I pull back my fist and deliver another punch to his gut. He jerks forward in his restraints, releasing an explosive grunt.

I continue with a series of jabs and uppercuts, filling the room with echoes of flesh hitting flesh.

His body jerks and shivers with the impact of each blow. Blood trickles down his nose and from his split lip. I take pleasure in his pain, in the way his body moves with each blow, and in the way his face contorts and twitches under my assault.

But it's not enough.

"Tell me something," I say. "How does it feel to star in a snuff movie, rather than jerk off from the sidelines?"

His gaze flickers, a fleeting moment of surprise, followed by horror.

"Did you think I would slice through your throat and carve

out your heart?" I ask with a laugh. "That would be too quick, too simple. You deserve a performance to rival X-Cite Media."

Hunter's body stiffens, his breaths quickening. Leaving him to stew on my words, I return to the table and pick up a nightstick.

"What?" he asks, his voice rising with panic. "You going to fuck me with that?"

"And give you the satisfaction?" I swing it at his temple, delivering a cracking blow that echoes through the room.

His head lurches to one side, with blood splattering against the concrete. His guttural scream rings through my ears like a symphony.

I strike again, this time hitting the side of his jaw. The weapon connects, and a tooth flies across the room in an arc before landing with a clatter on the metallic floor.

His body convulses, shaking against his restraints as I rain blows across his shoulders and arms and chest. A man like this is to be savored, not slaughtered. Screams echo through the room, the sound so animalistic and raw that my veins thrum with satisfaction.

I step back, observing my handiwork. All traces of the hardened officer are gone, replaced by a whimpering wreck. His body trembles, caked in a colorful mix of sweat and blood.

"What do you want to know?" he rasps.

"Ready to talk so soon?" I ask, feigning disappointment. "I was just starting to enjoy our game."

He blinks up at me, with blood-red saliva trickling from the corner of his mouth. "Tell me."

"Let's start from the beginning," I ask. "Who is Delta, and what is your relationship?"

He inhales a rattling breath and exhales. "His name is Dalton Grey. We trained together at the FBI Academy."

The revelation hits me in the solar plexus like a flying kick, but I hide my shock. Both at this fascinating insight into Father and at the confirmation of his real last name.

"Go on."

Information bursts out of Hunter like a sewage pipe, revealing the tale of a corrupt group of agents who decided to provide assassination services to the underworld.

"It started out as an undercover mission," he says through ragged breaths. "Then Dalton and the others decided to get organized and set up a firm called the Moirai Group."

I nod, already knowing Father was part of its management team.

"We recruited convicted and disgraced agents at first, offering them work. But paying for their silence proved too difficult." He gulps. "That's when Dalton got the idea to recruit teen runaways. We set up an academy and trained them to be assassins. They were loyal and dependent. Best of all, no one looked for them."

I swallow hard, forcing my features into a mask. It's a grisly mirror reflecting my own upbringing.

"What was your role in all this?" I snarl.

"I left the bureau to climb the ranks in the New Alderney Police Department. Someone needed to protect our interests from the inside."

He continues along these lines, explaining the early days of the Moirai, and how it built into the country's largest firm of assassins with Father's unique methods of recruiting and corrupting children. I glance at the camera's red light, making sure it's still recording.

"Tell me about X-Cite Media."

"Don't you see, boy?" he asks through rattling laughter.

My pulse drums in my ears, filling the quiet room with its deafening rhythm. I grit my teeth at his condescending tone, fighting to keep my features composed.

"What do you mean?" I ask, my voice tight

"He started X-Cite Media when he fell out of favor with his partners," he rasps. "The bastard son he fathered with one of our female operatives went rogue, poaching personnel from the organization and stealing clients. The others told him to handle you, but he failed."

My stomach drops. I had no idea my birth mother was another assassin. Hiding my shock, I snarl, "And?"

"When he failed, they wanted you and him both eliminated."

My jaw clenches.

I knew my acts of sabotage got him ousted from the firm, but Father was supposed to die, not skitter into another branch of crime like a cockroach.

"He left before they could kill him and bought a media company." Hunter's hollow laughter echoes through the room. "If you hadn't screwed with the Moirai, Dalton would never have gotten into snuff."

"Bullshit," I spit, my lip curling.

"It's true. X-Cite Media turned into a snuff site because of you. And your daddy issues."

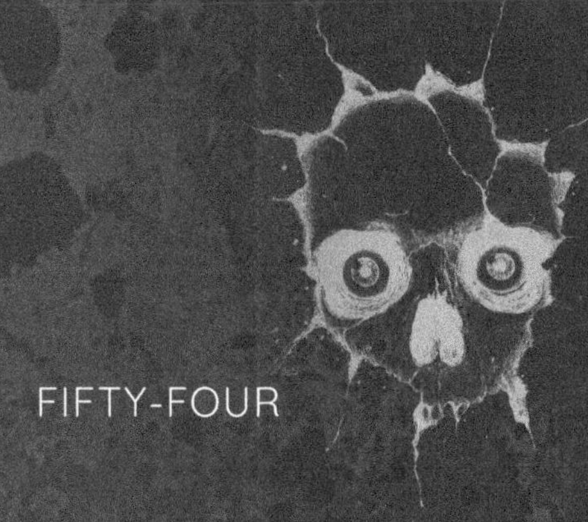

FIFTY-FOUR

AMETHYST

Squeals pierce the air. I turn around to find Myra emerging from around the corner, her eyes rounding with surprise. Her red hair is piled atop her head in a messy bun with tendrils framing her heart-shaped face.

"Amy," she says, her voice catching. She's wearing a black tank top and a matching pair of capri pants with a leather jacket slung over her shoulder.

Shock barrels through my system. My heart pounds so hard that every molecule in my body thrums. The only tie to my normal life is standing in this surreal environment.

I glance over my shoulder to where Xero withdraws to the house through a set of patio doors, and my throat tightens for the few heartbeats it takes for me to realize that I've become addicted to his presence. Him, not just the hallucination that kept me company at the asylum.

Myra rushes forward with her arms outstretched, her features mirroring my disbelief. I rise off the bench, still wobbly from being bedridden. Just as I'm about to collapse, she scoops me up in her arms and hugs me tight.

"Amy," she sobs. "Your mom was on the news. And your uncle. I'm so sorry. Shit. What happened to you? They said you were taken. I was so scared."

I stare straight ahead, watching Camila approach. She offers me an apologetic smile and winces. This is the first time I've seen her since the episode by the gate, and I suspect she knows what I've suffered. Everyone in the house has given me space. They all treat me well—kindly, with respect. But when someone throws their arms around me, oblivious or indifferent to my wounded state, my eyes well with tears.

Myra continues to pepper me with questions until I'm swaying on my feet. She draws back, her eyes widening.

"Are you okay? You look like you're about to drop."

I offer her a wan smile. "Just a bit weak."

Features softening, she lowers me to the bench, holding me snug around the waist. Myra has seen me through most of my life's struggles—she was there before and after I killed Mr. Lawson and kept in contact after I got expelled.

When Mom pulled me out of college after the incident with the Reed brothers—which I still can't remember—Myra was one of the first people to visit me at Parisii Drive. I was sleepwalking through a cocktail of powerful prescription drugs, but she was enthusiastic enough about my new home for both of us.

"What happened?" she asks. "All I know is what I picked up from TV and social media. There's all kinds of theories flying around, but Camila and Jynxson said they were all bullshit."

"If I told you, you wouldn't believe me," I say, my voice flat.

She grimaces. "Ugh... When I think back about how many times I tried to talk sense into you—"

"Don't." I squeeze her hand. "You didn't know what was happening. All those other times I was paranoid or hallucinating, it was you who kept me grounded."

Tears stream down her cheeks, and she pulls me into another hug. "I'm so sorry."

I lean into her embrace, my eyes fluttering shut. Somewhere on the edge of my consciousness, Camila's footsteps retreat into the house.

Myra is being too hard on herself. Everything that happened since the day of Xero's execution has been so surreal that even I questioned myself. She's been nothing but supportive.

"Don't apologize," I murmur. "You're here for me, which is all that counts."

She draws back, her eyes red-rimmed. "Do you want to talk about it?"

"I didn't kill my mom," I blurt.

"Of course you didn't," she replies, her brow creasing. In a much lower voice, she asks, "Was it him?"

I shake my head. "You remember how I don't have any memories from before the age of ten?"

Nodding, her breath deepens, her gaze fixed on mine. I swallow hard, trying to muster up the right words to explain truths I'm still struggling to believe.

"I have a twin sister." Pausing, I wait for her to protest, but she continues to stare, her eyes widening. "I don't remember anything yet, but she remembers me. At some point before I went to Tourgis Academy, I was in a car crash and ended up in an asylum. They subjected me to a bunch of treatments that wiped my memories."

She claps a hand over her mouth. "That polaroid was you?"

I nod, my throat thickening.

Myra draws closer, her hand clasping mine as I tell her everything I remember about the male psychiatrist who supervised my treatments. Then I tell her about the morning I escaped Reverend Tom, who turned out to be connected to X-Cite Media. When I get to the part about returning to Mom's house to confront her, thinking she was behind the polaroids, she gasps.

"That's when you saw your twin?" she asks.

Grief escapes my lungs in an outward breath, making me deflate. "I've never met anyone so malevolent. She blames me for everything that went wrong in her life."

"Did she ever say what she thinks you did?"

I raise my shoulders. "She wanted me to remember."

"But you don't?"

"It's always been at the tip of my awareness. You know that feeling you get when you turn out the light and sprint to bed, trying to outrun the monster?"

She shakes her head. "No, but I can imagine."

"I had the same thing with the mirror. If I looked myself full in the face, I felt like the monster behind it would climb out and kill me."

"That's..." She blows out a breath.

"Insane?"

"I was going to say insightful. Maybe even frightening. I can't imagine having an evil twin."

"From the way she talked, I was the evil one."

"My friend is not evil."

We fall silent for several moments, both staring into the vast garden. A squirrel scampers across the grass, pausing to look at us before it darts up a tree trunk and jumps from branch to branch.

"Why can't we be like squirrels?" I mutter. "They don't hold grudges. All they care about are nuts."

She bumps her head against mine. "Speaking of nuts, are you still with Xero?"

I draw back, staring into her warm eyes. She raises her brows, her smile widening the way it does when she pulls out one of the items she sells at Wonderland. It takes a minute to register that she's talking about Xero's dildo.

Warmth flares across my cheeks, and a giggle bubbles from my chest. I place a hand over my smile. "Myra!"

"So?" she asks, her eyes sparkling.

The initial rush of amusement fades, leaving behind a slowly burgeoning disgust. Silicone sex toys wielded by my best friend are one thing, but what they represent makes my stomach churn.

My mind dredges up memories of being force fed. I swallow hard, chasing away the mingled taste of gruel and semen, fighting the urge to gag. The last thing I want to talk about is anyone's penis. Not even Xero's.

"Myra, I can't."

Her smile falls. She pauses, seeming to process my words. Maybe she's piecing together what I'd told her earlier, before my abduction, about X-Cite Media capturing Lizzie Bath as a replacement for me, because there's a brief flicker of confusion before she rears back, her eyes widening with horror.

"Oh, my god. Amy, I'm sorry—"

I hold up a hand. "It's okay. Actually, it's nice to have

someone who doesn't walk around on eggshells. But maybe not that topic?"

She nods, her eyes spilling over with fresh tears. "You know I'm always here for you. This time, if you confide in me, I won't run off and tell my sister."

I laugh at the reference to the time I told her about killing Mr. Lawson. Most thirteen-year-old girls would freak out, maybe even call the police, but Myra tried to get me legal advice.

After her sister reported me to the police, her parents made up for it by helping Mom and Dr. Saint craft a defense strong enough to get me out of juvenile prison.

I squeeze her hand and smile. "Thank you for being such a good friend."

Her gaze flickers toward the house. "Will you be safe with him?"

How do I begin to explain that the man who tormented me for weeks, making me think I was the target of a vengeful ghost, is also the only thing holding my sanity together?

"He's saved me in more ways than I can count," I murmur. "Without Xero's help, I'd be dead. Even if those people kept me alive, there'd be nothing left to salvage."

Her brows knit together in a skeptical frown. "Are you sure?"

Pressure builds up in my chest. It's more gratitude than frustration. All Myra knows about Xero is that he escaped his execution, choked her personal assistant to death, and executed two men we met at the book fair. All the while trying to drive me insane.

"How many men could mobilize a small army to save you, sit at your bedside, keeping you company through nightmares and flashbacks, hold your hand when you're snotty, and read you to sleep, all the while providing a twenty-four-hour medic to heal your wounds and keeping your best friend safe?" I ask.

She shifts in her seat. "When you put it like that..."

Not wanting to rant, I peel myself off the bench, taking a few tentative steps across the stone patio. On its far right stands a trellis of red roses with twisting vines spreading in all directions. Myra follows me and places a steadying arm around my waist.

Leaning against her for support, we walk together toward the flowers. Their sweet, intoxicating smell fills my senses, masking the lingering scent of the asylum.

"What's happening with your life?" I ask.

"Me?"

"Last time we spoke, I made you move out of your apartment."

She huffs a laugh. "I was crashing on a sofa."

"But it had to be confusing to have two strangers turn up at your door," I say.

"Those pictures of Lizzie were convincing enough. After thinking about everything you said, it became difficult to ignore the truth."

I nod, almost missing the days when my biggest worry was being stalked by a vengeful ghost.

Myra draws in a deep breath. "Camila and Jynxson took me to a nice apartment overlooking the park and told me not to leave the building. There was a gym, a concierge who could get me takeout, plus the twenty grand wiped away all my credit card debt and left me with plenty to spare."

"You're not mad?" I ask.

She whirls around with a broad smile. "I was so depressed after waking up and not remembering what happened after the book fair that I did something stupid."

"What?

She squeezes her eyes shut. "Gavin."

My eyes widen. I picture the asshole who forced me to watch a man die on the electric chair before maxing out my credit card.

"Gavin, Gavin? Or some random stranger with the same name?"

When her cheeks turn a bright shade of red, my breath catches. Myra likes her men tall, dark, and dominant... And rich. Gavin, our red-haired, five-foot-five classmate shaped like a Funko pop, is none of those things. Last time I checked, she was obsessed with her boss who owned the Wonderland Fetish Store. Gavin was supposed to leave town after Xero amputated his fingers.

"Don't tell me you fucked him?"

She wrinkles her nose. "Shit... No!"

"Then what?" I ask, my breath quickening.

"He was depressed after... that thing with his hand. I took him down to one of the playrooms and showed him the ropes."

My jaw drops. "But I thought he was an inexperienced dom."

"I just flogged his back, made him crawl around and wash a few mugs. Now, he wants to be my sub, and he keeps calling me Mistress."

I wince. "Sorry."

She shakes her head. "That's just to say I hit rock bottom. I was even about to cave in to my parents' pressure on me to go to law school. That money and apartment was the break I needed."

Some of the pressure around my chest loosens. "I'm so glad it helped."

We exchange smiles. It's almost like old times, with her visiting me at Parisii Drive to share gossip. I used to wish my life was as exciting as Myra's. Now, I appreciate the peace and quiet.

She bumps my shoulder. "My old boss at the literary agency emailed me two days ago, offering me back my old job with a promotion."

"Really?" I ask, my voice breathy.

"I refused."

"Why?"

"My dad's cousin died and left Martina and me a bookstore with an upstairs apartment. I'm going to live there, set up my own agency, and sell the kinds of books I want."

Myra pulls out her phone, showing me footage she shot of us at the book fair. Three of her videos got over two-hundred-thousand views and a fourth got a million. She scrolls through the comments showing dozens of authors expressing their interest in collaborating.

"I threw up a form on my link page, and it's already gotten over a hundred responses."

"That's amazing," I say.

The words come from far away, and my gaze drifts to the roses. I'm happy to see my best friend thriving, but it feels like life is passing me by. We chat for hours, although it's mostly Myra catching me up with everything that's happened since I was taken. The book world moves so quickly, with new trends, new authors, and exciting new genres. Maybe it's too late for me to ever realize my dreams.

Myra pulls me into a hug. "You know, you'll always be my number one client. No matter what you want to write, I'll help it get published."

The door behind us opens, letting out the rich, mouth-watering scents of herbs and garlic. I turn around and lock gazes with Xero, who's wearing a black apron over his clothes. The sight of him, so dominant yet domestic, sends a thrill down my spine.

"Lunch is ready, ladies," he says in a deep voice that curls around my senses like sin.

Myra's breath catches beside me, and I smile. It's almost funny to think I was once struck only by his handsome face. There's so much more to him than his external beauty, a depth that draws me into his allure.

His gaze skips over my friend, lands on me, and he winks. That simple gesture, so casual yet intimate, makes my cheeks flare with heat. The butterflies in my stomach awaken, fluttering hard enough to make me shift on my seat.

Pride swells at our connection. I return his gesture with a tiny smile.

As Myra loops her arm through mine and walks us toward the kitchen, something in my heart lightens. Bringing the two people I love most in the world together fills me with a sense of belonging. I want to take advantage of my newfound freedom so my life can finally begin.

FIFTY-FIVE

XERO

I step back, letting Amethyst into the kitchen. Our eyes lock, and I see a flicker of the woman she used to be before her expression shutters into a blank mask.

My heart sinks, but I hide my disappointment behind a smile. It will take more than a week of bedrest to overcome her ordeal, and I'm determined to give her time.

Myra stares up at me with wide eyes. The last time I saw her was when they were both unconscious in the back of that limousine after the book fair. Isabel and Dr. Dixon picked them up in a triage van and put them both on saline until they regained a semblance of consciousness. After that, Camila transported Myra to her apartment, and I took Amethyst back to Parisii Drive.

Back then, I wanted to throttle Myra, both for retaining a physical copy of the manuscript I'd taken trouble to delete, and for leading Amethyst into danger. I let her live because she's the younger sister of my attorney and a loyal friend to my little ghost.

Amethyst gasps at the platter of arancini on the table. I made it with a marinara dipping sauce, based on something I read in the diary I obtained from the Salentino sisters.

"This is my favorite," she cries.

Myra frowns. "Really? I didn't know you liked Italian food."

Amethyst rubs the back of her neck and frowns. "Maybe I ate it at my other school?"

The pair continue to the table, where I've laid out a parmesan and arugula salad and jugs of lemon-infused water. Sun filters through the tall windows, casting a warm golden light over Amethyst's blonde curls. Her skin is paler than usual, with dark circles under her eyes, but the smile on her lips is genuine.

"So, how did you escape the electric chair?" Myra asks as I take my seat opposite Amethyst.

"With great determination and cunning," I reply with a flash of my teeth.

Camila sets down a platter of antipasto, takes her seat opposite Myra, and kicks me under the table. Ignoring my sister, I watch Amethyst, wondering if she'll eat. Isabel put her on a liquid diet because she wasn't keeping down solids. I hope this dish will make a difference.

"Did you make this, Xero?" Myra asks.

I turn my attention to the redhead. "Don't worry, Myra. No hearts were sliced up to create this arancini. I usually reserve body parts to serve with fava beans and chianti."

She shifts in her seat and pales.

"Xero, stop being a dick to my best friend," Amethyst says with more passion than she's expressed since the night she broke through the illusion.

"Sorry, my love," I reply with a smirk.

Amethyst flushes. "You should apologize to Myra."

I turn my gaze to the redhead, who shakes her head.

"It was a joke." She picks up a piece of arancini and pops it into her mouth. After taking several careful chews, she adds, "But your talents are more suited to cooking."

Grinning, I turn back to Amethyst, who shoots me a stern glare, but the corners of her lips twitch at her little friend's comeback.

She picks up a golden ball and studies it for several seconds. I lean forward, wondering if it triggers any memories. Melonie Crowley's diary was disturbing, and the mental torture Amethyst endured drew a surprising parallel to what I put her through when I first left prison.

Knowing what happened to her all those years ago might help her understand a little more about her sister. And Amethyst's own connection to Father. But I'm not sure she's ready to read the diary

On the subject of my bastard sire, some of the information from my recent encounter with Carl Hunter was unexpected. No one I've ever captured has given me such in-depth insight into Father's background. The Deputy Chief of Police was such a valuable font of information that I kept him alive for further interrogation. Now that he's started to talk, getting more background information on Father will be a breeze.

Cooking this dish from scratch was necessary to give myself something to do other than oscillate between my hatred of Father and fretting about Amethyst's mental state.

Amethyst finally takes a sniff, then a bite. She closes her eyes as she savors the mozzarella-filled rice ball. My breath catches as the corners of her mouth lift with a smile.

Satisfaction roars in my heart at having nourished the woman I love. The thought of lifting her mood ignites my heart with sparks of joy.

"My mom used to make these when I was little," she says, her voice wistful. "I liked this one, but my sister preferred the one she stuffed with meat."

Her eyes widen, and she sucks in a sharp breath. "How would I know that?"

"Are your memories returning?" Myra asks with a gasp.

Amethyst shakes her head, her brow furrowed. "No. Maybe... It just came out."

Silence settles around the table. I sit back, watching her take another tiny bite. Her features pinch as if trying to dredge up another memory.

"I don't actually remember Mom making this for me," she says, lowering her lashes. "She doesn't even like carbs."

Camila shoots me a glance, seeming to ask if Amethyst remembers her mother is dead. I give her a discreet nod.

Myra leans into Amethyst and places an arm around her shoulder. "Are you alright?"

Amethyst nods, her eyes meeting mine. "This is lovely. Thank you."

I return her nod and smile. Then the tension around the table lifts as my sister and Myra break into a conversation about the happenings in her apartment block. Amethyst returns to her arancini, takes another small bite, and chews.

"Are you still accepting clients?" Myra asks me.

My brows rise, and I suppress a surge of irritation that she even knows I'm an assassin attached to a clandestine organization. "Is there someone you want me to kill?"

She smirks. "Maybe?"

"Your boss?" Amethyst asks with a tiny smile.

"If you can throw my ex-boss in a truck and scare him into sending me a text, that would be perfect," she replies, her eyes dancing with mischief.

Amethyst chokes, coughing and sputtering. I rise off my seat, but she waves me off, still laughing. "Cesare from Wonderland?"

"Yeah," Myra replies with a nod.

"What's he done now?"

"I told him I wasn't coming back, and he said okay." Her features harden into a scowl. "No fight, no questioning, no bargaining. Just a bland 'okay'."

"Good riddance," Amethyst mutters. "Cesare Montesano is bad news anyway."

Camila nudges my arm. I turn to meet her meaningful look that I translate as a strong suggestion to tell Amethyst about her real family. I force back a grimace and nod, wondering how the hell she'll react when she discovers her birth father is a second cousin of the Montesano brothers.

Dessert is a red velvet cake to replace the one I destroyed on her birthday. Amethyst picks at her portion, but Myra dives in, her silver fork sinking into the creamy frosting.

"This is so good. Did you make it?" Myra asks.

I nod.

"I've never had a red velvet cake like this. What's the secret ingredient?"

"Blood," I deadpan.

She chokes, her brows shooting to her hairline. "What?"

"And a large quantity of criollo cocoa beans," I add.

Myra glances at Camila. "Is he joking?"

"Probably not." My sister takes a huge bite of cake.

Amethyst picks up her fork and begins to poke at the red velvet sponge, her brows knitted together. "It looks the same as any other cake."

"Have you ladies heard of cochineal?" I ask.

When all three of them shake their heads, I lean forward. "Once upon a time, there was a little bug who lived on a prickly pear cactus. One day, the bug was just minding its own business, inches away from a juicy, ripe pear when a human crushed it between his fingertips. As life drained out of its carcass, it dyed the man's skin red."

"This is bullshit, right?" Camila asks.

I shake my head, my grin widening. "The other humans saw the dye and were amazed by the radiant, deep red. Word spread, and soon humans used the cochineal bugs to dye their clothes, to make art, and even to color their food. And that is the secret ingredient to the red velvet cake."

Myra sets down her fork and grimaces. "Remind me not to ask how you make salted caramel ice cream."

Amethyst laughs. It's a rich, genuine sound that fills the kitchen and lifts my heart. She takes a generous bite of the cake and hums her appreciation. My chest aches that it was Myra who drew out this reaction and not me, but I appreciate it just the same.

After lunch, I light the fire pit outside, and Isabel joins us for coffee, where Amethyst repeats my tale about the red velvet cake. This time, she adds embellishments to the bug's backstory, and adds a love interest who seeks out the first human to get revenge.

I sit beside her on the bench, hanging onto her every word, enraptured by her story. This is the woman who captured my heart with her Rapunzel retelling. Amethyst made the time I spent on Death Row bearable, and here she is again, lighting up my life.

Guilt twists my heart at the reminder of how I unknowingly mirrored a trauma so heinous that her mother was forced to erase it from her mind.

If Amethyst is ever going to heal completely, then she needs to know the truth. About everything, from the root cause of her hallucinations to why my actions got her captured. If I hadn't aggravated that sore spot in her psyche, she might never have set her crawlspace on fire and escaped into danger.

The conversation lulls, and she leans on my arm, her eyelids drooping. Myra glances over at us from the other side of the fire pit and smiles. She may have reservations about her best friend being involved with a mass murderer, but she doesn't know the extent of Amethyst's darkness.

Amethyst slides her hand over mine, and the touch of her fingers infuses my veins with hope. Hope that she's on the way to recovery. Hope that she will overcome her tragic past and will still want me in her future.

As the fire dances and crackles in the pit, I gaze down into the curls nestled against my shoulder and wrap an arm around her waist. Inhaling her peach-and-vanilla scent, I luxuriate in this moment.

No matter what, she'll always be mine, and I'll follow her to the ends of the earth. I'll wait an eternity for my little ghost to return. And when that day comes, I'll cherish her with every fiber of my being.

Clouds drift over the sun, bringing with them a shadow of doubt. I tighten my hold on Amethyst, wanting to freeze time and keep her here, safe and unaware of the darkness that binds our souls.

This might be our last moment of closeness for a long time after she discovers how deeply connected I am to her trauma.

FIFTY-SIX

AMETHYST

I gaze into the fire, wishing it would both blaze through my memories and burn down the blocks around my past.

Nestling into Xero's side is so comforting that it almost feels like a dream. I don't remember the compound hallucination of him at the asylum having a heartbeat or such detailed skin. I slide my fingers over the back of his hand, feeling the outline of scars, bones, and raised veins beneath his warm, living flesh. The sensation is grounding, another reminder that he's real.

His muscles contract under my touch, and his breath catches. It's a small reaction that fills me with a thrill of satisfaction. He isn't just real. He's human. And despite suspecting I've been tainted, he's still attracted to me.

As I trace the lines on Xero's hand, my mind drifts to the asylum. The darkness of those days still clings to my mind, a shadow I can't shake. But here, in this moment, with his warmth at my side, I almost believe in a future where I'm whole.

He answers one of Myra's questions in a soft baritone that wraps around my senses like a comforting shroud. I could listen to his voice all day. It reminds me of another world when he was just a fantasy on the other side of the phone.

The fire's glow flickers toward the darkening sky, casting dancing shadows that mimic the turmoil in my heart. Cool air mingles with the scent of pine and burning wood, creating a cocoon of safety within the chaos of my thoughts.

As the sun dips behind the trees, Isabel excuses herself and rises, then Camila says it's time to drive Myra back to her apartment.

My best friend walks around the fire pit to give me a tight hug. I'm immediately transported to sleepy mornings when she would stay over at my place to decompress after a disastrous double date.

"Thank you, Amy," she murmurs, her voice laced with gratitude. "I hope you feel better soon."

Tears glisten in her eyes as she pulls away from our embrace, and my throat thickens. Our relationship has changed. We're both going in completely different directions. Myra is about to embark on an exciting new career as a literary agent with her own bookstore. I can't move forward while Delta and Dolly still live.

It takes every effort to focus on the positive, on how proud I am of my best friend, but I can't ignore that this is the end of an era.

I smile, trying to hold back tears. "Thanks for coming. I missed you so much."

She squeezes me once more, as if she knows this marks the change in our friendship, and draws back, committing my face to memory. With a sigh, she turns to Xero. "Thanks for lunch. You better take care of my girl."

"Always," he replies with a conviction that makes my heart flutter.

I used to think the most thrilling thing in the world was his attention. Now, what truly sends shivers down my spine is his care. The depth of his commitment is overwhelming, and for a moment, the gratitude I feel toward him morphs into fear.

What if I'm not enough? What if I'm too damaged to reciprocate? What if I can't meet his expectations—the ones I set up during our morning calls when he was in prison? My stomach lurches at the thought of that sex contract. I'm no longer that woman. Nothing about the fantasies I once craved is even remotely appealing.

Myra and Camila disappear around the corner, leaving me

alone with Xero and the flames. Firelight flickers across his chiseled features, casting patterns that make him appear god-like.

"Want me to warm up those balls?" he asks with a hint of a smirk. His gaze intensifies, his irises reflecting molten gold.

A laugh bubbles up in my chest. "That depends on if they're dipped in breadcrumbs."

His smirk widens into a broad grin. "How are you feeling?"

I take a deep breath, gathering my thoughts. "Overwhelmed. Seeing Myra was wonderful, but it also reminded me of everything I've been missing."

His expression softens, and he shifts closer on the bench, his body heat shielding me from the encroaching chill. "You've been through hell. This is your time to heal."

I nod, my gaze dropping to our joined hands. "I keep thinking about those men. How can I move forward with my life, knowing they're doing the same to another woman?"

Silence lingers, broken by the crackle of the fire. I glance up to see his jaw tighten, his eyes glinting with dangerous resolve.

"What is it?" I ask.

"We captured everyone we found in the asylum. Tell me which ones hurt you, and they'll die screaming."

The menace in his words makes me shiver. It's both comforting and threatening that he would do anything to keep me safe. But it's not enough. I need to be the one who draws blood.

"I want to end them myself," I say, my voice wavering. "But I'm not sure if I can."

His eyes meet mine with an unwavering confidence I'm not sure I deserve. "You're stronger than you think, and I believe in you."

My breath hitches. I want to say something to acknowledge that statement, but my mind goes blank. Xero takes my hand and leads me back into the kitchen, where he pulls up a laptop open at a webpage for arancini. After minimizing the browser, he fires up a program containing several screens, each showing photos of different men.

"These are the ones we captured," he snarls. "Which of them hurt you?"

I glance at the faces on the screen, my throat closing around a bellyful of bitter bile. They all look like regular men with families, girlfriends, and jobs. No one would ever conceive the monsters hiding behind the masks of normality.

Xero stays patient and silent, even though his chest heaves with restrained fury. It's comforting to know that I can point the finger and he'll exact vengeance, but I need to slay my own monsters.

"Take your time," he says.

Only one of the faces is familiar, a man about my age with a wispy mustache and a scar on his left eyebrow. My mind pulls up a flashback of him jerking off into my mouth, forcing up a wave of nausea. I yank my head to the side, my stomach heaving.

"That one," I whisper, pointing to the man with the scar. "He was one of the crew."

Xero double-clicks on the mousepad.

"Clyde Proctor. Graduated with a degree in film studies at New Alderney State University. Currently interning at the CNA Network."

I shudder. "How the hell does someone go from studying film to making snuff?"

"Let's ask him," he snarls. "But first, you're getting changed."

Xero takes me upstairs to a bedroom with charcoal walls and an ebony four-poster shrouded in a black silk canopy, along with matching furniture made of the same dark wood.

The setting sun streams in through the sheer black curtains, casting long shadows across the dresser.

He crosses the room, opening a closet filled with an array of black clothing.

"Pick something," he says before heading to the door. "I'll leave you to get dressed in peace."

I walk to the closet, taking in items I don't recognize. All the clothing I valued was packed in boxes in the crawl space I set on fire. Everything else I left upstairs would have been taken by Mom's removal people.

It's too late to cry about missing garments when I've already lost so much. After browsing through the clothes, I pick out a simple black turtleneck and jeans and pair it with some boots.

After I change and step out into the hallway, he hands me a waterproof coat. I already know it's because we're about to spill blood.

We walk in silence down the stairs, through the kitchen, and into a pantry that opens into another stairwell. He leans into me and says, "Don't push yourself. If at any time it's too much for you, say the word, and we leave."

As we descend, his gaze burns the side of my face. If I show any weakness, he'll take me back upstairs and put me to bed. I can't let that happen, so I square my shoulders, even though my heart pounds so hard against my ribcage that the sound drowns out the echoes of our footsteps.

We continue down a dimly lit hallway that feels like it stretches the length of the house and garden.

"I have a question," he says. "Why didn't you recognize any of the others?"

"Xero told me—" I shake my head. "Not you, but the hallucination."

"It's alright, I understand."

"He overheard them saying extras would be arriving soon, and Delta and Dolly would leave in a helicopter for an event. We decided to escape before they got the chance to shoot the main footage."

"So, the men we captured were newcomers to the shoot?" he asks.

I raise a shoulder. "Well, I killed half the crew."

He stops dead in his tracks, looking me full in the face, making me shift on my feet and stutter out an explanation of how I hid in a closet to ambush one man and fought another to the death in the jungle of weeds.

His eyes shine with admiration I don't deserve. I didn't kill the third crew member—that was Grunt, who shot him before carrying me off to escape.

"I saw you dart into the forest and then double back to steal the bus," he says, his voice breathy with awe. "That was the opening we needed to gun him down."

"You kept reminding me he wasn't to be trusted."

Xero taps the side of my head. "One day you'll realize the strategist who helped you escape that asylum wasn't me. It was all you."

A lump forms in my throat. I swallow, not quite believing his words. He wasn't there to see me when I was paralyzed by terror or bumbling and crying my way through that labyrinth of peril. I needed Xero to bark at me to keep moving.

I continue walking in silence, letting him hold on to the blood-spattered image of an action heroine. Eventually, we pass a fire exit that leads to another hallway lined with doors. The walls here seem to close in, and the air becomes colder, heavier, and charged with the weight of an impending confrontation.

My steps drag with dread. Xero's hand remains a steady anchor in mine, his presence keeping me grounded when my spirit longs to float into the ether.

I follow him to the one at the end, which he unlocks with his handprint. My heart pounds like it's punctuating a death march.

The heavy door creaks open, releasing a stench of sweat and despair that makes me gag. I clap a hand over my mouth to stifle a gasp. My stomach churns, every instinct screaming at me to retreat, yet I force myself to step inside on trembling legs.

A lone figure kneels at the back, his head bowed, with hands clasped as if in prayer. The flickering bulb casts eerie shadows, making him look almost ghostly. Despite the dim light, I recognize him in an instant.

My mind flashes back to the asylum. Bitterness clogs my throat, and I freeze, trapped by memories.

I force myself to move forward on wooden legs. With each step, my resolve dwindles, leaving only the man's whimpers and pleas for mercy. If Xero hadn't arrived with drones, that could easily be me, begging Delta and the others to stop. My heart resonates with his cries, transporting my mind back to the agony he and the others made me endure.

"Xero." My voice is a shaky whisper, inaudible over the pounding of my heart. Every shred of courage that had brought me this far evaporates, leaving me feeling small and powerless. "I'm sorry."

I step back, bumping into his solid frame.

When he turns me around, I expect to be crushed by the weight of his disappointment or the annoyance he displayed when I recoiled from the human centipede underneath my old house. But all I see is understanding. "It's too early. You don't have to do this now."

Tears sting my eyes, blurring my vision. I blink, and they spill down my cheeks. "Thank you," I whisper, my voice trembling with gratitude. "Can you hug me like you did at the asylum, please?"

He pulls me into a comforting embrace, his warmth enveloping my senses. His strong arms form a protective barrier against the debilitating memories.

"You're not alone, little ghost," he murmurs into my curls, his voice filled with sincerity. "I'm here for you. Always."

I lean against his chest, and the stench of sweat and despair is replaced by the familiar, comforting smell of Xero. The cell and its horrors fade away, and I lose myself in the rhythm of his steady heartbeat.

For the first time since I can remember, I let down my guard and release trembling sobs. The numbness around my heart shatters, and I let loose.

Xero places a kiss on my forehead, igniting a flicker of hope. It's fragile, barely visible in the darkness of my soul, but it glows steadily like an ember, ready to ignite into a flame. With Xero by my side, I know that I can face whatever comes next.

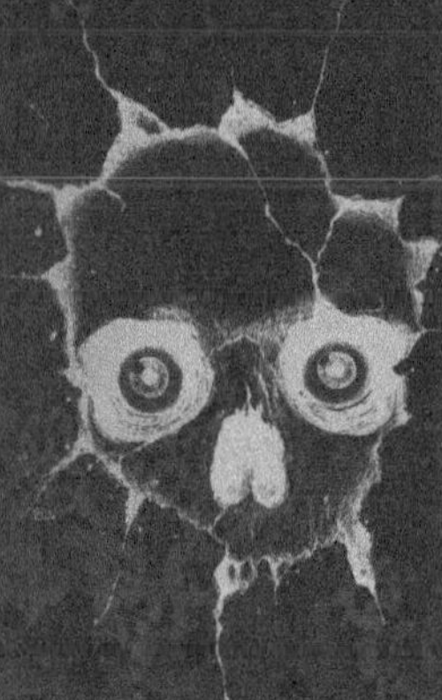

FIFTY-SEVEN

XERO

I didn't expect Amethyst to be able to kill that man. Her trauma is too recent, and her emotions are too raw. Seeing her friend doing so well must have pushed her into wanting to slay her demons before she was ready, but healing takes time.

Amethyst now sits in the kitchen, eating the warmed up arancini balls. Over lunch, she barely finished two, but now she's managed four. Her improved appetite is a step forward.

And she took comfort in my touch. Having her lean on me while we sat outside was unexpected, but a pleasant surprise. Having her turn to me down below was a balm to my soul. It feels like one step closer to regaining her trust.

I sit opposite her, nursing my black coffee, catching up on messages from the interrogation team. Deputy Chief Carl Hunter has revealed the address of a townhouse in Beaumont City Father uses for entertaining guests. I've dispatched a small team to reduce it to ashes.

Amethyst glances up at me from her plate, her eyes glistening but no longer filled with despair. Instead, they shine with determination. My little ghost is resilient. It's only a matter of time before she demands another chance to confront her abuser.

"Do you need anything else?" I ask.

She shakes her head, making her pretty curls bounce. "Did you like Myra?"

My brows pinch. She's insignificant, as are most people outside my immediate circle. A mild irritation, but otherwise unremarkable. Considering their connection, I choose my words carefully.

"You like her, and she's a loyal friend."

"What does that mean?"

"Anyone who makes you happy makes me happy," I reply, and it's true. Myra Mancini might have encouraged Amethyst into publishing the letters I wanted to keep secret, and led her into a limousine filled with predators, but she never gave up on their relationship.

Unlike Melonie Crowley.

I lean across the counter, my heart sagging at the reminder of that twisted story. Despite Amethyst's little breakdown, today has been a resounding success. Dare I ruin the mood by reminding her of Melonie's diary?

The selfish bastard in me says to keep her in ignorance and wait until she's healed. But hiding things from Amethyst will only erode her trust. The last time I concealed the truth from her, I woke up in a burning room.

We fall into a comfortable silence, with her dipping her fifth arancini ball into marinara sauce and me sipping my coffee. Now that she's out of the infirmary, her presence fills this kitchen with warmth. Bringing up the diary might stall her progress, but isn't it better for her to know about her past now rather than later?

Inhaling a deep breath, I force out a string of words I know will result in resentment. Her view of me will change once she realizes I'm not the first to drive her mad by pretending to be a ghost.

"Amethyst," I begin, my gaze boring into hers. "There's something you need to know."

She pauses, her fork in mid-air, eyes widening. "Is it about the sleeping arrangements?"

My eyes widen. I blink away the surprise. "What?"

"My treatment has finished, and the bed in my room is large enough for two."

"And?" I raise a brow.

"Xero always hugged me to sleep at the asylum," she murmurs, lowering her lashes. "He's not here, so..."

Jealousy and fear flare through my chest, even though the sensations are irrational. The thought of a hallucination comforting her instead of me burns. "Amethyst."

Her head snaps up. "Yes?"

"Who am I?"

"What do you mean?" she asks, frowning.

"My name. My relationship to you. My status in your reality?"

"You're the real Xero, and you're my..." She rubs the back of her neck. "I don't know what we are because I kind of broke up with you when I smashed that bottle over your head and left you for dead. But I know you're not Delta."

"And you want *me* to hug you to sleep?" I ask.

She glances away. "If that's too much—"

"I'll do it," I rasp.

She eats seven arancini balls in total before announcing she's full and rises from her seat. I take her back to the room and lay out a soft pair of pajamas and a robe.

Amethyst won't want me gaping at the cuts covering her body, even though Isabel assures me they're healing nicely without bandages. I leave her to shower and change before retreating to my room to prepare for the night ahead. After swapping my jeans and sweatshirt for a pair of soft cotton pants and a loose t-shirt, I pick up the red leather diary from my nightstand.

When I return to her room, she's already changed into pajamas and a pair of fluffy socks. She sits cross-legged on the four-poster, her damp curls piled atop her head. Her pajamas show glimpses of her tantalizing curves, which are at odds with the cute socks. Soft light from the bedside lamp casts a glow on her face, accentuating her serene beauty.

My breath catches, and sensation rushes south. It's almost impossible to tell she's gone through so much darkness. She's a vision of what I hoped life would be for us when I left Death Row. The kind of casual comforts of love and home that I yearned for but never thought I deserved.

I will my cock not to stir at her proximity, but the eager bastard has its own mind. She's so preoccupied with that red diary that she doesn't even notice my body's inappropriate response.

"What's that?" she asked.

"Something of your mother's I picked up from the women who referred you to Dr. Saint."

She frowns. "I thought she and my mom were friends."

"Perhaps, but these women knew her first."

"Who are they?"

"Aria and Elana Salentino." I cross the room and place the leather journal on the bed. "Your paternal aunts."

"Oh." She turns her gaze away from the diary and meets my eyes.

"You should read it. It explains a lot about your mother. And Dolly's animosity."

Swallowing, she closes her eyes. "Maybe later."

I place it on her lap and lower myself on the edge of the mattress, within touching distance but without crowding. "Whenever you're ready. I'm not hiding the truth anymore. If something is too painful, I'll let you decide if you want to know."

Nodding, she glances up from the diary and meets my eyes. "Did you hack into Dr. Saint's records?"

"They don't exist," I reply, smoothing a stray curl behind her ears.

She shivers, her breath quickening. I draw back my hand, wondering if she's ready for me to sleep in her bed.

"How do you know?" she asks.

"I've kept her in a holding cell since the night we went to the Ministry of Mayhem, and she hasn't yet changed her story."

Her jaw drops. She gapes at me, her eyes widening. "She's...she's been imprisoned all this time? Is she connected to X-Cite Media?"

"No."

"Then why haven't you let her go?"

"I was busy trying to find you," I mutter. "And I kept her in case you had questions about your mental state."

She licks her lips. "Did you record the interrogations?"

I nod.

"Can she add to the information in the diary?"

"Doubtful," I mutter.

"Then let her go. She's sneaky and unprofessional, but she doesn't deserve to be imprisoned like that. She must be terrified."

I hesitate for a few heartbeats, studying her features. There's a strength and determination I didn't see before her abduction, and a compassion for a woman who deserves to have her license revoked.

"Xero." She places her palms on my chest.

My pulse quickens. Amethyst is growing, changing, becoming stronger with each new revelation. Instead of hiding from unpleasant situations, she confronts them with courage.

"Fine," I say and pull out my phone. "Consider it done."

"Thank you."

She pulls her hands away from my chest, and my heart sinks at the loss. As she places the diary on the nightstand and slips beneath the sheets, I'm left rooted to the spot, my desire for her still burning.

I rise off the mattress and send a message to the operative in charge of the holding cells, ordering him to release Dr. Saint—with a discreet tracker and a warning not to report her abduction to the police.

When I turn my attention back to the bed, she's lying on her side, tucked into a ball. Her eyes are closed, and her curls spill out across the pillow. She looks so vulnerable that it hurts. I watch her for a moment, wondering if she's terrified or simply exhausted from her first day out of the infirmary.

Moving toward the four-poster on bare feet, I slip onto the bed beside her, careful not to jostle the mattress. Its springs groan beneath my weight, but she remains still, her breath steady and even.

She shifts, her lashes fluttering. "Xero?"

"Yes, little ghost?"

"Come to bed. I won't bite, unless you beg for it." She rolls onto her back, her eyes meeting mine with a mix of vulnerability and fear. When I don't make a move, she adds, "Hold me. Please."

Not wanting her re-traumatized, I place a hand on her arm.

She tenses, and I pause. When she relaxes, I slide my arm beneath her waist and pull her into my chest. I remain still, giving her a moment to settle into my presence, and she scoots backward, pressing our bodies flush. She's warm, soft, and inviting. Desire pulses beneath the surface, but I force myself to focus on her comfort. The tension from before dissolves into nothingness as she tucks her head beneath my chin.

Her rapid heartbeat resounds through my chest. I don't move, still wanting to give her time to adjust. As her heartbeat syncs with mine, her body relaxes, and my longing lingers as a smoldering ache, kept in check for her sake.

"Are you alright, little ghost?" I ask, my voice barely above a whisper.

"Hug me tighter," she murmurs.

I pull Amethyst closer, cradling her in my arms. Our bodies are pressed tightly, her ass flush against my hard cock. I'm almost certain the version of me she hallucinated at the asylum wasn't fighting off a raging hard-on.

"Like this?" I ask, my voice tight.

Nodding, she exhales a long sigh, her muscles melting. The warmth of her body seeps into mine, providing the comfort that's escaped me since she left. Relieved, I close my eyes and inhale her citrus and peach scent.

"Xero," she whispers, her voice trembling. "You're not going to change your mind, are you?"

I frown, my thoughts racing back through our last conversation. "About the shrink?"

She swallows hard, her fingers clutching the fabric of my sleeve. "About me. About what I did. Is this building up to a punishment?"

My heart squeezes. Betrayal is an integral part of her past. Even if she can't remember the events of that summer, her brain must cling to the idea that she isn't safe, especially with those she's supposed to trust.

I tighten my hold around her waist and press a kiss to the back of her head. "Never. I only wish you had confronted me, but I understand why you didn't."

Breath shuddering, she clings to my arm as if afraid I might disappear. "I wasn't thinking straight. I didn't know what else to do."

After all the information I've gathered on her past, I've become an expert on her deadly knee-jerk reactions. She's blameless. It's not even her fault. It's her stepfather's. And mine.

"Consider us even and focus on your healing," I murmur into her damp curls. "The only punishment I'm planning is my father's and anyone else who hurt you."

Nodding, she exhales a trembling breath, her grip on my arm loosening. "Thank you," she whispers. "For everything."

As she drifts into sleep, I keep my arms around my little ghost, feeling the steady rise and fall of her breath. Today has been a breakthrough. Tomorrow might not be so bright, after she reads her mother's diary. Whatever happens, however she reacts, I will help her through the fallout.

~

Hours later, an alert on my phone pulls me out of slumber. It's an urgent message from Jynxson, saying that a truck has pulled up to Harlan Stills's warehouse. He's X-Cite Media's content manager, the one who told us that was where Delta kept servers containing terabytes of illicit pornography, along with data on the members and every asshole who ever rented a snuff movie.

If we want to identify every bastard who directly or indirectly supported Father's snuff empire, we need to extract those names now, while the information is still accessible.

After giving him permission to intercept, I ease out of bed, careful not to jostle my little ghost, and rush to the door. I wake up Isabel, telling her to watch Amethyst, and change into bullet proof armor.

At this time of the morning, the streets are clear. I race through them in my car, ignoring the speedometer and every red light. Buildings blur past, flashing in and out of existence in the dim pre-dawn light as my car roars down the road.

My mind keeps drifting back to Amethyst, to the way her body molded against mine, the softness of her skin, and the intoxicating scent of her hair. The memory of her ass pressed against me stirs a familiar ache, and I grip the wheel tighter, trying to focus on the road ahead.

I reach the red-light district around the time most sex peddlers retire for the night and stop around the corner from the house. Glancing down at my phone, I find messages telling me that Tyler and his team are already inside, extracting all the useful data.

Slipping out of the vehicle, I walk around the block, keeping my eyes on the surroundings. Shadows stretch out from under the glow of the occasional streetlight, casting ominous silhouettes onto the cracked pavement. Five-story townhouses line both sides of the street, their windows too dark to tell if they're concealing Father and his cronies, but the moment he knows we're here, he'll attack.

As I approach Harlan's street, I spot the truck in question and take a moment to observe the scene from a safe distance.

Five figures emerge from around the corner, their movements stealthy and calculated. They're not our operatives. We raid buildings from underground, and Jynxson already confirmed he breached their basement.

Heart pounding, I step back into the shadows and speak into my Bluetooth. "Jynxson, we have uninvited guests. Four, possibly more, approaching the front door."

"Tyler needs two more minutes to empty the server," Jynxson answers. "We'll stall them."

I unholster my gun and attach a silencer. "No. Evacuate as soon as you get the data. I'll handle it."

Approaching the interlopers, I keep to the shadows. They move together in a formation, their bodies tense with anticipation. As they approach the truck, I take aim and fire a single shot towards the nearest man's exposed throat. The bullet slices through the quiet like a knife. The man drops, leaving his companions exposed.

The remaining men scramble for cover, their movements uncoordinated in the shock of the sudden attack. I fire again, taking out another of the bastards before they reach the dubious safety of the truck.

"Tyler has the data," Jynxson's voice resounds in my ear. "We're out."

I draw backward. "Detonate the explosives as soon as you're clear."

Another figure darts from behind the truck, trying to make a run into the house. I don't waste precious seconds lining up the perfect shot. Not when I need to escape before the building blows. Instead, I turn on my heel and run.

Gunshots fill the air as the assholes realize I'm retreating, but I round the corner and pick up speed.

"You clear?" Jynxson's voice cuts through the commotion.

"Just about," I say, my breath coming in ragged spurts. "Detonate in three... two..."

An explosion cuts me off mid-sentence, drowning out the gunshots. The house behind me is now a roaring inferno, with flames rising toward the starless sky. The truck is reduced to a smoldering husk, and the men are nowhere in sight.

The drive back is uneventful, save for the residual ringing in my ears. Jynxson and the others have taken the data to a processing center on the other side of town. Even though I plan to expose every bastard who ever paid to watch an innocent woman die, our priority is finding Father.

When I return to Amethyst, she's sitting up in bed, the open diary on her lap. I hesitate in the doorway, staring into her tear-streaked face, my heart aching for her.

"You read it?" I ask, my chest tightening with worry.

"Dolly thinks I'm the one who got her trafficked," she says, her voice flat and hollow.

I nod, trying to convey my empathy and understanding through my eyes. "I'm so sorry, Amethyst."

"Mom just handed me to some random psychiatrist with a grudge," she continues, her voice trembling.

I swallow hard, waiting for her to make the connection between my actions and the woman who pretended to be a ghost.

"And I killed my dad."

"He had stopped playing the role of father. You protected yourself from ending up like Dolly," I say.

She sighs. "At least I know why I hallucinate him. Even if I can't remember sticking those scissors into his neck, there's a part of me that can't forget."

"I'm sorry."

Trite words, but I hate to see her in pain. Stepping closer, I resist the urge to reach out and hold her, give her comfort, but the last thing she might need is my touch.

"Take me back to that man," she says, her chin rising, her voice hardening with determination. "I'm ready to confront him."

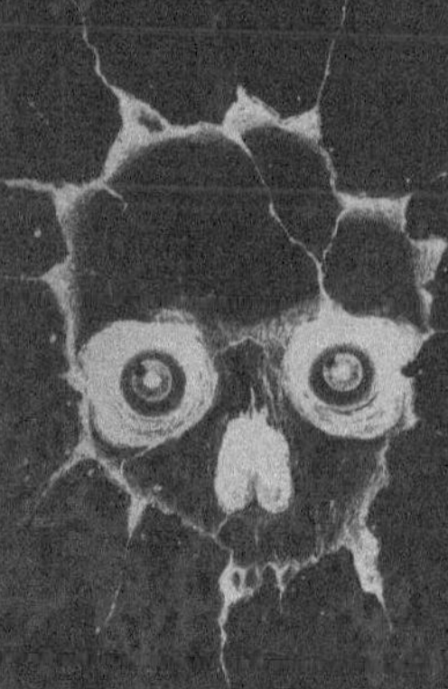

FIFTY-EIGHT

AMETHYST

I walk down the darkened hallway, aware of the weight of Xero's stare. He's worried about my mental state, but I've never felt more clear-headed.

Mom's diary might not have unlocked my memories, but they sure as hell uncovered the mystery behind her behavior.

And mine.

I now understand the origin of the hallucinations and why my mind only conjures up people I think I killed. Dad wasn't even my real father. It was some dead mafia guy. I can't believe a control freak like Mom could lose track of her children so easily.

Mom thought having another baby would cement them as a perfect family, but how on earth did she think Dad wouldn't find out about her affair?

Her last diary entry explains why she hated my guts. I was a reminder of all her mistakes—the murdered baby, her trafficked daughter, the Salentino family forcing her into sexual servitude. As time passed, the sacrifices she made to keep me safe must have felt hollow once the trail for Dolly went cold.

And when I turned into a killer, the love she had for me soured into hatred.

What the hell happened to Dr. Forster? I'm almost certain

he's the creepy psychiatrist in my memories. The diary just stopped abruptly, with no closure.

Xero opens the door, where Clyde Proctor curls up naked in a darkened corner. He flinches at the sight of us and cowers.

I picture myself hunched in the fetal position with only a hallucination to protect my sanity. The memory sends a jolt of emotion that makes me reel on my feet, but Xero's warm hand on my shoulder holds me steady.

"Amethyst," he murmurs.

I meet his concerned gaze. Whatever he sees in my eyes makes him draw back and straighten. That bastard belongs to me. This time, I won't fall apart. I'm so much stronger than my past.

Turning back to Proctor, I hiss, "Get up."

He shivers. "Who's there?"

"Take a look and see."

Proctor raises his head, meeting my gaze with a gasp. "Dolly?"

The insult hits like a slap. I step into the cell, my chest rising and falling with the force of my fury. "Take a closer look."

Recognition flickers across his features as he realizes I'm not his boss's wife, but the woman he filmed suffering a litany of indignities. All signs of hope morph into a grotesque mask of horror.

"Amy... Oh my God. I'm sorry. I didn't—"

"Didn't what?" I snap. "Didn't stand back while I was humiliated and tortured for B-roll footage? Didn't join the search party to recapture me when I escaped? Or are you going to deny jerking off into my mouth?"

Proctor lurches backward with a scream.

Snarling, Xero advances on the man, the heat of his fury burning at my back, but I raise a hand to ward him off.

"This is my revenge," I say.

In my periphery, Xero jerks a nod. He's practically vibrating with the need to tear this man apart, but he's holding back. For me. Moments later, he presses the hilt of a blade into my hand. His low growls echo across the cell, mirroring the feral beast that's taken residence in my heart. It rumbles with impatience, hungering for retribution.

Adrenaline surges through my veins, sending waves of power

that have my fingers trembling with anticipation of the kill. They tighten around the blade's hilt, ready to strike at a moment's provocation.

"Why, Clyde?" I ask through ragged breaths.

He shakes his head. "I didn't—"

I don't hear what he says next. Before I know it, I've already slashed him across the face with my blade.

"Gaslight me again, and I'll slice off your balls."

He screams louder than I ever did, and the blood pouring down his face doesn't give me a measure of satisfaction. Not while he still draws breath.

Leaning against the wall with his knees pulled into his chest, he closes his eyes and shudders. He shrinks into the corner, pressing himself into the concrete as if it would swallow him up.

"What do you want to know?" he rasps.

"Tell me how a man goes from being a film major to making snuff movies."

Proctor whimpers, and his sniveling fills the small room. Through halting breaths, he tells the story of a scholarship student who fell in with the wrong crowd.

His university roommate invited him to watch videos he rented from X-Cite Media. When he was invited to become a member, he allowed Clyde to use his computer to access more content.

They saw how other members uploaded videos of their exploits, and his friend persuaded Proctor to mount a multi-camera set-up in their dorm room to film him with a drugged student. When Proctor edited the video and uploaded it to the site, the roommate received praise for its cinematography.

"Delta himself reached out and discovered my background. He asked if I wanted to be a runner for one of his movies," Clyde sputters through tears.

I stare down at the pathetic man, incredulous. "How did you dispose of that first girl?"

"We didn't kill her," he replies, his voice tightening with offense. "She woke up confused and left."

"So, you don't murder innocent women," I say, my voice flat.

"That's right." He stares up at me, his eyes shining with a

sickening sincerity. "I'm a nice guy. I've never laid a hand on a woman in my life."

Never laid a hand on a woman.

What a nice, upstanding guy.

Something in my psyche snaps, and I laugh. Laugh to the edge of my sanity. Laugh so hard that I double over and tears spring to the corners of my eyes. I've never heard anything so flagrantly delusional, so utterly unhinged.

Xero steps forward and takes hold of my shoulder, but I shrug him off. This is between me and Proctor.

Proctor stares up, trembling, perhaps now grasping the explosive impact of his words.

I flash my teeth. "You witness the degradation of helpless women, you capture it on film. You dehumanize them. But because you don't stick them with the knife, that makes you a nice guy?"

His face freezes in a rictus of terror.

My laughter subsides, replaced by bitter contempt. "No, you just enable the rapists and killers."

When his gaze flicks to Xero's, I rush at him with the knife. "Don't look to him for help. He's not your fucking bro."

Screaming, he twists around, hiding his face in his hands. His vital organs now face the wall, and all I have left is the expanse of his back.

"How many?" I yell over his cries.

"What?"

"How many movies did you work on?"

"Just two."

"Don't lie to me." I punctuate the word with a slash of my blade, making slices across his shoulders. Blood pours down his back in thick rivulets.

"Five," he screams.

"How many?" I yell, making more slashes.

"Twelve. I swear it. Thirteen, if you include the one we made in the dorm room."

"What's the name of your roommate?" I ask.

"Nathan. Nathan Vance. He works for the DiMarco Law Firm as an intern."

I glance over my shoulder to find Xero raising his brows. That's the name of the firm that represented him when he went to prison. And where Myra's sister works.

"I can give you names of all the members. Anything. Just please, stop cutting."

"Too late," Xero drawls. "My people already downloaded all the data from X-Cite Media's servers."

I had a dozen more questions for him, wanting to know if murdering women made him feel powerful or if he just hurt them for sport. But he just repeats the same gibberish about not hurting the women directly. He doesn't have a clue that working on a snuff movie makes him a direct participant. Talking to him is worthless when he thinks he's one of the good guys.

He's no different from the dozens of people who pulled out their phone, recording Xero's brother the subway rapist, and who did nothing to stop him when he escaped into the tunnels.

"You're vermin, Proctor." I press the tip of my blade into one of the spaces between his ribs. "Since you worked on thirteen videos, you get thirteen chances to die."

"Please, don't," he cries into the wall.

"Turn around."

He shakes his head.

"Suit yourself." I push the blade deeper, sliding it between his ribs with satisfying ease. "Count them, or I restart."

"One," he gasps out, still cowering into the wall.

I pull out the wet blade and insert it into a different spot, this time with a little twist. The anguished cry he lets out is muffled by the roar of vengeance between my ears.

He chokes out, "Two."

The air grows hot, and my forehead breaks out in sweat. The body I slice into shakes uncontrollably as he moans the next number.

"Good boy," I say through my teeth. "You're taking this knife so well."

Xero breathes hard behind me, but doesn't intervene. This slow kill goes against all his principles as an assassin. But I'm not setting this bastard up for further interrogation—this is all about retribution.

My attacks pick up speed, and Proctor's voice becomes a garbled, choked whimper. At ten, his frail body convulses against the concrete wall, and I give him a moment to catch his breath.

"Three more," I say, my voice low. "Are you ready to face your death?"

His next word comes out a gurgled sob, and he turns around to meet my eyes.

When I look into his face, I no longer see a monster from my nightmares, but a pathetic coward who gets his kicks hiding behind stronger monsters. He's a vulture in human form, doing nothing to stop the evil because he's too preoccupied with getting a piece of the spoils. Blood streams from his lips onto his narrow chest and drips onto the concrete floor.

"I'm bored with you already," I snap.

Face crumpling, he squeezes his eyes shut.

"Stand up."

When he shakes his head, Xero steps forward and grabs him by the neck.

"Finish him," he snarls, his voice a low growl. Pale eyes burn with pride, locking onto mine with an intensity that makes my pulse race.

The line of his jaw hardens with satisfaction, making my breath catch. The way he dominates the smaller man makes my heart skip several beats. A part of me that's always been ashamed of my violent impulses rejoices at having found a kindred spirit.

I stab through Proctor's pathetic, limp penis, letting out a spray of blood. As it hangs from two pieces of flesh, I jerk the blade from side to side, slicing through the remaining strands.

His shriek rings in my ears, and he convulses once, twice, three times, before falling limp.

"Two more," Xero says.

I make a slash at the corner of his mouth, followed by the other to give him a grotesque smile. His body only twitches. Xero drops him to the floor. As he falls, so does a small piece of my trauma. It's only a tiny chunk in an unwieldy burden that won't shift until every bastard who touched me is dead.

"How do you feel?" Xero asks, his eyes shining with pride.

"Like I can finally take a breath," I reply, my throat raw.

He steps forward, his chest heaving, his heart beating so hard its vibrations resound against my skin. "I didn't know you could be so deadly," he says in a low purr. "You looked so beautiful when you were severing his cock."

I grab him by the collar of his bullet-proof jacket, pulling his head down to my level. Our gazes meet, his pale blue hues blazing with fiery intensity. His breath is hot on my face, fanning the flames of my desire. I want him so much, it hurts.

As I lean in for a kiss, an alarm rips through the air.

I jerk back. "What's that?"

"Perimeter alert," he snarls. "Someone is coming."

FIFTY-NINE

XERO

Just as we were making a breakthrough, we're interrupted by an alert. Pulling back from my little ghost, I step out of the pool of Proctor's blood and activate my Bluetooth headset.

"Report."

"A convoy of unmarked vehicles just passed Rectory Lane," says a voice I recognize from Tyler's team. "95% chance they'll take the turnoff to safe house Theta B."

"Fuck."

I whirl around and place a hand on Amethyst's shoulder. Her eyes are still glazed from the slow, sensual retribution she unleashed on that worthless bastard, and her lips are still parted, begging for that kiss. I hate to bring her back to reality, but there's no time to reconnect.

"What's happening?" she asks, her voice still breathy.

"We have to move out now. Intruders are approximately five minutes from breaching the grounds."

She nods, her jaw set with determination. She looks nothing like the broken woman who struggled to face her tormentor. "What are we going to do?"

"Don't worry. I have a plan." As we exit the room, I patch into the connection I share with my sister. "Isabel. Report."

"Already halfway down tunnel E. Do you have Amethyst?" she asks through panting breaths.

"Affirmative. We're heading toward the east bunker."

Amethyst hovers at the door, staring up at me through wide eyes. "Are we going back to the house?"

"We're going further underground, but first, I need to find out how the hell they located this safe house."

I stride down the line of cells, pausing at the last one occupied by Deputy Chief Carl Hunter. The old bastard glares up at me through the bars, his posture rigid with defiance.

It was him.

Rage ignites in my veins. I unlock the biometric security and stride inside. "Want to confess anything, Hunter?"

He raises his chin. "I knew Delta would come through. We're comrades, something an ungrateful backstabber like you could never understand."

"How did you do it?"

Hunter smirks. "I'll explain it all when you're the one sitting in the electric chair."

I search his bruised face for clues. We stripped every captive naked, scanned their bodies for devices, secured their limbs so they couldn't reach our communications networks, yet somehow this bastard managed to breach our security.

"One way or another, you're going to tell me how you did it."

When the smirk widens to a grin, I see it. A missing tooth.

"Let me guess," I snarl. "Your prosthetic tooth contains a mini faraday cage concealing a communications device?"

He chuckles. "Your father would be proud."

"Xero?" Amethyst says from the hallway.

Hunter's gaze snaps toward the door, his eyes widening. "Is that Amy? I'll look forward to taking my turn with you. Delta said your cunt was even sweeter than your sister's."

His taunt ignites a fury that consumes every fiber of my being. The world narrows down to a single point: this bastard who dares to lay claim to my little ghost. Before I know it, my gun is out. My vision is a haze of red. I fire a shot into his throat.

Hunter jerks backward, his smug triumph replaced by shocked gurgling. Blood sprays from the wound and pours from the sides of his mouth in rivulets. His eyes bulge wide with fear and confusion, only intensifying my wrath. I wanted to languish in his slow, agonizing death.

Amethyst grabs my arm. "You said they were five minutes away. Let's go."

Pocketing the gun, I let her lead me out of his cell. Hunter's words ring through my ears, and the question rises to my throat.

"I have to know," I rasp, my throat raw, "Did my father really touch you?"

Amethyst glances away, her chest rising. "I was drugged and didn't know what was happening until afterward."

Rage burns through my veins, hot and pulsing. I want to charge outside and meet the convoy of bastards if there's any chance of facing Father.

Amethyst cups my cheek, forcing our gazes to meet. "Xero. Where are we going?"

Her touch snaps me back to the present, and I swallow back a wave of all-consuming guilt. Vengeance can wait. My priority should be keeping my little ghost out of his hands.

Our eyes meet, and I see the fear in her green depths and a vulnerability that makes my heart ache. "No one will ever hurt you again, not while I draw breath. And if I'm dead, then I'll still watch over you like an avenging spirit."

She swallows, her eyes shining with unshed tears. "Thank you," she whispers, her voice choked with emotion. "I believe you."

The words hit like a punch to the chest, making my steps falter. Relief, guilt, and gratitude twist to tighten my throat. After everything, she trusts me. I swallow hard, forcing down the surge of emotion.

I lead her out of the cell and down the hallway in the opposite direction of the house. We pass another heavy door, leading to a lockout chamber. It's a large closet with a hatch on the floor that opens into a deeper tunnel.

As Amethyst climbs down into the darkness, I secure the airtight door and descend after her before sealing the hatch. Her feet hit the ground, triggering the tunnel's automatic lighting system. LED bulbs flicker to life, casting long shadows along the curved walls.

By the time I jump down, she's already sitting in the emergency cart. The four-wheeler's motor is just about fast enough to outrun the shitstorm I'm about to unleash if the chamber's seal fails.

"Where does this lead?" she asks, her voice echoing.

"Another bunker where we can launch our defense."

I unplug the cart, slide into the driver's seat, and fire up the engine. It hums to life, and we lurch forward at top speed.

Amethyst grasps onto the sides of the cart, her knuckles white. She breathes hard, her body leaning into mine for comfort. I wrap an arm around her shoulder, tucking her close. Her heart pounds against my side, its rhythm synching with my racing pulse.

"We're going to be okay," I say, my voice steady. "He'll die before he touches you again."

The tunnel's lights whizz past in a blur as we pick up speed through the darkness. Amethyst grips my thigh as if it's the only thing keeping her tethered to the present.

"Is Isabel safe?" she asks.

I grunt. "She escaped through another tunnel."

"Good."

"The crew members and investors we captured won't live to pose a threat." I pause, waiting for her to acknowledge my promise with a nod and then push down on the headset and order, "We're clear. Flood the Alpha bunker."

Tyler's voice sounds in my ear. "Acknowledged. Initiating septic tank sequence."

The tunnel vibrates beneath the cart, a low rumble that permeates our bones. It's the sound of gallons of waste flooding the bunker and drowning those bastards in shit. I glance over my shoulder for signs of sewage, but there's only the fading glow of the tunnel lights.

"Sequence complete," Tyler says.

I give Amethyst a gentle squeeze. "It's done."

She exhales, her grip on my thigh loosening. As we continue to speed down the tunnel, Jynxson updates me with the status of the approaching vehicles. They've passed the decoy gates leading to a long driveway that takes them around the woodlands and into the ruin that was the original house.

They're advancing toward a trap, but I'm not about to give them an easy ride.

"Detonate the road," I order.

"Those vehicles are armored," Tyler replies. "They won't go down easily."

I smirk. "Do it anyway."

"Acknowledged."

The explosion's rumble echoes through the tunnel, making the ground shake. Amethyst flinches, her fingers tightening around my thigh.

"Negative impact," Tyler says. "They're still advancing."

I lean back in my seat and place a kiss on Amethyst's temple. It's all going to plan. By now, Father or whoever Deputy Chief Hunter called to rescue him will advance toward the trap, thinking they've overcome our last line of defense.

We reach another part of the tunnel where the lights are red, indicating the entrance to the secondary bunker. It's located in a patch of forest land two miles away from the safe house.

I help Amethyst out of the cart and guide her toward the bunker's entrance. It's a nondescript steel door, tucked into the tunnel's side, secured by a biometric lock. I press a palm against it, and the seal breaks.

With a creak and a groan of hydraulics, it swings open to reveal a secure vestibule. I glance down at Amethyst, who stares up at me with so much gratitude that my breath catches.

It's bittersweet. She's appreciative because she's witnessed first-hand what could happen without my protection. But I would give anything to restore her to the resistant brat who threw cereal in my face. Regardless, I would never repeat the mistakes of her mother.

Red light floods the chamber before the final door clicks open, revealing a spacious, well-lit living area with leather sofas, a king size bed, and a large kitchenette with stainless steel appliances. At the very end of the room is a corner cubicle equipped with multiple screens already displaying live feeds from the perimeter cameras.

Amethyst glances around, her eyes widening, her blood-stained hands rising to her mouth.

I place a hand on the small of her back and guide her to the left. "Make yourself comfortable. There's a bathroom over there to clean up all traces of that bastard."

As she disappears to get washed up, I stride over to the surveillance cubicle. Drone footage displays men in armor piling out of a truck, advancing under the cover of trees toward the decoy house.

"Want to lure them all into the ruin?" Tyler asks.

I lower myself into a gaming chair. "Let's see how many we can take out along the way."

This part of the land is seeded with mines, snares, pit traps, and speakers to play the sounds of people trying to escape. It's a precaution we set up to protect the safe house. All maps and satellite images direct intruders into a danger zone to keep them busy while we evacuate.

I sit back, watching our drones either gun down the men or direct them into the trap zone.

"Xero. Are you there?" Camila's insistent voice cuts through the chatter.

"Go ahead," I reply, taking my eyes from the screens.

"Is Amethyst live on social media right now?"

I glance toward the bathroom door, hearing running water. "Why do you ask?"

"Then it's Dolly. She's cloned Amethyst's profile and is live streaming a murder confession."

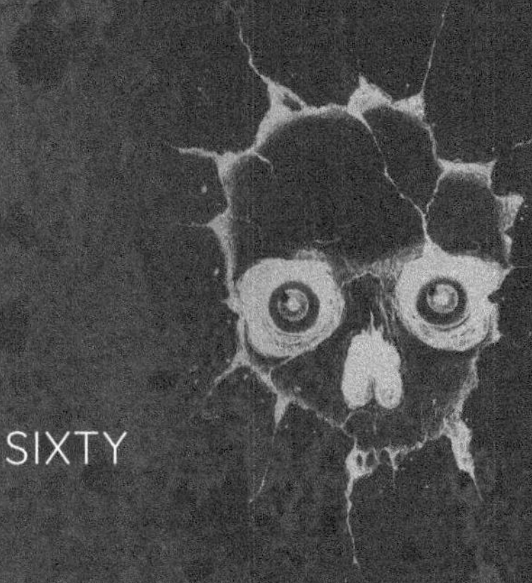

SIXTY

AMETHYST

I enter the bathroom, feeling like I'm walking on clouds. It's a bright space with white countertops, matching tiles, and a large glass enclosure for the shower.

Another of my abusers is dead. Somehow, I don't think my mind will resurrect him as a hallucination. He's too insignificant, and I needed to spill his blood. Good fucking riddance.

All four crew members who helped in the force feeding are dead, as is Grunt. Xero would have mentioned if he'd captured Delta or Dolly. I make a mental note to ask him about Barrett, Seth, and Locke.

A figure moves in my periphery, making me flinch, even though it's my own reflection. I turn to look at myself, and my stomach lurches.

This spectrophobia doesn't make sense. It's Dolly I fear, not myself, yet my brain hasn't caught up to the fact that I have an identical twin.

With a sigh, I peel off my blood-soaked clothes and place them in the laundry basket before stepping into the shower. The bandages on my limbs are now replaced by waterproof bandaids over the deeper cuts which split open during my struggles.

The hot spray hits my skin with a satisfying sting, washing

away Proctor's stench. I turn all the knobs, increasing the pressure until the water hits my flesh like a hundred tiny fists.

What I wouldn't give for Xero to appear behind me and wrap his strong arms around my waist. I want to feel his warm breath on my neck, and his hard body press into my back. His large hands would wash away the stains of my past, and he would reassure me in his deep, soothing voice, that everything will be alright.

That's not going to happen. I have more lines scored into my body than a map of the New Alderney subway, and more trauma than a demolition site. Killing my enemies might give me a measure of satisfaction, but I'm damaged beyond repair.

I reach for the shampoo and work it into my hair with vigorous strokes, trying to scrub away the smell of blood and fear. The lather drips down my face, stinging my eyes, but I barely feel it over the sting in my heart. I rinse and repeat, watching the frothy white bubbles swirl down the drain with the faintest tinge of pink.

A knock sounds on the door. I freeze, my heart stuttering. Ice water sluices through my veins, negating the heat of the hot shower.

He can't see me like this.

"Amethyst?" Xero's voice filters through the door.

Squeezing my eyes shut, I suck in deep, frantic breaths, trying to slow down my racing heart. I'll lose him if he discovers the mess they've made of my body. He'll turn away from me, disgusted. Xero already knows about me and his father. Now that I've confirmed that, he might be thinking about sending me away. Seeing me disfigured might be the last straw. My chest tightens with every exhale, fueling my mounting panic.

"Are you alright, little ghost?" he asks, the words laced with concern.

"I'm fine," I call back, my voice rising several octaves. With trembling fingers, I twist the knobs, cut off the hot spray, and grab a robe.

Rushing to the door on legs as brittle as twigs, I pull the robe around my body and fasten it tight. My fingers pause over the handle. I force in another breath and gather my composure before pulling it open.

He stands on the other side, a towering figure commanding every molecule of my attention. His piercing pale eyes lock onto mine, as if trying to unravel the emotions I struggle to conceal.

Forcing a smile, I ask, "What's up?"

"Let's dry your hair." Eyes softening, he steps forward, and I skitter to the side.

Ignoring my jumpiness, he strides past, reaches beneath the bathroom counter, and pulls out a stool. "Sit."

The soft authority in his voice has me lowering myself on the seat. I dip my head as he drapes a soft towel over my shoulders and works another through my unruly wet curls. His touch is feather-light, barely grazing my scalp, and an oddly comforting balm over my frazzled nerves.

My cheeks heat as I think about the last time he dried my hair, when he fucked my mouth and came down my throat. Shivers run down my spine, and I shift uncomfortably on my seat.

"You're trembling," he murmurs.

"I'm just cold." The lie tumbles out before I can rein it back.

Xero wraps my hair in the towel and pulls away his hands. The absence of his touch eases my discomfort and, at the same time, breeds a sense of longing.

Casting my eyes to my lap, I study the silk trim on my robe to avoid meeting the accusation in his gaze. He'll want details. How many times with his father? What did I do with the other men? What did I mean about letting them come in my mouth?

"I've made some tea."

He strides out of the bathroom, leaving me alone with my confusion. Was he expecting something more? I adjust the robe in the mirror, keeping my gaze fixed on my neckline to make sure I'm not exposing an inch of scars.

A moment later, Xero returns with a tray laden with two glass cups of chamomile tea, a matching pot filled with dried chamomile flowers steeping in hot water, and a small jar of honey with a wooden dipper. Next to it is a plate of shortbread. He sets it down on the counter next to me with movements so careful and precise that I can tell he's walking on eggshells.

Then he drops to a crouch, his eyes locking onto mine with a mournful intensity that makes my heart ache. I fight back tears, wondering if this is the moment he tells me it's over.

I'm corrupted by the men from the asylum. Why would he want me now that I've been tainted by the father he despises?

"Take a sip," he murmurs.

"What's wrong, Xero?" I ask.

His eyes squeeze shut, and he exhales a long breath. "Just drink the tea, please."

The vulnerability in his voice pulls at my heartstrings. I pick up a teacup, letting the warmth seep into my fingertips. The herbal scent of chamomile fills my nostrils, calming and grounding my spirit.

I take a small sip, the warmth radiating from my throat and spreading through my body. It tastes like comfort, like evenings spent at home curled up with an herbal brew and a book.

"Thank you," I manage to whisper, my breath shallowing in anticipation of the bad news. The words hang heavily in the air, filling the silence that stretches on into what feels like an eternity.

Xero remains crouched at my side, watching me consume the entire cup before asking, "Shortbread?"

I shake my head, searching his features for something—anything beneath the guarded expression.

"What's this about?"

A muscle in his jaw flexes. "Our enemies already made their next move."

My brow pinches. "They bombed the safe house?"

"Those bastards should be rotting around the decoy building. But this is different. Your sister went on social media and made a confession."

I wait for him to elaborate, but he reaches into the pocket of his jeans and pulls out a phone.

Its screen is open to a social media profile identical to the second one I set up before the book fair. The only difference is its username, which has a period between the name Amethyst and Ravenly.

According to Mom's diary, my name isn't Amethyst or even Crowley. Pushing away that thought, I look at the latest post, which has 11.5 million views. It's supposed to be me, in a corset like the ones I wear on my podcast, but I would never display so much cleavage.

It's Dolly, sitting against a green screen background of Xero's mugshot.

"Good evening, Xeromaniacs," she says in an exaggerated goody-two-shoes voice. "I have a confession for you all. Xero isn't dead."

My gaze flicks to Xero, who watches me, his expression grim.

Dolly continues. "I've been a bad girl. You see, I helped him escape the electric chair. Together, we've murdered a slew of enemies. Let's see... There was Roger Stern, who you'll know as Big Dick Johnson, Stephen Glick, the Well Hung Man, Jake and Dale Ryland, Paul Brantley..."

After finishing the list of men Xero turned into a human centipede, she follows with Grunt, whose real name is Fenrick Greer, and the crew members we killed together, including Clyde Proctor. My stomach churns as she lists a bunch of important-sounding men, starting with Reverend Tom and ending with Deputy Chief Carl Hunter. Their pictures flicker in the background, making me grind my teeth at the sickening display.

"And of course, I murdered my mommy and my Uncle Clive," she says with a practiced pout. "But you already know about that."

My gaze flicks to the stats on the right-hand side of the screen. 2 million likes, 10.5 thousand comments, 132.1 thousand saves, and 173.3 thousand reposts.

"That's more engagement than I've ever achieved on any of my content," I whisper.

"But don't worry, Xeromaniacs!" Dolly chirps. "I'm doing just fine. Xero and I are living the dream, taking out anyone who stands in our way. Isn't that right, Xero darling?"

Offscreen, a man's voice adds, "That's right, Amethyst, baby."

She leans into the camera with a conspiratorial wink and cups her hand on the side of her mouth. "Oh, and in case you think I'm B.S.ing, check the link in my bio for proof."

The video loops around to the beginning. I can't watch that evil bitch expose me for kills I committed in self-defense.

"What's on the link?" I ask through clenched teeth.

"A video she made of your mother and uncle's murder," Xero says, his words flat. "Conveniently, with no sound."

"Because Mom and Uncle Clive say her name before they die."

"Are you alright?" he asks.

I rise off the stool and yank the towel off my head. Any sympathy I might have had for the wronged little girl in the diary evaporates like the steam rising from the teapot's spout.

"Set me up with your best female fighter. I need a lesson in combat against an equal-sized opponent. It's time for Dolly to die."

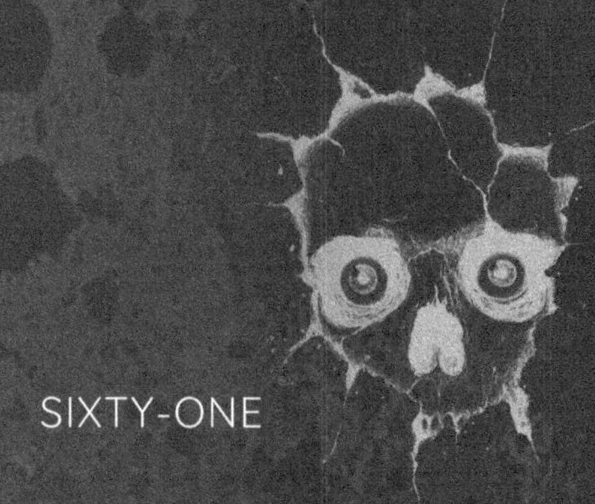

SIXTY-ONE

XERO

Amethyst didn't sleep that night. Watching Dolly's performance triggered a nightmare that had her thrashing beneath the sheets. When I held her, she fought back with inhuman strength.

The next day, she opened up about what happened in the asylum. Killing Proctor last night might have loosened something inside her psyche, but Dolly's fake confession released a flood of anger. Amethyst finally shared the extent of the horrors she suffered in captivity and cried on my chest.

She shook with her need for vengeance, every word she uttered laden with pain. By the end of her story, her green eyes blazed with fury. This was the most alive I'd seen my little ghost since I pulled her out of that bus.

Fire is good, as is anger. It means she's working through her trauma and will come out triumphant. But I wanted her to rest a little longer before resuming her training.

Now she lies on my chest, completely spent. I run my fingers through her curls, breathing hard through my own impotent rage.

Dolly will die for hurting my Amethyst. Father will suffer an eternity of torment.

Every man who touched my little ghost will die, too. As will every man who watched footage of her or Dolly. No one gets to leer at my Amethyst. Or by extension, her identical twin.

"Are you going to help me train?" she murmurs into my chest.

"I'll teach you to use firearms. They're safer and more efficient."

She shakes her head. "I want to learn hand-to-hand combat."

I slide a hand over her shoulder, which is covered in one of my shirts and a thick robe. "We need to be careful. Your stitches—"

"Have been removed. Isabel discharged me from her care. I'm well enough to start training."

My jaw clenches. I want to hide her away from the world. Keep her so deeply protected she never so much as stubs a toe. After losing her once, I want her permanently at my side.

"Let me capture them. I'll present you with their bound and beaten bodies."

She pulls out of my arms and sits up, her eyes still shining with tears. Breathing hard, she wipes her tears with the backs of her hands, then clenches her fists atop the covers.

"I can't keep hiding behind you. They stole so much from me. I need to face them myself." She exhales a shuddering breath. "Please, don't take this away from me, too."

The words hit like a dagger to the heart, and my breath catches. I force down every protective instinct, not wanting to be another man who causes her harm.

When she looks at me, her eyes aflame with determination, my resolve crumbles. I can't deny my little ghost. She needs to face them head on, just as I need to face Father. I want her to reclaim her power.

I nod, my throat too tight to form words.

"So, you'll help me?" she asks.

"Alright," I finally manage, "But it's training only. You leave the recapture missions to my operatives."

"Fine," she says, and lowers herself back onto my chest.

Hours later, Tyler messages that all personnel sent to the decoy house are disabled or dead. After turning off the traps, Jynxson and his team extract the survivors and dispose of the bodies.

I've ordered their teeth removed, just in case they're concealing communications devices. I've also summoned Camila.

Both my sisters are about Amethyst's size, but Isabel probably won't consent to fighting her patient.

After breakfast, Amethyst and I take the cart to a training facility a mile out from our hideout. Until Delta and his band of supporters are dead, we're still assuming the catacombs beneath the Parisii Cemetery are compromised.

Camila waits for us in a room surrounded by concrete walls, lit by harsh fluorescent lights. Around her are punching bags, sparring mats, and an array of combat gear mounted on the far wall.

She turns towards us as we enter, her brow creasing with concern. As the first person to have spotted Dolly's counterfeit confession, I'm not surprised Camila is worried. My sister might be cautious, but if anyone can understand the healing power of vengeance, it's Camila.

When I think about her alone in our childhood home with John, it makes me want to finish what I started with the urinal. Or at least execute him in the electric chair all over again.

"You're sure about this?" Camila asks, her gaze flicking toward Amethyst.

My little ghost pulls back her shoulders. "I need the strength to face my sister again."

Camila looks at her for a beat before she shrugs. "If it gets too much—"

"It won't." Amethyst punches into her palm. "And don't hold back."

My sister and I exchange glances. I've already had the rest of the night to come to terms with Amethyst's resolve, but my sister is taken aback. Camila has an idea of what Amethyst endured and likely doesn't want to add to her trauma.

Raising a hand, I cut off Camila's attempt to question her further and indicate for her to move behind.

"Alright, then," my sister says. "This time, you won't rely on leveraging a man's weight or strength. You'll face an evenly matched opponent, testing your skill and endurance."

Swallowing, Amethyst nods.

"We'll skip the boxing gloves. Based on the footage we downloaded last night, that's not Dolly's style. We'll focus on hand to hand. When you've got a grip on the basics, we'll escalate to knives."

My muscles tense as Amethyst marches forward, each step laden with determination. The urge to protect her claws at my insides, threatening to break free. I want to grab her, to pull her close and shield her from every conceivable harm. But restraining her would only stifle her progress, and she needs to reclaim her strength. So, I clasp my hands together and swallow back my frustration.

Camila assumes a fighting stance, which Amethyst mirrors. As the two women circle each other, Camila instructs her on how best to position her feet for balance and mobility.

"Xero?" says a voice in my Bluetooth headset. It's Jynxson.

"Report." I step away from the two women.

"Three of the personnel retrieved from the decoy house and its surroundings died en route to the holding cells. Two are critical and one is stable."

"Any ID on the survivor?" I ask, keeping my gaze on Amethyst and Camila's training.

"Moirai," he mutters. "All of them."

My brows rise. "Do they know they're working for Delta?"

"The survivor said her client's name was Fenrick Greer."

I nod. Father doesn't just use aliases, he steals identities. That's the name of the masked man who transported Amethyst out of the asylum in an old school bus. "And their mission?"

"To slaughter the occupants of the house and extract the prisoners. The client was particularly interested in saving Deputy Chief Hunter."

"Where were they supposed to deposit the prisoners?"

"The coordinates given were for a house ten miles away from Braye Airport. I've already sent out operatives to investigate."

"Be careful," I reply. "Delta is likely to set a trap."

"That's why we're sending the police to go in to perform a wellness check," he replies with a snicker. "I've told them their missing deputy chief went there with a young girl."

"Good thinking." Whoever's working with the corrupt bastard will go there personally to protect Hunter's reputation.

The sound of flesh hitting flesh turns my attention back to

Amethyst and Camila, who are now fully engaged in a sparring match. Camila swipes out a leg, but Amethyst side steps. This is an improvement from her last training session.

I expect this prowess is muscle memory from the summer camp from hell. Father, that slimy bastard, didn't even disguise the name of his facility. In Greek mythology, the Moirai is another name for the three fates. Strangely, none of the girls from Three Fates ever made it to the Moirai Academy.

Amethyst ducks Camila's right hook. She's getting faster, more adept. She spins on her heel, blocking another punch, and counterattacks with a direct jab that forces Camila to retreat.

"What do you want me to do with the injured personnel?" Jynxson asks.

"Put them in separate holding cells until we've handled Delta. The Moirai won't take on any more assignments from a client who's caused them mass losses."

Camila dodges a punch and jogs back. Amethyst lunges forward, falling into Camila's right hook. The force of the blow sends Amethyst crashing to the ground, her body splayed out like a broken doll.

Shit.

SIXTY-TWO

FOURTEEN YEARS AGO

AMETHYST

Why must I be stuck with an evil twin? I hate her.

She's staring at me from the other side of the back seat, breathing so hard I want to slam my fist into her nose. But that would get me into even more trouble.

Dolly got us expelled from school, even though it wasn't my fault. Mom can't cope with Dolly's antics, so we're both being banished to summer camp.

That's why I'm glaring out into the countryside. It's a nice day, with sunlight shining through the tall trees, but I can't appreciate it because Dolly's laser eyes keep burning through the back of my head.

Can't we just stop the car and release her into the forest like a wild animal? She'd be happier there, living like a female Mowgli among the wolves. Just as I'm picturing her picking ants out of honey, her foot lands on my thigh, leaving a dirty print on my khaki shorts.

"Are we nearly there yet?" she whines.

I twist around in my seat and kick her shin, wishing I could break the bone.

She shrieks, "Dad, Amy just kicked me!"

"Cut it out, both of you!" Dad snarls from the front seat. "Your mother is struggling enough. It's this behavior that made her reject you."

The words hit like a punch to the chest. Mom hates me, even though I did nothing wrong. I catch Dad's eyes in the rearview mirror and cringe. He thinks I started it, but I wish he knew the truth. It always begins with Dolly.

She's just like the shadow in that fairytale, always lurking and causing mischief that somehow never gets linked back to her. Why can't she just die?

We pass a creepy water tower that looks like a rusty kettle on stilts. Dad turns into a narrow space between two overgrown hedges, making me grip the seatbelt. Branches reach out and scrape against the sides of the car, sending shivers down my spine.

It's like we're in a carwash, except we're being attacked by nature instead of brushes. My breath quickens, and I jerk back from the window. Roots crunch under the tires like giant bones, and the foliage closes in around us like we're being swallowed by some monstrous beast.

Dolly screams, "Dad, stop the car. We're going to die!"

My heart pounds. I hate my sister, but maybe she's right. Maybe Dad is dumping us in the forest like we're Gretel and Gretel's cheap imitation, because he's finally getting a son. Maybe that's why Dad left the cases Mom packed for us with his assistant, Becky. What if we're going to spend the rest of our lives in an isolated shack?

When Dad ignores Dolly, I stare into the side of his face. His eyes are fixed on a path so narrow that it might as well be invisible, and his hands grip the steering wheel so hard that his knuckles turn white.

Dolly shoves me in the arm and screeches, "Say something!"

My lips part to form words, but I clamp them shut. Why should I help the girl who tried to gut me with a craft knife in front of our friends?

She's been mean to me for months, saying I broke or took her things when I never did. She blames me for wetting her bed, when I wouldn't go into her stinky room. Whenever I show someone she hurt me, they always come back to find she did the same to herself.

So, I keep my mouth closed and leave her to wail and whine like a banshee.

The ground beneath us evens out, and light streams in through the leaves. Dolly finally shuts her big mouth as the car drives out of the branches and down a gravel path lined with more of the hedges.

Out of the corner of my eye, I see her glaring at me like I'm the one who caused her panic attack. Ignoring her, I turn to Dad and ask, "Is this Three Fates?"

"Nearly there," he says, his voice light.

The corners of my lips twitch. I know better than to smirk when Dolly is in this mood. She'll probably rip out a chunk of my hair. Again.

This time, she won't even wait for Dad to turn his back. After the stunt she pulled with the knife at school, everyone knows she's got the problem. I'm just getting punished because I'm her identical twin. It's not fair.

We continue down the winding path until we reach a tall fence topped with barbed wire. Behind them are even more trees. They're so dense, I can't see what's on the other side. We could be headed anywhere.

Finally, we reach a gate. Dad stops the car outside it and picks up his phone to make a call. I steal a glance at Dolly, whose face is paler than diluted milk. Now is probably the time to ask what's happening, but what's the point? She's the one who got us into the mess.

The gate swings open, and Dad drives through.

Minutes later, I spot a concrete building hidden behind tall trees. It's made up of straight lines and square shapes, with narrow windows and a metal door. I can only see it because the sunlight bounces off the glass and making it sparkle through the leaves.

Dolly is too busy staring out into the grassy courtyard on the other side of the trees, where a group of girls in blue shirts practice fighting routines with a blonde instructor.

They're our age, but look like drones with their choreographed movements. My breath stills at the thought of joining their ranks.

"What are they doing?" Dolly asks.

I shake my head, my stomach churning. When Mom described Three Fates as a summer camp, I expected cabins, campfires, crafts, and canoes. This looks like an army training center.

Dad parks close to the weirdos, turns off the engine, and looks at us in the rearview mirror. "If you girls hadn't upset your mother so much, you'd be at school with your friends. If you follow the rules and obey your instructors, she might want you back."

My throat thickens. I resent Dolly so much for making Mom hate me.

"What if only one of us is good?" I ask.

Dad twists around in his seat and sighs. "Your behavior is harming your mother's pregnancy. She says this new baby comes first."

My stomach twists into painful knots. What if Mom decides she only wants one kid and we never get to go home?

"What does that mean?" Dolly asks, her voice trembling.

"If only one of you can behave, then you'll both stay here. You girls are a package deal. Understood?"

Dad steps out of the car, leaving his words hanging in the air like smoke. Dread sinks in my stomach as I picture myself trapped in this place with Dolly until I'm old enough to find my way home. The world will have changed, and it'll be just like Rip Van Winkle or that fisherman in Japan who ran off with that turtle.

I turn to my twin and catch her wide-eyed stare. She's trembling, looking like the message has finally sunk into her thick head. When she bites her bottom lip and stares at her lap, I want to punch her in the eyes. Her constant attacks and accusations drove Mom crazy. It's Dolly's fault, but she's the one trying not to cry.

Dad strides past the exercising girls and toward the building, leaving us both behind. I fold my arms, not daring to follow. Let Dolly go there instead of me. I'll stay here and return to Mom.

The blonde instructor leaves the girls to continue their routines and jogs over. She opens the door with a bright smile.

"Welcome to Three Fates. You must be Amy and Dolly. I'm Charlotte, your counselor, but you can call me Kappa." Her voice is chipper, as if she's trying to make a concrete box in the woods seem friendly. "Let's get you girls settled in."

Kappa leads us from the car into the main building. Inside, it looks like a prison with a long hallway full of locked doors and cold, gray walls.

We walk by an older girl mopping the floor with bleach, and another girl our age wiping the scanners on the metal doors. Now, I'm wondering if this place is a Kung Fu version of Annie.

At the end of the hallway is the only door that isn't metal. Kappa knocks on its wooden surface and waits for a male voice to tell her to come in.

She pushes open the door, leading us into an office lined with shelves filled with thick, leather-bound books. The wooden desk with a high-backed chair straight ahead of us is empty, so I glance to the sofas on the right.

Dad sits opposite a man so terrifying that my blood runs cold. He turns his head in our direction and stares through deep blue eyes that I'm sure can read minds. The air becomes heavy and thick. I inch closer to Dolly and stare at my feet, praying he won't speak to me.

"Amaryllis, Dahlia," he says in a hypnotic voice. "Welcome to Three Fates. You may call me Delta."

SIXTY-THREE

AMETHYST

Six weeks after arriving at Three Fates, Kappa drives us through the gates of a mansion. It's bigger than any house I've seen before, with its stone front covered in thick ivy and creepy marble statues standing on both sides of its wooden doors. Moonlight shines on its darkened windows, making them look like eyes peering out of a hood.

She hands us caffeine pills to wake us up because we fell asleep in the backseat during the long drive. They're bitter and make my heart race, but if we complete this mission, Mr. Delta says we'll be able to go home.

"I don't need to remind you of what will happen if you fail," she says.

"We won't," Dolly replies.

Kappa turns around in the driver's seat to look me in the eye. "Amy?"

"We won't," I whisper.

She nods, seeming satisfied, and hands us identical Alice headbands. They contain two syringes filled with a sleeping agent. Our job is to inject our targets so they can fall unconscious when the police come to search their house. As soon as we're done, she'll drive us home.

I once described Three Fates as an orphanage, like Annie, but it's far more brutal. Mr. Delta told Dad it was one big happy family and that he would take care of the 'beautiful twins' as if we were his own daughters.

The minute Dad left, Mr. Delta ordered us to join the other girls outside for fresh air. Kappa walked us back to the lawn, where the girls were exercising, and there was no sign of Dad's car.

Dolly and I went to the back of the procession of robotic girls and tried to follow their movements. It was so hot outside, and there were no breaks or water, just constant exercises under the sun. Every time we stopped, Kappa forced us to run laps.

It took two weeks to get used to the routines before the instructors called us out for one-on-one sessions, which were more like wrestling than combat drills. They pinned us down on the mats and we had to wriggle free. If we failed, the consequences were disgusting. And painful.

"Do you hear me, Amy?" Kappa's voice cuts through my thoughts.

"Go in there, do what they want, and wait until we get them alone," I say, my voice flat. "Then we pull the syringes out of our headbands, knock them out, and leave."

She nods.

"Then we go home," Dolly adds.

"That's right," Kappa replies with a bright smile.

Dolly opens the door and steps out into the courtyard. I'm about to shuffle across the back seat to follow her, when Kappa grabs my wrist.

"Don't crease your pretty pinafore," she says, her smile vanishing.

Nodding, I swallow down the lump in my throat and open the door. My feet crunch on the gravel in these weird patent leather shoes that pinch around the toes, but I ignore the discomfort.

This time tomorrow, we'll be back home.

Back in our rooms, where we're left alone to be normal kids. Where the only man we have to deal with is Dad.

Dolly waits for me on the mansion's front steps. Three Fates has beaten the evil out of her, and she finally acts like a sister instead of a monster. I heard that's because the girls in her dorm are bullies. The ones in mine just leave me alone.

"Ready?" she whispers.

I give her a shaky nod.

As she rings the bell, Kappa reverses down the driveway and disappears through the gates. We'll rendezvous with her after our mission in the back of the mansion where she'll be parked.

We've practiced this a hundred times with our instructors. The moment our targets take us to a separate room, we need to strike. Failure to take advantage of the element of surprise will lead to an ordeal worse than their nasty punishments.

The door opens, and a gray-haired butler stares down at us with cold eyes. "Karen and Adele?" He doesn't give us a chance to answer. "Follow me."

Dolly and I exchange glances. Our instructors gave us these made-up names, but they didn't tell us there would be a butler. My sister steps over the threshold first. I grab her hand, needing some of her courage.

We trail after him, our shiny shoes echoing through a foyer that seems larger than our entire house. Giant chandeliers hang from the ceiling like they're about to crash over our heads, and the walls are lined with portraits of men whose eyes I'm sure are following as we pass.

I shoot my sister a frown and flick my head to the shoes. How are we going to escape in such noisy footwear? Her lips tighten as if the answer is obvious. We'll have to take them off.

The butler stops at a door and slides it open, revealing a large dining room filled with men wearing suits. All the chatter stops, and every head turns to gape at us like we're circus freaks.

My stomach drops. Our targets were supposed to be alone.

"Take your seats at the ends of the table," the butler says.

Dolly turns to the right and walks toward a bald man who has risen from his seat. He's dressed in a black suit with a face shaped like a boiled egg. I'm about to follow her, when the butler grabs my shoulder.

"You're over there." He turns me to the left, where a man identical to the first one holds out a hand.

The men around the table chuckle. Our instructors also didn't tell us our targets would be twins like us. In fact, they didn't even give us names. Swallowing hard, I walk on trembling legs toward the man, passing his friends, who stare at me like I'm going to be the next course.

Remembering everything I was taught, I take my target's hand. He squeezes back in a grip so tight that I force myself not to wince.

He drags me onto his lap and murmurs into my ear, "Which one are you, Karen or Adele?"

"Adele."

"Call me Cass."

I stare across the table at my sister, who sits on the man's lap, her eyes mirroring my terror. My fingers tremble, and my palms become slick against the cold fabric of my dress. This isn't what they told us would happen. We were supposed to go in, take out our targets, and then leave.

The men restart their conversations, their laughter echoing through the room. Cass brings a tumbler to my mouth, filling my nostrils with the stench of liquor that smells worse than Mom's nail polish remover. I let the liquid wet my lips but don't swallow.

Across the table, Dolly meets my eyes again. She's also pretending to drink.

"Relax," Cass says, his arm tightening around my waist. His touch feels like a threat.

I breathe hard, reminding myself this isn't much different from the private lessons. All I need to do is endure. When servers arrive with dessert, Cass adjusts me on his lap and tries to feed me a spoonful of chocolate mousse. I shake my head, remembering the instructors' warning about drugged food.

"Worried about your figure?" he asks with a smirk, making the man beside him chuckle.

Shaking my head again, I glance across the table, where Dolly is eating the same dessert. The man feeding her takes a big spoonful for himself before offering her another, so I accept a tiny bite of the mousse. It might as well be whipped dog shit.

"Good girl," Cass murmurs into my ear. "You and I are going to get along well."

I force back a shudder. The rest of the dinner carries on with the men discussing finance, cars, and vacations, seeming to forget we exist. Then Cass's hand slides down to my thigh, making every fine hair on my body stand on end. I block out his touch and focus on Dolly's every move.

By the time the meal ends and the guests leave, my eyes are drooping from exhaustion. Cass scoops me up in his arms while his twin brother, Paul, does the same with Dolly. As they carry us out of the dining room and up a grand staircase, I fight to stay focused and alert.

Cass's arm tightens around my waist even more as he and his brother part ways at the top of the stairs. When they walk in opposite directions, I twist around in his hold. Dolly's eyes meet with mine for a heartbeat before Cass grabs my chin.

"None of that now," he growls, his voice low and menacing. "Your attention is on me."

I stare into his cold gray eyes, my heart pounding so hard that every inch of my body trembles. I need to remember the training. The moment we're alone, I'll strike. Then Dolly will meet me in the hallway, and we'll escape together. I've rehearsed this in my mind a thousand times.

Cass pushes open the door to a dark room. Moonlight filters through a gap in the heavy drapes, casting eerie shadows on the antique furniture. As I scan for possible escape routes, he runs his fingers through my curls and removes the headband containing my hidden weapons.

"What's this?" he asks, studying the object with a furrowed brow.

I freeze, my blood running cold.

He squeezes me tight around the middle, leaving me gasping for air.

"Cass," I rasp. "I can't breathe."

He flicks a switch with his thumb, releasing a blade. With a roar, he tosses the headband on the floor and grabs me around the throat. "Tell me who sent you."

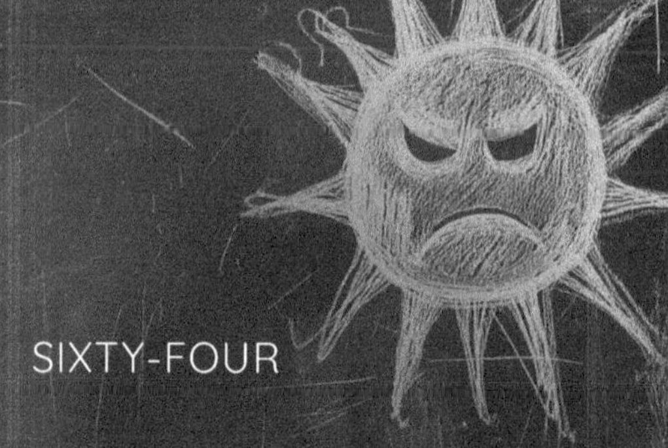

SIXTY-FOUR

AMETHYST

Cold shock turns my veins to slush. I struggle within Cass's iron grip, my heart pounding like it's about to explode. Eerie shadows fall across his face, making him look even more monstrous. My instructors never told me what to do if the target seized my headband.

Cass carries me across the room and throws me onto the bed with a force that knocks the breath from my lungs. He grabs my arms and binds them with rope. I twist and pull, but the rough fibers dig into my skin.

Alarm bells ring in my ears.

I can't fight—he's too strong.

Everything I've learned is useless.

He glares down at me, his face twisting with rage. Foam gathers in the corners of his mouth and veins stand out on his temples like bolts of lightning. I freeze, staring up into his manic eyes, trying to think up a way out of this mess. Panic winds around my chest, pulling even tighter than the ropes.

"Give me a reason why I shouldn't kill you," he snarls.

My ears ring. Every instinct screams at me to make something up.

"I-I don't know what you're talking about," I whisper, my voice trembling.

He leans in close, his face inches from mine, the alcohol on his breath stinging my nostrils. "Don't play games with me, little girl. Tell me who sent you, or I'll rip the truth out of you, piece by piece."

My heart pounds, each beat echoing in my ears as I scramble for a convincing lie. "I didn't know that was in my headband. I swear it."

He snorts, his expression darkening with disbelief. When he pulls back, I fight against my bonds, but they're too tight. He returns, waving the needle in my face, jabbing its point so close to my eyes that I squeeze them shut.

"This says otherwise."

Shivers run down my spine, and my skin breaks out into a sweat. This is it. The moment I die. Mom will never know what happened to me, and I'll never meet my baby brother. Cass might even tell his twin to kill Dolly.

I can't get Dolly into trouble. I need to stay calm. I need to think. But his grip tightens around my throat like a vise. I try to breathe, but nothing comes. My lungs burn, and my vision starts to fade.

My thoughts scatter as my eyes roll back. I'm slipping away, thinking of a place where girls go to school, not to kung fu camps where they get hurt every day. The fear takes over, and everything goes dark.

A crash sounds on the other side of the room, making Cass release my neck. My eyes fly open, and I suck in a deep breath. Dolly rushes in through the door with a dart gun.

Before I can even scream at her to run, she pulls the trigger. The dart flies, embedding itself in Cass's neck. He staggers back, pulling out the object, but it's too late. The tranquilizer takes effect, and he collapses to the floor, unconscious.

"Where did you get that?" I whisper.

"Paul." Dolly jogs to my side, looking paler than death. She unties the ropes around my wrists, her fingers trembling. "We need to get out of here."

"Where is he?" I ask.

"Dead," she replies, her voice a strained whisper.

My stomach lurches. They told us to drug the targets, not kill them. I rub my wrists where the ropes had cut into my skin. We head for the door, but footsteps echo down the hallway, making us freeze.

"What are we going to do?" I ask Dolly, my voice tight.

She glances around the room. "Grab his legs."

We drag Cass's heavy carcass to the corner, so he's out of sight. My arms strain, and sweat breaks out across my brow. When he's in place, I grab a rug and cover him up.

The footsteps disappear, and Dolly slips off her shoes. I do the same and place them in my pinafore's pockets. She walks to the door, opens it a crack, and peers out into the hallway. I wring my hands, my insides twisting into painful knots. This is a disaster. What will the police say when they raid the mansion and discover Dolly killed her target?

"It's clear," she says.

We slip out of the room, clinging to the shadows as we creep along the dark corridor. Footsteps echo from below, but no one seems to notice we're escaping.

At the end of the hallway, we push open a door leading into a stairwell and descend. Every time one of the steps creaks beneath our feet, I cringe. My breath shallows, even though my heart pounds loud enough to summon the butler.

At the bottom, there's a door leading to a courtyard. Dolly pushes it open, and we slip outside. The night air cools my clammy skin, and I finally inhale a deep breath. Outside, the gardens are unlit, but we run hand in hand through the dark toward the distant trees. Behind them is an iron fence. We slip through the railings and sprint toward a parked car.

When we open the back door and scramble inside, I want to howl with relief. It's over.

Kappa turns around from the steering wheel, her eyes wide with worry. "Did you do it?"

"Yes." Dolly fastens her seat belt. "Let's go."

Kappa speeds away. I breathe hard, watching the mansion shrink in the wing mirror. The tires crunch against the gravel drive, putting more distance between us and the nightmare we escaped.

As the tension drains away, I collapse against the seat, my

body trembling with exhaustion. I can't believe I almost died. Dolly reaches across the back seat and takes my hand.

"We did it," she murmurs, her voice a soothing balm. "We're going home."

"We'll see Mom," I whisper, already picturing her and the new baby growing in her belly.

I let my eyes flutter closed and melt into the back seat. The hum of the car's engine lulls me into a state of calm. As I drift off, my chest relaxes. No more Three Fates. No more exercise drills. No more grabby instructors. No more fighting with Dolly.

We can go back home and be normal sisters for Mom and Dad.

Hours later, sunlight streams through the car window, pulling me out of sleep. I wake up in the back seat and spot the rusty old water tower. Heart sinking, I squeeze Dolly's hand. This isn't New Alderney. We're minutes away from Three Fates.

My sister wakes up, blinking the sleep out of her eyes and leans forward in her seat. "I thought you were taking us home."

"Not until you give Delta a debriefing," Kappa says.

This time, when she takes the turning in the hedges, neither of us flinches. From what I heard from the other girls, Three Fates is an extension of a law enforcement agency. It recruits delinquents and turns them into contributing members of society.

Because of kids like us, criminal organizations around the country are falling. But our facility has to remain top secret to protect the world.

Kappa walks us back through the concrete building, where Mr. Delta waits in his office. There's no sign of any of our instructors or Dad. The headmaster sits behind his desk, staring at his tablet while we wait for him to pay us attention.

Shuffling on my feet, I rub the back of my neck, which still aches from being choked.

Dolly clears her throat.

He flicks his eyes toward us like a whip. I flinch, but my sister holds still.

"Hand over the headbands," he demands, his voice as cold as ice.

Dolly marches over to his desk and places her headband on its wooden surface. When it's my turn to step forward, my heart sinks into a pit of dread. Cass ripped it off my head. I didn't think to pick it up before we escaped.

Mr. Delta raises his brow. "Where is it?"

Tears well up in my eyes. I swallow over and over, struggling to stay composed. Three Fates girls don't cry. We also don't make excuses.

"I-I left it behind," I stammer.

Mr. Delta's gaze hardens, his eyes piercing through my chest. "Do you realize what this means?"

Nodding, I loosen two fat tears that spill down my cheeks.

"I'm sorry," I whisper.

Beside me, Dolly stiffens. I can't stop thinking of what Dad said about us being a package deal. We've both screwed up. Dolly killed her target, when she should have left him unconscious for the police. I left behind my headband.

Mr. Delta leans back in his seat, his cold eyes fixed on mine. "You failed on multiple counts. You didn't strike fast enough. You froze in the face of challenge." When he turns to my sister, only a fraction of the tension eases. "And Dolly, you failed too by saving Amy from the consequences of her stupidity."

Dolly's hands ball into fists. "But we completed the mission."

"Barely," Delta snaps, the word cutting like a blade. "I've already informed your father of the sub-par performance. You won't leave Three Fates until every mission you complete is flawless."

My stomach plummets at the implication of further ordeals. "But that's not fair."

Ignoring me, Delta turns to Dolly, his expression stern. "As a sole operative, your performance on its own was passable. You'll need to be stronger to compensate for your sister's weakness. Do you understand?"

She nods, her face set with determination. "Yes, sir."

"Dismissed."

Kappa steps forward, placing a comforting hand on Dolly's shoulder. "You did well. I know you'll do even better next time."

I trail after them into the hallway, my feet dragging. Failure hangs over my head like a dark cloud. I can't believe it's me who's screwed up. It's all my fault.

We reach Dolly's dorm, and Kappa opens the door, letting my sister in. "Good night, sweetheart."

When the door closes, she stares down at me, her features hardening. "Delta doesn't give second chances. Don't waste it."

I nod, my heart shattering. At this rate, we'll never see Mom and Dad again. Never meet my new baby brother. Pulling up my shoulders, I steel myself for more training, more missions.

Next time, I won't fail.

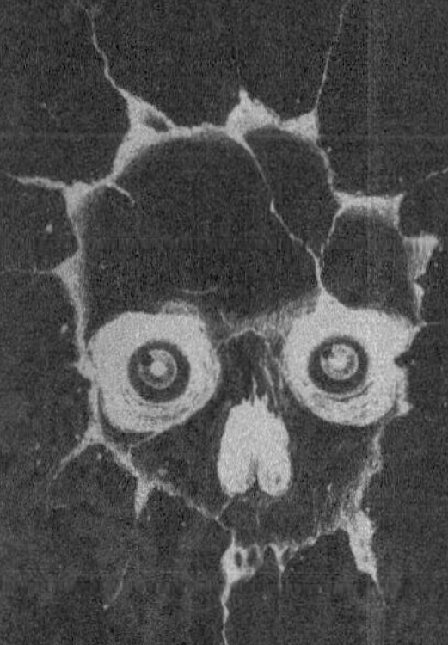

SIXTY-FIVE

XERO

I kneel beside Amethyst, my heart pounding as I check her pulse. She's breathing, but she's out cold. Each second feels like an eternity as I wait for her to wake up.

Camila crouches beside us, breathing hard. "Xero, I'm sorry."

"Don't." I squeeze my sister's arm. "This is what she wanted."

Turning my attention to Amethyst, I place a hand on her shoulder. The warmth of her skin reassures me that she's still with me. "Baby, can you hear me?"

Her curls have spilled loose, fanning around her beautiful face like a halo of darkness and light. The sight of her, even in this vulnerable state, takes my breath away. My heart squeezes. She's so brave, wanting to face her sister, but she's doing too much too soon.

Stirring, her lashes flutter. Then she gazes up at me through dilated pupils ringed with a tiny circle of green.

"Xero?" she whispers, her voice weak. The sound of my name on her lips is a lifeline.

I cup her cheek. "It's me. Are you alright?"

She nods, her eyes unfocused. "I had a new memory."

Exhaling my relief, I sit back on my heels. She tries to rise, but I push her back down to the mat. "Not yet. You can tell me about it while resting."

She inhales a deep, shuddering breath. "I remember some of what happened before the diary. Mostly the summer camp. That's where we first met Delta."

Her voice cracks, and I can feel the pain behind every word. I squeeze her hand, grounding her in the present. "You're safe now, Amethyst. He can't hurt you anymore."

"It was in a campus in the woods. He supervised our training and sent us out on missions."

A sharp breath whistles through my teeth. Camila gasps but remains silent. We've both picked apart the diary we received from the Salentino sisters. It's the most damning evidence we've had in years, indicating that Father didn't discontinue the Lolita assassins, but hearing that the events are true puts them into a horrifying new perspective.

"My dad..." She shakes off that thought. "My stepdad drove us to the Three Fates Boarding School. That's where we met Delta for the first time."

I listen to her story, my eyes widening as I piece together the fragments of her past. Every word she speaks is a knife to my heart. Father told the girls the same lie he told us to make their missions more palatable. The syringes never contained sedatives but poisons.

We boys at my underground facility had the luxury of injecting our targets as we walked past them in public. Lolitas had to enter their private spaces.

Fury pounds through my veins as Amethyst describes three assignments. Each one she recounts brings up a wave of anger, but I force myself to stay calm. The first was a dinner party the twins had to endure before they were taken upstairs to kill the hosts. The second was a house event where children were treated like party favors. They performed the third mission together, killing a high-ranking police officer.

I breathe hard, forcing myself to process my anger. Amethyst needs my support, not my rage. I can't let my emotions overshadow her need to be heard. I don't want any of my reactions to feel like judgment.

"Do you remember any landmarks from when you were at Three Fates?" Camila asks from my side.

Amethyst pauses for several heartbeats, her brow furrowing. "We passed the airport... I remember Dolly asking if Three Fates was overseas. When we were outside, we could see and hear planes landing and taking off."

I nod, processing this new detail. "That's good. It gives us a location to start with." I glance over at my sister, who's already messaging Tyler. "Anything else?"

She licks her lips, a nervous habit I've noticed before. "There was a water tower shaped like a kettle. And Dad... He had an assistant called Becky Taylor. He dumped our suitcases at her house by the airport when he drove us to Three Fates. On the way back, he picked them up."

Camila taps down the details.

"Thank you," I say, my chest tightening. The words feel inadequate for the gratitude and sorrow I feel for what the hell she's endured.

I squeeze her hand. "You're incredibly brave, little ghost. Thank you for sharing this with us."

Amethyst sits up, her eyes brightening with determination. "I want to continue sparring."

Seeing her push herself is like a knife to the chest. "You need to rest and recover."

"But fighting is the only thing that's brought back my memories," she says, her voice cracking.

The pain in her eyes tugs at my heart, making it hard to deny her. But I can't let her continue to get hurt. I need to find a safer alternative. "There are other ways to access your memories that don't involve getting knocked out. Do you want to talk to someone?"

She shakes her head and sighs, her lips tightening. "I'm sick of psychiatrists. Talking to Dr. Saint never got me anything but frustrated."

"Let's see Dr. Dixon. He's our Chief Medical Officer."

Camila leaves to help Tyler with the new leads, promising to keep me updated. I drive Amethyst through the tunnels to our infirmary. This is our most expensive safe house, equipped with operating theaters and state-of-the-art scanners. Thanks to my connections with the Moirai's support staff, we're always up to date with the latest medical advancements.

"Stay with me?" she asks as we take the stairs through the basement.

My gaze drops to her huge, green eyes, which shine with a vulnerability that makes me want to wrap her up in cotton wool. I reach out, taking her hand in mine, offering the comfort of my touch.

"Always," I say, my voice choked.

I stay with Amethyst throughout her MRI scan, neurological exam, and final toxicology screen. When Dr. Dixon gives her a clean bill of health, he advises against forcing new memories.

Amethyst frowns. "But I might remember another clue."

"You've given us enough," I say.

"Please, Xero."

I turn to Dr. Dixon, who sighs. "Ginkgo Biloba and Panax Ginseng can help with mental clarity. That's the best I can recommend to stimulate your memories."

"What about hypnosis?" she asks, her voice quickening with desperation.

I squeeze her hand. She's pushing herself too far. I can't let her get hurt on our account.

He rubs his chin. "The Moirai has a method for debriefing operatives' suppressed memories. It's intense and involves taking a large quantity of drugs before entering a white room. It's another form of torture, designed to unlock what's been repressed."

Her breath hitches, and her skin turns pale. "A white room... like a tent?"

My brow furrows, and several knots form in my gut. There's only one way she'd know about that technique.

The doctor leans forward, his eyes widening. "Is that familiar?"

"That's what Delta did to me," she whispers, her head dipping toward her chest. "I don't want to go through that again."

My blood boils with the overwhelming need for vengeance. I want to present Father's beaten and bound body to her in chains so she can work out every minute of trauma he made her suffer with rusty razor blades.

Squeezing her shoulder, I lean in to give her reassurance. "No one is going to force you into anything. You don't even need to take the herbs."

We leave the infirmary and drive back to the hideout through the darkened tunnels. My mind is in a turmoil, plagued by the torments Father made her suffer, both as a child and an adult.

I spent years wondering what happened to the Lolita assassins, only to fall in love with one. Where are the others, and can I save them when the one I have is still struggling?

Amethyst grabs my arm. "I need to erase Delta's touch," she says, her voice trembling. "It's like he's still here."

My chest burns with a mix of anger and sorrow. The thought of Father still infesting her is unbearable. "When we catch up with him, I'll let you spill his blood."

"That's not what I mean."

I turn to meet her green eyes, her features etched with pain. Her vulnerability in this moment is a raw wound that needs careful tending. I swallow hard, forcing my eyes on the tunnel ahead and school my features into a mask of calm.

"What do you need from me right now?" I ask, my voice steady.

"I need you inside me. That's the only thing that will make me feel clean."

Her plea slices through my chest, leaving me torn between desire and the need to protect her from herself. Touching her before she's ready will only deepen her wounds. I can't allow my need for her to cloud my judgment.

"Xero?"

"I won't cause you permanent harm," I murmur.

"I've faced worse," she counters. "I can handle this."

But I know she can't. Some of our female operatives who slept with men as part of their duties at the Moirai can't face the opposite sex. What Amethyst went through was brutal, nonconsensual, raw. She's already fresh from bringing up childhood wounds.

My protective instincts rear up, telling me to override her demands. I need to be sure she's not just pushing herself out of desperation. "How can you be ready for this after everything that's happened?"

"I have to be," she says, her voice firming. "I can't continue with these thoughts as my last memories of being with men."

"And the long-term impact? On you, on us?" I ask, my eyes searching hers for any sign of doubt.

"We'll figure it out," she mutters.

Guilt gnaws at the frayed edges of my conscience. If I have to think about those creeps, I'll tear off someone's skin. All that bull-shit I did to her in those first weeks after prison has weakened her mental state. Touching her now will only add me to a list of predatory bastards.

"I'm not about to take advantage of your vulnerability."

"You're helping me heal." She clings to my arm, her grip both a plea for help and a lifeline.

I take a deep breath, my resolve hardening. What am I really afraid of? Losing control? Breaking her trust? I'm better than that. I need to be strong for my little ghost. "One step at a time. Let's start with something simpler."

She nods, her breath quickening. "Like what?"

"If you can get into the tub and let me bathe you, then we can talk about taking the next step," I say.

She hesitates, her body stiffening. I peer at her through the corner of my eye, watching her determination morph into fear.

"Alright," she finally says, her voice faltering. "Let's have that bath."

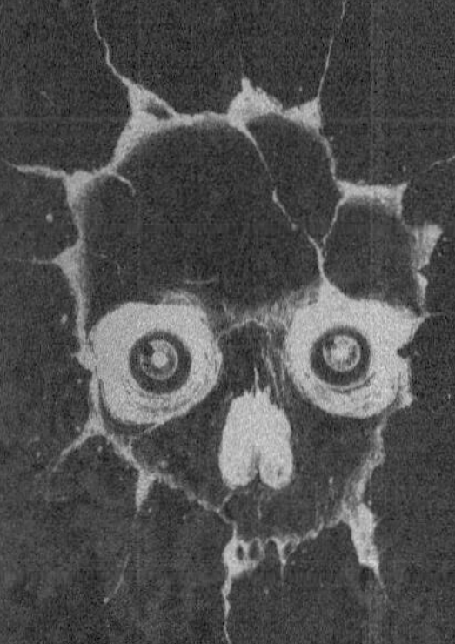

SIXTY-SIX

AMETHYST

I shift in the front seat of the cart, my throat tightening with dread. The tunnel walls rush past in a dizzying blur, and Xero's presence beside me is a heavy, palpable force. His silence is unnerving, each passing second amplifying the tension wrapping around my throat like a noose.

Of all the things Xero could have asked for, why a bath?

How the hell is he going to react to my scars? It's too late to back out. At best, any signs of skittishness will have him coddling me like I'm a broken toy. At worst, he'll decide I'm too tainted by his father and relegate me into his sister's care. Or move me into an apartment, so he won't have to see me as a constant reminder of his father's victory.

When we arrive at the hideout, he guides me to the changing area, where there's a robe in the closet. It's fluffy and long enough to cover the bulk of my lacerations. He places a kiss on my forehead and leaves for the bathroom, where I hear running water.

This is a test. If I can't withstand a simple bath, then it proves I'm still that broken, deluded woman he pulled out of the bus.

I can't let that happen.

He can't know I'm really that sniveling little girl everyone used as a pawn. If I'm ever going to face Dolly, then I'll have to push forward, get this over with so I can move on with my life.

With a glance over my shoulder to make sure he hasn't left the bathroom, I strip off my exercise clothes. By now, all traces of that concussion are gone. My gaze drops to the scars crisscrossing my skin, and I force back a wave of humiliation and fury.

Helplessness overwhelms my psyche. Limbs stiffening, I feel the slice of Delta's blade. Imaginary blood trickles down my skin, making me want to scream. I clench my teeth, forcing back the memories of Delta, of Dolly, of those leering scumbags.

One day, they'll all pay.

One day, it will be their blood coating my skin.

Turning my gaze back to the closet, I put on the robe and sigh as the soft fabric caresses my skin. I imagine my body unmarked, save for the scars I've had since I was ten. He already accepted those blemishes when we thought they came from the car crash. Picturing myself as whole is the only way I can face Xero.

As I walk to the bathroom on trembling legs, my mind drifts to Mom and her mental gymnastics. Those cuts on my back and stomach were the work of a disturbed little girl, and not a car accident. I never asked myself how a child could get thrown out of a windshield and not get a single scar on her face.

The bathroom is lit by candles, which cast a soft, warm glow on the tiled walls. Xero sits at the edge of the bathtub, testing the water temperature with his hand. Steam rises from its surface, filling my nostrils with the scent of lavender.

Our gazes lock as he rises off the ledge, making my steps falter.

He's breathtaking, bare-chested, with a tiny towel clinging precariously to his hips that barely conceals the outline of his cock.

My chest tightens, my skin prickles, and my pulse quickens. The fine hairs on the back of my neck stand on end. The air between us thickens, charged with an electric intensity that makes my heart race, making it impossible to look away.

What the hell was I thinking? I'm not ready to have sex.

Swaying on my feet, I tighten my grip on the robe, trying to steady my breath. Steam swirls throughout the room, wrapping around my body like restraints. My pulse races as I feel his eyes on me, my skin tingling under his gaze. The air grows thick with tension, making it impossible to breathe.

Xero's eyes soften. "Would you like some privacy?"

"What do you mean?" I blurt.

"Anything you want. I can leave you alone to get into the bath, leave you alone to bathe, or come in later to scrub your back."

The tension around my chest loosens, and air floods my lungs. "Is this a trick?"

He shakes his head. "You can even say no to the bath."

"And have you thinking I'm fragile?" I snap.

He raises a brow. "Amethyst."

"I want this." The words tumble from my lips before I can stop them.

He takes a step forward, making me flinch. Instead of approaching me, he walks toward the towel rail. Taking advantage of the opening, I rush behind him to the bath. My heart pounds as I slip off the robe and submerge myself in the warm water.

It sluices against my skin like a warm caress, encasing me in its floral fragrance. But I'm too busy staring at Xero's tattooed back to appreciate it fully.

He takes his time selecting the towels. I track the way he strokes the soft fabric before placing them on the counter. He peels open a bar of soap with the kind of loving caresses that make my heart flutter.

I lie back in the tub, wondering how it would feel to have those fingers on my flesh. As he continues fondling the inanimate objects, my skin aches for his touch. Steam rises, creating a cocoon of lavender that soothes my frayed nerves.

"Ready, little ghost?" he asks with his back still turned.

"Yes," I squeak.

He turns around, and our eyes meet for a brief, electrifying moment. The intensity in his gaze makes my spine shiver with both fear and anticipation. I grip the edge of the tub, trying to steady the whirlwind of emotions.

The room shrinks, the air thickens, and the world condenses to Xero, me, and the frantic beat of my heart.

When he finally breaks eye contact, I drop my gaze to his tattooed chest, and my lips part with a tiny gasp. It's silly because I've committed the prison photos to memory. We've seen each other naked hundreds of times, but everything feels new.

It's like I emerged from that asylum as a different woman, still shedding layers of who I used to be, discovering who I am now in the heat of his gaze.

"Are you alright?" he asks with a frown.

I slide beneath the water, submerging myself to the neck. "It's my scars. They're ugly."

The word 'ugly' hangs in the air like a storm cloud, threatening to rain on what should be a special moment. Then my scars throb. I can't tell if the pain is phantom or if the memories of getting them have crystallized into my flesh.

Xero's chest heaves, and he closes the distance between us to cup my cheek with his warm fingers. Tears sting my eyes, and I lower my lashes. In a minute he'll realize I'm a burden. Then it will be just like it was with Mom. Xero will make an excuse to move me away, and all I'll have of him are memories.

"Amethyst, look at me," he says.

I force our gazes to meet.

His pale eyes lock onto mine with a tenderness that makes my breath catch. I search his face for traces of impatience, but all I see is unwavering love.

"Nothing about you could ever be ugly. Not your past, not your trauma, and certainly not your body."

My shoulders rise to my ears. "You haven't seen it yet."

"Doesn't matter. Those scars tell your story, just as much as Rapunzelita. They're proof of your strength and your survival."

"You don't have to say that," I mutter.

"Do you know why I replied to your letter above all others?"

I shake my head, my curls bouncing, my gaze dropping to the water.

"You said you were also a killer. That's something a man like me can't resist."

"I thought it was because of the scented pages," I mutter and peer up at him through my lashes.

He grins, his blue eyes sparkling. "True, but it isn't your heavenly scent that keeps me addicted. It's your resilience. You're a scarred warrior. My other half."

My throat tightens, and my gaze travels over the tattoos adorning his chest. "All I see is perfection."

"Give me your hand."

"Why?"

"Because you need to feel my scars."

I sit up a little, pulling my arm out of the water. Xero takes my fingers and traces them over his temple, letting me feel an invisible ridge.

"Two boys knocked me off my feet in the school hallway to impress my older brothers. They kicked me there until I fell unconscious."

"Xero, I'm so sorry—"

"Save your pity for those bastards who hurt you. I plan on keeping them alive long enough to regret being born."

He moves my fingers into his hairline, behind his ear, down his chest, telling me the story of every scar. My chest burns once more with fury at how Delta could have engineered Xero's miserable childhood. He ruined so many of us, including me.

"It wasn't your fault," I murmur. "You were at those people's mercy and did everything to survive."

He gives me a crooked smile. "I can say the same to you."

That's when it finally sinks in. We both have so much in common that it's uncanny. Both former child assassins. Both with siblings who doled out unimaginable betrayal. Both equally scarred. Both looking to wash away our pasts with blood.

Delta has already taken so much. I can't let him taint my relationship with Xero. I won't let him take my happiness.

Gathering all my courage in a deep inhale, I rise from the water. My hands drop from my chest, exposing my scars. Cool air swirls around my heated skin, making it pucker, and trepidation skitters through the lacerations.

Xero steps back, his eyes fixed on mine.

"You can look," I say.

He hesitates for several heartbeats before allowing his gaze to sweep down my body. I search his features for any hint of revulsion. Instead, he exhales the longest sigh. It's sorrow, acceptance, and shared pain.

"All I see is the woman I love." His words wrap around me like a warm blanket, and his eyes meet mine again. "But every man who ever touched you will die screaming."

My heart flutters. I picture the two of us maiming and killing Barrett, Locke, and Seth, saving Delta and Dolly for the grand finale.

"Come into the water with me," I murmur.

Xero loosens the towel around his waist, and my heart lurches. I don't dare to look down to see if he has an erection. He enters the tub behind me and pulls me down, so I'm sitting on his lap.

The heat of his body envelops mine, melting away my tension. I relax against his broad chest, close my eyes, and whisper, "Wash away his touch."

"I will never see you as tainted or dirty," he murmurs against my ear.

"Xero—"

"But I will replace his touch with mine, only when you're ready."

He picks up the bar of soap and rubs it between his hands, creating a thick lather. Smoothing his sudsy palms over my neck, he massages the tight muscles with strong fingers. I moan against his touch, wanting more.

Maybe I should tell him I'm ready to go further. Maybe I should shut the hell up and allow things to unfurl.

When he washes my arms, his fingers graze my breasts. His touch is delicate, reminding me of how Delta handled my body when slicing into my skin. The memory rises to the surface, and I cringe against the sting of the blade.

Panic claws at my mind. Tears build behind my eyes. I hold my breath, not wanting Xero to notice, but it's like holding back a dam. As his hands glide down my belly, I release a sob.

Xero's strong arms encircle my waist, tethering me to the present. "It's okay, little ghost. I'm here to catch you when you fall."

Grief spills from my chest like a torrent, bringing up the

buried memories that I'd dissociated. Memories that the hallucinated Xero locked up until I was ready to cope resurface with vivid intensity. The bathroom fades away, replaced by the asylum's bright lights. My muscles tense. My breath quickens. My pulse pounds in my ears to the beat of my panic.

"You're safe now. I'm right here. Breathe with me." Xero's voice is the anchor I need to process that memory.

As I force the breaths in and out, Xero assures me that I'm beautiful, I'm strong, I'm a survivor. I shatter in his arms, only for him to hold together my broken pieces.

I focus on his voice, his calm presence, his unwavering support. It's pulling me back to the present, reminding me I'm safe. Panic ebbs away, replaced by a deep sense of relief. I'm not in Delta's clutches anymore. I'm with Xero.

"That was so intense," I say, my voice trembling.

"Want to tell me about it?" he asks.

I blow out a long breath. "Give me a minute."

He presses a kiss on my temple. "Take your time."

The warmth of the bath returns to my awareness, as does Xero's strong body and steady guidance. I melt against his body in a puddle of gratitude.

After the bath, Xero helps me out and wraps my body in warm towels. He places me on a stool and kneels at my feet, drying me off like I'm his most precious possession.

He gazes up at me and smiles. "I'm so proud of you."

"Thank you for helping me," I murmur. "And for not pushing for more."

"I won't touch you like that until you're ready," he says.

"How will you know that?"

He brings his mouth down to my foot, his lips brushing my big toe in a kiss that sends sparks of pleasure up my inner thigh and into my core. My breath catches, and I squeeze my thighs together, trying to contain the surge of desire. Our eyes meet, and the air crackles with electricity. His gaze darkens, pulling me deeper into the moment, making it impossible to think of anything else but how much I want him.

"I won't fuck you until you beg for it," he says, his deep voice making my nerves sing.

My clit swells, and the pulse between my thighs pounds. I part my lips to ask for more, but a buzzing sound breaks the tension. I flinch backward. "What's that?"

Xero's features harden. "An update from Tyler about your father's assistant." He turns toward a panel behind the counter and says, "Report."

"We've found several women aged thirty and above named Rebecca Taylor living in New Jersey." Tyler's voice comes through a speaker. "We need Amethyst to identify them,".

Xero looks back at me with furrowed brows. "Are you up for this?"

I swallow hard, the calmness from the bath evaporating. "Yes, let's go."

We move out of the bathroom and into the living space, passing the bed and sofas to reach the workstation. The computers line the desk, each with blank screens. My heart stutters as I sit on the chair with Xero holding my shoulder, keeping me rooted to the present. I shouldn't be nervous. Becky was always nice to Dolly and me, yet there's a part of my mind that wonders if she knew Dad was a trafficker.

DMV photos pop up onscreen, each displaying different women. I scan images of so many with variations of Dad's assistant's name. Each face blurs into the next until I stop at one.

My breath catches. She's a round-faced woman with pink cheeks and frizzy auburn hair. It's parted in the center but could rival Relaney's blonde afro.

"That's her," I rasp.

"Rebecca Taylor, Apartment 5B, 432 Elm Street, Carmel, New Jersey," Tyler says.

"What else do you have on her?" Xero asks.

"One second."

The line goes silent. I stare at Becky's photo, remembering our last encounter. Dolly and I sat in the back seat of Dad's car while he parked outside her house. Becky came to the door with our cases and several boxes of arts and crafts. I didn't notice the car that pulled up behind us until Kappa, our instructor—who Mom called Charlotte in the diary—stepped out. She walked past us to Becky, took the items, and loaded them into the trunk of Kappa's car.

"Are you okay?" Xero asks.

I inhale a deep breath, trying to shove away a slew of memories. "Becky was really nice. She once took Dolly and me to volunteer at a shelter and got us to hand out cereal bars to the homeless kids."

"You remember that?" he asks, his brows rising.

My hand finds the back of my neck, and I chuckle. "You'd think memories would just download like files, but it's more like fishing them out of a black hole."

The corners of his eyes crinkle. "What else do you remember?"

Before I can answer, Tyler's voice fills the speaker. "Rebecca Taylor works for the Sacred Hearts Adoption Agency, run by a woman named Charlotte Banks."

The name hits me like a punch to the gut. We both shoot to our feet. "Charlotte?"

"Show us a picture of her," Xero growls, his voice tight.

Seconds later, Tyler pulls up a photo of a beautiful blonde with her hair swept up in a chignon. She smiles into the camera, but there's no mistaking those cold eyes. Memories crash through my mind like a tsunami, making my eyes sting. Seeing Charlotte brings back a torrent of terror that's never left my body, even when I had no memory of her cruelty.

"That's her," I choke out. "The instructor who always praised Dolly and not me. The nanny who haunted my nightmares and tried to drive me insane. The bitch who murdered my baby brother."

As I hyperventilate, Xero holds my shoulders. "We'll get her. She'll pay for everything she did to you and your family."

I stare into space, trapped in nightmare after hellish nightmare. Somewhere on the edge of my consciousness, Tyler asks for instructions. Xero demands more information on Charlotte and her adoption agency. The words filter through the fog, but I'm consumed by a burning need for revenge.

SIXTY-SEVEN

XERO

Just as we make a breakthrough with the bath, Amethyst's childhood monster appears and hampers our progress.

She freezes, her eyes turning glassy. I place a hand on her shoulder, and she snaps out of her fugue with a clap of anger. Her fury fills the room, crackling like a live wire. It blazes in her green eyes, burning brighter than the night she attacked me in her sleep.

"Amethyst?" I grip her shoulders, concern tightening my chest, but she shoves me aside with surprising strength.

Fists clenched, she paces, each step radiating barely contained violence. "That bitch is still alive," she hisses, her voice filled with venom. "I want to go to her house now and cut her into pieces."

Pain twists inside my gut like a coiled serpent, each movement constricting my breath. I would give my little ghost the world, but Charlotte is a valuable lead. "Amethyst," I murmur, my voice low. "We can't rush. She knows the facility's location."

She stops, her wild eyes locking onto mine, blazing with rage, desperation, and grief. "She killed my baby brother," she screams. "Right in front of me."

Guilt gnaws at my conscience for putting the mission before her immediate revenge. I can't let that deter us from our goal. Stepping closer, I bear the intensity of her emotions and grasp her by the arms. "You remember the Three Fates Therapeutic Boarding School? That facility might still contain children groomed to become assassins."

Blinking, she releases tears and stares up at me through glistening eyes. Breathing hard through her parted lips, she whispers, "What?"

"We need to rescue those girls," I say.

It takes a moment for her to register my words before her defiance crumples into devastation. She collapses against my chest, her body shaking with sobs. "You must hate me for being so selfish."

I wrap my arms around her back, holding her so tightly that her anguish bleeds into my heart. "I could never hate you." I punctuate the words with a kiss on her temple. "You're brave, resilient, and the strongest woman I know."

We stand together in silence, our hearts beating in sync. I long to assure her we'll take down our enemies, one by one, but promises only stretch so far. Charlotte is within reach, but capturing her now risks alerting the facility she's been compromised. I can't jeopardize Father and the instructors moving the children elsewhere.

"Give me three days," I murmur into her damp curls. "Three days of tailing her. If she doesn't lead us to the facility, we'll raid her home."

Amethyst pulls back, meeting my gaze with watery eyes. "Promise?"

"I swear it. Let me give Tyler the order."

She nods.

Turning back to the computer, I send out a string of instructions. Tyler will dig up every piece of information about Charlotte Banks. His team will station devices in her neighborhood in preparation for the raid. The Spring brothers will infiltrate her street and keep an eye on her movements. Jynxson will attach tracking devices to her vehicle.

"Three days," she repeats.

I inhale deeply, feeling the weight of my promise. "Yes, three days." I guide her to the kitchenette, hoping to ground her in normality. "Let's make an early dinner."

Amethyst sits at the counter in silence. Sometimes, the best medicine is time. I leave her to process the recent influx of memories and the return of her childhood abuser. After finding the right recipe, I open the refrigerator and gather butter, eggs, pancetta, pecorino and parmesan cheese.

"When did you get fresh ingredients?" she asks.

"Our maintenance staff supplies groceries to occupied hideouts." I fill a saucepan with water and set it on the stove.

"Did they teach you to cook at the Moirai academy?" she asks.

Chuckling, I extract a knife and slice open the wrappings. "They taught me to follow instructions. After months of cleaning up after their assassinations, recipes are child's play. Want to help?"

She nods, a tentative smile breaking through the gloom. I slide over the knife and pancetta. "Dice this into small cubes."

As she works, I grate the cheese, crack the eggs into a bowl, and whisk them until they're fluffy. Amethyst opens the spaghetti and places it into the boiling water. I add salt to the pasta and black pepper to the eggs.

She crushes the garlic and fries the pancetta without prompting. I glance at the recipe and frown.

"It says two cloves."

"You're making carbonara, right?" she asks.

"How did you know?"

"It's obvious from the ingredients," she replies with a smirk.

"I could have been making Pasta Alfredo."

"There's no cream." She adds a block of butter to the pancetta without measuring.

"This recipe is ruined," I mutter, unable to hide a smile.

"It's going to taste amazing."

Warmth fills my chest as I grab the plates and set them on the counter. Amethyst is making more progress than I ever expected. For a moment, I'm awestruck by her resilience. Then, reality hits me—being abducted by Father and her sister isn't her first encounter with trauma, or even her second. This time, though, she'll face it head-on and retain her memories. She'll emerge stronger.

"I can't believe how much we have in common," she says, her eyes misting.

"Kindred spirits," I reply, drawing closer.

My heart pounds with unwanted intensity. It's too early for us to have this kind of moment. It stretches for several heartbeats, charged with desire. Every instinct screams at me to close the distance, to taste her soft lips and make her forget her past, but no amount of kissing can erase the deluge of new memories. They might even set back her progress.

But then she blinks, breaking the spell, and turns back to the stove. "So, tell me about the facility you lived in before the academy."

Disappointment clogs my throat at the abrupt shift. I swallow hard and push the feeling aside. I tell her about the exercise drills, the bunks, and the other boys. She laughs when I recount the stories of how Jynxson used to get on my nerves, rearranging my possessions until I had to rearrange his face.

"What did the facility look like?" she asks.

"Underground, with fluorescent lights, concrete walls, and a rec room that served gigantic meals. It was in the forest. I only caught glimpses of trees when they transported me to missions."

Silence stretches, broken only by the sound of bubbling water. I glance up to find her staring.

"What?"

"Do you think it's the same building?" she asks, her voice tentative.

"It's possible." I pick up my phone and scroll to an image of Father with all the instructors and boys and set it on the table. "Do you remember any of them?"

Amethyst expands the image with her fingers and studies each face. "Only Delta. I'm not sure about the rest."

"Don't push yourself. We'll figure out the truth when we get the location from Charlotte."

She hums.

"Do you want me to bring in Becky?"

"What if it makes Charlotte suspicious?" Her expression hardens, exposing a flicker of rage. "We should wait. Becky was nice, but if she knew the adoption agency was trafficking children, she'll die like Charlotte."

I smile, my chest swelling with admiration and pride. "You've come a long way from the woman who couldn't face torture."

"You're talking about the human centipede," she says, her eyes rolling. "When I get hold of Charlotte, there'll be no silly games. I'll keep her alive and in constant pain until she's the one hallucinating."

My heart flutters. "That's my girl."

The next days pass in a blur of sparring, shared meals, and shared baths. Amethyst allows me to massage her back and pepper her neck with kisses. Every night, she wakes up screaming, remembering a new sick method of torture, courtesy of Charlotte. It takes several moments to reassure her she's safe before she nestles against me and recounts the nightmare.

Tyler's research on Charlotte is extensive. She took over the adoption agency shortly after Lyle Bishop died. Since then, she's ostensibly devoted her days to removing children from the streets and putting them in permanent homes.

The team cross-referenced images of adoptees from Charlotte's database with movie stills from X-Cite media. It's hard to tell because of the age difference, but Tyler thinks there's a pipeline from the agency to Father's facility to dying on camera.

That's probably what happened with Dolly, except she fought back. Surviving on camera brought her popularity and kept her alive. Instead of directing her rancor where it belongs, her resentment festered and turned toward Amethyst.

I almost understand. Father has a way of brainwashing children until they don't know what's right or wrong. At one point, he got me thinking my mother's death was a mercy killing. But that doesn't mean I'll show Dolly clemency.

But the end of the three days, Charlotte doesn't lead us to the facility, so it's time to move out.

With Tyler's help, we cut off the power and approach the building under the cover of darkness. Infiltrating a townhouse the size of Charlotte's requires more finesse than force. Amethyst is at my side, clad in night-vision goggles and bullet-proof armor. We don't expect a welcome party, but I won't put my little ghost at risk.

We enter through a basement conveniently linked to the sewers and make our way through the ground floor. It's a modest residence for someone who peddles human lives. The Spring brothers reported that she returned from work hours ago and her lights have been off for long enough to assume she's asleep.

We pass by a study containing a filing cabinet and a computer I itch to explore, but our immediate target is Charlotte.

There'll be time to come back for the other information after capturing her treacherous carcass.

After ascending the stairs, we head down the hallway to her bedroom. Passages from the diary return to my mind with renewed horror. What kind of operative accepts such a heinous mission? I can't wait to watch Amethyst slay her demon.

"Stay back," I whisper into her ear.

She nods, her breath quickening as she grips my hand.

Movement sounds from the other side of the door, and I fling it open. A streak of blonde hair flashes as a petite figure disappears into a closet.

I charge after her with Amethyst on my heels. As the door swings shut behind us, the room fills with the sound of faint clicking. I kick the closet, but it's reinforced.

"Fuck," I snarl.

"What is it?" Amethyst asks, her voice rising with alarm.

"She has a panic room."

Beams of red light cut through the darkness, crisscrossing the entire space. Alarm shoots through my gut. I leap on top of Amethyst to shield her before the room erupts into chaos.

SIXTY-EIGHT

AMETHYST

I freeze, my eyes widening as beams of red light target my chest. Before I can even register the ambush, Xero shoves me down. I hit the rug with his larger body crushing mine, then my ears ring with the roar of automated gunfire.

My heart thrashes. All the air escapes my lungs. Bullets fly from wall to wall, and Xero flinches.

On instinct, I rear up, but he presses my head into the carpet. "Stay down."

My breath shallows. "Xero, you're hurt."

He tenses, but neither confirms nor denies. His breath is hot against my neck, making me shiver. I can't tell if it's out of pressure or pain, but we can't continue to lie here, exposed.

Staring out into the dark, I eye the room for shelter or escape. The bed lies a few feet ahead. Its mattress is the only thing that isn't exploding. I elbow Xero in the ribs and yell, "Hide under there."

"I'm not leaving you exposed," he snarls.

Desperation fuels my next words. "Then we move together. Under the bed, now!"

With a grunt, he crawls across the floor, covering every inch of my body like a shield. Bullets whizz past, embedding into the wall and nightstand. We make it to the bed just as a round hits the nearby rug.

"Did you think you could break into my house, assholes?" A female voice sounds over the speakers.

Her words trigger a slew of fresh memories, making every fine hair on my body stand on end. It's the bitch who came to my bedroom every night, telling me to kill my baby brother. Some days, she'd appear as a wraith. Others, a disembodied voice.

Once again, Charlotte has gotten the upper hand.

"Ignore her," Xero rumbles, shoving me further under the bed. I close my eyes, trying to shut her out, but the memories keep coming more vividly than a dream.

One time, she sat on my chest, crushing my lungs until I passed out. When I woke up the next morning, my mind was filled with images of her pale face, her blood-spattered gown, her red fingers. Mom looked around my room and told me it was a nightmare, but I could still feel the lingering pressure on my ribs.

Another voice fills the Bluetooth in my ear. It's Tyler's and he sounds urgent. "Shutters just fell across every door and window in the building. What's happening?"

"Charlotte's placed us in lockdown," Xero snarls. "She's in a panic room, attacking us with remote-controlled weapons."

"We turned the power off. She might have a generator." Tyler replies.

"Or she's siphoning power from a neighbor like a parasite," I say, remembering how Charlotte used to cozy up with Dad when Mom was upstairs resting.

Xero snorts. "If you can't shut her down, we'll expire long before she runs out of ammunition."

Bullets pierce the mattress and hit the metal bed frame. How the hell can anyone be so calm when we're stuck in a killing room? Xero might be protecting me, but how long will his armor continue to protect him?

"Give me a few minutes. Let me override the lockdown," Tyler says.

"No time. Activate the EMP."

"But that will fry our tech," Tyler says.

"Then protect as much of it as you can. Start the countdown."

Xero plucks my night vision goggles off my head, along with the attached Bluetooth, and pulls the comms device from my jacket. "Stick these in your left pocket. It's the only one that's shielded."

With trembling fingers, I do as I'm told and place a hand over that pocket for extra protection. Xero shifts on top of me, moving his devices. Seconds later, my ears fill with a high-pitched ringing, and then the bullets stop.

We slump at the sudden stillness, both releasing identical exhales. The next few heartbeats stretch out like minutes. Our breathing synchronizes, and the butterflies in my chest flutter. Knowing he would sacrifice his life to save mine does strange things to my heart.

When he rolls off my back with a soft grunt, I already miss his comforting weight.

"Are you okay?" I whisper, patting him down for wounds.

He catches my hand, his touch infusing me with a jolt of electricity, and brings my knuckles to his lips. "I'm fine."

"But you flinched."

"My armor absorbed the bullet, but not the impact. How are you holding up?"

I gulp. My heart is racing, I can barely breathe, but I'm not about to add to his worries. "This is still less terrifying than my last memory of Charlotte. Are you sure you're okay?"

"Worried about me?" he asks, his voice lightening. I don't need the night vision goggles to tell that he's smirking.

Heat rises to my cheeks. The fear of losing him was a knot in my chest, tightening with every flying bullet. "Of course, I worry. Who else would keep me warm at night?"

He leans in, pressing a quick kiss to my lips. The contact is brief, but it leaves me breathless, sending a flush of sensation low in my belly.

"Let's capture Charlotte. Then I'll keep you warm all night long."

Heat spreads to my core, awakening parts of me I thought were long dead. The muffled sound of crashing has me jolting back to the present, and I crawl out from under the bed and slip on my night vision goggles.

Charlotte's room is a mess of bullet holes and debris. The rug we lay on now has a hole in its middle and the mattress we hid beneath is cratered. I glance at the metal door leading to her panic room, which is unsurprisingly intact.

"What are we going to do?" I ask.

Xero reaches into his backpack and pulls out an ax. It's a lightweight, titanium model with an edge that looks sharp enough to split a hair.

"We're going to get her out," he snarls, the resolve in his voice sending a thrill down my spine.

"What if she's armed?"

He flashes me a grin. "I have you to watch my back."

Before I can react, he moves to the door and swings the ax. I unholster the pistol with trembling fingers, wondering if his confidence in me is misplaced. I'm about to confront a demon of my past.

What if I freeze?

Xero hacks at the door with the ax like he's auditioning for a part in *The Shining,* and I ready the gun. The moment he penetrates the metal, I'll be there to shoot Charlotte before she has the chance to retaliate.

I adjust my goggles, letting the Bluetooth slip back in my ear. The volume is quiet, but Tyler's voice screams through the headset, "She's escaped! There's a convoy of trucks approaching. Evacuate, evacuate!"

Alarm kicks me in the gut, sending my pulse ratcheting up to a hundred. "Xero, we need to go. Charlotte's already left."

He whirls around. "What?"

"Camila's giving chase," Jynxson's voice resounds through the device.

"Fuck!" Xero rushes to the door leading to the hallway, attacking it with frenzied swipes of the ax. The metal buckles under his furious assault, leaving massive dents.

Three swings later, the door crashes onto the floor, and we rush through the hallway and down the stairs. Shutters cover every opening, enclosing us in the dark. We continue down to the basement, toward a vent leading to the sewer, when Xero's feet skid.

"Change of plan," he snarls.

"Why?" I peek out behind him.

Lurking on the floor is a device the size of a cell phone, flashing with a countdown from 49 seconds.

My heart skips a beat, fear clawing at my insides. "Is that a—"

"An explosive she activated when evacuating the house?" he growls.

"Shit."

Xero grabs my arm and spins me around, sending me racing ahead back up the stairs.

"Head for the front door. Now!" he roars.

Panic punches me in the chest, propelling my movements. I thunder up the steps to the ground floor. Xero barks orders at Tyler, who says something about the EMP blast taking out the remote-control bomb he planted around the perimeter.

We're trapped. Trapped in a house about to explode. Xero will die, never reaching his goal, and Dolly, Charlotte, and Delta will go unpunished.

We reach the front door, and my last hope shatters as Xero's ax fails to make a dent. Cursing, he rushes into the living room to hack at the window shutters.

I stand in the hallway, paralyzed by terror. My skin breaks out in a cold sweat. We have less than thirty seconds left before that bomb detonates.

"Tyler," I stutter into the Bluetooth. "Can one of your team fly over a grenade?"

"Affirmative. Stand back from the front door. Drone incoming. Ten... Nine... Eight."

"Amethyst!" Xero charges out of the room, scoops me off my feet, dives into the kitchen, and slams me against the wall. His large body covers mine completely, a solid shield against the impending explosion. His breath is hot and ragged against my ear, mingling with the acrid scent of gunfire and fear.

"Four... Three... Two..."

An explosion rips through the house with a deafening boom. Debris flies from the walls as a shockwave rattles the floor. Plaster and dust rain down on us like it's Armageddon.

As I'm reeling from the impact, Xero picks me up again and launches us both through the smoky hole. The night air hits me like a punch, but I barely have time to register the change in atmosphere before we're moving again.

Xero picks up speed, clinging to me like his life depends on it. We race down the street, passing houses, trees, and cars that whip by in a dizzying frenzy. My heart pounds so hard in my ears that it muffles the second explosion.

Fire brightens the sky, followed by a gust of heat that knocks Xero off his feet. He dives behind a truck, cradling me so tightly that I'm at risk of suffocating before the bomb can do its work. My breaths come in shallow gasps, my heart hammering a furious rhythm against my ribs.

Sirens blare. People scream. Car alarms ring. The toxic stench of smoke fills the air. A vehicle screeches toward us in reverse. Its back door swings open, revealing Jynxson.

"Get in!" he shouts from the driver's seat, his face illuminated by the horrifying glow of the fire.

Xero rises on shaky legs and tosses me into the vehicle, climbing in as the tires screech away from the scene.

He grabs me by the throat, his grip tight but not threatening. "Amethyst," he snarls through gritted teeth, scanning my face with frantic eyes. "Never do that again."

But I saved us, didn't I?

My lips part with a protest, but he silences me with a kiss.

SIXTY-NINE

XERO

If I don't kiss Amethyst, I'll throttle her for interfering.

We were on the brink of escaping. I'd just created a hole in the shutters when she ordered the explosions.

Sure, her move was effective, but it was also premature and reckless. We had seconds to spare and could have escaped through the window before the bomb in the basement detonated, but Amethyst had to jump the proverbial gun.

She tenses beneath my lips, and for a moment, I forget she's fragile. Not only traumatized from being assaulted at the asylum, but from resurfaced memories, each one a raw nerve, pulsing with excruciating pain. I draw back, needing to erase the unwanted touch, but her arms encircle my shoulders, drawing me closer.

Her lips are tentative, soft, yet they ignite a fire that I've been trying to keep banked. The truck rumbles down the road, making a sharp turn that knocks us both into its metal wall, but I barely notice our surroundings.

"What was that for?" she asks, her voice breathy against my lips.

"I almost lost you," I snarl. "We could have gotten out seconds before the explosion if you hadn't interfered."

She gazes up at me through dilated pupils, looking so vulnerable and needy I almost forget my train of thought.

"But I saved us. I couldn't leave you to die in a burning house again."

I stiffen, my anger replaced by surprise. I hadn't expected her to bring up that past, the one we'd both agreed to bury and forget.

When she grips the lapels of my bullet-proof jacket, pulling me closer, heat rushes to my cock. Who am I to argue when I've brought out her protective instincts? Every fiber of me roars to claim her—to take what's mine. To erase Father's touch with mine exactly as she demanded, but a bump in the road breaks me out of those thoughts.

I'm about to pull back from the kiss when her teeth sink into my bottom lip. The sharp burst of pain has my knees buckling as all sensation rushes south. I twine my fingers into her curls, holding her in place as our tongues twist with desperate need.

"Stop fucking about," Jynxson snaps, his voice cutting through the haze. "There's a convoy of attackers up our ass. Xero, man the drones."

With a groan, I tear myself away from my little ghost, my gaze lingering on the soft swell of her mouth. Her cheeks are flushed, and she's breathing hard through parted lips, her eyes darkening with desire.

"We're going to finish that kiss," I growl, forcing myself to resist the pull.

Her eager nod sends a jolt of anticipation to my throbbing cock. I drag my feet to the console just as bullets hit the side of our truck. Jynxson swerves to avoid more incoming fire, making the tires screech.

Amethyst falls into the seat beside me and fastens her belt. On-screen, an armored truck chases us through a country road bordered by fields. Dust kicks up in a thick cloud behind us, obscuring part of our view, but not enough to hide the persistent bastards.

"Report," I command, fingers flying across the laptop keyboard.

The drone feed comes to life, displaying a bird's-eye view of our surroundings. Its thermal imaging picks up heat signatures inside a trio of pursuing vehicles. The front one has three individuals leaning out of the windows, shooting at us, while a fourth drives.

"There's another truck chasing Tyler and his team," Jynxson replies. "They're fending off their attackers with drones."

"Damn it," I mutter, adjusting the drone's altitude for a better angle. "And the Spring Brothers?"

"They're pursuing Camila who went after Charlotte."

"Any updates from her?" I ask, directing the drone to zoom in on our pursuers' engine.

"Charlotte is driving toward Courtland Bridge. She could be leading them into an ambush," Jynxson reports, his voice tense.

"Cut her off before she gets to her destination," I snarl, locking the drone's target. "Even if that means crashing into her from behind."

"Copy that."

Switching to manual control, I align the targeting system with our attacker's hood. With a click of a key, the drone releases a burst of small charges. The screen lights up with the explosion, debris flying as the lead truck swerves and crashes into a ditch.

"Direct hit!" Jynxson shouts, but there's no time for relief.

Amethyst's eyes are glued to the screen, her breath coming in shallow gasps. The truck lurches as Jynxson makes a sharp turn, trying to shake off the remaining pursuers. I glance at her, my heart pounding not just from destroying our enemies but from the promise reflected in her gaze.

The second truck rams us from the back, making us jerk to the side. I maneuver the drone towards the next target, releasing another barrage of explosives. Jynxson speeds ahead, leaving them in flames.

Up ahead, the road narrows, lined with thick trees. Headlights emerge from the darkness on a collision course. Jynxson swerves, narrowly avoiding a crash. After deploying a drone against the third vehicle, I send another ahead to scan for obstacles. It looks like we're clear.

"Are we safe?" Amethyst asks, her voice trembling.

I turn to meet her eyes, letting her fingers intertwine with mine. "Eager for that kiss?"

She whacks me on the arm, her smile intoxicating.

Camila's voice sounds over the comms. "Xero, Charlotte just crashed into a tree."

"Approach with caution. It could be a trap." I sit back in my seat, my lips quirking. As a former instructor, Charlotte can definitely lead us to the facility's location. We're baby steps away from catching up with Father.

Amethyst squeezes my hand. "Why are you smiling?"

My smile morphs into a grin. Kissing Amethyst might have to wait a little longer. If her vengeance on that crew member is anything to go by, Charlotte might not survive long enough to regret her actions.

"I can't wait to see you take care of Charlotte."

An hour later, after administering basic first aid and cutting the tracking devices from Charlotte's limp body, we move her into an interrogation truck. As a precautionary measure, we've extracted all her teeth. They now reside in a ditch, miles away from where she crashed.

She sits on a chair welded to the metal floor, her mouth a gory mess. Her ankles and wrists are shackled, rendering her completely immobile.

I lean against the wall, watching Amethyst approach her with the knife. My little ghost stands proud despite the emotions bubbling beneath the surface as she faces her former abuser.

She backhands Charlotte hard across the face with a force that makes the woman's head snap to the side. The blonde jerks awake, her eyes wide with fear.

"Charlotte Banks. Or should I say, Kappa," Amethyst sneers.

Recognition flickers across the blonde's features. She breathes hard, her face paling.

"You remember me?" Amethyst asks.

Charlotte coughs up a mouthful of blood. "I don't..." she slurs, the words garbled by the mess we've made of her mouth. "I don't know what you're—"

Amethyst cuts her off with a slash across the face. "Don't lie to me, Kappa."

Charlotte blinks, trying to focus. "Dolly?"

My little ghost flashes her teeth and slaps her again with more force. Blood flies out of the older woman's mouth, staining her chest.

"Amy," Amethyst snarls, her voice dripping with venom.

Realization finally dawns on Charlotte's features. Her eyes widen, and her face leeches of color. I nod, satisfied. She's starting to understand the depth of her predicament.

"Amy... You've got to understand. I was a victim, just like you. I was under orders when I did those things. It's haunted me every day. I didn't mean it. Delta would have killed me if I'd refused. I was a recruit, just like you and your sister."

I frown, my gaze bouncing to Amethyst. Will she show Charlotte any compassion?

Child assassins follow orders, yes, but Charlotte was an adult during the events of the diary. By then, she knew the implications of that mission. Charlotte should have chosen to die rather than terrorize an innocent child and murder an infant.

Breath quickening, I wait for Amethyst's response. Her jaw tightens. Her features flicker with the resurfacing of old wounds. The rawness of her emotions tugs at my heart. I remain silent, unwilling to intervene. If Amethyst forgives Charlotte, I will continue the interrogation.

Amethyst turns to me, and our eyes lock. Her pretty features contort in a pained expression of indecision. She's torn between her sense of morality and her desire for revenge.

I ache to tell her it's alright. That she doesn't need to go ahead with the interrogation. I love her the way she is.

The sound of her fist smashing into Charlotte's wounded mouth goes straight to my cock. My chest rumbles with satisfaction, and I swallow back a groan.

"Cut the crap. I remember how much you enjoyed terrorizing me at night," Amethyst spits. "Back then, you were so creative. Now, you're just saying anything to save your worthless hide."

Charlotte's frightened facade morphs into the cold, calculating gaze of an assassin. This is the true identity of a killer molded through years of manipulation and abuse. The lower half of her face is too swollen to form a sneer, but her eyes scream defiance and a fierce will to survive.

This is the predator Father created, so corrupted that she's lost her humanity.

Amethyst will have to work hard to break her spirit. If she succeeds, she'll emerge as a completely different woman. She'll be one step closer to vanquishing her demons. One step closer to facing Father and Dolly.

SEVENTY

AMETHYST

Charlotte's existence feels more like a nightmare than a memory, but now that she's dropped the facade, everything snaps back into place.

This is the woman who taunted Mom and made her seem crazy while cozying up to Dad and Dolly. The same instructor who praised my sister for not freezing during our missions while deriding me for struggling to kill. The same creature who smothered my baby brother.

I stare into her cold eyes, seeing the bitch who tormented me at night. Confronting her is more intense than facing the monster in the mirror. She's aged a little since the days of pretending to be our nanny, and the swelling around her mouth has distorted her features beyond recognition, but this is Charlotte.

The truck rumbles over the uneven road, each jolt sending vibrations through my bones. Dim light casts eerie shadows on her mottled skin, making her contorted features appear ghostlike.

Xero stands behind me, a constant reminder that I'm not alone in this battle against my past. His fingers brush my shoulder in a gesture of support, infusing me with a jolt of warmth.

He doesn't need to offer his help. I already know he's ready to step in if I falter. But this is my fight—my past to confront. I'm determined to see it to the end.

"No more bullshit," I say, my voice flat. "You're going to tell me everything about the children you train and traffic. After you help me rescue them, you'll lead me to Delta."

Her eyes burn with hatred. "Or else, what?"

"Or you'll die slowly for everything you inflicted on my family and me."

She shakes her head, her gaze dropping to the floor. "You're wasting your time. I'm just a pawn."

Gripping her chin, I force her to meet my gaze. My stomach churns at the contact. Even though I'm wearing gloves, the heat of her skin soaks through the latex.

Wincing, she tries to pull away, but I tighten my grip.

"Tell me about the adoption agency and all the children you trafficked."

"Some of them actually found homes," she spits, each word bringing up splatters of blood.

"With pedophiles?" I sneer.

"With families. Wealthy ones. People who could give them better lives than they had on the street."

Bile rises to my throat. Does she even believe what she's saying? Any organization connected to Delta has to be corrupt. Pushing forward, I make a mental note to demand her records. Tonight is all about finding Three Fates and rescuing the child assassins. We can check in on the adopted children after we've handled Dolly, Delta, and their corrupt organization.

"What about the other kids?" I ask. "Where did they go?"

She clamps her mouth shut, her eyes flashing with defiance.

"Answer me, bitch," I hiss through clenched teeth.

When she closes her eyes, it's like striking a match that ignites an explosion of anger. Charlotte never gave me the chance to hide from her nightly taunting. She would wake me up and stand over my bed, wearing that bloody nightgown. When I hid under the covers or in the closet, she would repeat the same words over and over, urging me to kill Heath so her spirit could rest.

I step back to the table where Xero has laid out a selection of tools. He moves aside, giving me room to choose my weapon. Ignoring the bloody pliers, I select a syringe filled with clear fluid and return to her side.

"What is that?" she asks.

"I have no fucking idea."

"An experimental drug to increase pain sensitivity," Xero replies, his tone clinical.

Her eyes widen, and she shrinks into her seat, the defiance on her features flickering. She drops her gaze to the syringe, breathing so hard that the vein in her neck pulses.

"Anything to say?" I ask.

At her silence, I slide the needle into her vein and press the plunger.

A shudder runs through her body, causing beads of sweat to form on her skin before she convulses.

Frowning, I glance over my shoulder, wondering if I've done something wrong, but Xero's reassuring nod tells me everything's going to plan.

"Give her a few seconds for the drug to take effect," he says.

While Charlotte gets accustomed to the infusion, I return to the table and pick up the pliers. She makes a strangled noise, and my heart thrums with satisfaction. After Xero used them to extract her teeth, I'm not surprised she finds them triggering.

"Maybe this will jog your memory." I return to her side, clamping its jaws into her fingers.

A scream rips from her throat and echoes across the truck's walls. My breath quickens. The sound only makes me want to inflict more pain.

I lean closer until our noses are almost touching. "Where. Are. The. Children?"

"Only a few go to patrons who want a pet," she says through ragged breaths. "Those who fail to meet the beauty standards are sent for organ trafficking."

The words hit like a punch to the gut, and my world tilts sideways. I knew what they were doing to the girls. Knew that some of them ended up in snuff movies. But cutting them up and selling their body parts is a level of depravity I hadn't fully grasped.

Behind me, Xero stiffens. I don't need to turn around to feel his rage. It radiates off him like a storm, dark and heavy and violent. His breathing deepens, each inhale sharp and controlled, a clear sign of his restrained fury. The air around us crackles—not just with his anger, but with mine. Every instinct in my bones wants to beat this woman to a mosaic of blood and broken pieces.

"Where are the children?" I snarl.

"Lyle was on his way to dispose of you when he died," she replies, her voice dripping with contempt. "You were dead weight, ruining Dolly's performance. Delta said you were worth more to him as body parts than as a Lolita."

Her words land like a punch to my gut, and I flinch.

She smirks, revealing her swollen gums. "You always were weak, Amy. Crying every night, freezing during missions."

Her manic laugh turns my body rigid. This is the same cruel taunting she subjected me to when I was a child. Every instinct screams at me to plunge a knife into her face, not stopping until she shuts her filthy mouth.

"I was a child, you sick fuck!"

Out of the corner of my eye, I spot Xero stepping forward to intervene. I raise a hand, and he draws back.

My grip tightens on the pliers, tearing into her finger. Bones crack beneath the metal, and her screams turn hoarse. The absence of those hateful words sends pleasure shivering down my spine.

But the screams turn to laughter. "Dolly was strong. She's thriving now, and married to Delta. But you paired up with the son he rejected for becoming a janitor."

Xero snorts.

I glance over my shoulder to find him grinning.

"We prefer the term cleaners," he says.

Despite her taunts, Xero stands tall, his expression unyielding. Watching him face her without flinching fills me with a surge of strength. I draw on his resilience, lifting my head to meet her gaze, refusing to be cowed.

She leans forward as much as her bindings allow. "Do you think Xero loves you? He's just using you to resolve his daddy issues. You're nothing but a stepping-stone in his quest to find Delta."

Her words cut deep. Cold dread settles in my stomach, but I hold my features in a tight mask. I know I'll eventually have to make Xero listen to why I left him to die in flames, but that can wait until we've dealt with our mutual enemy.

"Your attempts to manipulate me won't work, bitch," I snap. "I'm no longer that frightened child."

She cackles, but it soon stops when I bring the pliers to her nose.

"What are you doing?" she asks, her voice rising several octaves.

"You took everything from me. I won't let you do the same to the children. Tell me where they are, or you'll lose what's left of your looks."

"What's the point?" she asks through ragged breaths. "I'm dead, either way."

I squeeze the pliers, cutting into her flesh. She shivers, her breath coming in panicked bursts.

"You tormented me until I started hallucinating. Because of you, every person I kill haunts me as a delusion. That's fourteen years of agony I've suffered, which is how long I'll keep you alive."

Her pupils dilate, and her face freezes in a rictus of terror. It's not just about the psychological damage. Heath would have been fourteen by now. Because of her, I lost my baby brother. She knows I mean every word.

I lean in close, my voice a low growl. "Give me the information I want, and I'll make it quick."

Her eyes widen, her features flickering with fear. She swallows hard, her voice trembling as she whispers, "What do you want to know?"

"Where is the Three Fates Boarding School?"

Eyes squeezing shut, her swollen face etches with pain and fear. "I have a daughter there," she whispers, her voice breaking. "You have to promise she won't suffer because of me."

Disgust churns in my gut, and I can't help but bare my teeth. "I'm nothing like you," I snap. "I'd never take revenge on an innocent child."

Xero steps forward and places a hand on my shoulder. The warmth of his touch grounds me to my humanity. My head clears, and the grip on the pliers loosens.

"We're going to rescue all the child assassins," I say. "Regardless of their parents. Now, tell me where to find Three Fates."

"It's off Highland Lane. Stop torturing me, and I'll help you avoid the traps," she rasps.

"Where is Delta?" I ask.

"I don't know," she sobs. "He hasn't met me in person since I told him about the baby."

Xero and I exchange glances. The corners of his lips tighten. I expect it's because of the implication that this little girl is another of his siblings.

"How do you communicate with him?" I ask.

"He calls or emails. You took my phone... Use it."

"Give us the coordinates of the entrance," Xero says.

She slumps in her chair, her entire body trembling. Tears roll down her cheeks as she stutters out a string of numbers. Xero taps them into his phone, bringing up a patch of forest. His fingers expand the map, revealing nothing but trees.

"Is this accurate?" Xero holds the phone in front of her swollen face.

Wincing, she scans the screen. "Yes."

"If you lead us into a trap, we have enough drones and backup to wipe out a small army," I snarl. "And don't think Delta will come to your rescue. Your daughter isn't the only child of his he's exploited."

She nods. "Now, will you kill me?"

My eyes narrow, and I glare at the pathetic creature, sobbing and trembling in her seat. "Oh, Charlotte, my revenge has only just begun."

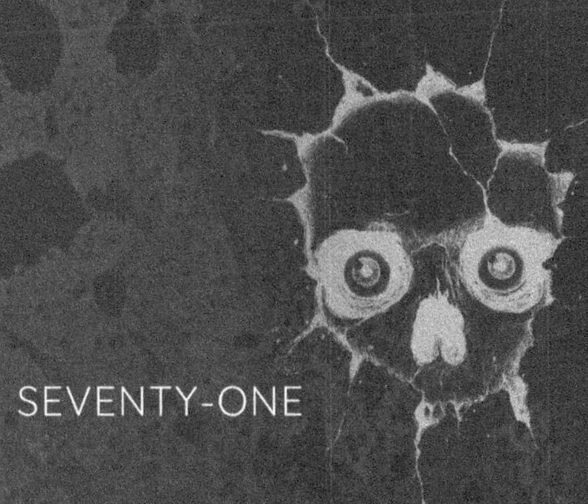

SEVENTY-ONE

XERO

Thirty minutes after Charlotte's intel, I'm pressed against the side of the truck, the cold metal seeping through my jacket. The hum of the engine vibrates through my bones as I coordinate the teams for our assault on Three Fates.

Jynxson is in the front seat, also buried in his phone. He's confirming satellite and surveillance images with Tyler. Our tracker team sent out drones to the coordinates, in search of thermal activity.

Their latest update buzzes in my earpiece, confirming multiple heat signatures. Every operative within fifty miles is on their way, and it's all thanks to my little ghost.

My chest swells with pride at the thought of Amethyst's contribution. We wouldn't have advanced this far without her. She's tackled Charlotte's emotional manipulations with a strength that has me on my knees. I knew she was special when I received her first letter, but I never guessed she would make my every dream come true.

She continues working on Charlotte, extracting every scrap of intel she can about Father's organ trafficking operations. We're recording the interrogation with a view to sending out operatives after surgeons, hospital administrators, brokers, social workers—anyone enabling Father to exploit children.

With confirmation from the last team, I issue the command. Charlotte guides us through a narrow gap in the hedges. The truck jolts over uneven terrain, its wheels bouncing rhythmically. Dense foliage encroaches on the windshield, transforming the world outside into a shadowy blur.

"Are you sure this is the place?" Jynxson asks from the driver's seat.

"It wouldn't be a secret entrance otherwise," Charlotte replies through pained whimpers.

"How do you get in supplies?" he asks.

"Underground passageways."

I glance at Amethyst. "Is this familiar?"

She nods. Charlotte's comment about bringing in supplies underground also makes sense. In the four years Jynxson and I lived in the facility, they never let us out for anything other than missions. When they did, we traveled mostly through tunnels.

Eventually, the road evens. Amethyst moves to my side, and we look out through the windshield into a clearing. Beyond the stretch of lawn, the headlights illuminate snatches of a gray building hidden within the trees.

Trucks park on either side of us, and a swarm of drones hover around the building. Charlotte assures us that most instructors don't live among the child assassins, but we're monitoring heat signals in case her information is out of date.

I turn to Amethyst. "Stay here with Charlotte. Make sure she doesn't slither out and escape."

Her pretty features harden. "She doesn't need a babysitter, and I don't need coddling."

"Amethyst," I snarl.

"I need this last chance to face my past." Her voice breaks, and my heart splinters at the sound of her pain.

A lump forms in my throat. I swore to protect this woman with my life, but facing her pain is something even my promises can't prevent.

I cup her cheek. "What if coming here triggers another flashback?"

"Then I'll handle it," she says through clenched teeth.

I study her features for any signs of hesitation. The past few days have been tumultuous. Less than an hour ago, she almost got blown to pieces. Amethyst is strong, but everyone has limits.

Her jaw tightens, and her eyes blaze with an intensity that cuts through the tension. "Let me get this closure."

I take a deep breath, and what's left of my resolve crumbles under the weight of her gaze. "Fine, but at the first sign of trouble, I'm sending you back. Understood?"

She nods.

"All units in place," Jynxson says. "An EMP blast already took out their electronics. Ready whenever you are."

I hand Amethyst a sedative strong enough to knock out an elephant. She turns to Charlotte, who whimpers and trembles in her seat. Without a word, Amethyst injects her former abuser and places the syringe back on the table.

Exiting the truck with Amethyst at my side, I step into the cool night air. Team leaders, clad in body armor, gather by the front doors. I signal them to spread out and find entry points.

My protective instincts rear up to shield Amethyst, but I shove them down, needing to trust her skills. The lives of those children depend on my ability to lead this mission, but it's hard when all I want to do is keep her safe.

The Spring brothers remain by the front doors, awaiting instructions. I direct them to the nearest window. One rushes forward with a crowbar to pry at its edges, while the other cuts through the metal grating with a portable electric saw.

"Any movement inside?" I ask into my Bluetooth.

"Negative," Tyler replies from wherever he's stationed. "Heat tracking detects twelve motionless bodies in the rear."

"And the basement?"

"The drones are showing it's heavily shielded or insulated—could be the concrete or some other materials. I'm picking up something, but it's faint and inconsistent."

"Does it matter?" Amethyst asks. "Charlotte already confirmed that's where they keep the boys."

The Spring brothers open the window, and we climb into a small gymnasium. I rattle off instructions for them to follow our lead. Nodding, they slip into position.

With Tyler guiding us by tracking heat signatures, Amethyst

and I navigate through the dimly lit facility, encountering locked doors at every turn.

Her steps falter, and she stops to point toward the far end of the hallway. "That was Delta's office. Our dormitories were on the left and right."

Her voice is strained, as though she's holding back a torrent of painful memories. I squeeze her hand in silent support, then motion for our team to split up and approach the room on the right.

We step into the darkened dormitory on the left. Bunk beds line one wall, and young girls huddle in the corner, their faces contorted with terror. I step back, letting Amethyst approach the children.

"It's okay, we're here to help you," she says, her palms raised.

Camila pushes past me to join Amethyst. I leave the room, directing the female operatives to extract the girls. If their experiences are anything like the memories my little ghost shared, the last thing they'll need is the presence of a man.

"Xero!" Jynxson yells from down the hallway. "We've found an entrance to the basement."

Movement in my periphery catches my attention. I turn just in time to see a door open and a man in full body armor emerge, with an automatic weapon aimed at Jynxson. He fires, bullets hitting Jynxson square in the chest.

Fury powers my steps. I charge at the shooter, tackling him to the ground. The machine gun skitters across the floor, the clatter drowned by the roar in my ears. We grapple, his fists pounding at my ribs, but my vest absorbs the impact.

I tear the helmet off his head, exposing a face I nearly recognize—sharp features, dark hair, and a distinctive tattoo near his right eye.

My fist lands into his face, breaking his nose with a satisfying crunch.

"Give me a reason why I shouldn't kill you right now," I snarl, my hands tightening around his throat.

"Xero, right?" he chokes out through clenched teeth. "Kill me, and all the information you're looking for dies with me."

I press harder on his windpipe, savoring his gasps for air. "You should have thought about that before you shot my friend."

Another figure rushes out from down the hall, but disappears under a pile of my operatives. I strip off this asshole's armored jacket and shove him aside.

"Get him up," I snarl.

As I stand, two of my operatives haul him to his feet. "Show me where the other instructors are hiding from our sensors."

Jynxson stumbles toward us, clutching his chest but waving off help. "I'm fine. Just a bruised rib."

I clap him on the shoulder. "This asshole is yours. Make him pay."

Jynxson and the others drag the captured man to another room, and the rest of us move toward a stairwell. It's narrow and unlit, clearly meant only for the instructors. When I lived here, I had no idea Father kept the Lolitas upstairs.

We reach a heavy door, and I motion for an operative to drill through its lock. The girls might have been receptive to Amethyst, but things will be different with the boys. I was happy here, and so were the others. For me, this facility was a haven from an abusive stepfamily. For Jynxson, it was a home away from the streets.

"Be ready for anything," I say over the whirr.

The drilling stops, and the operative opens the door with a swift kick. We pile into another hallway. Adrenaline surges through my veins. It's so familiar, I could navigate it in my dreams.

This is it—I'm seconds away from saving the boys.

My heart pounds. My thoughts oscillate between the state we'll find the children in and how Amethyst is coping with confronting her past.

We continue to the dormitory I once shared with Jynxson and the others and signal for my team to prepare. "Remember," I say, my voice low. "Half the kids here don't even know they're assassins."

I force the lock and push the door open. The dorm is clean, orderly, and lit with flashlights. Twelve boys, aged between ten and fourteen, stand in a defensive formation with their backs to the wall. Though they look scared, they're prepared to fight.

"Stand down, operatives," I order, using language they should find familiar.

"Identify yourself," demands one of the taller boys. He's dark-haired, already six feet tall, though his features are still a child's. He can't be more than fourteen.

I step forward. "Xero Greaves. Former graduate of this facility. I'm here to move you to an above-ground home where you'll be safe and free."

The boys exchange skeptical glances, their defensiveness palpable.

The older boy clenches his fists. "How do we know this isn't a trap?"

"Your instructors are dead. Delta has gone into hiding. If you want to survive, come with me to my safe house."

They remain in place, and I can't fault their suspicion. These boys have been conditioned to trust no one except their instructors. I take a step closer, wishing I'd brought Amethyst or another female operative to add credibility.

"I know what you've been through," I say, pointing to my former bunk. "I lived in this dorm for four years before Delta moved me to another facility. Children shouldn't do the work of adults. They also shouldn't be held prisoner underground. I'm here to set you free."

Silence stretches out across the dorm as the boys process my words. Their leader glances at his companions before turning back to me. "What do you want us to do?"

"Go to school with children your age. Play games outside. Make friends. Read books not related to combat strategies." I shrug. "Meet girls."

Some of the boys snicker. Others' expressions are longing, telling me I've struck a nerve.

"Will we have a dorm like this?" asks a smaller boy.

I shake my head. "No bunks. No more dickheads kicking your mattress while you're trying to sleep. No more waking up in a cloud of some asshole's farts."

They laugh.

The leader bites his lip and glances at his friends again, who shrug. "Okay," he finally says. "We'll come with you. But if this is a trick..."

"It isn't." I raise my palms. "You have my word."

When the boys break formation, I motion for my operatives to start moving them out. Jynxson and Camila will scan the children for trackers before taking them to a safe house.

As the last of the boys file out of the room, I take one final look at the facility that was once my prison. The happiness I experienced here is tainted by the manipulative tactics Father used to keep me compliant.

I'm so close to retribution that it simmers beneath my skin, a buzzing anticipation to face him after all these years. I'll make him bleed for what he did to us all, but he'll lose body parts for touching my Amethyst.

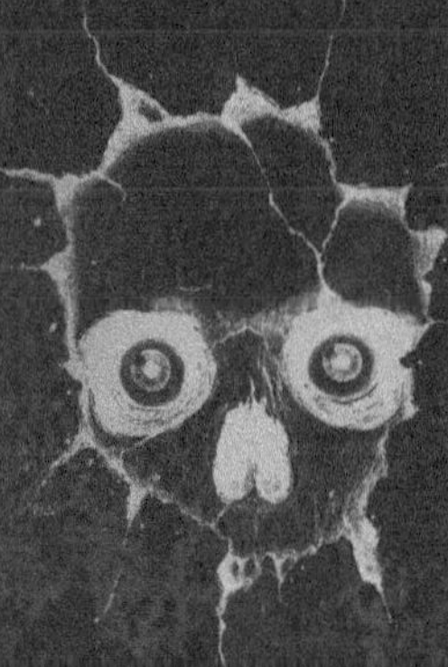

SEVENTY-TWO

AMETHYST

Hours after the raid, I follow Xero into a cottage nestled within a sprawling estate. My limbs drag like lead weights, each step a monumental effort. Sunlight floods the wood-paneled room, casting warm golden hues, but my heavy eyelids struggle to stay open.

The adrenaline that once coursed through my veins has long since drained away, leaving me hollow. Every inch of my body aches with exhaustion, burdened by memories I can't escape.

We spent the rest of the night transporting and settling the children into a safe house on the grounds of this estate, guarded by Xero's people. There were only twenty-four child assassins, yet over seventy operatives arrived to help.

Navigating the old summer camp was like walking through old memories. It wasn't just the location that pricked my mind, but the anguish etched in the girls' eyes. Their faces reflected the pain and fear of that terrible summer, mirroring my own haunted past.

Xero turns around and cups my cheeks. "You alright, little ghost?"

I can barely hear him through the ringing in my ears. "Just exhausted."

That's an understatement. Last night was intense—from

nearly getting blown up, finding and interrogating Charlotte, to returning to Three Fates—the weight of it all drapes heavily on my shoulders.

Eyes sparkling, Xero gazes down at me with a soft smile. "You did well for your first mission."

I lean into his chest. "Thanks."

"Anything hurt?"

"Just the usual aches. It feels like I've fought my way through hell," I mutter against his shoulder.

"Did you win?" His arm slides around my waist, pulling our bodies flush.

"This round was a victory," I reply with a yawn. "Making Charlotte scream was so satisfying."

Chuckling, Xero walks me past the cottage's cozy cream furniture and sits me on the edge of a bed. Kneeling at my feet, he unlaces my boots. His touch is gentle, almost reverent, and my heart aches with the intensity of my gratitude. What did I do to deserve this man? How did I become so entwined with someone who sees the broken pieces of me and still chooses to stay?

He slides off my socks, his fingers grazing the sensitive skin of my soles. Shivers erupt along my spine. The exhaustion fades away, replaced by a flicker of arousal.

"What are you doing?" I ask with a smile.

He meets my gaze with dancing blue eyes. "Such pretty feet need attention after their trip through hell."

"You think so?" I giggle. "Maybe they could use a massage."

He chuckles, the sound soothing and rich. "It's the least I can do for my brave little warrior."

Kneading his thumbs into the arch of my foot, he unravels knots of tension. I moan, the muscles of my core tightening. Every touch of his fingers is just another reminder of what we used to have, and I long for the time we spent together on Parisii Drive.

"Thank you, Amethyst," he says, his voice thickening with emotion. "Without you, I might never have achieved one of my biggest goals."

Pride swells in my chest. Maybe this breakthrough can make up for not trusting Xero after seeing that video. Apologies can't compensate for what I did. I wish there was a way to make things right.

My hand trembles as I reach up to brush his platinum hair. "It should be me doing the thanking," I say between ragged breaths. "I owe you my life."

Our eyes lock, and the air between us thrums with tension. My gaze drifts down to his lips and I lick my own in anticipation.

Xero's eyes darken, mirroring my longing, and the space between us closes. My heart pounds, echoing my need to be in his arms. With him, I feel invincible, loved, desired. His presence chases away the demons and makes me feel like I can conquer anything.

"What are you thinking?" he asks, placing my feet on a soft rug.

"About how much I want to kiss you," I murmur.

Rising, he draws closer until our breaths mingle. His scent—citrus, spearmint, and cedarwood—overwhelms my senses, leaving me dizzy with desire.

"You want my mouth?" he whispers against my lips.

His fingertips graze my jawline, leaving my skin prickling with goosebumps.

"Yes," I whisper, inching closer.

The kiss starts with a tender brush of lips that makes my skin tingle. There, Xero's mouth moves against mine, soft and coaxing, drawing out another moan.

I wrap my arms around his neck, wanting more, needing it, and he slips his tongue into my mouth. As the kiss deepens, his hands travel up my spine, making every nerve ending sing. My fingers tangle in his silky hair, holding him in place.

His heart thrashes against my chest, mirroring the rhythm of my desire. I want this man so badly that it hurts. I pour a lifetime of gratitude into this kiss, and Xero returns it with a passion that makes my toes curl.

Shutting down Three Fates released a dark void in my psyche I never even knew existed. Making Charlotte bleed vanquished the ghosts of my past and brought me one step closer to closure.

"I've missed you so much," he groans against my lips, his touch igniting my skin with sparks.

The kiss becomes more heated, unleashing a fire that burns through years of trauma and pain. The flames consume my past, and, as I kiss back, I arise from the ashes a new woman.

His large hands glide up the backs of my thighs, his fingers digging into my skin as he grips my hips. His body heat seeps through our clothes, branding me as his. When he pulls me closer, my heart races, each beat a desperate plea for more. This kiss is hotter than the one in the truck, and I crave more. I want him with an intensity that borders on madness.

"You're wearing too much," I say.

We fumble with each other's bulletproof jackets, my hands trembling with urgency and desire. The garments drop to the floor with heavy thuds. Xero lowers me onto the mattress, his touch charging my skin with sparks of desire.

My breath quickens as he straddles my hips, his limbs creating a cocoon of security and warmth. I slide my fingers beneath the fabric of his shirt, wanting to remove every barrier between our bodies. He draws back, letting me yank it off, revealing his tight abs and bulging pecs.

Sunlight streams through the windows, bathing Xero in golden light and casting a glow across the dips and contours of his muscles. He looms over me like my own personal deity, and I can't help but trace the tattoos on his chest. His breath quickens with an intensity that goes straight to my clit.

"Tell me what you want," he says.

"All of you," I reply, my voice breathy.

He blinks. "Sure you can take it all?"

I give him an eager nod.

With a low growl, Xero captures my lips once more, deepening the kiss with a passion that leaves me breathless. His hands roam down to where my vest has ridden up to expose my belly, his touch igniting sparks of desire.

"Fuck, Amethyst. You're driving me crazy."

His hands move lower, and his fingers trace over the waistband of my pants before slipping beneath them. His touch is electric against my bare skin, sending shivers down my spine. Anticipation coils low in my belly, tightening with every heartbeat. If I don't have him right now, I might die.

When I reach for his belt buckle, he breaks away, leaving me panting and flushed. His pale eyes survey my features as if checking that I still consent.

"Please," I whisper, my back arching.

Can't he see I'm no longer the jumpy woman fresh from the asylum? I've evolved into someone stronger, fiercer, in control. Someone who knows exactly what she wants, and that's Xero. I want to say all of this, but I just don't have the words.

Instead, I unbuckle his belt, my fingers shaking with anticipation.

A smoky chuckle escapes Xero's lips. He leans forward to whisper in my ear, "Impatient, little ghost? You beg so prettily?"

"Like you wouldn't believe."

I pull down his pants, revealing his chiseled thighs and the outline of his impossibly thick cock. It strains through his boxers, begging for release.

Xero kicks off his pants, leaving himself only clad in his boxers. The lining of my stomach flutters. I can't tell if it's butterflies or nerves. Ignoring the peculiar sensation, I pull him in for another kiss.

Our lips collide with a rush of urgent desire. I squeeze my eyes shut and lose myself in the intensity. Sunlight streams through my eyelids, bathing my inner world in light. For a moment, it feels like we're the only two people in existence.

As Xero's erection presses into my belly, a memory from the asylum hits me like a punch to the gut. I'm paralyzed in a tent of light, with Delta's probing fingers removing the pessary filled with drugs. Seconds later, he pushes into me and groans.

A sob catches in my throat. I flinch, jolting out of the memory, my eyes flying open. It's like waking up from a nightmare, half-dazed, half-confused, yet still haunted by the lingering memory of Delta's touch.

Xero pulls back, holding my face in his hands, his gaze searching mine. His eyes, clouded with desire a moment ago, are now filled with worry.

"Talk to me, Amethyst," he says, his voice soft, his thumb wiping a stray tear.

"I'm sorry." My throat tightens. "I just kept picturing him."

Xero's features harden. "My father."

"It was a flashback," I croak.

Xero pulls me into his chest, wrapping his arms around my shoulders in a protective shield. He runs his large hand up and down my spine, his caress a balm on my nerves.

"He will die painfully for touching you," Xero growls, his deep voice resounding through my chest. "Every one of those bastards who took from you will pay in blood. I will carve out their hearts and present them to you as offerings."

My eyes flutter shut, and I relax into his embrace. "I know you will."

His hold is steady and grounding. The warmth of his palms on my skin anchors me to our connection. The past doesn't dictate my present. I'm safe. I'm sane. I'm strong.

With a shaky breath, I draw back and focus on his face. The terror ebbs away, and I lose myself in his gaze. Xero's irises are a pale blue lit up by bolts of lightning, reflecting the depth of his fury.

"Kiss me again," I murmur.

He leans in, his lips pressing against my forehead. "I'm so proud of you."

"Not like that," I say, my voice barely above a whisper. "I want to move forward with our relationship."

"Don't push yourself before you're ready," he says.

"But I'm tired of being traumatized."

Drawing back again, he nods, his eyes filled with understanding and a touch of hope. "We'll take it slow. The moment you're uncomfortable, I'll stop."

"Thank you," I whisper, a weight lifting from my chest. It's minuscule, the tiniest shift in my psyche, but I'm a step closer to healing.

He kisses me again, this time with a gentleness that makes my heart ache. His lips move slowly, reverently over mine, as if sealing a promise. We'll move forward together, our love strengthening with the blood of our enemies.

Xero's fingers trace gentle patterns on my back, bringing with them tiny shivers. The warmth of his touch contrasts with the cold hands that once held me captive. I close my eyes, trying to focus on the present, on the safety of his embrace. But the memories claw at the edges of my mind, threatening to pull me back into the darkness.

"Eyes on me," Xero says, bringing me back to the present.

Xero's eyes lock onto mine, a blend of desire and concern. I lose myself in his gaze, surrendering to the moment, feeling Delta's presence dissipate until all that's left is us.

"Tell me what you want, little ghost," he murmurs.

My throat thickens. I swallow hard, trying to muster the words. "Can I watch you touch yourself?"

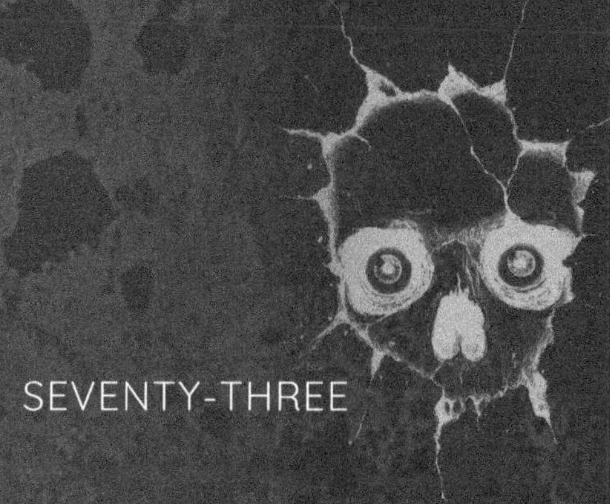

SEVENTY-THREE

AMETHYST

Xero hesitates for several heartbeats, his gaze locked on mine as if he's weighing the gravity of my simple request. We lie on our sides, facing each other. The silence between us stretches, and I almost regret confessing what those men did during the force-feeding.

Just as I'm about to tell him to forget about it, he nods, a slow, deliberate movement that sends a shiver down my spine.

He shifts back on the mattress, the muscles in his torso bunching and rippling with every movement. I drink in the sight of his sculpted pecs, the defined lines of his abs, the raw power in his broad shoulders. His intricate tattoos come alive in a mesmerizing dance of shadows and ink.

Anticipation and nervousness thrum through my core, my pulse quickening with each breath. I can't tear my eyes away as he raises his hips, his boxers sliding down to reveal his hard length. His cock springs free, the piercings catching the sunlight and sending a cascade of shimmering reflections around the room.

"Is this what you want?"

Breath hitching, I bite my lip and nod. Nothing—not even that silicone dildo—could ever capture his full grandeur.

Xero's gaze never wavers, his eyes boring into mine as if he's reading my every hidden thought. The air between us thickens, charged with a tension that crackles against my skin like static electricity.

"See something you like, little ghost?" he asks, his deep voice eliciting a delicious shiver.

My breath quickens. My gaze fixes on the hand wrapping around the base of his cock. "Lots of things, actually."

He runs his fingers up and down his shaft once, twice, setting a slow, sensual rhythm that makes my clit swell.

"You're so fucking beautiful," he says, his words wrapping around my senses like tendrils of smoke. "I want to worship every inch of your body. I want to kiss every scar, every mark, because you're the only goddess I worship."

Heat pools low in my belly, and my breath shallows. His words are intoxicating, an auditory aphrodisiac. For the first time, I feel seen—not as a broken woman, but as someone worthy of love and desire.

"Show me how much you want me," I murmur from the other side of the mattress.

Xero's gaze drops to my bare breasts, his strokes quickening around his shaft. "I want to kiss those glorious tits."

I arch my back. "These?"

"Yes," he growls, his voice raw with desire, "They're perfect."

Pleasure skitters down my spine as he runs his tongue across his lip. I want that mouth on my nipples. I want those hands stroking my breasts.

As if sensing my thoughts, he slows his motion up and down his length in a gesture meant to tease. In response, the muscles of my core clench.

"I want to make you writhe beneath me. I want to hear you moan my name," he continues, his voice thickening with lust. "I want to taste your sweet nectar, feel your body tremble as you come undone, just for me."

My heart races at the raw honesty in his words. I want all those things, too.

"Fuck, I want to bury my cock in your tight cunt," he growls, his hand moving faster, his eyes darkening with need. "I want to feel your wet heat, see your face as you shatter with pleasure."

His dirty talk ignites a fire within my libido, burning through the lingering fear. Heat builds in my core, and my pussy becomes slick with arousal. My nipples tighten. My breath shallows. Without meaning to, my body scoots toward him across the mattress.

"Xero," I whisper, my voice trembling with need.

His gaze remains on mine as he quickens his strokes around his cock. "Talk to me. Tell me what you want."

"I want you," I moan, my voice barely audible. "I want you touching me, too."

"Stroke that pretty pussy. Make it purr," he commands, his voice a throaty growl.

Pleasant shivers run between my legs, making my clit ache. As I part my thighs, he leans in to take a closer look. I slide a finger between my swollen lips, and we both moan.

"Good girl. Are you wet for me?" he rasps.

"Yes," I whisper.

Xero's gaze never leaves mine. The muscles in his arm flex and contract with each motion and his breaths grow heavier, matching the rhythm of his hand.

I mirror his strokes, exploring my wetness, my fingers running down from my clit to my soaking entrance.

The air between us buzzes with tension, and every sense heightens. The room fades away, leaving only the two of us, locked in this bubble of pleasure. But it's not enough. We're too far apart. The space between us on the mattress feels like a chasm.

Xero's lips part with a low moan that I feel as a caress against my skin. As it increases in volume, the sound sends a jolt of longing straight to my core.

"I want my tongue on your pussy, tasting you, making you scream my name. Would you like that, little ghost?"

"Fuck," I groan. "Yes."

Drifting closer, he presses his lips on the tip of my shoulder, igniting an explosion of sparks. "More?"

"Please."

His lips trail down toward the swell of my breast, searing my skin with a path of desire. Every stroke of his tongue sends electric jolts to my needy clit.

He doesn't touch me with his fingers—just his mouth. I scoot closer until the hand stroking his cock bumps against my thigh. The muscles of my pussy clamp around nothing, needing his fingers.

"I've never wanted anyone—anything—as much as I want you," he says before sucking my nipple into his hot mouth.

Sensation hits my solar plexus with an intensity that draws out a strangled gasp. Xero's tongue swirls around my hardened nipple before sucking with a pressure that makes me jerk against his larger body.

This contact earns me a pleased growl. I grab onto his hair, pulling him closer, wanting him to never let go.

His tongue continues to tease and torment my sensitive peak until every nerve feels like it's been set alight. My hips grind against the mattress, desperate for more contact. I arch into his touch, a pleading whimper escaping my lips as he continues to lavish my body with his tongue.

When Xero's mouth leaves my nipple with a soft pop, I want to scream. But then his lips trail downward, each touch igniting waves of ecstasy.

"Tell me what you need, little ghost," he murmurs against my skin.

"Your mouth," I say between ragged breaths. "On my pussy."

His lips move lower, down my belly, pausing to swirl his tongue around its button, and then further down to my pubes. He kisses, nips, sucks, and teases my skin, making me roll on my back and pant for more.

When his hot breath grazes my pussy, my hips buck on instinct, seeking more of his touch. The tip of his tongue teases at my slit, and my eyes roll to the back of my head. My body trembles, my mind consumed by overwhelming need. Every nerve catches fire, consumed by the raw desire for his next move.

"Come undone for me. Fill my ears with the sound of your pleasure."

His nose bumps against my clit, and I cry out. "Xero!"

The vibrations of his chuckle against my wet folds hit me with a fresh wave of arousal, and I shiver. Then his tongue dips between my folds and swirls around my clit.

I tighten my fingers in his hair and moan, "Yes! Right there."

"You taste so fucking good," he murmurs around my heated flesh. "Just like you were made for me to eat."

I buck against his face, chasing my pleasure.

"That's right, baby. Use me. Take what you need. I'm yours."

Tossing my head back, I shiver. Each lash of his tongue sends waves of pleasure through my core, pushing me closer to the edge. Xero alternates between soft licks and firmer strokes, his hands never intruding.

"More," I cry out. "Please."

His tongue slides down to my opening and plunges in with wild abandon. I groan, gripping his platinum hair. As he fucks me with his tongue, his finger makes slow, teasing circles around my clit.

My hips jerk and spasm, increasing the friction. Pressure builds, and sensation coils deep in my core. This is it. I'm going to climax. Pleasure swells, growing more intense with each frantic heartbeat. I'm babbling incoherently, not sure if I'm begging him for more or to never stop.

Xero keeps his rhythm steady, holding me suspended in so much pleasure that my body convulses. I claw at the sheets, teetering on the edge of oblivion.

"I'm close," I whisper, my voice trembling.

"That's it, baby. Come all over my face," he growls into my pussy.

Sensation mounts, cresting into a storm that crashes through my core, leaving every nerve electrified. An orgasm rips through my body, making my muscles clench and spasm. Euphoria overwhelms my senses until my vision turns white.

As the waves of ecstasy subside, I reach down, threading my fingers through Xero's platinum hair, guiding him up from between my legs. My body still hums with lingering pleasure, and my breaths come in frantic gulps. When our lips finally meet, it's an all-consuming kiss, desperate and hungry, as if we're trying to meld into one.

I taste myself in his mouth and groan. Xero deepens the kiss, his tongue twisting, exploring my mouth. I clutch at his shoulders, pulling him nearer, craving the feel of his entire being, and revel in his growl.

My existence narrows to just the two of us, our mingled breaths, our joined lips, the slick slide of our bodies. His hands explore my skin, leaving trails of fire that make me want to burn in the heat of our desire.

"You're my addiction," he moans into the kiss. "Every taste of you leaves me wanting to overdose."

"That was incredible," I whisper against his lips, my voice still trembling with the force of that orgasm.

"Was?" he growls. "I haven't finished with you yet."

SEVENTY-FOUR

XERO

Amethyst's climax will be forever seared into my memory. The way her body responded to my touch was so intoxicating that I almost came to the thought of being the one to restore her sexuality.

She gazes up at me, breathing through parted lips, her green eyes still dilated with lust. A flush stains her cheeks, and her pretty curls lie damp against her brow.

"There's more?" she whispers.

"I could worship you day and night, and it wouldn't be enough," I say, my voice rough with need. "But I want more than your body. I want your mind, your soul—your everything."

Her eyes widen. "Even with my scars?"

My chest tightens with a surge of fierce protectiveness and the need to destroy every bastard who ever made her doubt my commitment. Those scars haven't diminished her worth. They only make her more precious. My arms tighten around her waist, pulling her close.

"I almost lost you," I snarl, my voice shaking with restrained rage. "If you think those scratches will lessen my desire for you, then you're mistaken."

She lowers her lashes, but I'm not about to allow her to slide back into despair. If I have to tell her a hundred different ways how much she makes me burn, then I will.

"Place your hand over mine."

Raising her gaze to meet my eyes, she places trembling fingers over the hand fisting my cock. "Like this?"

Her voice is tinged with curiosity, reminding me of the skittish girl who first answered my call during a thunderstorm. She was so nervous that morning, yet I coaxed her into climaxing with my voice.

"Just like that," I say with a groan.

Amethyst's hand rests atop mine as I stroke my shaft, and her breath quickens. That's all I need to tell she's excited.

"Does this feel like I'm put off by your scars?" I ask.

She gives her head a vigorous shake, making her curls bounce. One of her fingers wanders off mine and slides against my cock, sending jolts of pleasure through my core.

I hiss through my teeth, my gaze locked with hers as I wait for her courage to bloom. Her touch is hesitant at first, with just the barest trace of a fingertip grazing my shaft. When a second joins, my breath hitches.

"Is this okay?" she asks.

"More," I groan, my hand continuing along the same rhythm.

The sensation of her fingers on my cock is almost too much to bear. When she licks those swollen lips, I groan.

My hips buck, wanting her to add another finger. "That's it, little ghost," I say, my voice thick with lust. "You're doing so well."

Her eyes spark with determination and desire as she looks up at me. Slowly, she replaces my hand with hers, taking full control. Her strokes become more assured, more deliberate, each movement a calculated promise of ecstasy. My balls tighten, the intensity of her touch sending shivers up my spine.

"Fuck, Amethyst," I groan, my breath hitching. "You're driving me crazy."

The corners of her pretty lips lift with a smile, radiating confidence. "Are you going to come for me, Xero?"

Her voice is so sultry that I'm on the brink of release. When did my little ghost get so bold?

"Answer me," she says.

Anticipation, mixed with the slow and sensual rhythm of her hand, pulls me into a whirlwind of pleasure. I'm drowning in her seductive green eyes, drowning in her scent, drowning in her touch.

"Fuck, yes," I groan, barely recognizing my own voice.

Her hand pauses, leaving me teetering on the edge of madness. My body shivers, the desperate need for release coursing through every vein, pooling like liquid fire.

"Why did you stop?" I rasp.

Her eyes glint with mischief before they narrow into dangerous slits. "Because I can. Because I want to see you beg."

"Amethyst," I growl, my body thrumming with need.

My heart pounds like a caged beast, ready to break through my ribs. It matches the rhythm of my throbbing cock. I have never had to beg a woman, but Amethyst has a way of making me break my own rules.

She licks her lips again, and I imagine that little pink tongue swirling around my crown. Her fingers tighten around my shaft, reminding me of what's at stake.

"Enjoying yourself, little ghost?" I grind out.

"Yes," she answers, her eyes glinting with wickedness. "I love seeing you so needy."

The primal instinct to take control rears forward, but I clench my jaw, fighting back the urge to demand satisfaction. This is her test, her way of exerting control. I force myself to stay calm, to obey.

"Go on. Beg for it," she murmurs, her voice sending shivers down my spine. "Beg me to continue."

Rage and desire mount within my soul, bringing up my drive to dominate. But I swallow it down, focusing on her delicate trust. This is more than a test—it's a chance to prove I will never take more than she's willing to give.

"Please, Amethyst," I rasp, my voice raw with need. "Please don't stop. I need it. I need you."

Her eyes darken, and her lips curve into a satisfied smile. The fingers around my shaft loosen and tighten, shocking me with jolts of pleasure and pain.

"More," she demands, her thumb sliding back and forth beneath my Prince Albert in a maddening rhythm.

"Please, little ghost," I repeat, my voice cracking with desperation. "I'm begging you. Don't torture me like this. Let me come for you."

Her hand glides over my shaft in a slow, deliberate rhythm, each stroke delivering ripples of sensation. A low moan escapes my lips, mingling with her excited panting. I want to buck my hips, fuck her hand and take my pleasure in an almighty explosion of rapture. Instead, I ball my fists, letting Amethyst set the pace.

She pumps me faster, her eyes locked with mine, her lips so close that we're breathing the same air. She's feeding off my desperation. I never knew my little ghost could be so predatory. But then, this is the same woman who tortured a man to death and a woman to the brink of insanity.

The thought of her taking what she wants from me ignites a fire across my libido that spreads through my veins like lava. Tension coils tight within my core, and I teeter on the edge of release.

Her hand halts, depriving me of pleasure. My muscles tremble, straining to obey the silent command to stay still.

"Amethyst," I moan against her lips, choking back a groan of frustration. "Fuck... Please..."

"You're so close, aren't you?" she murmurs, her breath hot against my ear, her lips brushing my skin like the softest silk.

"Yes," I groan, my body trembling with the effort to hold back. "So close. Please, little ghost. I'll do anything. Just say the word, and it's yours. You own me—please, just let me have this."

She continues forcing me to beg until my words become an incoherent babble. Her thumb rubs back and forth over my slit, each stroke driving me closer to madness. Her gaze locks onto mine, the connection between us almost unbearable in its intensity. Tension mounts. The hunger in her eyes mirrors my desperation, amplifying our shared desire.

Rage rumbles like distant thunder at being teased so mercilessly. But it's nothing compared to my overwhelming need to make her happy, to prove myself worthy of her trust.

"You're doing so well," she finally whispers, her voice a balm to my frayed nerves.

Her hand moves with renewed purpose, faster and firmer, driving me back to the brink of ecstasy. My breath comes in strangled gasps, my body straining towards release, every muscle taut with anticipation.

If she stops one more time, something inside me will crack. I need this woman more than I need air—more than I need the blood flowing through my veins. I need her more than I need the strength in my limbs or the electricity powering my heart.

Every second without her touch felt like a lifetime of hell, every moment without her love an eternity of torment. As though sensing my perilous state, she leans closer, melting her naked body into mine. Citrus, peach, and vanilla flood my senses, consuming what's left of my sanity.

"Who do you belong to?" she asks, her strokes quickening.

"You," I say through clenched teeth.

"Say my name," she says.

"Amethyst. Amethyst Crowley. My little ghost."

"Say my real name, too."

I swallow hard. "Amaryllis Salentino."

"Come for me, Xero," she commands, her voice a siren's call that shatters my last vestiges of control. "Come apart for your little ghost."

With a final, shuddering groan, I explode, my release spilling over her hand. The pleasure is overwhelming, an inferno igniting every nerve, leaving me breathless and utterly spent.

Every muscle in my body trembles in the aftermath, my mind blank with ecstasy. I collapse onto the mattress, gasping for air, trembling through the aftershocks.

Her touch is the only thing anchoring me to reality, her fingers still tracing patterns on my skin. The room spins, the intensity of the moment overwriting everything that's gone before. My body resonates with my slowing heartbeat, a reminder of the connection we just forged.

I lie on my side, trying to catch my breath, and turn to the woman who's become my life's purpose.

She smiles, her eyes shining with affection and triumph. "You're mine, Xero. And I'm yours."

The bond between us solidifies in that moment, and I know this truth, deep in the marrow of my bones. I will die for this woman, kill for this woman, slice through every living being on this planet for this woman. I would steal fire from the gods just to see the flames reflected in her eyes. I would tear apart the heavens to keep her safe, and face any measure darkness to hold her in my arms.

In her gaze, I find my destiny, my reason for existing, and nothing else in the world matters but her.

I thread my fingers into the back of her hair and pull her into a kiss that rivals the intensity of my climax. Her lips mold to mine with a burning fierceness. I've unlocked a new level of confidence in my little ghost that didn't exist before, and I've never been so proud.

As we pull apart, our breaths coming out in ragged gasps, I know we haven't just crossed a threshold. We've forged a bond that no other can break.

And I will do everything in my power to protect it.

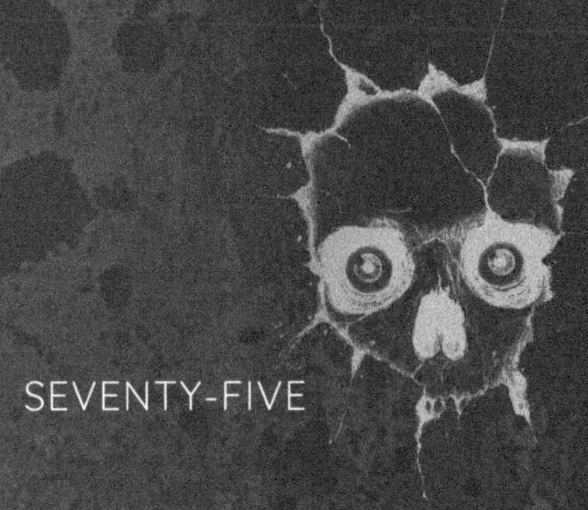

SEVENTY-FIVE

AMETHYST

The exhaustion of the night catches up with us, and we spend the rest of the day sleeping. Xero assures me that his Chief Medical Officer and Isabel will make sure the children we rescued get help with their trauma.

For the first time since leaving the asylum, it feels like I've regained pieces of my past I thought were lost forever. Xero was extremely patient, allowing me to navigate my feelings at my own pace and not pushing me beyond what I could handle.

He stirs beside me, his arms tightening around my waist. Gratitude swells in my chest, threatening to spill over in tears. I turn toward him and bury my face in the crook of his neck, wanting to stretch out this feeling of closeness and safety and warmth.

"Awake?"

His soft murmur sends a tingle down my spine. I hum against his skin, never wanting this moment to end. His fingers trace a slow path along my bare back, eliciting a quiet sigh.

"Thank you," I murmur into his neck. "What you did for me earlier meant everything."

He draws back and places a kiss on my temple. "Any time you feel the urge to come, I'll be there with my body at your disposal."

A giggle bursts from my chest. "You're volunteering to be my personal sex toy?"

"I'm the only man for the job. Always eager and ready to satisfy my little ghost."

Heat rises to my cheeks. I squirm against his chest, wanting to give him the same assurances, but the words die in my throat. I feel great right now, perfectly capable of enjoying Xero's touch, but what happens if I reach my limit? What happens if I can't handle any more?

"Hungry?" he asks, pulling me away from my thoughts.

"What time is it?"

Hesitating, he shifts on the mattress and pulls his phone off the bedside table. "Five."

My stomach chooses this moment to rumble, answering Xero's question. I finally open my eyes, finding the room dimmed by fading light. Through the window, the sun sets behind the distant trees, casting long shadows across the lawn.

"Is this the same safe house from before?" I ask, remembering its vast gardens.

"It's a secondary facility a few fields away from the first one." He eases us both up to sitting. "It's even more difficult to approach from the road."

We shower together, taking time to explore each other's bodies before changing into matching jumpsuits. Xero's maintenance crew—the same people who kitted out my crawl space—keep them stocked in all their hideouts, along with basic underwear.

I study my reflection in the mirror, still unable to look myself in the eyes. The woman on the other side looks more vibrant, with reddened lips and flushed skin. I feel stronger, more capable, more in control.

Xero comes up from behind, his hands settling on my hips.

"You're perfect," he murmurs, pressing his lips into the nape of my neck, and sending shivers skittering across my skin. His palms glide up my sides, warming the cool fabric of my jumpsuit.

Turning around in his arms, I look up into his eyes, finding them filled with adoration and a hint of mischief. I give him a peck on the lips. "I could say the same about you, but that would just give you a big head."

His blond brows quirk. "That's not the only thing about me that's big."

"Your ego?" At his grin, I place a palm on his chest and add, "Your heart."

Gaze softening, he brushes a curl off my forehead. "That's one of the reasons why I love you so much," he murmurs. "You look beyond my monstrous acts and see the man."

"You're not a monster, Xero," I murmur.

He breaks eye contact. "I've been killing since I was a child, and I run an organization that murders strangers for money. That at least makes me a villain."

His words hang in the air. I stare into his profile, my chest squeezing at the weight of his confession. Xero doesn't give me the chance to answer, turning away before I can process his meaning. By the time we leave the cottage and walk across the darkened lawn and through the trees, I'm still reeling, and his words echo in my mind like lurking ghosts.

Aren't we almost the same? Delta broke down Xero over several years. Dad did the same to me, with the help of Delta and Charlotte, in the space of months. Xero might be a trained assassin, but my past makes me the closest definition of a serial killer.

We reach the main building, a sprawling log cabin that blends into the forest. A canopy of tall oaks hangs over the roof, creating the impression of a tree house.

Armed guards patrol the perimeter, their silhouettes darting like specters in the dim light. As we step through the main entrance, Xero pulls me closer, his fingers interlacing with mine.

"Charlotte's in an underground holding cell. What do you want to do with her?" he asks.

"Don't you need her to access all the adoption records?"

He shakes his head. "Tyler already hacked into them. Another operative is interrogating Becky Taylor to see how much she knows."

We pass a reception desk at the entrance, manned by two guards, male and female. They nod at Xero as we head deeper into the heart of the building. He stares at the side of my face, waiting for me to object.

"As Dad's assistant, Becky had a vested interest in being nice to us," I say. "All I remember about her is a facade."

Xero nods. "What should we do if she's involved with the trafficking?"

"She should die," I reply.

We continue through a hallway lined with wooden panels, dimly lit by soft wall lights. The scent of pine fills the air, mixed with the lingering aroma of cooking. As we advance toward the end, my mouth waters at the mingled smells of roast chicken and freshly baked bread.

"This place is more like a summer camp than Three Fates," I mutter.

The corners of his mouth lifts into a rueful smile. "We wanted to create a nice atmosphere for the children."

Xero opens a door to reveal a vast, wood-paneled dining room with two sets of long tables. The girls we rescued sit on the left among only female staff, and the boys on the right sit with a mix. On the far end of the space is a head table on a podium, where Dr. Dixon sits with Isabel and two more of Xero's people.

"This looks familiar," I say, lifting my chest with nostalgia.

"Our maintenance staff might have gotten some inspiration from *Harry Potter*." He places a hand on the small of my back and guides me toward a serving hatch to the left of the room.

A middle-aged couple with kind smiles serves us tomato soup, grilled cheese sandwiches, and slices of apple pie. The woman adds an extra chicken leg on Xero's plate before he leads us to the head table.

Isabel scoots down two seats, giving us space to sit in the middle, while Dr. Dixon greets us with a tired nod. Xero settles into the chair next to his Chief Medical Officer, while I sit beside his sister.

"No incidents last night," the doctor says. "And the young operatives are in excellent health."

"Children," Xero mutters, tearing into his grilled cheese.

The older man nods, his gaze settling over the tables. "Although some of them are showing the beginnings of PTSD."

I lean close, my heart sinking as I scan the dining hall, taking in the haunted looks across both sets of tables.

"A trauma specialist will arrive tomorrow," Dr. Dixon murmurs.

Xero's lips tighten. "Do whatever's needed. We'll provide the resources."

The two continue talking in low voices about the logistics of bringing in additional staff and implementing counseling strategies, but my attention is fixed on the children. Not all of them pick at their meals. Others chat with each other and the older staff, although the atmosphere is subdued.

"How are you doing?" Isabel's voice breaks me out of my musings. I turn to face her, meeting dark eyes filled with concern.

"It's hard to see them like this," I say, offering her a weak smile.

Her gaze never leaves mine. "Did returning to the Three Fates Boarding School jog any extra memories?"

"Not as many as getting cold-cocked by your sister."

She snorts. "Camila has a powerful right hook. But if you need to talk to anyone about what you're experiencing, I'm here."

Swallowing, I nod my appreciation and take a large spoonful of my soup. While I appreciate the gesture, talking only gets me upset. The only thing that seems to make an impact is Xero's presence. And his touch.

And shedding the blood of my enemies.

"Think about it," Isabel says.

"Thanks," I murmur. "I will."

I tune back in to Xero's conversation with the doctor. An older woman has joined them; she seems to oversee this facility. They're already discussing curriculums and ways to ease the children back into society.

"Tyler told me how you helped us locate Three Fates," Isabel says. "What percentage of your memories would you say have returned?"

I pick up my sandwich. "There are still major holes. Sometimes it's hard to know what I'm supposed to remember."

She nods. "Understandable. What do you recall about the day of your abduction?"

I pause, the sandwich halfway to my mouth. Those memories exist in my mind in vivid technicolor, every gruesome detail etched into my subconscious. They don't haunt my thoughts because I keep myself busy, and Xero's presence beside me overwhelms that darkness.

"Everything, unfortunately," I say with a sigh.

She stills, her gaze sharpening. "Then perhaps you can tell me whether it was you or Dolly who started the fire that gave my brother permanent lung damage?"

SEVENTY-SIX

AMETHYST

The past few days have been a whirlwind of data gathering. Tyler and his team unearthed the names of everyone who ever rented a movie from X-Cite Media or became a member, while Jynxson and Camila extracted a list of wealthy families who adopted children from Dad's old agency, as well as the version Charlotte ran with Becky.

It turned out that Becky knew what was happening to the children, yet she allowed it to continue because each recruit earned her a thousand-dollar bonus. Camila shot her between the eyes and handed Tyler her bank details for him to plunder.

While Xero follows leads on Delta, I help interrogate the instructors Jynxson captured about their training methods. Two of the men who molested me are in the cells and have already given us names of the other men who turned little girls into Lolita assassins.

I also spend time with Charlotte, going through every manipulative tactic she and Dad used to break up our family. When I'm not torturing my personal demons, I'm training with Camila and any other female operative about my size.

My priority right now is avoiding Isabel. The other night, her question caught me off guard, and I nearly choked. Xero rushed in and saved me from further interrogation and changed the subject by volunteering for another round of tests. It only distracted his sister for a short time before her eyes were back on me with silent accusation.

I barely tasted my soup and sandwich after that, and the apple pie slid down my throat like cement. That single question has left me riddled with guilt.

Every time I bring up the morning I tried to set Xero on fire, he cups my cheek and tells me it wasn't my fault. Then he blames himself for the underhanded way he plagued my life, pretending to be a vengeful ghost.

One afternoon, days after Isabel confronted me about attacking Xero, I sift through Dolly's social media page. She's added three additional videos since the one where she pretended to be me and confessed to killing Mom.

They're all similar in format: her, dressed in a black corset, sitting in front of a green screen of my previous videos. She sips champagne, taunting the internet with names of other men I supposedly murdered.

My former fans leave hateful comments, asking why I haven't been arrested. Others try to siphon traffic by replying to those comments with think-pieces speculating that I was Xero's accomplice in the murder of his stepfamily all along.

It's infuriating how everyone's getting clout from something I built up with Xero.

"What are you doing?" asks a deep voice.

My heart leaps to the back of my throat. I whirl around, meeting a pair of smiling blue eyes. "Shit, Xero, don't sneak up on me like that."

Chuckling, he massages my shoulders and peers at the screen. "Why are you watching that?"

"Looking for clues," I mutter.

He shuts the laptop. "My father is an expert in staying hidden. And in psychological warfare. Those videos exist to manipulate your state of mind."

My shoulders sag. I know he's right, but the anger and frustration still wriggle around inside me like a nest of vipers. Which proves Xero's point.

"I wish I could reach through the screen and rip out her throat," I mutter.

He slides his fingers through my curls, his touch electrifying my scalp with tingles. "How's the training going?"

"I've sparred every five-foot-five woman on the campus," I say. "If they're not too busy helping you track down Delta, or on assassination missions, then they're helping out with the kids."

"Have you tried the boys?" he asks with a smile that makes the corners of his eyes crinkle.

I rear back, my jaw dropping. "I can't fight children."

"They're eager to train, faster, and have more explosive power than the average female operative."

Sighing, I consider his words. "It might be helpful to get a variety of opponents."

"And you can always spar with me again." He leans forward, his lips brushing mine.

Heat warms my cheeks, and the pulse between my legs quickens. "Your sparring always ends up the same way."

He grins against my lips, his eyes sparkling with amusement. "Is that a complaint?"

"Maybe we can save your kind of training for the evening."

He laughs, the sound so rich and warm that my heart flutters. "Valid point, but we should get one sparring session where I'm coming at you full strength. Just in case you end up fighting my father or one of his men."

I shudder, all traces of amusement vanishing, replaced by mounting dread. "You're right. We'll have to face them eventually."

"Any new memories today?" He massages my temples.

"Just some incident where one of the instructors molested me in Three Fates," I mutter.

His fingers still. "Which one?"

"I killed him after squeezing out the names of the other men who trained the girls."

Xero studies my features for several heartbeats, as if he's expecting me to crumble. Or explode. I slide a hand over his and give it a gentle squeeze.

"Don't worry about me. Those memories don't hurt, and they

weren't too much of a shock because of the time Camila knocked me unconscious. Before that, I'd already guessed what might have happened from the diary."

His gaze softens, and his thumb traces gentle circles over my cheekbone. "I want to gather every man who hurt you and bury them in a pit where they'll spend the rest of their lives in agony."

"You already drowned Reverend Tom and the investors in sewage," I reply with a smile.

"That reminds me." He draws back and walks to the cottage door, where a white box sits atop a side table. It's two feet wide and secured with a black ribbon.

"What's that?" I ask.

He carries the box over to the desk and places it on my lap. "A few gifts for my good girl."

The butterflies in my stomach take flight in a burst of excitement, their soft wings tickling my insides with delight.

"You've already given me so much," I say, my voice breathy with awe.

Safety, healing, acceptance, protection, a purpose, a home. Thanks to Xero, the black hole that I had for a childhood is now filled with memories. They're mostly unpleasant, but I finally have answers about the events that shaped my personality.

"This is something different," he says, his smile turning mysterious. "Go on. Open it."

My heart races as I unravel the ribbon and lift the lid. Inside are several more boxes. I open the first, a slender ten-inch rectangle, to find a big, red dildo.

Giggling, I pull it out and place a kiss on its tip. It's anatomically accurate in all ways but size. Somehow, the silicone always reduces its length and girth.

"Why did you make it?" I ask.

He raises a shoulder. "You've been asking for more than fingers recently. I thought that might satisfy you until you're ready for me."

A lump forms in my throat, and my chest constricts, making it hard to breathe. Tears prick at the backs of my eyes, threatening to spill over. Overwhelmed by his thoughtfulness, I can't help but feel unworthy of a man so considerate, so attuned to my needs.

"Xero..."

"Open the others," he says, his voice gruff.

The next box contains a leather overbust corset he bought from my Wonderland wishlist. It's black and fitted with laces at the back and steel hooks that fasten around the front.

"It's gorgeous," I whisper. "Thank you. I love it."

"Open the next one," he prods, his gaze wavering with a hint of vulnerability.

It contains a replica of the collar he gave me before the Ministry of Mayhem. My breath catches at the memory of how I lost the original in the fire, but I hold back from ruining the moment with another apology. Beneath that box is another containing a skirt that matches the corset, and next to that is a pair of red-soled heels.

"This is so extravagant," I whisper. "Why?"

"My little ghost deserves nothing but the best." He leans down and places a soft kiss on my lips.

I gaze up into his pale blue eyes, which shimmer with affection. "Thank you seems too weak in the face of such generosity—"

"What you give me is worth more than money," he replies.

My brows crease, and my mind dredges up Charlotte's taunts. She said Xero saw me as a project—a stepping stone to reach Delta. I shove that thought aside. So what if that's true? We're exactly what each other needs.

Before I can stop myself, I blurt, "But I don't give you anything."

"Watching you grow stronger isn't just rewarding for me. It gives me hope that I might regain what I've lost, too, once we've dealt with Dolly and my father."

My throat thickens, and I swallow back a surge of emotion. "It might take some time, but I think we will."

Eyes never leaving mine, Xero brings my knuckles to his lips and lavishes each one with soft kisses. "You are my anchor, little ghost. You give me more than you could ever know."

The raw honesty in his voice makes my heart thud. I take a deep, steadying breath, fighting the overwhelming wave of warmth. Xero always knows how to reach me with his words. His openness is both exhilarating and terrifying. But I'm not an inspiring warrior princess, just a screw-up trying to pick up the pieces.

He steps closer, releasing my hand to cup my cheek. "You deserve something beautiful. Tonight, let's take a break. I want to show you somewhere special."

"Are we going on an undercover mission?" I ask, my breath quickening.

He shakes his head. "No, a date."

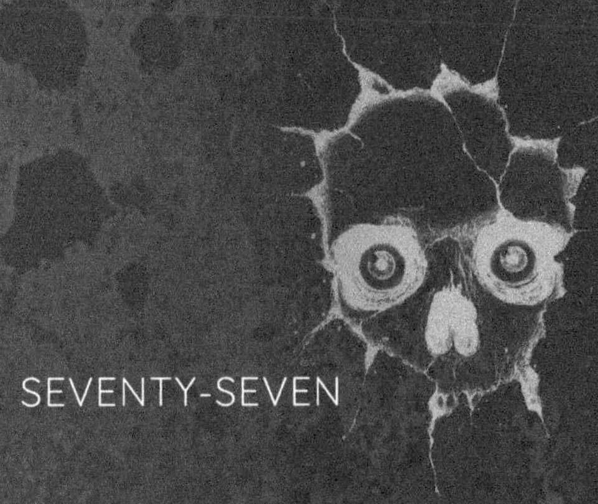

SEVENTY-SEVEN

XERO

I planned Amethyst's outfit to the last detail, knowing the tight leather will hug her curves, making her feel like the kind of woman who would pluck up the courage to write a killer on death row.

She's been making great progress, both in her combat and interrogation skills. Each time I watch her succeed on camera, I'm overwhelmed with a surge of possessive pride.

This transformation is everything I wanted for Amethyst from the beginning. My only regret is that it's been forged by pain and abuse. After tonight, I want my little ghost to see herself as my fierce goddess. She needs to acknowledge her burgeoning power, the power that's blossomed with each act of vengeance.

Amethyst belongs to me—not to Father, not to her psychotic sister, not to any of the people in her past. She's mine. And tonight, she'll understand that with every fiber of her delectable body. I'll show her the version of herself that's cherished and worthy of being worshiped.

I adjust my suit in the mirror. It's black and tailored to my physique, paired with an emerald green tie that matches Amethyst's eyes. In my pocket is something I've wanted to give her since I was imprisoned.

When she steps out of the bathroom covered in black leather, my breath catches. It's like my fantasy woman from the lonely nights in my cell has come to life. The leather corset hugs her torso, pushing up her breasts, and the skirt clings to her hips, accentuating every curve. My heart swells and heat rushes south. This is the woman I wanted to see waiting for me with the prison chaplain.

Amethyst is a vision, my dream made flesh.

She's tamed her curls so they frame her pretty face in soft waves. The left side is tinted the same shade of green as her eyes, which sparkle with anticipation. Beneath the excitement is a flicker of doubt I plan to extinguish.

"Xero?" Her voice wavers with an unspoken question of her worth.

"You look exquisite." I close the distance between us and brush a stray lock from her face, eliciting a pretty blush. Pride flares in my chest at how I can reduce this deadly little killer to shyness. She's strong, but still vulnerable. To me, that makes her even more precious.

"Where are we going?" she asks.

"You once wanted to know what happened to the liberated operatives who didn't choose to join our group. Some live quiet lives, others fight their own causes, and a few create things of beauty."

I offer her my arm and guide her toward the door. "Tonight, I'm going to show you the latter."

We step out into the balmy evening air, still warm from the day. The sky is a deep indigo, sprinkled with stars. The vintage BMW is parked outside with its top up, ready for our journey. Once we're settled in, I drive Amethyst out to Lake Alderney, where a former Moirai operative I freed purchased a vineyard after retiring.

As we approach the valley, Amethyst sits up in her seat at the sight of fairy lights illuminating the grapevines. The magic in her eyes is beyond my wildest hope.

"Is this a vineyard?" she asks, her voice breathy with wonder.

The corner of my lips lifts into a smile. "I always wanted to take you to Armagnac. Our trip there will have to wait until we've slayed our enemies. Until then, this is the next best thing."

She sits forward in the front passenger seat, her breath quickening. "This is stunning."

I chuckle. "You haven't even seen it yet."

We pass through wrought-iron gates shaped like curling vines, opening onto a cobblestone path. The air is filled with the sweet scent of grapes, mingling with the earthy aroma of vineyard soil. The wheels of the car bump along the stones, alerting my former colleague to our presence.

"Who owns this place?" she asks, her gaze moving from side to side, drinking in every detail of the illuminated grapevines and ancient olive trees lining the path.

"A man named Vinzent."

"Vincent?"

"Vinzent. With a Z."

"I can't hear the difference."

I grin. "You will when you meet him."

We pull up to a white mansion at the heart of the vineyard, where Vinzent is already striding out of the doorway. Like most former members of the Moirai, he prefers black, a stark contrast to his tanned skin and golden hair. I expected him to dress more like a vintner.

I wind down the window, letting in the sweet scent of ripe grapes. Vinzent approaches with a smile, his sharp gray eyes meeting mine before flicking to Amethyst.

"Xero," he says, clasping my hand in a firm grip. "Welcome back from death row. I see you've brought the president of your fan club."

Amethyst shifts in her seat, visibly cringing at being recognized from social media. I immediately squeeze her hand, letting her know she's safe and protected.

"Thanks to Amethyst, we've broken up a snuff-movie ring," I say with a touch of pride. "Seized over eighty-million dollars in bank deposits and rescued twenty-four child assassins. She's gotten us closer to capturing Delta than anyone before."

Brows rising, Vinzent's gaze moves back to Amethyst, his eyes softening with newfound respect. "Welcome, Amethyst, and thank you for advancing our cause. It's an honor to have you visit my humble abode."

She offers him a weak smile, and I give her hand another reassuring squeeze. Vinzent then gives us directions to his summer house at the edge of his vineyard.

We continue in silence down a driveway lined with grapevines toward a small grove of olive trees around the back of the property. Moonlight bathes the vineyard in a silver glow, casting long, rippling shadows across the cobblestone path. My little ghost stares ahead, seemingly lost in thought.

I turn to her and say, "Vinzent didn't mean any harm earlier."

She rubs the back of her neck. "I know, but it's scary to think that my social media exposed me to the whole world and left my enemies a trail of breadcrumbs."

The tremble in her voice makes my heart sink. I know she's thinking about Dolly, Delta, and her degradation.

"Don't blame yourself." I give her a comforting squeeze, wanting to remove her regret and replace it with resolve. "The drugs you were taking at the time affected your judgment."

She blows out a long breath, releasing a fraction of her tension. "True."

I wait for her to say something else, but she remains silent.

"Do you want me to bring in Dr. Saint?" I ask, my chest tightening with concern.

She shakes her head. "There's no point. All she ever did was keep me medicated under my mom's orders. I don't want her harmed, because she did help me get away with killing Mr. Lawson and the Reed brothers."

"You remember them now?"

"Vaguely." She raises a shoulder. "I remember going to a college party and dancing with Sparrow. Then Wilder joined us later with drinks. There's a gap, then the next thing I remember is calling Mom from a dorm room with two dead bodies."

My brow furrows. This is a breakthrough, but forcing her to unearth a trauma she might not accurately remember could ruin the surprise I set up for my little ghost. Tonight is about moving forward. We can talk about her time at college in the morning.

Deciding not to poke at that memory, I park beneath a sprawling olive tree and help Amethyst out of the car. We walk alongside rows of grapevines, their leaves rustling in the slight breeze, until we reach the French doors of a summer house overlooking the lake.

Opening the doors, I guide her into a spacious living room lit by a crackling fire. The table is set with a selection of Vinzent's wines and an elaborate charcuterie board piled with cured meats, cheeses, olives, pickles, and freshly baked breads.

"I hope you brought your appetite," I say with a reassuring smile.

Amethyst freezes in the doorway, her eyes wide with wonder as she takes in the surroundings. I had planned an elegant evening reminiscent of the wine tastings I enjoyed in France, complete with a gourmet spread and Vinzent's finest bottles.

"You arranged this for me? It's beautiful," she whispers, her voice breathy with awe.

"I wanted to give you a break," I say, my heart soaring at her happiness. "Just for tonight, let's forget everything outside this vineyard."

She steps further into the room, her gaze sweeping to the fireplace before settling on me. "Is there a bedroom?"

My brows rise at her boldness, and sensation surges to my cock. "Are you trying to seduce me, little ghost?"

Closing the distance between us, she places her palms on my chest and murmurs, "Maybe I am."

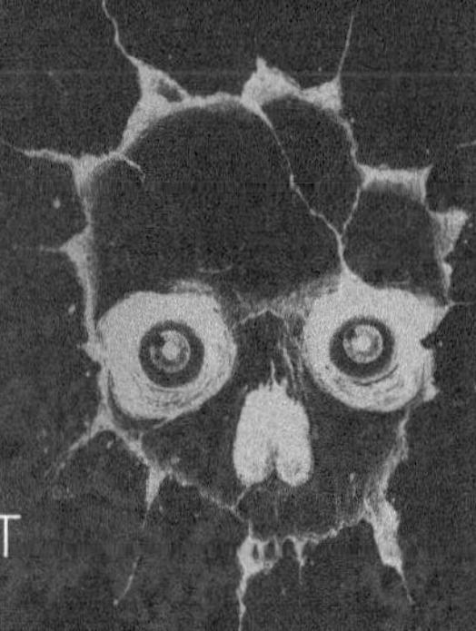

SEVENTY-EIGHT

AMETHYST

Xero gazes down at me, his pale blue eyes burning brighter than the fire. He might be surprised at my forwardness, but I'm not the same person I was even last week.

It's just like he said—I've furthered his cause and faced down a handful of my former abusers. The trauma of my past feels distant, replaced by the satisfaction of retribution. Each confrontation has stripped away the layers of my old self, leaving me stronger.

He steps closer, his hand cupping my cheek, his touch both gentle and possessive. "Are you sure about this, little ghost?"

"You've teased me for long enough." I turn my head to press a kiss to his palm. "When you gave me that toy, all I could think about was how much I wanted the real thing."

Gaze flickering with desire, he wraps an arm around my waist, pulling me flush against his erection. Its length and heat and girth soak into my belly, making me swallow back a groan. Heat rushes to my core, which clenches in anticipation.

With his thumb, he traces the line of my jaw before sliding it onto my bottom lip, sending shivers down my spine.

"This is a dangerous game you're playing," he growls, his voice a husky whisper. "You know the way I fuck... I'm not a gentle man."

His words hang in the air, a dark promise that makes my pulse race. Tremors course through my core, and my pussy becomes slick with arousal.

"I can handle three fingers. Why can't I handle you?" My voice comes out more challenging than I intended, even though I need him to push my limits.

Silence stretches, broken only by the soft crackle and pop of burning wood. Outside, the wind rustles through the grapevines. Xero's gaze darkens, taking on a predatory glint. His fingers slide down from my lip, tracing the column of my throat and lingering at the hollow base. The touch feels possessive, and I shiver at the thought of him claiming me as his.

"I'll warn you, once I start, I won't stop until you're mine in every way. There's no holding back with me, no halfway. You want this? You'll take all of me, or nothing at all."

My breath catches at the raw promise in his voice, but I manage to keep my gaze steady, my body aching for the danger he's offering.

"Ruin me, Xero," I whisper.

"Pick a safe word," he rumbles, his lips grazing my ear.

Shivers skitter down my spine, and my breath hitches. "Why?"

"Because when I fuck you, it will be with all my heart. I'll erase the touch of any man who thought he could lay claim on what's mine, and I won't stop until you're sobbing my name. If you can't take it, you need a way to stop me before it gets too intense."

As his words sink in, my pulse thrums in my ears. I swallow, my mouth suddenly dry. "McMurphy?"

"What?" he draws back, his lip curling in distaste. His eyes narrow, searching mine.

"Too much?" I ask, my voice trembling with uncertainty.

His features tighten. "That word is like being doused with ice water."

"Good," I say with a nod. "What happened to her?"

"She lost an eye." He lowers his mouth onto mine, his kiss searing and possessive, claiming me completely.

All thoughts of that pervy prison officer disappear as his

tongue ravishes my mouth. His kiss is fierce and commanding, with an intensity that leaves me breathless. I melt against his larger body, surrendering completely to his desire.

His hands find their way to the front of my corset and unfasten the hooks. His touch is electric, each brush of his fingers igniting my skin with sparks. The leather falls away, revealing my breasts to his gaze.

A draft swirls around my exposed skin, making my nipples tighten. Groaning, Xero rolls them between his thumb and fingers, igniting waves of ecstasy.

"Xero." I arch into his touch, a moan escaping my lips as I crave more of his intoxicating caress.

His lips graze my neck as he unzips my skirt. My skin tingles as the leather slides down my thighs, a chill rushing over my skin before it's warmed by the fire. I step out of the puddle of fabric, standing before him in just my boots and panties.

His eyes roam over me, taking in every inch of my figure. I try not to squirm, pushing away thoughts of the cuts marring my skin. I'm no longer damaged, but battle-hardened. A warrior, just like Xero.

He leans in close, his breath warm against my ear as he whispers, "You're exquisite. Every inch of you is perfect."

The warmth of his breath against my neck makes my skin tingle. Then his lips find my collarbone, trailing lower to my breasts, each kiss a burning brand. I cling to his biceps, losing myself in the sensation of his touch.

"Get on your knees," he growls, his voice a low, commanding rumble.

Obeying, I sink to the rug, feeling the heat from the fire seeping into my back. Desire coils in my belly as I meet his gaze, his eyes now pools of black with just the barest ring of blue.

His erection strains against the fabric of his pants, the outline of his pierced, thick cock clearly visible and tantalizing.

With trembling fingers, I reach for his waistband, unbuckle his belt, and pull down his zipper. His cock springs free, its piercings glinting in the firelight.

Suddenly, memories surge to the forefront of my mind. I'm back in that chair, my mouth wedged open with steel, surrounded by men jerking off at Dolly's command. I flinch, my heart stuttering.

"Are you still with me, little ghost?" Xero asks, his voice snapping me back to the present.

I shift on my knees, the memory fading. "Sorry," I mutter. "Flashback."

He slides his fingers through my curls, making my scalp tingle. "Look at me."

I glance up at Xero, seeing those pale eyes filled with banked fury. The firelight catches his platinum hair, giving him an unearthly glow. He looks like a warrior god crowned with flames. The sight is both terrifying and breathtaking. As I lock gazes with him, every other man fades into insignificance, leaving only the intensity of his presence.

"You're with me, understand?" he asks, the conviction in his voice unwavering.

Gulping, I nod, my heart pounding in my chest.

"I will castrate every bastard who ever touched you and burn their balls on a pyre," he growls, his voice menacing and low. His fingers tighten in my hair, his eyes burning with fierce protectiveness.

"Why not set fire to their dicks?" I ask, with a spark of defiance.

"Because you're going to stuff those cocks down their throats," he replies with a sharp grin.

Bubbling laughter erupts from my throat, breaking the tension. A crushing weight lifts from my chest, and my spirits soar. How could I ever feel bad about myself with Xero watching my back?

This isn't even dark humor. It's a fucking plan.

I wrap my fingers around his shaft and pull him closer, making him jerk forward with a soft grunt. As I continue to stroke him, he lengthens and thickens at my touch. The temptation is too great, and I can't resist adding a playful comment.

"What if I want yours? It's so tempting. It even comes with lots of pretty jewelry."

"My cock is not pretty," he growls.

"Yes, it is," I say, holding his gaze. "Everything about you is pretty. Even your balls." I grin, drawing my thumb along the sensitive skin beneath his Prince Albert.

He shivers. "How about you put it in that smart mouth?"

Licking my lips, I lean forward and swirl my tongue around the head of his cock, savoring the way he feels before taking him deeper. His taste is intoxicating—a blend of salt and musk, heightened by the heat of his arousal. I relish the way he twitches in my mouth, each movement igniting a spark of desire.

"Slow down," he murmurs, his hand resting on the back of my head. "Take your time. Feel every inch."

I open wider, letting him guide me slowly, as my mouth adjusts to his size.

"Good girl," he groans. "That's it. Let me feel that perfect mouth."

I hum around his shaft, my heart soaring.

"Use that tongue," he growls, his voice rough with desire. "Make me lose control."

My clit throbs with anticipation, and the muscles of my pussy tighten. I lash my tongue from side to side, my folds becoming painfully slick.

"Good girl," he groans, his fingers tangling in my curls. "Now, part those pretty lips and take me all the way."

His voice is deep and commanding, sending a pulse of excitement straight to my core. I open wider, taking in as much of him as I can without gagging. His deep groan sends me a thrill of satisfaction as he hits the back of my throat.

Bobbing my head, I continue to take him in, using just the right amount of pressure and suction to drive him wild. With each swipe of my tongue, I control his reactions.

"You're incredible," he moans, his hips jerking. "So tight. So wet. So utterly irresistible."

I hum, the vibration making him shudder. Even though he's fully dressed and I'm the one kneeling before him only in my panties, I feel empowered. Right now, I control Xero's pleasure. I own him.

Every swirl of my tongue causes his breath to hitch and his body to tremble. I hollow my cheeks, sucking him harder, my mouth working in tandem with the strokes of my hand.

His grip tightens in my hair, guiding my movements as I take him deeper, his crown pushing against the muscles at the back of my throat. Tears prick at the corners of my eyes, but I push through, determined to bring him to the edge.

"Eyes on me."

I pull back just enough to lock gazes. His expression is raw, filled with a need so intense it makes my breath catch. His eyes burn with a molten intensity, and in them, I see my own reflection—a goddess, a temptress, a woman unafraid of her desires.

Gaze darkening with lust, he thrusts into my mouth. "You look so beautiful with your lips wrapped around my cock."

Moaning, I swallow around his length, my own arousal building with his shudders and groans. They mingle with the snap and crackle of the fire, and the soft rustle of the wind.

"I'm going to take your throat, Amethyst. Do you want that? Do you want me to use you?"

"Yes," I say around my mouthful. "Please."

He tightens his grip in my hair, holding my head steady as he pulls back his hips. With a powerful thrust, he drives deep and hard into my mouth, meeting the resistance of a ring of muscle.

"Relax your throat, baby," he says softly, his thumb caressing my cheek in a tender gesture. "Let me in."

Nodding, I surrender to him, forcing my muscles to loosen, letting him slide further down my mouth. As he passes my gag reflex, we both groan.

"Just like that," he rumbles.

He moves back and forth, taking control, each powerful thrust delivering a wave of pleasure. His taste, his scent, the feel of his cock stretching my lips—it's intoxicating, making my core throb harder with need.

"Ah... you're my good girl. My very special, little treat."

With my free hand, I slide my fingers into my panties and rub a circle around my swollen clit. Arousal coats my fingers, slick and hot as I pleasure myself, matching my movements to the rhythm of his hips.

"That's right. Stroke it nice and slow."

Every moan, every gasp from Xero heightens my own pleasure, and I press harder, needing my own release.

"You're taking me so deep, so well. Fuck, little ghost, you're going to make me come."

I want to push him over the edge, to feel the power of his climax, to take control of this awesome being. His cock throbs, his abs tense, his breath comes in ragged gasps. Just as he's about to climax, he pulls back, his cock slipping out from my lips with a wet pop.

"Xero?" I ask, my voice breathy.

He leans down, his eyes locking with mine. "You've been such a good girl for me, I'm going to give you what you want."

My eyes widen.

"Lie back for me, baby. I'm going to take your sweet cunt."

SEVENTY-NINE

XERO

Amethyst gazes up at me through bleary eyes. Mascara has run down her cheeks, making her look beautifully wrecked. My balls draw up at the sight of her, so eager and flushed and ready for my cum. It's almost enough to have me spilling over the edge.

Almost.

But I don't plan on climaxing before my little ghost.

Her breasts bounce as she sits on her ass, and I guide her onto her back. Seeing her laid out for me on the rug with the fire casting a warm glow over her skin is nothing short of heavenly.

Amethyst is a masterpiece of soft curves and dips. I take in the sight of her beneath me, her body trembling with need. Her breasts are full and round, her nipples hardening for attention. I glance between her thighs and groan, captivated by the wetness glistening on her pink folds, slick and inviting.

Her body, which was once an intoxicating blend of innocence and beauty, is now one of an equal. The scars adorning her skin tell tales of battles she's survived, and the vengeance she'll wreak on our mutual enemies.

Breathing fast and shallow, she reaches for my shirt. I move closer, positioning myself between her creamy thighs. My fingers trail down her belly, making the muscles beneath her flesh quiver.

"Xero," she whispers, "You're wearing too much."

A smirk pulls at the edges of my lips. "Think you can handle what's underneath?"

At her eager nod, I add, "Then you know what to do."

She slips her fingers through the opening of my shirt and pulls hard, sending buttons scattering across the rug.

"I love it when you take what you want," I murmur, my breath catching as she continues tugging until she's exposed my chest and abs.

She moans, making me chuckle. "Impatient, little ghost?"

As she runs her hands over my pecs, I trace my fingers over the slick contours of her pussy. Pride swells in my heart at her desperate cries.

"Tell me what you want," I whisper, teasing her clit, making her hips jerk. Her gasps of pleasure are all the encouragement I need to slide two digits into her wet heat.

"Xero," she moans, rolling her hips in time with my strokes. "I want more."

"You think you've earned it?" My lips quirk when she snarls. "Then who am I to deny the woman I love?"

I add a third finger, savoring the way she trembles and arches at my touch. "That's it. Take it all. I love how your body responds to me."

Whimpering, she clenches the digits.

Over the past few days, she's become less skittish, more responsive, and bolder than ever. I can't tell if it's the torture she's been inflicting, her trust in me deepening, or the passage of time, but her confidence makes me lightheaded.

"Fuck, you're so tight," I growl, my voice thick with desire. "You were made just for me."

She moans, her hips moving against my hand, and I lean down to press a kiss to her inner thigh. The scent of her arousal is intoxicating, a mix of musk and sweetness that drives me insane.

Her body arches with tension, with an urgent need, but I want to take my time and make sure she's ready. I slide my fingers in and out of her tight heat, curling them to hit just the right spot. I revel in the way her face contorts with pleasure.

"Xero, please," she says, her voice a desperate whisper.

"Tell me what you need," I snarl.

Her breath quickens. She jerks on her back, making her breasts jiggle. "Please, Xero. I need you inside me."

Desire overwhelms my senses. Arousal shoots straight to my cock at her raw need, and the edges of my vision go dark. Every instinct screams at me to pull out my fingers and replace them with my cock, but I force myself to resist.

"Not yet, baby. I want to hear you beg for it."

Part of me still reels from the time she mistook me for Father. I know she's no longer under the influence of hallucinogenic drugs, but I need to be sure this is what she truly wants. We're on the precipice of a breakthrough. This has to go at Amethyst's pace, not mine.

"Xero," she cries.

My name on her lips sparks a primitive urge to claim and mark her as mine. Clenching my teeth, I snarl, "Sure you handle it?"

"Yes," she gasps out, her voice barely louder than a breath. Her fingers take my shaft in a death grip, pulling it closer to her sweet, wet pussy. "Please."

My cock twitches.

Not yet...

Not until she demands it.

"You think you're ready? Let me make sure."

"Xero!"

"But I'm already inside you." I scissor my fingers, resisting the urge to position myself at her entrance. She mumbles something incoherent, making me add, "What was that? I didn't hear you."

Her breath hitches, and she squirms around my fingers. "I want you to fuck me, Xero. Please. I need to feel your cock."

My digits slide out of her slick pussy. I take hold of my shaft and rub its tip of my cock against her folds. "Is this what you want, little ghost?"

She shivers. "Please, Xero." Her voice breaks. "Fill me up. I need your cock. Fuck me."

My chest thrums with satisfaction. There's no doubt about it —she's ready. But I've become addicted to the sound of her begging.

"You can do better than that," I say, my breath shallowing. "Come on, I want to hear every word. Beg me like you mean it."

Tears well up in her eyes and she cries out, the sound a mix of frustration and need. "I want you more than anything. I've been dreaming of this, needing this. Please, Xero, I'm begging you. Fuck me hard. Fill me with your huge dick."

Her desperate pleas break the last of my restraint. "You asked for it, baby. Now take all of me."

With a growl, I thrust into her, feeling her tightness envelop my cock. The sensation is overwhelming, almost too much. I'm on the verge of coming, but I grit my teeth, not wanting to disappoint my little ghost.

"Fuck, you feel so good, I might not last."

Her pussy muscles clench and spasm around my shaft, pulling me closer, milking my every inch. I hold still, wanting to imprint this memory forever.

"Fuck, you're so tight," I groan, my voice rough. "So perfect around my cock."

She whimpers beneath me, her body trembling. "I almost forgot you were so big."

I push down to the hilt, and her pussy quivers around my shaft, adjusting to my girth. We lie together on the rug, gazing into each other's eyes. This is the moment I thought we'd have during our conjugal visit. I planned on claiming her in the visitation room and telling her in person not to mourn my passing because I had a way for us to be together forever.

Her muscles stop adjusting around my shaft, leaving her body open to me completely. Only then do I move with deliberate thrusts, driving into her slick heat with a careful rhythm.

"You're ready for me now, aren't you? I'm going to make you remember this."

Clenching around my cock, she moves her hips in counterpoint to my thrusts, giving back as much pleasure as she's receiving. The rhythm quickens, our bodies moving as if we've been together for years instead of weeks.

"Tell me how it feels," I growl, my lips brushing her ear.

"Incredible... So deep... so good... but not enough," she moans, her body trembling.

I move faster, spurred on by her cries for more. Her body arches into mine, and I can't get enough of my little ghost. Her tight, wet heat grips me like a vise, pushing me to the edge.

"Amethyst, you drive me wild," I groan, my voice thick with desire. "Fucking you is like teetering on the brink of madness."

Her moans grow louder, and I can tell she's close. "Please, Xero," she begs, her voice desperate. "Touch me. Make me come."

I reach down, my fingers finding her swollen clit, and circle it in time with my thrusts. She cries out, her inner walls clenching so hard that my eyes roll to the back of my head.

"That's it, baby," I murmur, my own voice shaking with need. "Come for me. Show me how good it feels."

Her orgasm rips through her walls, making her body convulse as she screams my name. I continue rubbing her clit, drawing out her climax.

While she's still trembling from the aftershocks, I pull out, shifting her onto her hands and knees. The sight of her wet pussy from behind sends a surge of heat through my veins. Every primal instinct rears up to claim what's mine. This time, I can't ignore my urges.

Gripping her hips, I thrust back inside her, hard and deep, and she gasps, her pussy still quivering. Her tight heat envelops my shaft, and the sensation is almost too much to bear.

"Who do you belong to?" I growl, as I pound into her perfect cunt.

"You, Xero," she moans, her voice breathy and raw.

I quicken my thrusts, driving into her harder, the beast inside me rutting in a frantic rhythm. "Say it again."

"Xero. I belong to Xero Greaves," she screams.

Her words send a thrill straight to my balls. I'm so close to coming that every nerve thrums.

"That's my girl... That's my sweet, wet, tight girl. Take it. Take it all. To the fucking hilt."

I reach around, finding her clit again, and rub it with rough strokes, making her scream. We fuck like animals, our bodies slick with sweat, filling the room with the sounds of flesh smacking on flesh.

"Amethyst," I growl, my voice hoarse with need. "I'm close... come with me."

Her body tenses, and I feel her tightening around my shaft. Over and over, she squeezes, those powerful muscles clamp and spasming.

"Yes. Just like that. Milk me, drain me, take my soul. Fuck... you're killing me. Clenching so tight. You don't know what you do to me. I'm going to... I'm going to... Oh, fuck."

I hold back, teetering on the precipice, wanting this moment to last, but it's more than I can resist. Her climax grips my cock so hard that no force on earth could stop me from tumbling over the edge. With a final, powerful thrust, I explode inside her, shooting ropes of cum into her tight heat.

Afterward, we collapse together on the rug, our bodies spent and trembling, the fire casting a warm glow. I hold her close against my chest, feeling the rapid beat of her heart in sync with mine. Our breaths mingle as I brush my lips against her forehead, inhaling the sweet scent of her hair.

Whispering words of love and adoration, I tell her how much she means to me, how every moment with her feels like a gift. My fingers trace gentle patterns on her back, each touch a promise of my unwavering devotion.

For a moment, the world outside ceases to exist, and it's just me and my perfect match, wrapped in the cocoon of our shared intimacy.

"Amethyst," I whisper into her curls, my breath catching. "You have no idea how much I love you."

She lifts her head, her eyes meeting mine with a softness that steals my breath. "How much?"

The vulnerability in her voice triggers every protective instinct. "I love you more than the blood in my veins. I love you more than the air in my lungs. You're the first thing I think about when I wake, and the last on my mind when I sleep. I love you so much that every moment without you feels like burning in the pits of hell."

"Xero," she whispers.

"I love you more than words could ever capture, because you've always been mine. Mine long before we even met. No one has ever completed me the way you do. You're it. My everything. My perfect match."

Her eyes well with tears, but they're from joy, not sorrow. Instead of demanding a response, I hold her tight, not wanting to push her before she's ready. We lie together, entwined, savoring the fire's glow and the depth of our shared feelings, cherishing our rare and beautiful connection.

An alert breaks through our special moment. With a groan, I grope around the rug for my pants and find my phone. One glance at the screen makes me stiffen.

"Who is it?" Amethyst asks.

"It's from HQ. Dolly sent you a new video."

Her brow furrows, concern etching lines on her beautiful face. "What's it about?"

Another message pops up:

Dolly's people just posted bail for Relaney Cymbal. Permission to pursue?

Amethyst's breath catches. "We need to do something."

I nod, my mind racing. "We will. Get dressed."

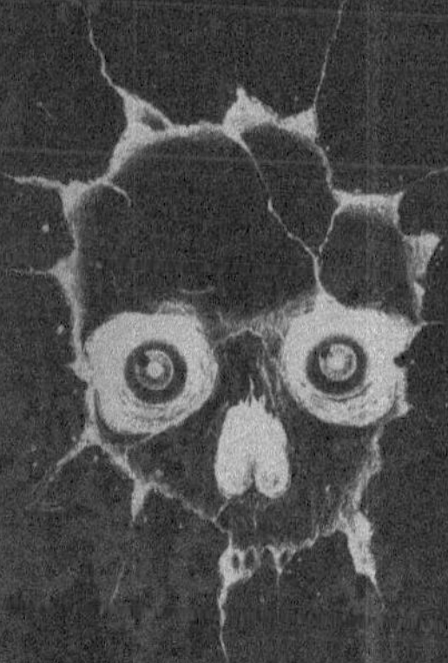

EIGHTY

AMETHYST

The next several seconds are a scramble to put on my clothes. My hands shake so badly I can barely fasten my leather skirt. Even my corset crushes my lungs, forcing my breaths to shallow. I'd completely forgotten about Relaney's existence until now, assuming the strange woman who lived next door on Parissi Drive was still in prison for the cannabis farm she'd created in her basement.

Xero slips on his suit pants and boots, but his shirt is a lost cause since I ripped it open. He exits the summer house bare-chested and helps me into his car.

Silence stretches out for the tense seconds it takes to exit the vineyard. Each bump in the cobblestones sends jolts through my gut and rattles my nerves. I ball my fists so tightly that it hurts.

Worry gnaws at my insides. I clutch at my chest, not believing those bastards targeted my neighbor just to use her as a pawn in Dolly's misguided vendetta. Hasn't Relaney suffered enough?

Xero's car tears out of the vineyard onto a narrow, winding country lane. He's struggling to stay composed, but his white knuckles and the veins on his temples telegraph his fury.

The fear that gnaws at my insides fights a losing battle against the anger boiling in my veins. My gaze drops to the phone he left on the center console.

"What's in the video?" I ask, my voice tight.

"Take a look. Maybe you'll spot something useful."

I pick up the phone and click the URL, which directs to a private social media page. My nostrils flare. There's a reason why Dolly didn't post publicly. This bullshit would probably get her arrested.

The screen lights up with a POV shot of a man walking into a police precinct and signing over some papers. A door at the back opens, and Relaney steps out, clad in a jumpsuit that hangs off her skinny frame.

My breath catches. She's barely recognizable without her round glasses, and her blonde afro is now a backcombed mess. Dark circles ring her eyes, and she's lost so much weight that her facial bones have become even more prominent.

"Who are you?" Relaney asks, her voice wavering.

"A friend of Amethyst Crowley," replies Locke's snide voice. "She felt really terrible about your arrest and raised money to get you out of jail."

My heart plummets into my stomach. I fight back a slew of memories from the asylum to focus on Relaney.

Locke's hand comes into the frame as he guides her through the precinct and towards its exit. The video cuts to her approaching a black SUV. Its back door opens, revealing a grinning Dolly.

Nausea churns in my gut. I glance away at the sight of her psychotic features, only for the scene to shift to Relaney in her living room, clad only in her underwear and hogtied across the three mattresses on her floor. Tears stream down her pale face, and her lips move but make no sound. The dim lighting casts sinister shadows, accentuating her terror.

The camera pans to Dolly, posing with a knife between two masked men. "Show yourself," Dolly says. "Or Relaney becomes our next star."

Guilt presses down on my chest, crushing tighter than any corset. I suck in a trembling breath, but it barely reaches the tops of my lungs. Dolly has completely lost her mind. She's putting every woman connected to me in danger.

"I'm going to be sick," I mutter. "Relaney got dragged into this nightmare because of me."

"No, it's because my father and Dolly are vicious psychopaths," Xero replies, his fingers tightening on the steering wheel.

We merge onto the highway, and he picks up speed. Streetlights flash by in a blur of white and yellow. I barely register the passing scenery, my mind flooding with intrusive thoughts.

If I'd continued ignoring Relaney, she would never have become a target. I only stayed over at her house because I thought mine was haunted. Now, her life hangs in the balance.

Tears sting my eyes and blur my vision. "You're wrong. She got arrested because of me."

"She was growing cannabis in her basement," Xero says, his tone gruff, but barely penetrates my fog of guilt.

They only discovered the weed farm because Xero murdered Chappy. If he hadn't been so psychotically overprotective, then the police wouldn't have searched her house and arrested Relaney. She would still be surrounded by her strange men.

I shake off that thought. This isn't Xero's fault. Not completely. The blame lies with Delta and his cohorts.

Xero places a finger on his Bluetooth earpiece. "Tyler just hacked into police surveillance to obtain their registration. Jynxson and Camila are already en route to intercept Dolly."

The journey takes forever. Lake Alderney is nearly thirty miles away from my neighborhood and the highway seems to stretch into eternity. The tension inside the car climbs with each passing second, thick enough to make me choke.

Suddenly, Xero's phone vibrates with a notification, which pierces my heart with an icy shard of trepidation.

"Accept body cam from Jynxson?" I ask, glancing over at Xero, whose gaze is still fixated on the road ahead.

"Do it," he says.

I tap the YES button and brace myself for what I might see. It's footage of Jynxson moving behind Camila through a darkened hallway lined with skulls.

"They're approaching the house from the catacombs," I say. "Will they be able to access Relaney's crawlspace?"

He grunts. "Through a hatch."

It's probably how Xero entered Relaney's house whenever I visited. I don't dwell on that thought for long, because another notification comes up from Tyler. When I accept it, an additional screen appears on the phone, displaying drone footage of Parisii Drive.

"They've surrounded Relaney's house," I murmur.

As two more notifications bring up screens of operatives approaching my old road via vehicle and on foot, Xero directs them using his Bluetooth headset.

I sit back in the front passenger seat, feeling powerless. Everyone is storming Relaney's place, and all I can do is watch from a distance.

One of the screens displays footage of someone attacking number 11's front door with a battering ram. The wood splinters, sending shards flying in all directions. Another figure tosses in a smoke bomb that fills Relaney's hallway with thick fog.

"Spring team, proceed with caution," Xero says into his Bluetooth.

I switch to a screen from the drone's point of view as it hovers above number 11. Its infrared camera picks up heat signatures scrambling around the house. Red figures charge into its interior, while a trio of green markers remain stationary. I can only guess one of them is Relaney.

"What does it mean if a heat signature is green and unmoving?" I murmur.

Xero glances across the front seat at me, his steely gaze softening. "Either they're tied up, unconscious, or already dead."

"If they were dead, wouldn't they be cold?"

He shakes his head, turning his attention back to the road. "A human body can stay warm for at least three hours."

Choking back a sob, I glance down to the screen, willing Relaney to move. A fresh wave of red figures approaches the building from the catacombs, then they stop moving.

My brow furrows. If Relaney is green, then what color are Dolly and her henchmen?

"What?" Xero roars and clutches his earpiece.

I jerk backward. "What's happened?"

"It's Jynxson."

Heart hammering, I switch to the other screen displaying Jynxson's body camera. It's filled with twisted metal and piles of debris.

"All I see is rubble. Is he trapped?" I ask.

"Yes. Rewind," Xero snarls.

I scroll back the stream of the body camera, passing the footage of rubble, debris, smoke and dust. The image shakes as the feed rewinds, stopping at a moment when Jynxson is still on his feet, charging out of the catacombs and into the concrete tunnel stretching beneath our backyards.

He's running fast, his breath echoing in the enclosed space. Ahead of him is Camila's smaller figure. Two people appear from the shadows at the far end of the tunnel. It's a man and a woman, dressed in identical armor.

In the feed, Camila and Jynxson skid to a halt, then the smaller of the newcomers tosses an object. In the blink of an eye, the speakers fill with the sounds of explosion, and the screen fills with white light.

The body camera feed shakes violently, as if Jynxson is thrown off his feet. Debris falls all around him, obscuring my view of Camila.

"Someone must have thrown a grenade," I yell. "Jynxson and Camila are trapped."

Xero leaves the highway, and we speed through the streets. The city becomes a blur as we race toward the house. Xero directs his team through the Bluetooth, his voice terse.

I breathe hard, my gaze fixing on a third screen displaying drone footage of a helicopter hovering over our backyards. If Xero wasn't busy driving and coordinating his troops, I would ask if this was his rescue team or another threat.

The answer comes when the drone fires on the helicopter, and two figures emerge from a crater in the ground. As the shorter one, who I suspect is Dolly, sprints toward a ladder dangling from the helicopter and ascends, the taller one secures a small, unconscious figure into a rescue harness and attaches it to the ladder's lower rung.

"They're escaping," I say with a gasp.

The drone follows the helicopter, displaying footage of the man climbing the ladder after his smaller colleague, then reaching the top where he helps hoist the unconscious figure into the aircraft. The cabin crew pulls them in before turning gunfire on the drone until it spirals into a free-fall, the feed whirling before blinking out completely.

"They shot the drone," I rasp. "And they took someone into a helicopter."

"It's Camila," he grits out. "They've abducted my little sister."

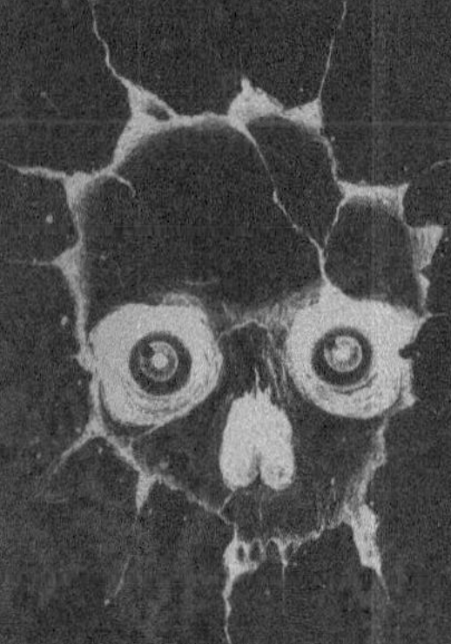

EIGHTY-ONE

XERO

I pull into the courtyard of St. Anne's Church, shaking with impotent rage. Jynxson and his team are still trapped under the rubble, but there's no sign of the bastards who took Camila.

Every drone we sent after the helicopter was shot down, leaving us blind. All we know is that they've gone west.

The Spring brothers retrieved Relaney Cymbal, along with two other men from number 11. All three had been shot with tranquilizer darts, which explained why they were unmoving. Ms. Cymbal is now en route to Simon Memorial Hospital, while the men found with her await us inside the church.

Amethyst hasn't said a word since we lost sight of my sister. If she blames herself for Relaney's abduction, then she'll be even more devastated about Camila.

St. Anne's is the late Reverend Thomas's workplace, which backs onto the Parisii Cemetery. It's a gothic stone building hidden within a copse of weeping willows. I ordered the Spring Brothers to move them to the altar for questioning, because I plan on using a former member of X-Cite Media's place of worship to send a message to Father.

She places a hand on my shoulder. "Xero, are you alright?"

"Ask me again after we've found Camila." I turn off the engine.

My emotions are on lockdown. I'm far from okay, and my little ghost wouldn't believe a platitude. While Dolly won't recognize Camila, Father might. The best-case scenario is that he'll use his own daughter as a hostage. I don't want to consider the worst.

If Charlotte told us the truth about the daughter she had with Father being used as a Lolita assassin, then Camila's potential fate is too chilling to contemplate.

Amethyst stares at my profile for a few seconds before opening the door and stepping out into the darkened courtyard.

Cold rage powers my steps as I stride toward the church. I push open its wooden door and step into the gloom.

The Spring brothers meet me on the aisle, avoiding my gaze as they mutter about needing to join the search for my sister. At the altar, they've set up a makeshift interrogation space. Dolly's accomplices hang from the ceiling by ropes, their naked bodies swaying under the weight of their guilt. Next to them is a table laden with instruments.

Moonlight filters through the stained-glass windows, casting multicolored shadows on the two captives. Their heads are bowed, their limbs immobilized by shackles.

Amethyst's steps falter. She claps both hands over her mouth and suppresses a gasp.

I turn to her, my brow furrowing. "What is it?"

"Those two are from the asylum," she whispers.

"These are the men who hurt you?" I snarl.

She points a trembling finger at the pair. "The one with the long black hair is Seth. The other one is Barrett."

"Tell me everything," I say through clenched teeth.

She swallows hard, her voice quivering. "Those two strung me up so Delta could cut into my skin. Another time, they strapped me to a chair for forced feeding."

Her face tightens with disgust. "Seth came to my cell with a bottle of water. When I went to the door, he stuck his dick through the hatch and came all over my water bowl."

A red haze clouds my vision. I stride to the altar, my thoughts raging like a violent storm. These bastards will die screaming for what they did to my little ghost, but I have to keep them alive long enough to gather information on Camila's location.

"Wake up," I yell.

Neither man twitches.

I grab a knife from the table and slash their bellies deep enough to jolt them into consciousness. They jerk backward, filling the church with screams.

"Look at me," I yell above their howls.

Barrett, the one with the shaggy brown hair, is the first to speak. Recognizing his sharp features from the graveyard video makes me want to stick the knife into his throat.

"What do you want?" he asks through ragged breaths.

"Where did Dolly take Camila?"

His eyes widen. "I don't know any Camila."

"Dolly took my sister. I want to know where she went in that helicopter."

Barrett's gaze darts to Amethyst, who stands at my side. Realizing she's not his boss, his face leeches of all color.

I grab his jaw. "Look at her one more time, and you'll lose an eye."

He stiffens. "Look, man. I don't know what's happening. One minute, I was standing in that woman's living room. The next, I'm being strung up in some fucking church."

"Where did Dolly come from?" I press my blade into his chest.

He shakes his head. "I don't know. I swear."

"Try again." I slice off his left nipple.

"We never stay in one place!" he screams.

"Not good enough." I slice off the right.

Barrett sobs, his features crumpling. "Ask Seth. He'll know."

I glance at a long-haired man, who stares at me with cold, black eyes. He was the man who attended the mixer with Dolly and appeared more loyal to Father than to his X-Cite Media colleagues. He's another one from the graveyard video I recognize, but I wanted to leave him intact for Amethyst.

"How about you, Seth?" I ask.

He remains silent, glaring back with defiance. His breaths come out in labored gasps, yet the pain in his abdomen isn't enough to break his spirit.

"Your loyalty to the man who left you for dead is commendable," I sneer. "But my people found you already unconscious, abandoned by your supposed ally."

Fear flickers across his features before they harden.

I can't help but grin at his naivety. "You think I'm lying? Our drones found three motionless figures in that house. Dolly and her accomplice left you both there to die."

Beside Seth, Barrett whimpers.

Amethyst steps forward. "It's true. I saw the footage. And before Grunt died, he told me Delta leaked videos with your faces to make you wanted by the police."

Seth pales at the revelation, while Barrett breaks down into harsh sobs. Despite the overwhelming evidence against them, Seth keeps a stoic mask.

"I don't know what you're talking about," he says.

"You weren't his elites, you were just his puppets," I reply.

"You're wrong." He swallows, his throat bobbing. He's the kind of asshole who doubles down, even when they know they've lost the argument.

I scoff. "You're still under Delta's spell. Did he recruit you from the outside world, or are you a former child assassin?"

Seth turns his head, refusing to meet my gaze. His silence speaks volumes. No one shows such bravery in the face of interrogation without training.

"What about you, Barrett?" I turn to the sobbing man. "Are you also a trained killer?"

He shakes his head, loosening tears that stream down to his mutilated chest. "No," he chokes out between ragged sobs. "I'm just an adult movie star."

"Who Delta left behind to get tortured to death by his enemies?" I ask, my brows rising.

He shivers. "What do you want to know?"

"Where can I find Dolly and Delta?"

"If I knew, I would tell you—"

I cut him off with a fist into his gut wound, relishing his pained howl. "Explain."

"Delta never stays in one place for longer than a few days," he screams. "He has hideouts all over town."

"What are you doing?" Seth barks, his eyes flashing with fury.

Satisfaction thrums through my chest at the confirmation. Ignoring him, I ask, "Where are they?"

"I don't know," he stammers. "Apartments, mostly."

"Start with the last one."

"It overlooked the wrought iron gates of Beaumont Park." His words come out in a frantic rush. "Eleventh floor, but they would have already moved."

I turn to Amethyst, who's already typing out a message on my phone. "Send it to Tyler."

She nods.

I turn back to Seth, who glares through eyes burning with hatred. His stubbornness isn't just stupid—it's suicidal. He's about Amethyst's age, which means I might not have met him if he resided at the underground facility. Either way, he's completely brainwashed.

"Delta isn't any kind of father figure worth protecting," I say. "Many of the girls killed in those movies were former assassins like Dolly who became too old to be Lolitas."

Seth gathers saliva in his mouth and spits, but his aim is off, and it lands on the altar floor. "You're just jealous. Delta valued his adopted sons more than the bastards who were disappointments."

The insult barely lands with a sting. I've had years to come to terms with Father's Machiavellian antics. He's affected so many people, I can't take anything he does personally. Despite this, a laugh rises in my chest. It's half-grief, half-madness, and all fury for Camila.

"You're still defending a man who left you to die?" Losing interest in Seth, I turn back to Barrett. "Is there anything else you can tell us?"

Barrett's entire body convulses. "Are we... Are we really going to die?"

Cold fury settles over my spirit, and I give him a smile that could freeze fire. If he thinks this information will absolve him for hurting Amethyst and all the other women who suffered at the hands of X-Cite Media, then he's deluded.

"Delta discarded you like trash. You can decide if you die tonight or in a few months, after your body gives up from torture."

He shivers. "I overheard Dolly tell Locke they could hide out in a property Delta's company owns."

My eyes narrow. "X-Cite Media?"

Barrett shakes his head. "Hades Holding Company. I don't know what kind of building it is or its whereabouts in Beaumont City. All I know is that it's empty."

Satisfied with the leads, I step back and sweep an arm towards Amethyst. "I'm going to start researching Hades Holdings. Feel free to mutilate them, but leave Seth for last."

Amethyst nods, her pretty features twisting with malice. I take my phone from her and turn away, leaving the altar echoing with screams.

I would sit back and watch the show, but I have a sister to rescue.

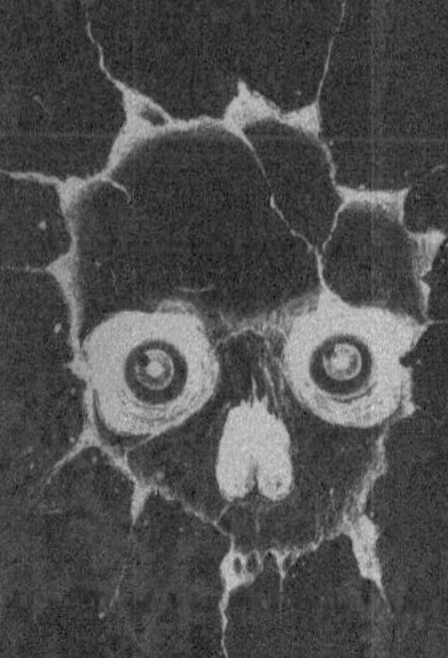

EIGHTY-TWO

AMETHYST

As Xero leaves to investigate, I take a moment to steady my breath, my gaze locking onto Barrett and Seth. The fear in their eyes is satisfying, but it isn't enough. They need to suffer—to feel the pain they inflicted upon me a thousandfold.

I approach the table of instruments, my fingers brushing over the cold metal of surgical equipment and knives. I pick up a scalpel, feeling its weight, imagining the way it will slice through flesh.

I turn to Barrett first, since his whimpers grate on my nerves. "What do you have to say for yourself?"

"What... what do you want?" he croaks, his voice thick with pain.

"You remember me, don't you?"

He nods, his eyes streaming with fat tears. "Please, I'm sorry. I didn't—"

I silence him with a slap, the sound of skin hitting skin echoing in the hollow space. "Sorry doesn't erase what you did."

He flinches, his cheek reddening as his eyes widen with shock. His breath comes in ragged gasps, and he stammers, "I-I didn't mean—"

"Why did you do it? Why did you hurt me and the others?"

He whimpers.

I run the scalpel across his ribs, making him flinch. When he squeezes his eyes shut, I slice a line up his chest and over to the pulse thrumming in his throat. He shudders, his breath coming in shallow pants. He knows what's coming.

"Tell me, Barrett," I say, circling his hanging carcass. "How does it feel to be helpless?"

He sobs, his body shaking. "Please... I can tell you something important," he says, his voice hoarse with desperation. "Just... just don't kill me."

"Speak," I snap.

"I didn't want to do any of this, you know." He gulps. "I joined thinking it was just acting. When I got there and the girl died, it was too late. I became an accessory to murder."

Seth snorts.

I tighten my lips, already sick of the bullshit. These second-rate predators only ever show regret when they've fallen out of favor with Delta. "Funny how you didn't seem reluctant when you were joining in on all the fun at the asylum."

"Dolly, I didn't—"

I cut him off with a slash to the face. "Don't call me by that name!"

He chokes another sob.

Fury flares across my chest. I return to the table, snap on a pair of disposable gloves, and grab a serrated knife.

His eyes widen. "Wait. What are you—-"

My fingers close in around his flaccid penis. Jerking hard, I saw it with my serrated knife. The screams ringing through my ears soothe my inner predator. Warm blood oozes over my fingers, washing away a fraction of my trauma. Its metallic tang overwhelms my senses, leaving me light-headed. I slow my movements, making sure every cut is agonizing and precise.

Barrett jerks and spasms and twists toward Seth, trying to squirm away. This only makes me grip harder and stab the tip of my blade into his balls.

"Shut the fuck up. You deserve worse than this," I hiss.

When I've liberated his genitals, Barrett's body goes limp. I hold up the severed penis and turn to Seth, who watches through bulging eyes. All the color has leached from his sallow features, leaving his jaw hanging.

"Remember the hatch?" I ask, my lip curling.

He swallows hard, trying to maintain some semblance of control. "Can't you take a joke?"

"Well, how do you like this prank?" I hold the severed penis in his face. "Put it in your mouth."

He swings backward, all signs of bravado faltering. "No."

I rush to the table, set the balls to one side, grab a taser and test its trigger. The room fills with an electrical crackle. When I turn back to Seth, he stiffens. Sweat breaks out across his skin, and his chest rises and falls with rapid breaths. Even a former assassin can't be stoic in the face of losing their genitals.

"Did Lizzie feel like this when you electrocuted her?" I ask, pressing the taser's electrodes to his side.

I press the trigger again, releasing screams that stoke my thirst for revenge. Smoke rises from his skin, filling the air with the acrid scent of burning flesh.

"Stop," he rasps.

"Then eat it," I say through clenched teeth.

He shakes his head again and wheezes, "I can't..."

I press the taser back into his burnt side, setting off a surge of electric shocks that make him convulse. "Do it!"

"I... I can tell you something Barret doesn't know," he says, his voice straining with desperation. "Just... just stop."

Silence stretches for several heartbeats, broken by the rasp of his breath. Xero hovers farther away in the background, deep in conversation. I turn my attention back to Seth, wondering if this is a bluff.

"Speak." I punctuate the word with another blast of the taser.

"It's about D-Dolly," he stammers. "Everything we did... it was for her revenge. She came to Parisii Drive to capture you. She'll probably trade you for Camila."

His words hit me like a sledgehammer, even though I shouldn't be shocked. "What do you mean?"

Seth nods. "She'll release Camila if you go to her."

My breath catches. "How do I arrange a swap?"

"She added you as a friend on her social media. Just send her a message."

"That's it?"

He nods.

"Thank you." I bring the severed penis to his mouth. "Now, eat. Unless you want me to fry your brain."

Eyes burning with betrayal, he gags and chokes on the cock meat, letting blood and bits of flesh dribble down his lips.

I scrape the debris from his chin and bring it back to his mouth. "Spit it out and I'll slit your throat."

Tears roll down his cheeks as he eats.

"Good boy," I say. "You're taking Barret's cock extremely well."

He squeezes his eyes shut and whimpers.

Satisfied, I step back and wait for him to swallow. As his throat bobs, I return to the torture table to set down the taser, place a scalpel between my teeth, and pick up a tourniquet. Barrett will probably die of blood loss, but I need Seth alive a little longer.

I return to wrap a tight band around the base of his penis, making him twist around. "Stay still," I mutter around the metallic hilt. "Don't ruin your dessert."

"Wait!" he cries out. "I have information on Delta!"

I take the scalpel from between my teeth and press its blade into the pulse point beneath his jaw. "What is it?"

"Release me and I'll take you. I can even help you get back that girl."

I glance over my shoulder to see if Xero overheard. He's busy on the other side of the church with his phone, unaware of the exchange. I return to Seth and press my blade beneath his chin.

"How do I know this isn't bullshit?"

Seth shivers, his breath coming in ragged pants. "It wasn't Delta who left us for dead. It was that two-faced bitch, Dolly. Help me take her down and I'll—"

"What the fuck is this?" Xero's bellow echoes across the church.

My heart skips several beats. I whirl around, my eyes widening.

Xero's eyes lock onto mine, his fury palpable even from across the room. He strides down the aisle, the intensity in his gaze making my pulse race.

I step back and bump into the table of instruments, the cold metal pressing into my skin. Unpleasant shivers race down my spine. He's about to ruin my plan.

"What are you telling her?" Xero snarls, his voice menacing and low.

Seth trembles, his face pale. "I was just... I was just trying to stay alive."

Xero's expression hardens. "You think you can negotiate your way out of dying?" He turns to fix me with a glower. "What did he tell you?"

"He has information on Dolly and Delta," I say, trying to keep my voice steady.

Xero's eyes narrow. "You trust him?"

"No, but it's worth hearing him out," I reply, my grip tightening on the scalpel. The metal hilt bites into my palm. It's the only thing keeping me grounded in the face of his anger.

Xero steps closer to Seth, standing so close their faces are inches apart. "Start talking. Fast."

Seth swallows hard. "I can broker a swap. Amy in exchange for the other girl."

"Out of the question," he snaps.

Frustration roils through my insides, building in intensity until it bursts out in a scream. I whirl on Xero, wondering how one man can be so stubborn. "How else are we going to save Camila?"

His jaw tightens, his eyes darkening like thunderclouds before a storm. "I nearly lost you once. Losing you again isn't an option. I would die before handing you over to those monsters."

Guilt crushes my chest, making me choke back a sob. How many times has he put himself on the line for me? "You can't keep coddling me or making such huge sacrifices. I've already cost you so much."

"You're wrong," he snarls.

"If that's true, then when will you confront me for nearly setting you on fire?"

Xero's features harden. His eyes bore into mine, filled with a pain I rarely see. He slams his fist into Seth's gut wound, earning himself a pained groan. "You think I haven't wanted to scream at you for jumping to conclusions?"

His words cut deep, flaring up my guilt. I always knew the resentment would eventually surface. My throat tightens, and I gulp. "Then let me fix this. Let me go there. You can even provide back up."

Xero grabs my throat, making me gasp. His skin is hot, the pulse in his fingers beating wildly against my skin. "I was disappointed. After everything we went through together, you didn't trust me."

My eyes widen, and I use his confession as ammunition. "Then let me fix this. Use me as bait to save Camila. Let me show you just how much I trust you. See that as my way of making things right."

His eyes flash with anger, his features tightening with hurt. "You want to apologize for leaving me in a fire to die? Then you can stay here while I burn down this fucking church."

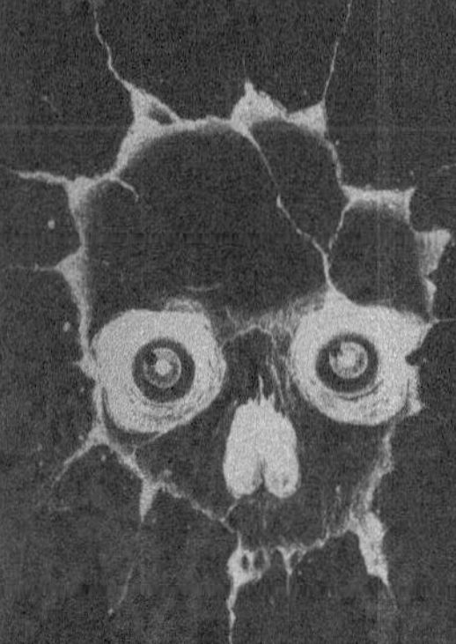

EIGHTY-THREE

AMETHYST

I stare into Xero's eyes, trying to ignore the volume of my pulse pounding in my eardrums. They're black pools surrounded with the barest traces of blue that crackle with the white heat of his fury. I've never seen him so angry.

"Burning down a church won't save Camila," I say.

His fingers tighten around my throat, cutting off my air.

"Do you think I'll let you throw your life away so easily?" His voice is a dangerously soft rumble that makes my blood run cold.

Every instinct screams at me to drop down on my knees and beg for forgiveness. My vision blurs, but I hold my ground, forcing myself to breathe through his crushing grip.

"Let me do this," I say through clenched teeth. "Don't forget, I knocked you out, set the basement on fire, and left you for dead. You brushed over that like it was nothing when you should hate me."

His eyes narrow into slits. "Hating you would be like hating my own heart. Since you don't believe in forgiveness, then you will take this punishment."

My breath catches. "What does that even mean?"

He releases his grip around my throat, leaving me swaying on my feet. Gasping for air, I stare at his broad back as he advances toward the torture table, wondering if burning down the church is a metaphor for something else.

But when he bends down and picks up two canisters of gasoline, my instincts kick in and I step backward, not knowing what the hell he'll do next.

"Xero," I whisper, my voice hoarse from being choked. "What the hell are you doing?

He sets both canisters on the table with a jarring clink. Without looking in my direction, he snarls, "Giving you the chance to make amends."

Dread rolls in my gut like thunder I struggle to understand his twisted logic. "I didn't mean meeting Delta alone. I'll be the bait, but you and the others will be a few feet away, watching my back."

He slams his fist on the table, making me flinch. "Never."

My mind races, trying to comprehend his madness. Xero's sisters are the only positive part of his childhood. Why would he risk either of them for a woman he's barely known for a year? He can't dismiss an opportunity to save Camila just because it puts me in danger.

When he rips off the lid of one canister, I take another step back and bump into something solid. Barrett's unconscious body swings from the ropes, still streaming blood from multiple cuts.

Flinching, I turn back to Xero. "What are you doing?"

Ignoring my question, he unscrews the second canister and walks both of them around the altar's perimeter, pouring out a stream of gasoline onto its wooden floor.

I stiffen, my veins surging with cold fear. "Xero, please... don't do this."

"You asked for punishment. Now, you will receive it." He jumps down from the altar and strides along the far side of the pews, spilling more of the flammable liquid on the floorboards.

"Untie me," Seth croaks from where he's hanging. "It's not too late for me to take you—"

A knife whizzes past my face and lodges in his chest. Jumping back with a yelp, I turn to the other side of the church, where Xero picks up his canister and continues dousing the floor with that infernal liquid.

"He's bullshitting," Xero snarls at me.

I swallow over and over, wondering why the hell I'm not getting through to Xero. Maybe he's right. Maybe Seth is saying whatever can buy him an opening to escape. I can't think straight with my psychotic boyfriend creating a ring of gasoline.

Turning back to Seth, I say, "Xero has lost his mind. Give me something and I'll at least stop you from burning to death."

Features tightening, he strains against the ropes. His head dips, and he chokes a sob before meeting my gaze. "Cut me down. Please."

Xero's laugh reverberates through the church, a manic sound that chills me to the bone. Despite everything, the sight of him burning down a building with us inside is strangely captivating.

"If he knew something, he would have said it earlier. Now he's just desperate."

A shiver snakes down my spine. There's only one way to find out if Xero is right. I grab Seth's flaccid penis. "Don't fuck with me and don't think I've forgotten how you slid this into the door hatch and told me to suck it in exchange for a bottle of water."

He shudders. "I'm not the danger. It's him."

"You have a choice," I snarl. "I can stab you in the heart and give you a quick death, or you can bleed out through a gaping wound in your groin."

Fear floods Seth's eyes, his pale face turning green, his gaze darting to Barrett. His lips tremble, but he makes no sound.

"What it's going to be, Seth?" I ask. "A quick death or slow agony?"

"You're as insane as that cunt," he spits. "Delta didn't stab me in the back. It was her. Ever since they got married, she's made him weak. She's the puppeteer."

"So, nothing useful?" I make my first slice into the base of his shriveled dick.

"Her left eye is made of glass!" he screams.

"Something about her location." I press the blade deeper, freeing a torrent of warm blood. His scream echoes across the church walls.

When all he does is jibber, I sever the rest of his penis and bring it to his lips. "Dessert."

He jerks his head to the side. "You crazy bitch."

"And you're a liar." I whack him across the face with the severed appendage. "A rapist." I punctuate the word with another dick-slap. "And a murderer."

His shrill laugh rings through my ears. "And what does that make you, huh? Torturer? Executioner?"

"A survivor." I bring the bloody stump to his mouth. "And the one who's giving you your last supper."

Before I can stuff the penis down Seth's gullet, Xero grabs my wrist in an iron grip and whirls me around. His eyes are wild, almost feral, radiating a dangerous mix fury and insanity.

Unable to withstand his gaze, I glance at the flame flickering at the tip of his lighter, casting a dancing light that illuminates the shadows of the old church. The heat from the impending fire and the intensity of his stare make my skin prickle with a surge of adrenaline.

"Are you playing with another man's cock?" he growls.

My stomach drops.

Shit.

"Xero," I whisper, my voice trembling, "Turn off that lighter, or I'll—"

"You'll what?" Xero interrupts with a grin sharp enough to cut throats. "Bad girls who leave men to die in burning basements are in no position to make threats."

Behind us, Seth's laughter morphs to wracking sobs. I toss the severed penis at his face, which only makes him cry harder.

Ignoring him, I turn back to Xero and his still-burning lighter. He breathes hard, his eyes dancing, their depths reflecting the flickering flames of madness.

My heart hurls itself against my ribcage, threatening to burst out of my chest. I breathe hard, struggling to keep calm enough to make him see reason.

"Let's go to the car," I say, trying not to provoke him further. "We can get out of here together."

The grip on my arm tightens, and he leans close with a dark chuckle. "And why would I deprive you of a punishment?"

My lips part, and I struggle to form an answer. Before I can think of something to say to soothe this beast, Xero tosses the lighter over his shoulder with a sadistic smirk. The flame flies in an arc before landing on the altar cloth, which sets alight with a loud whoosh.

Panic bubbles up in my chest as the fire spreads across the church's perimeter with the speed of falling dominoes. Wrenching my arm from Xero's iron grip, I dart toward the edge of the altar, desperate to outrun the flames.

"Running won't save you from me, little ghost."

Snarling, Xero charges after me, grabs my waist, and lifts me off my feet. He spins me around and grabs my chin, forcing our gazes to meet. His features twist into a rictus of fury, sending a thrill of terror that goes straight to my clit.

"No one takes you from me. Not even you," he snarls, his voice dark and possessive. "And no one gets to escape me. You're mine, in every way."

Flames crawl up the altar's walls and up to its wooden ceiling. As fiery particles drop down like ashes from hell, I scream, "Oh my God!"

"That's right, little ghost. I'm your god. There's no higher power. I'll burn this whole place down if it means keeping you, and tonight you'll pray to me for deliverance."

I push at his chest, trying to wrestle free, but his grip tightens around my waist. I claw at his eyes, but my gloved fingernails only slide down his face. He bites down on my chin, delivering a burst of pain that makes me shriek.

"That's it, scream for me. I want to hear how much you love it."

"Xero, we need to leave."

My mind dredges up the safe word, but my lips refuse to cooperate. The pulse between my legs throbs in sync with the frantic beat of my heart, and the muscles of my core throb with anticipation. A sick, curious part of my psyche craves to know how far Xero will push this punishment.

He walks us past the altar rails, which burn like hellfire. Pulling up my leather skirt to my waist, he exposes my pussy to the hot air. Cold fear trickles down my back, and I shiver. It only makes him grin.

"Afraid, baby? You should be terrified."

He positions my legs around his waist and strokes my aching clit. Sparks detonate across my core as his digits glide down my dripping slit.

Somewhere on the edge of my consciousness, the clink of his metal belt unbuckling mingles with Seth's hoarse screams. I'm too preoccupied with the psychopath stroking my pussy to heed to the words of a dickless rapist.

"Look at you," Xero snarls, his breath hot against my ear. He slips two fingers into my opening, creating delicious friction. "So eager and wet for your punishment."

I bite back a groan, refusing to give him the satisfaction. "Fuck off."

"You want to fuck, baby. As you wish. I'll give it to you nice and deep. Just how you like it." He pulls out his fingers and replaces them with his thick cock. "Now take it all."

His first forceful thrust has me gasping for air. The stretch is incredible—almost too much to bear. My eyes roll to the back of my head, and I stifle a moan.

"I love you so much that nearly losing you cost me my soul. I won't risk it again," he snarls.

"Xero, please," I moan into the side of his neck.

"Please, what? Use your words."

I shake my head and clamp my mouth shut. If I speak, I might beg him for more when I should be begging him for mercy.

He pounds into me without compassion or restraint. I cling onto his shoulders, fighting back a barrage of pleasure. This isn't a baptism of fire or some kind of sacrament—this is suicidal. This is insane. Those thoughts are cut off when Xero's thick Prince Albert piercing rubs against a spot that has me seeing sparks.

As if sensing that I want more, he unhooks the front of my corset. My breasts spill out into his hands, then he squeezes the left one hard enough to make me gasp. The pain is sharp, and my pussy tightens around his thick cock, triggering a surge of arousal that makes us both groan.

"Xero, we're going to burn," I say with a whimper.

"There's no place I'd rather die than inside your heavenly cunt."

I grip his shoulders and buck my hips, not knowing if I'm

trying to wriggle off his cock to escape or increase the friction. Either way, pleasure surges through my core, mingling with cold adrenaline and raw fear. It's a dangerous cocktail of emotions that has my mind spinning out of control.

"You feel so good, little ghost," he groans, his hands gripping my hips hard enough to leave bruises. "So hot and tight and wet."

The fire rages around our entwined bodies, and the heat from the flames makes my skin break out in sweat. I'm burning up from the inside, and every thrust from Xero feels like a brand.

His mouth descends on my neck, the teeth grazing my sensitive skin before he bites down, eliciting a shock of pleasure-pain. I arch up, pressing myself against his chest, my hips lifting to fuck that impossibly thick cock.

"That's it, baby," he growls, his voice raw with desire. "Ride me through this inferno. Ride me till my knees buckle. Ride me to our fucking salvation."

Ecstasy burns through what's left of my good sense, leaving me teetering on the edge of oblivion. Pressure builds, and the walls of my pussy quiver around his shaft. All thoughts of survival and escape disappear into the flames as I chase my orgasm.

By now, the church has erupted beyond a ring of fire, with flames consuming its walls and spreading across its ceilings. Some of the wooden pews have caught fire, crackling with dancing sparks. I squeeze my eyes shut and cling onto his shoulders, imagining us both together in hell.

Just as my eyes roll to the back of my head, the crazy bastard stops thrusting and snarls, "Do you want to come?"

"Fuck, yes." I reach down between our bodies to stroke my clit, but he snatches my wrist.

"Then tell me you're mine."

My eyes snap open. For a heartbeat, I hesitate, my gaze locking with his amidst the chaos. Silence stretches across the burning church, broken only by the crackle of flames and the snap of burning wood. His eyes burn with a need so raw and carnal, it makes me shiver despite the surrounding heat.

"Xero... I've always been yours," I grind out, my voice hoarse with desperation and desire. "Maybe even before I saw your mugshot. I knew a man like you was out there, waiting to rescue me from my tower."

"Then tell me you'll never leave. Swear it, or I'll leave nothing but ashes."

My throat tightens at this glimpse of vulnerability. Half-assed declarations flicker through my mind, but I can't dredge up the right words. The fire rages and wood splinters and cracks from above, reminding me that time is running out. At this rate, the church's roof will collapse on our heads.

"Never."

In the past, I might have loved him for the way he looked, or the way he made me feel, or even for protection, but that was when I was incomplete. A dangerous mix of gaslighting, suppressed memories, and prescription drugs kept me from uncovering the depth of my emotions.

Now, as I'm stripped bare and on the brink of death, everything is clear. Every time Xero said he loved me was the truth. I belong to him, and he belongs to me. It's simple.

"I won't ever leave you again. You're the only man I trust."

"Good girl. Now, prove it."

He wants me to claim him in the heat of this burning church. Our relationship went sideways when I jilted him at the altar. It's only fitting that we commit to each other in the flames of our desire.

Seeming to read my thoughts, he nods. "Ride me, baby. Show me you're mine. Make the flames jealous."

I move against him, each roll of my hips a promise, each gasp escaping my lips a vow. Xero Greaves is mine and I am his—forever, until the end of time. When time no longer exists and we're just fragments floating in chaos, our love will be the primordial anchor keeping us intertwined.

His lips descend on mine, sealing our union with a kiss that tastes like redemption and sin. My eyes flutter shut, and I revel in the depth of our connection.

"Xero, I'm yours," I pant against his mouth, each word punctuated with a desperate thrust. My nails dig into his shoulders as my movements become more frenzied, the friction driving me closer to the edge. The heat, the danger, the sheer force of his possession—it's all too much.

"Oh, fuck... Xero, I'm going to..." I gasp, my body trembling.

"Come for me, little ghost. Make these walls collapse with your screams."

His words send me over the edge, and I shriek through an orgasm, every muscle in my body tightening as if bound by an unbreakable force. My legs wrap tighter around his waist, clinging to him, my senses alight with flames of pleasure. I revel in the heat, the scent of burning wood, the feel of our bodies pressed so tightly we become one.

Xero's groans are low and guttural and primal as he comes with powerful thrusts, filling me with spurts upon spurts of warm fluid. The intensity of it leaves me trembling, my legs quivering around his waist with the aftershocks of our shared ecstasy.

I'm spent, utterly consumed. As I catch my breath and open my eyes, the world comes back into focus. We're no longer in the church but in the moonlit courtyard where he parked the car. Acrid smoke billows through the night like escaping phantoms, and I glance over my shoulder, finding the stone building engulfed in flames.

Before I can ask when he took us out of the fire, he flinches and curses under his breath.

My brow pinches. "Xero, what's wrong?"

A sharp sting pierces into my neck. I hiss.

Xero plucks out a small dart, his features twisting with rage, and snarls, "We're under attack."

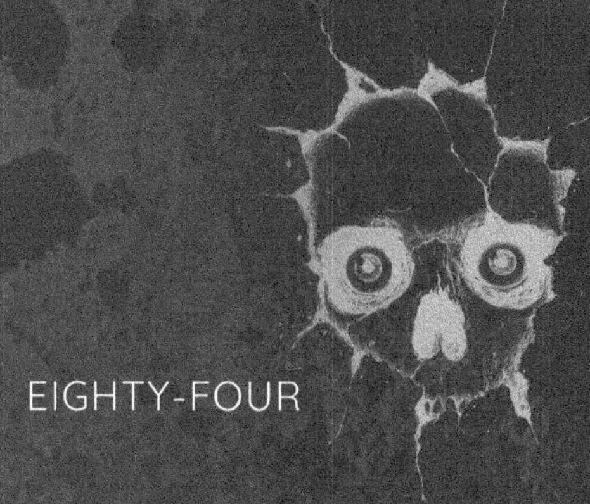

EIGHTY-FOUR

XERO

My head throbs. I slow my breath, trying to feign unconsciousness as I take stock of my surroundings. I'm strapped to a wooden chair with leather bindings at every joint. A cold draft blows across my bare skin, carrying the faint scent of brandy and cigar smoke.

It triggers memories of sitting in Father's study, surrounded by tall shelves stuffed with leather-bound books. Throat spasming, I fight against residual terror from being ten years old, thinking he would inject me with the same poison he used to kill Mom.

Compartmentalizing my fear, I focus on survival. Amethyst is in the hands of our enemies. The question is, which one?

Thanks to Dolly's counterfeit confessions, we're both wanted by the police. Law enforcement officers don't use tranquilizer darts unless they're dirty, but then, the death of Deputy Police Chief Hunter would have opened up a vacancy for another corrupt official.

It could be the Moirai. My organization's primary source of revenue comes from work we steal from our former employer. Not to mention the number of operatives we've killed or poached.

The third option is too ridiculous to contemplate.

"I know you're awake, son."

My blood chills at the sound of that familiar voice. Then my heart accelerates, filling my veins with molten fury.

A current surges through my skin, delivering bolts of electricity. Muscles clenching, I open my eyes and lock gazes with a face I want to erase from existence.

My heart pounds. My skin breaks out in a cold sweat. He's a little older than I remember, and the lower half of his face is covered with a cropped beard, but there's no mistaking those cold, blue eyes. Father stands in the middle of the room, dressed in a navy-blue smoking jacket with black silk lapels, cosplaying the gentleman we both know he isn't.

"Delta," I grit out, the word tasting like acid.

Father's lip curls in a derisive sneer. "You've gotten sloppy. Returning to an enemy location with your pants down."

"Where are they?" I ask.

"Such hostility. I taught you to be more specific."

"You didn't teach me a fucking thing."

His features fall in a mockery of disappointment. "That's where you're wrong. Your childhood conditioning, the rigorous training... even my elusiveness was all part of your education. Skills that were supposed to serve my purpose."

"What the hell do you mean?"

"You were supposed to eliminate the leadership of the Moirai." He brushes imaginary lint off his arm. "Create mayhem and take down my enemies so I could resume ownership of the firm I started. To think all it took to distract you was something sweet and wet."

I grit my teeth. "Where are Amethyst and Camila?"

"You'll see them soon." He turns to a table, picks up a syringe, and flicks its barrel, loosening a drop of red fluid.

My throat dries. I'm no expert on chemicals, but the only drugs I've seen of that hue are propofol and Dr. Dixon's blend of epinephrine. The first is a powerful anesthetic, the second a potent stimulant. In the hands of a man like Father, neither prospect is good news.

"What do you want from me?" I ask.

"Your complete ruin. Just as you engineered mine." He advances on me with the syringe. "Once I've broken you into a loyal and obedient submissive, you will return everything you stole from me. With interest."

I thrash within the bonds, the chair scraping against the concrete floor, but it only slams into a wall. It takes a second to realize this is the same device they used to electrocute Lizzie Bath.

Father plunges the needle into my neck, releasing liquid that crawls through my veins like icy fire. Muscles stiffening, I recoil.

"Good boy," Father murmurs. "You were my greatest creation. The perfect blend of myself and your mother."

"You didn't know her," I snarl.

Drawing back, he stares down at me, his head tilting. "Your birth mother. Not the woman who took you into her home. That was your aunt."

This isn't news. Mom already told me my birth mother died in childbirth. With a leap of logic, I can guess her association with Father wasn't entirely romantic. The room spins. Reality distorts, blurring at the edges and stretching out of proportion. I fight against it, trying to cling to sanity, but Father's words echo and warp until the words form a blur.

Time passes in a distorted haze of disjointed thoughts and images. Dismembered memories intertwine with broken fragments in the room. When my muscles tire of struggling, I throw my head backward and fixate on the lightbulb. Its filament flickers on and off, creating a haze resembling an evil eye.

Throughout this, his words reverberate through my head like a broken record. I hold on to the thought that Father might leave Camila and Amethyst intact.

The hours stretch like melting clocks, dripping wax into the chasm of my thoughts. After an eternity, the drugs fade, and my vision returns. I glance around the room, looking for some form of escape. The space is spartan and white, save for a screen hanging on the wall straight ahead.

Black cables lead from my chair to a power point beneath a metal table by the door, which is far beyond reach. There are no windows, and the only source of illumination comes from the dim light bulb hanging from the ceiling, casting long, twisted shadows.

That drug Father injected into me had a single purpose—to

keep me bound and disoriented. But to what end? He could be shooting another movie with Amethyst or Camila, or arranging their grisly deaths.

Anguish washes through my veins like acid. How the hell were Father's men able to sneak past my operatives and get so close to the church so soon after Dolly escaped with Camila?

Because the two men Amethyst castrated were merely bait. In my desperation to find out what happened to my sister, I'd become sloppy. I dropped my guard and became overconfident after so many victories against Father.

The door swings open. As if summoned by my very thoughts, Father walks in, holding a remote. He closes the distance between us and gazes into my eyes as if checking for something within their depths. I can't help but wonder if he's searching for traces of the drug.

My pulse quickens to a slow, sluggish beat. I jerk forward against the leather restraints.

"If you don't release Camila and Amethyst, I'll kill you," I manage to spit out, my words still slurred.

He saunters across the room, seeming unfazed by my threat. The sight of him looking so composed is a knife twisting in my chest. Closing the small gap between us, he leans in close, his breath hot against my face. "Is this the beginning of a negotiation, dear boy?"

"Sure," I say through clenched teeth. "But I want to see my girls first."

He draws back and snorts. "Predictably weak, just like your mother," he sneers, his voice dripping with contempt. "She was one of my finest assassins, until she grew sentimental and fled with our unborn child."

My jaw clenches. My blood boils beneath the surface, yet I force my features into a mask of cold restraint. "Taunting me about a woman I never met? If you still remember her after all this time, she must have been your weakness, not mine."

A flicker of emotion crosses his features before he veils it with indifference. "I hunted your mother down and shot her in the head. You, however, might still prove useful."

"Where. Are. They?" I snarl.

The door creaks open. Camila stumbles inside, looking dazed but unharmed, followed by Amethyst holding a gun.

Shock and hope surge through my system, crashing like violent waves. My heart lurches against my ribs, racing with disbelief at the sight of my salvation. I jerk forward, straining against my bindings, my eyes wide and searching. My little ghost—has she truly rescued my sister?

Amethyst turns to me and smirks. Then she points her gun at Father.

And fires.

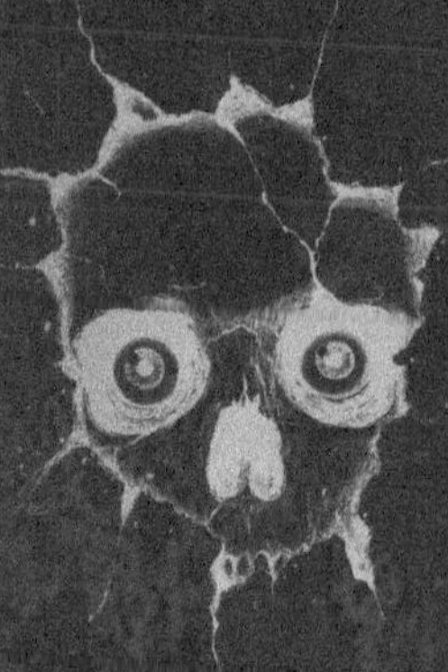

EIGHTY-FIVE

XERO

The bullet lodges into the wall, missing Father by inches. I turn back to Amethyst, expecting her to try again, but she doubles over and laughs.

Just laughs.

Several things are wrong with this scenario. The woman holding the gun has a full head of dark hair, while my little ghost colored the left side of hers green.

Father's only reaction to her near miss is an indulgent smile. It's the kind a man makes to a beloved pet. My heart plummets, and all hope that Amethyst is safe shatters like glass.

Father chuckles, the sound cutting like blades through the fragile threads of my sanity. I turn my gaze to Camila, who slumps against the wall in a tank top and a pair of fitted leggings many operatives wear beneath their bullet proof armor. She stares through glassy eyes, oblivious to Dolly and Father.

I don't know how much time has passed since they hit us with tranquilizer darts, but I can only hope she's been drugged and not broken.

"Where's Amethyst?" My voice cracks.

Father's smile fades. "That girl was a bad influence who kept you from fulfilling your true purpose."

"What the hell does that mean?" I snarl.

Rage surges through my veins, fighting the effects of the drugs. I jerk forward, trying to break free, but the leather straps around my chest dig into my flesh.

Dolly's laughter becomes shrill. "Didn't you tell him?"

"Tell me what?"

"Amethyst had to die," Father says.

His words land with a blow that knocks all the air from my lungs. I recoil, my chest tightening around my shrinking heart.

"You're lying," I say, my mind rejecting the very notion.

"She's distracting you from your destiny," Dolly adds.

"What?" I snap, my gaze bouncing from her to Father.

He steps closer, his eyes boring into mine. "After you and your rag-tag gang of defectors kill the Moirai's management team, you will return everything you stole from me and take your place at my side."

"You're deluded," I rasp.

"You'll come to terms with your position in life the moment you accept that Amy is dead."

I shake my head. "You wouldn't kill someone so important to me without turning it into a spectacle."

Father points his remote at the wall. "See for yourself."

The screen lights up with footage of Amethyst lying on a brown leather couch in a white room. Her eyes are open, but she's dazed, with her arms encased in a grubby straitjacket. Its fastenings at the bottom are undone, revealing her pubic hair and legs encased in compression bandages.

I stiffen, my pulse pounding so hard I can barely hear the audio.

Father appears on screen and positions himself at the edge of the couch. My breath stills as his hands slide up her legs.

My heart thrashes. She told me Father had raped her in the asylum, but seeing it unfold is another level of hell.

His fingers probe her vagina, making her whimper. I can't tear my eyes from the screen, as if looking away would abandon Amethyst to her fate.

"You sick bastard," I snarl. "I already know what you did."

"She was as tight as a virgin," Father says.

I strain so hard against the leather straps that my wrists bleed. "Monster. I'll make you die screaming!"

"Tighter than me?" Dolly asks with a pout.

"You are a queen among women," Father says without conviction. "Amy could never compare."

On screen, Father extracts a thick rubber ring from inside Amethyst and sets it aside before unzipping his fly and positioning himself between her spread legs.

Anguish grips my chest. I can't breathe, can't move as the horror unfolds on video. He violates the woman I love with jerky thrusts, while the camera captures every flicker of pain and fear and resignation across her anguished features.

I want to tell myself this is Dolly, but this is exactly how Amethyst described one of her flashbacks. I watch, helpless and impotent, as Father steals from yet another woman I love.

After an eternity, he climaxes with a shudder, and the video switches to a different scene. It's of Amethyst lying bound to a metal table. A blond man stands over her, holding a knife. The camera cuts to him making a stabbing motion, then back to Amethyst, whose wound oozes blood.

Adrenaline surges through my veins, bringing with it a rush of panic and denial. This has to be another one of Father's twisted games.

It can't be real. I can't lose her. I won't lose her. She's all I have left. My mind clings to this hope, refusing to accept what I'm seeing.

"Bullshit," I snarl. "This is makeup and special effects."

Father picks up another syringe from the torture table and plunges its needle into my neck. Its sting barely registers, but a flood of cool liquid sends my heart galloping. My senses sharpen, my breath quickens, and my limbs surge with power.

He strolls to the door and holds it open. "Xero thinks we fake deaths. Show him we mean business."

Before I can ask what the hell he means, Dolly points her gun at Camila's chest and fires. Blood splatters across the white wall, and my sister's body collapses.

"No!" I thrash against my restraints, my scream echoing off the walls.

Camila falls to the floor in a heap, her brown eyes still glassy.

Dolly blows smoke from the barrel of her gun and steps over Camila's body. She approaches me, her heels clicking over the floor. Satisfaction shining in her eyes, she leans close and grins.

"I'll kill you," I scream.

"Can't wait to be your special reward. I hope you're a better fuck than Delta."

"Dolly, time's running out," Father says.

Straightening, she turns on her heel and saunters across the room without a backward glance.

White-hot fury courses through my veins, bringing another surge of power. I thrash, ripping off a leather wrist restraint.

Just as Dolly disappears into the hallway, the second one follows with a snap. The door swings shut, leaving me alone with my sister's lifeless body.

With trembling hands, I unbuckle the leather straps around my chest and ankles, my movements still numb with shock. I break free and crawl into Camila's expanding pool of blood.

Grief seizes my chest in a punishing grip, robbing my lungs of breath. My vision blurs with unshed tears, leaving me blind to everything except my sister. I fumble at her neck, finding no pulse.

I kneel beside Camila and cradle her head in my lap, my heart shattering into a thousand shards, each one pulsing with raw pain. Every memory of the smiling little girl rises to the forefront of my mind, crushing my chest with despair.

Her kindness, her laughter, her acceptance of a boy rejected by his father and stepfamily—all gone. It was Camila who invited me to stay with Isabel and her mother, tempering my misery with compassion.

When she arrived at the Moirai academy, traumatized from having been molested by John, I swore then to protect her.

And now she's dead.

How the hell will I explain my failure to Isabel? Or to Jynxson?

Tears stream down my cheeks as her blood pools beneath my legs. Its coppery scent fills my nostrils with the metallic tang of torment.

The air cools, but my anger heats as the walls close in around what's left of me and my sister. My mind reels with the weight of her death. I can't comprehend how anyone could harm such a pure soul.

Father ordered a kill on his own daughter just to prove a point. He recognized her, but chose to extinguish his own flesh and blood.

Hate and disgust battle within my psyche. My world narrows to a pinpoint of pure, searing rage. Every nerve screams for vengeance, every muscle trembles with the urge to retaliate.

I failed Camila. I failed Amethyst. I failed every operative who defected from the Morai, believing in the promise of freedom. Retribution burns through the last vestiges of my humanity. My thirst for revenge consumes my soul, leaving only a shell of pure wrath.

"They'll all die," I snarl, my voice trembling with the force of my conviction. "I'll kill every one of them with my bare hands."

The room spins, but I'm already on my feet. Already moving, already at the door, already planning what I need to do next.

Father wants a monster?

Then a monster will be the last thing he sees before I rip Dolly and him to pieces.

EIGHTY-SIX

AMETHYST

Everything hurts. My body feels like it's been stuffed in the washing machine and gone several rounds on the spin cycle. My aches go bone deep, and I'm sure the muscles attached to them are shredded.

The surface under my back is unforgiving and hard, with the faintest scent of bleach. I try to move, but my limbs won't cooperate. Artificial light pulses against my eyelids, matching the throbbing of my head. Dread pushes through the haze. This is no hangover—it's something far more terrible.

I have no idea how much time has passed since that dart hit me outside the church. It could be an hour, a day, or longer. Based on the cool air swirling over my skin, whoever took us has stripped me of what was left of my clothes. The ache from rough sex with Xero has faded, and that part of my body is still intact.

Footsteps approach, an ominous click-clack of heels that makes every fine hair stand on end.

My heart races, and a burst of adrenaline pushes through the grogginess to a state of semi-alertness. I crack open an eye to find myself on the floor of a marble-tiled bathroom.

A breath catches in the back of my throat as I dart my gaze from left to right.

There's no sign of Xero.

The door slams open, letting in ruby-red stilettos attached to legs identical to mine. My stomach lurches and churns with a debilitating mix of nausea and dread. I don't need to look this woman full in the face to know it's Dolly.

Her footsteps draw closer, clicking against the marble floor, and ringing in my ears to the thunderous beat of my heart.

"Wake up, you lazy bitch." She punctuates the order with a sharp kick to the ribs.

I can't even flinch, even though I want to grab her ankle, pull her down to my level, and demand to know what she did to Camila and Xero. No matter how much I try, my body won't move.

Dolly reaches down, twists her fingers into my curls, and hauls me up by the hair. Before I even process the pain ripping across my scalp, she delivers a hard slap with a sting that snaps me fully awake. Flinching, I draw back under a wave of dizziness.

The shock fades, giving way to an overwhelming despair. Once again, I've fallen back into Dolly's clutches. At best, Xero is in another room, being tortured by Delta. At worst, he's dead.

"You cowardly cunt. What the hell did you do to our investors?" she screeches.

I grind my teeth, refusing to give her the satisfaction of an answer.

"Look at me when I'm talking to you!" she screams, her voice echoing across the tiled walls.

Not while I'm helpless. Not while I'm still drugged. Not while she holds all the power. Whatever they put in that poisoned dart has left me unable to fight back, and I'll be damned if I give her the satisfaction of a response.

"Get in here!"

She drags me across the cold, hard tiles to the shower cubicle, each step aggravating my aches. With a sharp twist, she turns on the taps, releasing a cascade of icy water. I gasp at the shock, my teeth chattering. My limbs tremble and convulse from the cold. I force every ounce of determination into my extremities, but they can't escape the punishing chill.

The door creaks open again, letting in a set of male footsteps.

My insides lurch, hoping to everything it's Xero, but knowing in the pit of my stomach I'll be disappointed.

"You called?" asks a male voice that turns my blood to ice. It's Locke. The golden-haired pretty boy they put in charge of the drugs. He chuckles. "What are you doing?"

"Trying to give this bitch a bath, but it won't cooperate," Dolly says.

"Did you administer the antidote?" he asks.

Dolly releases a flirtatious giggle. "I forgot."

"Understandable. There's a hundred and one things to do before the auction."

My breath stills.

Auction?

As they move further into the bathroom, their voices become muffled. I squeeze my eyes shut, trying to focus on their conversation through the roar of running water.

From the snippets I manage to catch, it sounds like Delta is staging another drinks reception where he's brought together a new group of investors to watch a private showing. I listen out for any mention of Xero, but all I hear is about a hot new superstar who will tear me apart for the audience, then the highest bidder will desecrate my corpse.

Dolly steps into the shower. "Give her half."

"Are you sure?" Locke asks.

"She'll be weak, but not so much of a dead weight," she replies. "I'll inject her with the rest before the bidding."

The cold water stops, leaving me gasping. Panic roils in my gut as a needle pierces my biceps. Warmth spreads from the injection site and trickles down my forearm, infusing my limbs with the sensation of pins and needles.

Locke steps out of the shower, pausing to kiss Dolly.

"Give it a few seconds," he murmurs against her lips.

When I try to move my fingers, they twitch. I send a similar message to my toes, which curl. As the pair continue kissing, I ball my hands into fists and try to shift my arms.

Muscles trembling, I push myself up to sit, but I'm still too weak to stand.

I slump against the cold tile, pouring every ounce of hatred into my glare. Now that I'm upright, I can get a better look at Dolly. She's colored the blonde side of her hair dark brown and styled it into pigtails, making her look more like Mom.

Her dress is a low-cut gingham-blue pinafore, which she's paired with white socks and red shoes. It's a grotesque Wizard of Oz cosplay, which makes me want to vomit.

Tears prick the backs of my eyes, and my sinuses burn. Why the hell am I dwelling on her choice of attire when I'm going to die?

More importantly, what will they do to Xero?

Dolly pulls away from the kiss, smooths down Locke's lapels, and gives him a pat on the ass. I would scream that she's a backstabber, but he already knows—he was part of the duo who tranquilized Barrett and Seth, leaving them to be tortured and killed.

He exits the room, leaving me alone with Dolly, who kicks off her red heels and slides off her pinafore dress. She's naked underneath, her body a map of faded scars. They might be identically shaped to the ones Delta inflicted on me, but his cuts were clean and precise enough to heal into thin lines. Dolly's are jagged and cruel, a canvas of torture and pain that's twisted her into a maniac.

Swallowing hard, I shrink to the edge of the shower, my insides roiling. Now that I have most of my memories, all I can think of is her being sent to Three Fates, then suffering untold torment for fourteen years. Her vitriol is misguided. We were both pawns. She needs to direct her need for vengeance where it belongs.

"Dolly," I say, trying to stop my voice from trembling. "Did you know Charlotte is still alive?"

She picks up a bottle of shampoo. "What are you talking about?"

"The nanny you found murdered?"

"Kappa?" She enters the shower and squeezes half a bottle of shampoo over my head.

I gulp. "Yeah."

"It was a prank, but you went psycho and smothered the baby. Then you killed Dad."

"I didn't—"

"Hold still and stop talking." Dolly sticks her hands in my hair and works the shampoo into a lather. "I can't present you to the auction with green hair, stinking of sex and smoke."

"I didn't kill Heath. It was Kappa."

"Nobody gives a fuck. Because of you, Dad didn't pick me up from Three Fates. I stayed there, seducing and murdering assholes. Then I spent the rest of my teens getting raped and stabbed by sick perverts. All because of you."

"That's not how it happened. Dad—"

Her fist lands in my face, making me reel backward from an explosion of pain.

I struggle against her brutal assault, trying to pull away, but Dolly holds me with an iron grip. As she digs her knuckles into my scalp, each twist sends searing agony down my neck. I stutter out the true version of events, my voice desperate and strained.

Water stings my nose, forcing me to gasp for breath. Shampoo soap stings my eyes, making them water. Despite the burning sensation and my frantic pleas, she turns on the spray to full blast and refuses to listen. I reach out blindly, trying to ward her off, but she's relentless.

"You've had fourteen years to work out an excuse with Mom." Dolly slams my head against the wall, delivering a burst of pain that makes me see stars. "Don't think for a second that I'll swallow your bullshit."

With a final vicious tug at my hair, she slams my head against the wall. Pain explodes, sharp and blinding, and I wince. When she steps back, I collapse onto the shower floor, gasping for air while my vision blurs and my head spins. Dazed and disoriented, I shiver against the onslaught of chilling water, which mingles with my tears.

The next several minutes blend into a blur. Dolly drags me out of the shower to style my hair, drowning out my explanations with the dryer. She's colored the left side of my hair the same shade of dark brown as hers, making us once again identical.

Nothing I tell her about Delta and Dad's shared history with the FBI is a surprise, yet she refuses to believe we were both pawns in a sick game of vengeance.

I clench my teeth as she forces me into her gingham dress. Since reasoning has failed, maybe she'll respond to antagonism.

"If you stabbed Dad like I did, he wouldn't have taken you to Three Fates," I say.

"What are you talking about?" she spits.

"You sat back, knowing where you were going, and let it happen. It's your fault you didn't live with Mom and me."

I cringe as I say the words because they're untrue. Dolly was just a child. But so was I, and I can't allow my compassion for her to get me killed. Maybe she's braced herself for a barrage of excuses, or maybe cruelty is the only thing she understands. Either way, I won't allow her to feed me to those predators.

She draws back, her eyes widening. "You bitch. It's not enough for you to have stolen my life, but now you're blaming me for not being a murderer?"

Guilt knots in my throat and winds around my chest. I need to push forward, despite these hateful words. "Don't you get it? Dad set us up. Mom was having an affair with her therapist, and he did all this for revenge. We were just collateral damage."

She slaps me hard across the face, and I nearly topple off the chair. "Do you think I'm stupid?" she hisses. "I pieced together the truth years ago and married that sick old bastard to take him down from the inside."

I stare up at her, my jaw falling slack. "You want to destroy Delta, too?"

"I brought Xero here to beat him to death," she spits. "Don't you know the enemy of my enemy is my friend?"

"What about me?" I whisper.

Crouching to my level, she grabs my chin, forcing our gazes to meet once more. The lining of my stomach trembles. This is my worst nightmare, come to life. The monster wearing my face, reaching through the glass to steal my soul.

Looking into her eyes is like confronting an infinite mirror of self-loathing, a nightmare I thought I'd never escape. The reflection stretches to eternity, dredging up memories I'd kill to forget. Years of festering resentment smolder in her glower. Until now, I didn't truly understand the meaning of hell.

"He thinks you hurt his dowdy sister."

The word hits like a knife to the gut. "What?"

"So, you'll die and I'll live happily ever after with my sexy son-in-law," she replies with a smirk.

"No?"

"We have so much in common," she says as if I haven't spoken. "Both child assassins, both with vendettas against Delta. Both murdering unworthy siblings. Xero won't notice a thing."

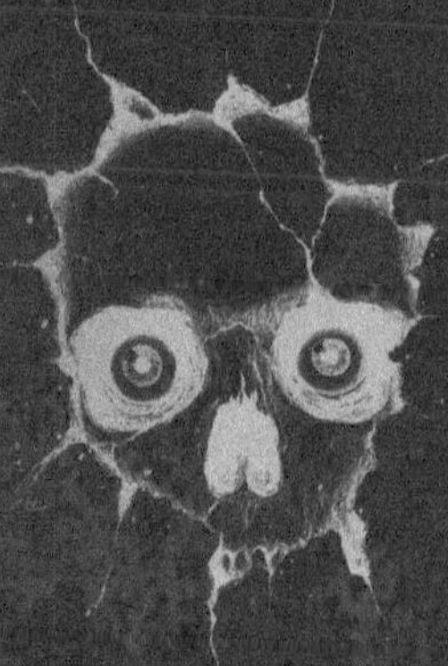

EIGHTY-SEVEN

AMETHYST

Dolly's declaration hits me harder than that cold shower, making my breath catch. What the hell did she do to Camila? Releasing the arm holding me steady, she steps back, letting me slump to the floor with a painful thud.

Even though the thought of her touching Xero makes my skin crawl, it still might happen. We're almost identical. He might not even notice the physical difference until he examines our scars.

"What's wrong, Amy?" she asks, her voice a mocking singsong, her painted lips widening into a broad grin. "Finally unable to yap?"

"Eventually, he'll work out the truth. You're exactly the sort of person he despises."

She turns toward the mirror, the absence of her gaze loosening my chest. I inhale a deep breath to gather my strength. Dolly fluffs her curls and applies a fresh coat of lip gloss. "Xero Greaves has a weakness for victims, and he's fixated on Delta. He'll love me since I've been under that monster's thumb since I was ten."

My breath shallows. I shake my head, unable to form a denial. Xero and I might share a connection that's been forged over months, but Dolly has a point. As a former Lolita assassin who was forced to perform in snuff movies, her traumatic past might make her seem more sympathetic. But nothing can compensate for her diabolical personality.

"There's a difference between having a tragic background and becoming a monster," I say, my conviction wavering. "Charlotte was also one of Delta's pawns, but now she's dying in a holding cell."

She whirls around, her gaze sharpening. The sudden eye contact makes me wince. Even though I know Dolly isn't some mythical mirror monster, seeing her look me full in the face is still jarring.

"I'm the only one capable of giving Xero his heart's desire," she says.

"Oh, and what's that?"

"His father's head on a platter. He'll be so grateful to me that he'll forget all about you. He'll fuck me in Delta's blood."

My stomach churns, but I manage to huff a laugh. "He's more likely to cut your throat."

She scoffs. "You're nothing special. You never were. The sooner Xero learns you're just a pale imitation of me, the sooner he'll discover I'm his perfect match."

Before I can even respond to that ridiculous comment, the door swings open, revealing Delta.

Panic punches me in the chest, and my muscles go rigid. I can't pull enough oxygen into my lungs. I can't even exhale. The only part of my body able to move is my heart, which hurls itself toward my spine.

His gaze flicks over Dolly before sweeping over to me and my exposed legs. Then a cold smile curls his heartbreakingly familiar features. I sit on the floor, frozen by trauma and drugs, my gaze fixed on his deep blue eyes, high cheekbones, and trim beard. He looks so much like Xero in disguise that it hurts.

Delta strides across the bathroom tiles, clad in a velvet smoking jacket. It's a luxurious rich navy with black collars and two frog closures at the front to sculpt the fabric around his frame. The attire is fitting, considering he's the Hugh Hefner of death.

"How are the preparations going?" he asks, his voice making my skin crawl.

Casting me a nervous glance before facing her husband,

Dolly raises trembling fingers to the back of her neck. "She's been uncooperative."

"She looks perfect." Delta looms over me, his eyes darkening, and reaches for my biceps.

Time stills. My mind transports me back to the asylum. I'm standing on my tiptoes, tied up with my arms stretched high above my head. Delta's warm hands grip my flesh as he slices into my skin with a blade. Pain lances across my skin, followed by a warm trickle. Then my limbs are trapped within a straitjacket, and he pounds into my body, crushing my lungs with his superior weight.

Panic seizes my throat in a paralyzing grip. I can't move. I can't breathe. I can't see anything but white.

Then his large hand moves to my shoulder, triggering a burst of adrenaline that has me shuffling backward on my ass.

"No," I scream, my voice raw. "Get away!"

My heart pounds so hard that its beats echo in my ears like a drum. I pull away from Delta's grip, my mind still thrashing within the throes of traumatic memories. In a flashback that feels like it's still happening, a man pins me to the kitchen table, while his friends close in around us like the walls of an open grave. Another time, another man in black, crushes my body to the kitchen floor with blood streaming from his throat on my face like rain. Every shitty thing that ever happened in my life is connected to this monster.

Delta draws back, his brow furrowing. "Is she having a bad trip?"

"Maybe Locke should take her to meet the investors," Dolly says, her voice wavering.

My gaze snaps to her paling face. It's strange how my childhood monster looks mild compared to this predator. Her features are no longer mockingly triumphant, but now held in a stoic mask. I don't need a psychic bond to know she doesn't want me alone with Delta so soon after revealing her plans to use Xero to murder her husband.

"Nonsense." Delta reaches down and scoops me into his arms, his touch igniting a riot of revulsion.

I shift in his grip, my stomach lurching, but he pulls me closer to his chest. "Easy now, Amy," he murmurs into my ear, his hot breath making me cringe. "Be a good girl for Daddy Delta."

Dolly walks at his side, following us out into a spacious bedroom of mahogany furniture and burgundy drapes. The last vestiges of sunlight stream in through the window, letting me know I've spent an entire day in captivity.

Her breath quickens, reminding me of the time she slashed me with that craft knife. She wore the same trapped expression back then, when the other students stared at her like she was a psychopath.

Delta pauses mid-way to place a hand on her shoulder. "Stay in the master suite. The investors can't know there are two of you."

She halts, her eyes wide with fear, her fingers twisting at her sides.

Delta continues toward a heavy door that leads to a black-and-white-tiled hallway, and my pulse quickens to a drumroll. Now's my chance to say something—anything—to stop the auction.

I clutch at Delta's lapel, making him pause. "Mr. Delta," I say, feeling like I'm ten again and reporting back from a mission. "Dolly's planning on having you killed."

He stares down at me and grins. "Worried about me, Amy?"

My throat tightens, and I gulp. Didn't Xero say something similar to me under Charlotte's bed? I shake off that thought. "Don't you want to know what she's planning?"

His dark chuckle makes every fine hair on the back of my neck stand on end. "Dolly is my second greatest creation, and I'm well aware of her ambitions. Why else would I have eliminated her most loyal followers?"

My jaw drops.

He gazes down at me, his eyes dancing. "Any questions? Anything further to negotiate?"

Bile rises to my throat. I don't need to ask about his greatest creation. This cold-hearted bastard subjected Xero to mental and psychological torture since he was seven. And if Delta already knows about Dolly's plot, then I have nothing to offer him to save my life.

He pushes open a heavy oak door and steps into a spacious room filled with the clinking of glasses and the low hum of conversation. The scents of brandy, cigar smoke, and expensive cologne mingle with the stench of corruption and decay.

I stare out at dense trees through a wall of leaded glass windows, then at a group of older men lounging on leather sofas, nursing drinks.

Their chatter ceases as we cross the room and head toward a bed set up opposite the wet bar, surrounded by studio lights on tripods. All eyes turn to me, making my heart want to break through my chest and leap out of the window.

The men rise off the sofas, approaching like hyenas catching the scent of carrion. I shiver, feeling exposed in this gingham dress and more vulnerable than I did at the asylum.

Back then, the crew members were more interested in creating the movie, and I was just another victim sent to die.

Here, I'm the main attraction.

Delta sets me down on a rubber sheet. "Gentlemen, give us a few minutes to set up the auction."

Twelve men form a small crowd around the bed. Their ages range from late thirties to about eighty, yet they all stare with the same predatory gleam. A sick hunger thickens the air, making every molecule tremble with unleashed tension.

"Dolly," one of the men rasps. "Suck my cock."

The others snicker.

My limbs are still heavy from the drugs, but there's nothing wrong with my jaws. If he brings that putrid penis near my lips, I'll bite it like a sausage.

As Delta draws back, I grab his lapel, making him raise his brow. "I only got a half dose of the antidote."

Frowning, he beckons to someone standing by the wet bar. "Come here. Administer Dolly a full shot of Nano Epinephrine."

Moments later, Locke slithers through the crowd, holding a syringe. He slides its needle into my arm, delivering a sting, followed by warm liquid. It courses through my veins, restoring my strength.

As he draws back, a man with a bad comb-over tries to mount the bed. He's just like the hallucinations of my dead music teacher, only this time, my mind is clear. I kick out at him, making the others chuckle.

BANG!

Everyone's attention swings to the other side of the room. A second crash confirms the source of the sound—a set of double doors secured by a wooden crossbar.

It sounds like someone's attacking it with a battering ram.

My breath catches. I move my limbs, infusing them with sensation and strength.

Is that a rescue party?

"What the hell is that?" asks a silver-haired man in a burgundy smoking jacket.

Delta chuckles. "That's my new star, Xero Greaves, making his grand entrance."

Nervous laughter ripples through the room, prompting several men to retreat from the bed. Mr. Combover stays put, as if eager for a front-row seat to the unfolding drama. Shivers race down my spine, my insides oscillating between hope and fear.

Delta claps a hand on Locke's shoulder before retreating from the bed. "Start the auction."

Locke describes Dolly in dehumanizing terms, recapping the movies she survived. But my focus is on the double doors. The wood holding them together creaks under pressure, and I shift on the mattress, sliding a hand beneath a rubber pillow. Something sharp pricks my finger, and I flinch. When I fumble with the object's contours, I realize it's an ice pick.

As the men bid for first dibs on me after Xero, I reach beneath the second pillow and find the shaft of a bladed tool. It's heavy, with an edge that feels like a cleaver. Movement out of the corner of my eye catches my attention. It's Delta sneaking past the wet bar and disappearing through a door.

My brow pinches. Why isn't Delta warning everyone else to run? Slipping the ice pick into the pocket of my pinafore, I scoot to the edge of the mattress with the cleaver behind my back.

The men continue bidding, and the room erupts in excited chatter. Some rub their hands as the crossbar cracks. My breath catches. Xero is seconds away from breaking down the door. With my heart pumping adrenaline and power, I roll my shoulders, my veins thrumming with anticipation. The moment he charges in, I'll strike.

"Sold for five hundred thousand," Locke cries to a round of polite applause.

The winner is the silver-haired man in the burgundy jacket. He extracts his phone and taps a few commands onto its screen. I can only assume he's transferring payment.

Locke strides to the doors and lifts the barricade. They fly open, revealing Xero, platinum-haired, naked, and covered in blood. The men scatter across the room like rodents.

My jaw drops. What the hell did they do to him?

Xero's face is a mask of madness, streaked with tears and blood. When our eyes meet, his features twist into a rictus of unbridled hatred.

EIGHTY-EIGHT

AMETHYST

All plans to stab my way to freedom vanish when Xero charges across the room—not toward Locke or the sexual predators. But toward me.

His hair flies in all directions like a bloody halo. His face is red with rage, with veins protruding from his brow. The muscles in his neck expand like the hood of a cobra, making him look fresh from an asylum.

My heart leaps into the back of my throat. From the way his eyes still lock on mine like I'm the only other person in existence, it almost looks like he's about to pull me into his arms... until he pulls a fist.

I dart to the side before the punch lands.

"Xero!" I scream, but my voice fails to reach him through his haze of fury.

He spins, lurches, grabs me by the hair, and the audience erupts into cheers. Realization slaps me in the face, and every drop of blood drains from my head and into my pounding heart.

Xero thinks I'm Dolly.

Using everything I learned from our training sessions, I drop to the floor and twist out of his grip, yanking out dozens of hairs by the root. As Xero advances toward me, I snatch the cleaver and aim it at his chest.

The audience coos.

His gaze swims from side to side, triggering long-forgotten flashbacks of male inmates on psychotic rampages. This time, there's no small army of men in white to subdue them—just me.

"Xero?" I repeat, my voice trembling.

I'm so accustomed to sparring with Xero and the others that his movements are clumsy in comparison. I dodge to the side, narrowly avoiding a right hook. A rush of air passes just above my head, signaling the strength behind his blow.

The cheers of the audience grow louder, spurring him on. I lunge to the side, narrowly missing another punch. If I don't pull him out of this drug-induced frenzy, he'll continue to attack me, thinking I'm Dolly.

"Xero, it's Amethyst!" I yell over the chaos.

He lurches forward, his hand shooting out to grab my throat. I twist to the side, his fingers grazing my shoulder.

"Xero Greaves, snap out of it!"

His other hand catches my wrist, making pain explode through my arm as he yanks me into his chest. His heart beats so hard, its reverberations echo through my back. I twist and turn, trying to wrench free, but his grip is iron.

As his free hand wraps around my throat, desperation drives me to kick backward. My foot connects with his shin, but he barely flinches. I run through all the moves we practiced, trying to find one that won't hurt Xero, but as he cuts off my air, I hurl my bodyweight forward, throwing him off-balance.

Xero tumbles forward, stopping himself before he falls. He pivots and swings his fist again, forcing me to duck.

The audience roars with laughter.

I walk backward, raising the cleaver like a shield, but Xero advances on me with the determination of a tiger. I'm trapped in a demented dilemma. The only man capable of saving me thinks I'm a woman he wants dead. If I attack him in self-defense, Delta and a dozen other predators are waiting in line for my demise. If Xero kills me in a drug-fueled rage, it will break his spirit and Delta wins.

"Xero, please listen to me!" I scream, my voice raw.

His arm strikes out like a rattlesnake and grabs the wrist of the hand holding the cleaver.

I could punch him, but that would only confirm in his mind that I'm an enemy. I could break free of this hold, but he'll continue chasing me until he passes out. Then we'll both be vulnerable.

Maybe the only weapon I have is my surrender.

Fingers clenching around my wrist, he walks me backward until my hamstrings meet the edge of the mattress. His free hand wraps around my throat and squeezes.

"Xero," I rasp. "It's Amethyst. Your little ghost."

Too far gone in his delusion to listen, he cuts off my air. Spots dance before my eyes, my vision darkening. In my periphery, the men press in closer, their excited breaths penetrating the roar of blood between my ears.

I stare into Xero's eyes and stroke the hand trying to strangle me to death, pouring every ounce of love into the caress.

"McMurphy," I whisper into his ear.

Xero flinches at the word, his grip loosening a fraction. His eyes remain wild and unfocused, but my chest brightens with a spark of hope.

I whisper the safe word over and over, and each time, his hold slackens enough for me to draw in a rush of air. He breathes hard, his features forming a grimace.

"That's right, Xero," I say, my palm sliding up his arm. "It's me. I'm Amethyst."

Recognition flickers across his features. He looks into my eyes, his brow furrowing with confusion, followed by a glimmer of the man I love.

Around us, the men clap and chant for Xero to tear me apart. He's oblivious to their presence, his attention honed only on me.

When his fingers loosen around my throat, I grab his wrist. "Don't make it obvious."

He hesitates, his breathing ragged, his gaze darting from side to side. The madness in his eyes dims, replaced by a burst of rage. Without a word, he throws me onto the bed. The mattress springs squeak under my weight, and I scream.

The movement jostles studio lights and cameras on tripods

surrounding the bed, filling my vision with a blinding glare. I blink over and over, my eyes watering.

Xero positions himself between my spread legs, his hands sliding up to the neckline of my dress. He grabs the fabric with both hands and pulls, tearing it apart.

The audience's raucous cheers become a distant roar, my world narrowing to Xero's touch. He looms over me, his hands caressing my exposed breasts. His touch ignites my skin with sparks of electricity, and my breath quickens. I bite my lip to keep from moaning.

Does Xero even know what's happening?

A foreign hand touches my knee, making me flinch and shriek. Xero's head snaps up, his eyes narrowing.

The groper is the man whose comb-over hangs down in wisps beside his ear. In a blur of movement, Xero grabs my cleaver and slashes his throat.

Blood sprays across the bed, splattering on my chest. I gasp, my eyes widening. The men crowding around the bed skitter backward to the farthest corners of the room.

Xero turns his focus on me, then climbs back onto the bed and places the cleaver in my hand. Heart fluttering, I close my fingers around its hilt. Grabbing the torn fabric of my dress, he wipes the blood off my breasts.

With trembling hands, I reach up to cup his face and whisper, "What did they do to you?"

Xero hisses through clenched teeth, making me flinch. Is he hallucinating? Before I can work out a way to get through to him, the hand that was holding the fabric slips between my spread legs.

My gaze travels over his muscled chest and down his abs to his thick erection. I shiver, the muscles of my pussy tightening. Xero slips his fingers through my slick folds, his eyes darkening with anger and need.

"You want me?" I curl my fingers around his shaft.

He answers with a low, rumbling growl and moves closer, allowing me to position his cock at my entrance. When I rub his crown over my swollen clit, we both groan.

Before I know it, Xero pushes into my pussy with a thrust so forceful that I scream. He pulls back, not giving me time to adjust, and snaps his hips.

His thrusts are hard, unyielding, delivering jolts of pleasure and pain. Wrapping my legs around his hips, I cling to his biceps. His breath is hot and erratic against my cheek, mingling with the smell of sweat and blood.

"Harder, Xero," I groan, my fingers digging into his shoulders. "Make me come."

He draws back, his eyes meeting mine in silent understanding. Pulling away, he flips me onto my front and enters me again with another violent thrust. His hands grip my hips hard enough to bruise, and he pounds into me, his movements furious and frantic.

I push against him, meeting him thrust for thrust. As I turn around, some of the men from earlier enter my periphery, stroking their erections.

My fingers tighten around the cleaver. The first bastard to come in touching distance will be the next to die.

The rhythm becomes erratic, his breath hot and ragged against my neck. His chest rests flush against my back, his arm tightening around my waist.

Pressure builds in my core, fueled by the strangers' imminent deaths. I picture them crawling onto the mattress, wanting their turn and getting sliced open with my cleaver.

As Xero's rough fingers stroke my clit, the men venture closer. I wonder how much they paid to watch and ask myself if it was worth their lives. They're waiting for the grand finale, where Xero kills me in the throes of my climax.

Just as I'm about to come, he pulls us both backward so I'm sitting upright on my knees with him pounding into me from beneath.

I turn to the silver-haired auction winner and lick my lips. As he grins, I imagine him rushing forward, his erection within the range of my blade.

Xero's fingers find my throat again and he squeezes hard. My eyes widen, and I clutch at his fingers, trying to pull them off.

The men edge closer, their faces monstrous.

Darkness clouds my vision again. I open my mouth in a silent scream. Xero quickens his thrusts, as though excited by my impending death.

An orgasm tears through my core, and my muscles clench and spasm around Xero's shaft. Eyes rolling to the back of my head, my body falls limp.

The room erupts into raucous applause, but I stay still, wanting them to believe I'm dead. Xero's strokes become erratic, fucking me so hard that my body jerks across the mattress.

With a final snap of his, his cock throbs once, twice, three times, before erupting in an explosion of warm cum. My ears ring with his roar. He continues pounding into me through his climax, stretching out my orgasm.

As his movements slow, he strokes my curls, still breathing hard. I peek through my lashes, watching the men approach.

Xero pulls out of me, plucks the cleaver from my fingers, and turns on the crowd. The room echoes with shouts and screams and the sounds of slicing flesh. I continue playing dead throughout his wild rampage as the men scramble to escape. All the doors, including the double ones that were barricaded, are shut.

As he works his way through the men, I resist the urge to join in with my ice pick. The man we both want to kill is missing.

Just as I'm ready to take another peek, the carnage stops, and Xero drops to the floor with a thud.

Delta rises from behind the wet bar with a tranquilizer gun. "Apologies for that, gentlemen. The winner of the auction is now deceased. Would you like to bid again for a rare opportunity to fuck Dolly while her corpse is still warm?"

EIGHTY-NINE

AMETHYST

I lie on the mattress, holding my breath as Delta orders Locke to take me to another room. He tells his patrons to help themselves to drinks while he settles Xero into an appropriate cell.

The room erupts into nervous chatter, although it's a lot thinner than before Xero's rampage. That's partly because half the men are either dead or maimed. Sweat and blood and death stain my nostrils, making me want to gag. The surviving men don't seem to give a shit that their comrades got slaughtered—they're all itching for a chance to fuck Dolly's corpse.

I peek through my lashes, watching Delta dragging Xero out of the room, wishing I had the manpower and strength to cut them all into pieces. Since all I have is an ice pick, I'll have to play dead and strike from the shadows.

When Locke's fingers close around my ankles, I force myself not to flinch. He drags me off the mattress, and I land on the floor with a painful thud. I close my eyes, focusing on the sensation of being pulled across the room and through the door leading to a tiled hallway.

As we enter a bedroom, Locke lifts me off the floor and tosses me onto a mattress. I land on my back, the ice pick in my pocket bouncing on my thigh.

Locke retreats, leaving me alone in the lavish, dimly lit room.

The moment the door clicks shut, I reach for my weapon and secure it in my palm.

All I need to do is wait for the auction winner.

When I've killed him using the element of surprise, I'll wait for the next man to come and check up on him, then he'll be the next to die.

Before I can even complete that plan, the door swings open, and I stiffen. Dolly steps in, her figure in silhouette. She switches on the light and strides to my bedside.

Her hot breaths make every fine hair on the back of my neck stand on end. I close my eyes, my heart pounding so hard and fast I'm sure she knows I'm faking.

"How typical of you to fall dead after less than twenty minutes. You were always weak." She reaches down and yanks me up by the hair. "Always getting off lightly. I had to perform in those movies for years, fighting off hundreds of those bastards, yet you can't even survive a single one."

My heart sinks at the reminder of everything she suffered. When warm spittle lands on my cheek, I force myself not to flinch. I hate Dolly, even though she's a victim as much as she's a monster. But I wish there was a way I could make her understand the truth.

"I begged Delta to be the one to kill you, to slay the last of my demons, but he wanted to make money from your death. It made me fucking sick," she hisses.

I stiffen, my throat tightening. Can't she see Delta is her enemy and not me?

"Since I can't kill you, I'll desecrate your fucking corpse!"

She releases me with a hard shove, and I fall back onto the mattress. I crack open an eye to find her with her back turned, rummaging through a dresser by the wall and extracting a serrated knife.

Alarm kicks me in the chest, and I launch myself off the mattress. All notions of compassion crumble in the face of my imminent mutilation.

I lunge at Dolly with the ice pick, aiming for her throat. She turns around to dodge, but not fast enough. The pointed tip pierces the side of her neck, releasing a spray of blood.

Dolly staggers back with a scream, her eyes widening as she clutches the wound. She slashes wildly with the knife, but I leap out of reach.

"Cockroach," she snarls, her voice harsh with venom. "You were playing dead all along. You two-faced, pampered princess."

My jaw clenches as every memory of her attacking me first rises to the surface, bringing up a bellyful of resentment. Even if Dad smashed her possessions and made it look like I was the culprit, we could have talked things through. Instead, she struck out at me like a psychopath.

"What are you going to do now, Dolly?" I ask, my fingers tightening around the ice pick. "Even things out by stabbing me in the neck?"

Flashing her teeth, she charges. Blood pours from the wound and onto her white dress, but she doesn't seem to care. Pushing forward everything I learned from sparring practice, I steel my jaw, widen my stance, and ready myself for impact.

She swings the knife in an upward arc, aiming for the gap between my ribs. I block, sidestep, and strike at her throat. She stumbles backward, crashing into the dresser.

"You bitch," she screeches.

Still facing me, she reaches behind her back and fumbles through the drawer, presumably looking for a weapon more deadly than a knife. I charge at her, narrowly missing an attempt to gouge my eyes.

"Wake up. All I ever did was exist." I kick her wrist, making the knife fly across the room.

She whirls on me, her face twisted into a rictus of rage. "You've never suffered a day in your life!"

"Bullshit."

With a scream, she charges. I pivot, but she adjusts course and tackles me to the bed. The mattress sags under our combined weight, and we roll across its surface, grappling for control. She gets on top, her hands wrapping around my throat.

"If you think a month in the loony bin matches years of being raped while killing and nearly being killed for Delta, then you're insane."

"Then team up with me and kill him," I snap.

She draws backward for a head butt. At the last minute, I punch her neck wound, releasing another spray of blood. She cries out, her grip loosening enough for me to twist free and roll off the bed. Landing on my feet, I glance around the room and rush to where she dropped the knife.

Dolly leaps off the bed and jumps on my back. "Mom handed you everything on a golden platter." She tries to cut off my air. "I had to fight and fawn and fuck to stay alive."

I charge backward, slamming her into the wall, making her cry out. When she doesn't release her grip around my neck, I back us into the wardrobe, knocking over a small table covered with cosmetics.

Releasing her grip, she drops to the floor, panting hard. "Is that all you've got?"

Ignoring her, I pick up the fallen knife. "I'm sorry your life was a misery, but it wasn't my fault."

"Bullshit!" she screams, clutching her neck.

Her gaze is unfocused, and I wonder if it's just the blood loss or if she's also under the influence of drugs. I can't imagine existing alongside Delta without needing chemicals to muffle the horror.

"Mom's diary explained it all. We weren't even Dad's kids. He was an FBI agent—"

"I know," she snaps.

I flinch. "What?"

"Delta told me everything. You don't have to tell me what Kappa did, or that Lambda plotted to steal everything away from Mom and leave her destitute, because I already know."

My brow pinches. Lambda must be a code word for Lyle. "Then why—"

"Because we were supposed to be together," she screeches, her eyes streaming with tears. "Three Fates and what happened after would have been bearable with you!"

Her words trigger a slew of memories where she was always praised for succeeding, while I was chastised for minor failures. The instructors made a point of breaking my spirit, stroking Dolly's ego while offering me nothing but denigration.

Gripping the knife, I nod. "I was supposed to be the scapegoat, while you basked as the golden child."

"What the hell is that supposed to mean?" she snarls.

"I don't expect Delta taught you the intricacies of narcissistic abuse."

She rises to her feet on shaky legs, raising the ice pick. I flinch, not knowing when she wrestled it from my fingers.

Charging at me like a banshee, she screams, "You were always a book nerd. Why don't you just die?"

Time stills, and the space between pounding heartbeats expands. I stand in place, imagining myself as a matador, facing a furious bull. Dolly aims the ice pick at my eyes, her features a rictus of fury.

She won't change.

She never will.

I exist to serve as the whipping girl for everything that's gone wrong in her life. But I refuse to take the blame for the actions of our stepfather and his corrupt associates. Refuse to waste another second of my time explaining my truth to a murderous woman who won't listen.

Dolly might be a victim, but she's far from innocent. She sat by, allowing Delta to create more snuff movies. She could have killed him any time during their marriage, including today, yet she turned her anger on me.

As she comes within reach, I remember Seth's comment about her glass eye. Shifting my weight backward, I wait for the hand holding the ice pick to approach. At the last minute, I leap into her blind spot, grab her arm, and slip my knife between her ribs.

Time snaps back to normal as she drops to her knees, her eyes widening with shock.

"Amy?" she whispers, sounding just like the twin I remember.

"I hope you find peace in death, because you're too dangerous to keep alive."

Blood wells at her parted lips, and she gazes up at me with wide eyes filled with betrayal. She falls onto her side, her body convulsing.

Bile rises to my throat. I stumble back, gasping for breath as life drains from Dolly's eyes. Her body twitches once before falling limp in a pool of spreading blood.

Dolly. My stalker, my tormentor, my twin. The monster in the mirror. The woman who should have been my lifeline but chose to make me suffer.

Finally, it's over. At least for her.

I fall to my knees beside her, grief crashing down like a lead weight. Harsh sobs tear from my throat, mingling with hot tears. I place a hand on her face, feeling warmth that will soon dissipate. No matter how much I try to stem the emotion, it won't stop.

There's no time to mourn. Xero is unconscious, alone, and at Delta's mercy. What if Delta is murdering him or letting those sickos access his unconscious body?

But I can't stop crying.

I cry for the girl she was, for the sister I lost, for the monster she became. My tears soak into her dress, mingling with the blood.

Dolly deserved better. We both did. So did Mom. But this is our reality. Pulling back, I blink away the tears and gaze down at her through swollen eyes. Her face is peaceful—free from rage and pain. I want to hate her, but all I feel is overwhelming sadness.

Wiping my eyes, I peel off my torn dress and strip Dolly's corpse. After forcing her into my outfit, I lift her corpse onto the bed and stumble into the bathroom.

In the mirror is a wild-eyed woman I barely recognize. I'm spattered with blood and my curls fly in all directions. Dark circles ring my eyes, and bruises are already forming around my neck.

With trembling fingers, I turn on the faucet and splash cold water on my face, but it does nothing to cool my nerves. My body is so jittery I can barely scrub off the blood.

Once I'm clean, I rinse the knife and take another look at my reflection. All I see is myself. I'm pale, exhausted, and out of breath, but the monster in the mirror is dead. Any reactions to killing her will have to wait until I've rescued Camila and Xero.

It's going to take more than a knife to get past Delta, and I think I know where to find it. Earlier, Dolly must have been searching for a gun in the top drawer. Slipping on a robe, I step out of the bathroom in search of a weapon, only for my feet to stumble to a stop.

Locke stands at the foot of the bed, staring at Dolly's corpse. He turns his head, his brow rising with recognition.

Oh, shit.

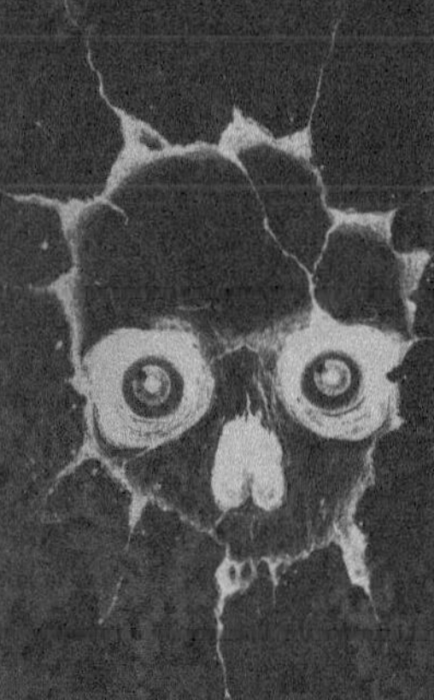

NINETY

AMETHYST

Panic floods my veins. I freeze in the doorway, staring at Locke. Any minute now, he'll raise the alarm, telling Delta I'm an impostor and his precious wife is dead.

The golden-haired pretty boy glances from me to my deceased twin sister and smirks. "What did you do?"

Swallowing hard, I steady my breathing, trying to channel Dolly's insanity.

Huffing, I say, "After everything she took from me, I had to work off a little steam."

He steps closer, his brows pulling together. "Your eyes are red. Have you been crying?"

"Despite everything, she was still my twin."

He shakes his head. "That was reckless, baby. We agreed you'd play along until the time was right for Delta to die."

My mind races, and the room tilts on its axis. Dolly mentioned wanting him dead, but I didn't realize she had a plan.

"Dolly?" Locke moves from the side of the bed, closing the distance between us, and places a hand on the arm that holds the knife at my side.

My skin crawls at his touch, and I fight the urge to recoil. Raising my other hand to the back of my neck in a gesture of awkwardness, I grimace. "I lost it."

"Have you changed your mind?"

"No," I say.

"It's normal to trauma bond with an abuser. Delta's only giving you freedom because you're helping him capture Xero. Don't be fooled by this truce. It's only because you're giving him what he wants. Once Xero is under his control, he'll truss you up like Grunt again and pimp you out to anyone he wants to impress."

I bow my head, trying to force back crashing waves of sympathy and guilt. I don't know why it didn't occur to me that they would have treated Dolly worse than Grunt. It looks like my going viral on social media triggered a series of events that elevated her into a position of power.

"Talk to me," Locke says.

"You're right," I reply, my fingers tightening around the knife.

"Good girl." Locke pulls me into a hug that makes me want to heave. "Once he's dead, we'll take control of Xero and the assets he stole from Delta. Then we'll discard him and live the rest of our lives together in luxury."

This star-crossed love story might be believable if Locke didn't participate in snuff. If he gave a shit about Dolly, he would have helped her escape. Instead, he sold her a dream. Bringing up the knife, I plunge it into his gut, making him stumble backward with a shocked cry.

"Dolly?" he whispers, his eyes widening.

"Guess again."

I slash at his chest, sending out a spray of blood. It splatters across my face, giving me a thrill of satisfaction.

Recognition flickers across his features. "Amy."

"What was the plan?" I ask through clenched teeth. "Manipulate Dolly into signing over Delta's assets, sell her to the highest bidder, and run off alone into the sunset?"

"She was a broken whore."

My lip curls, and I raise the knife again. "What does that make you?"

"I can explain." He lifts a shaking palm.

"You have ten seconds."

"Delta blackmailed me to drop out of medical school so I

could take care of Dolly." Lips trembling, he darts his gaze to her corpse, cooling on the bed. "I had to keep her medicated, heal her wounds, and keep her alert for the patrons."

Nausea churns in my gut. I clench my teeth, resisting the urge to strike. He's describing the worst kind of pimp.

Locke licks his lips. I've never seen him look so nervous. "We grew close. She told me about her past. Then someone on the membership forum saw your posts and asked if she'd set up some social media."

"Hurry up," I snap, my grip tightening on the knife.

"It was all her idea. She knew Xero had stolen from Delta and knew he was desperate to get back everything he'd lost. So, she convinced Delta to use you as bait."

"What's your point?" I sneer.

He breathes hard through the pain, his golden features turning gray. "It was all her idea. If you want to blame someone, look at her. Or Delta."

Disgust coils through my insides like a constrictor, poised to strike. "You'll say anything to save your hide."

"No—"

I rush forward, plunging the knife into his gut, eliciting a satisfying gasp. "What was it you told me about having four holes? I'm about to give you five." I twist the knife for good measure, savoring his choked scream.

"Please—"

"I wish I could draw out your death after everything you did to me at the asylum, but I need to save the man I love."

Locke falls on his face. Dropping to my knees beside him, I roll his carcass to his front and plunge my knife into his midsection once more, making him groan.

"That's for injecting me with all kinds of drugs." I deliver another stab to his chest.

"Fuck," he says, coughing up a mouthful of blood.

"That's for the mockery." I slash across his pretty face, turning his mouth into a giant grin.

"And that's for violating me with the pessary." My blade digs into his groin, eliciting a gurgling scream.

He stares up at me, his face frozen in a mask of agony.

Rising to my feet, I roll him under the bed. Blood soaks the front of my robe, but I'm too far gone to care. I rush to the dresser and close my fingers around the gun.

Cold washes over my senses, slowing my heartbeat and bringing a newfound sense of power. After this baptism of blood, I'm ready for anything.

I walk through the bedroom, trailing bloody footprints out into the hallway. A door up ahead opens, and Delta steps in with a man I recognize as one of the spectators.

He's a middle-aged blond with round glasses, who raises his arm and points.

"I thought Dolly was dead."

"Obviously, she survived." Features hardening, Delta strides toward me, his eyes flashing.

I raise the gun and shoot him in the leg.

When the man behind him turns around, I shoot him in the back. He falls flat on his face with a groan.

"What the hell do you think you're doing?" Delta snarls.

"Take me to Xero, or the next thing I shoot won't be a leg."

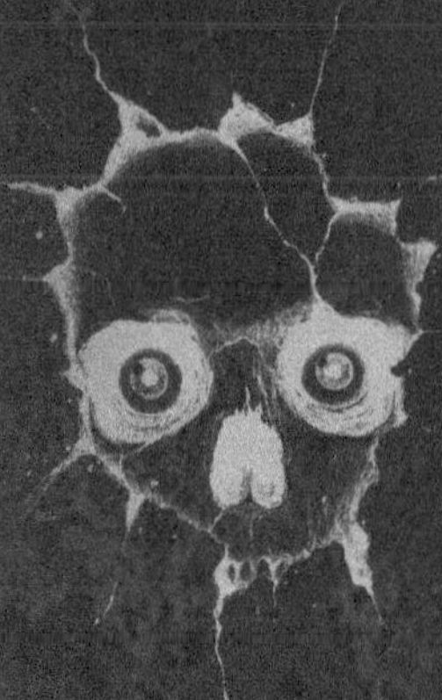

NINETY-ONE

XERO

I wake up feeling like I'm living the same hellish day on repeat. Agony pounds through my temples, and my throat is raw from screaming. I'm staring at the electric chair through the bars of a cage, already plotting my escape.

My gaze wanders past the dried blood pooled across the floor to Camila's motionless body. A cold knife of grief slices into my heart, breaking through the haze. The last thing I remember was cradling her as she died, before everything went sideways.

Father's drug pulled me into a violent nightmare where I fucked Amethyst, killed Dolly, and hacked through a crowd of bodies. I felt untouchable, powerful in my vengeful rampage until everything turned black.

Raising stained hands to my face, I wonder if there's more to the dream than just my tortured imagination. There's too much blood to be Camila's. It's on my cheeks, encrusted in my hair, on the tips of my lashes. If I tore through Father's associates, then which twin did I fuck and kill?

I scramble to my feet, my heart lurching with a jarring rhythm. The mere thought of betraying my delicate ghost is inconceivable. The prospect of harming her—even unintentionally—is unfathomable.

The door swings open, and a short man pokes his head into

the room. His eyes widen as they land on mine, and he takes a step inside.

"Xero Greaves," he says, his voice breathy with reverence. He wears a plain gray suit with a matching tie, the outfit as unremarkable as his fawning. "Delta said I'd find you here, but he also said you'd be unconscious!"

My jaw clenches.

"I'm a huge fan of your work," he continues, his gaze lingering on my chest. "The stepmother murder videos were... impressive."

Rage surges through my veins, a hot, burning inferno. I grind my teeth at the implication that Father is treating my captivity like a fucking zoo.

Forcing myself to remain calm, I snort. "How much did you pay for the privilege to grope me in my sleep?"

Cheeks pinking, he scurries closer to the cage. He doesn't reply, but the way his gaze sweeps down my form confirms my suspicions. My heart pounds, and blood roars in my ears, threatening to drown out all rational thought. Sucking in a deep breath, I shove down my outrage and focus on using him to my advantage.

The man stops out of grabbing range and gazes up at me through his lashes. "Did you get those piercings in prison?"

"Only one of them," I reply, forcing myself not to cringe at the sensation of being infested by crawling ants.

He steps close enough that I can see the thread-like veins across his cheeks and how the spaces in his sparse hairline fill with sweat.

"Which one?"

My hand slides down my abs, making his breath catch. I lift my cock and point at the patch of skin where its base meets my balls.

He gasps. "You have a scrotal ladder?"

"Can't you see the flesh tunnel?" I ask.

Brow furrowing, he leans closer and squints. "What am I supposed to be looking at?"

"Step closer and you'll see," I say, my voice lowering an octave.

The fanboy's breath quickens. He glances up to meet my eyes

and I raise my brow in challenge. Licking his lips, he steps closer to the cage. Then he raises a trembling hand and whispers, "May I?"

I snatch his wrist, yank him closer, and slam his head into the metal bars, creating a satisfying thud. Blood gushes from his nose like a broken faucet, and he screams. I deliver two more blows, each one more satisfying than the last.

The air thickens with the scent of iron as he crumples to the floor. I guide him down beside the cage and rifle through his pockets until I find a phone. With trembling fingers, I dial Tyler's number, my breath coming in short, sharp gasps.

He answers on the first ring. "What?"

"It's me."

"Where the hell are you?" he asks, his voice filled with worry. "Xero, we've been looking for you two everywhere."

"Hold on." I put Tyler on speaker, reach for my Prince Albert ring, and unscrew its bead. The deputy police chief isn't the only person capable of making faraday cages—I prefer to keep mine in my piercings.

A tiny metal tracker falls to the floor.

"Got a lock," Tyler says. "Hades Holdings owns a condo in Woodland Suites. It was the next location on our list. ETA ten minutes."

"Send a medic—Camila's been shot," I say, my voice breaking. I remove the top barbell of my Jacob's ladder piercing, shivering as the metal slides through my skin. "What about Jynxson?"

"A concussion and a few broken ribs. How's Amethyst?"

Tyler's question lands with the force of a gut punch, leaving me winded. "I... I don't know."

The thought I might have raped and murdered her is unthinkable, no matter how powerful the drugs, and yet the possibility hurts worse than a knife twisting in my gut. I can barely stand to consider that this nightmare might be real. Instead, I focus on picking the lock so I can find Amethyst.

Tyler falls silent, giving me the mental bandwidth to focus on unscrewing the barbell, removing a pin, and manipulating the lock's mechanism. The steady click of its tumblers falling into place provides a little reassurance. My sister might be dead on the other side of the room, and the woman I love might have died painfully at my hands. When the cage door springs open, I shake off the lingering traces of self-pity.

I step out and rush to Camila's side to check her pulse. It's weak and thready, and her skin is clammy. Her lashes flutter, and my lungs release a breath of relief. My eyes sting with tears as she moves her lips, unable to make a sound.

Stroking her cheek, I murmur, "Hold on. Help is on the way."

"Isabel and the others will arrive in seven minutes," Tyler's voice chimes through the phone speaker.

"My tracker and this phone are in the same room as Camila," I say. "She's barely conscious. Keep her updated."

"Got it."

Returning to the fanboy, I snap his neck and tear off his jacket. I lay it over Camila, walk to the table of tools, where I pick up an ax, and leave my sister in the care of Tyler's disembodied voice.

I run down a short corridor, my insides roiling with dread. Father might have already left by now, having murdered Amethyst or taken her hostage. He could have left her corpse discarded on a bed.

Adrenaline rages as I burst through a door at the end of the hallway and enter a room as spacious as the penthouse hotel in Helsing Island. My eyes immediately fix on the bodies piled up on the empty bed to my left.

I catch sight of five men gathered around a wet bar, their features etched with shock. Anger burns through my veins as I channel every ounce of aggression and charge at them with the ax.

"Where's Delta?" I snarl. They scatter in all directions like vermin. Some of them have the nerve to scream. I sprint toward a man whose face I recognize from the New Alderney Police Department. "Where the fuck is my father?"

"Here."

I whirl around in the direction of that hateful voice.

Father steps in through a door behind me, holding Amethyst at gunpoint. My heart stops beating for the seconds it takes me to absorb the blood splattered across her face, soaking the front of her robe and covering her feet.

At least, I think that's my little ghost. The woman standing beside him, looking shaken, could easily be her identical twin. The last time I saw Amethyst, the left side of her hair was green, while Dolly was a full brunette.

Father looks too comfortable to be bluffing, but he's always had the upper hand. He cocks the gun against the woman's temple, making her whimper.

My blood boils. The desperation in her eyes fuels my mounting fury. Her expressions belong to the woman I love, but this could also be an elaborate trick.

"What do you want?" I ask.

"There's a convoy of armed vehicles approaching the condo. Call them off."

"Or you'll kill your wife?" I ask, my brows rising.

"She's dead," Father says, his voice flat. "Murdered by her evil twin."

My throat tightens. "You and Dolly told me you'd already killed Amethyst."

His features pinch the way they did whenever I earned his displeasure. "We lied. It was a ruse to get you to kill Amethyst under the influence of epinephrine and PCP."

I glance at the woman Father holds hostage, looking for a sign, a plea, a flicker of recognition, but she holds her features in a stubborn mask. It's almost as if she wants my operatives to storm this penthouse.

She has to be Amethyst.

"Fine," I say, my mind racing for a plan. "Get me a pair of pants."

Smirking, Father drags her to the wet bar, toward a stack of towels.

I move closer, my fingers tightening around the ax. Sweat prickles across my skin, which cools against a blast of air conditioning. I need to time this right. Attacking too soon will only get Amethyst hurt.

As Father reaches for a towel, Amethyst ducks beneath his

arm and stabs an ice pick into his side. Howling, he fires his gun into the ceiling.

Heart racing with hope, I sprint toward the bar. It's her. My little ghost.

"Bastard." Amethyst grabs his arm while he's still off balance and flips him over her shoulder. He flies over the bar, landing on a shelf of glasses.

Righting himself, Father lunges at the fallen gun. I swing the ax, sinking the blade into his shoulder. He screams, just as the air rings with gunshots.

I pick up the gun, turning my ax's blade around and slam its butt against his skull, making him crumble to the marble floor. We'll deal with him later.

Amethyst runs into my arms, her body trembling against mine.

"Is it really you?" I croak.

She gazes up at me, her green eyes shining with unshed tears. "It's not McMurphy."

At the reminder of our safe word, I laugh.

"Xero," snaps a female voice. "Put on some fucking clothes."

Relief floods my system. I turn around, finding Isabel storming in with a crowd of operatives.

Pointing at the doorway leading to where I left Camila, I smile. "She's over there."

Isabel leads a small team to the back room, while the rest of the operatives apprehend Father's guests. I bury my head in Amethyst's hair and inhale her heavenly scent.

"I'm so proud of you, little ghost," I murmur.

She rests her head on my chest. "Take me home, Xero."

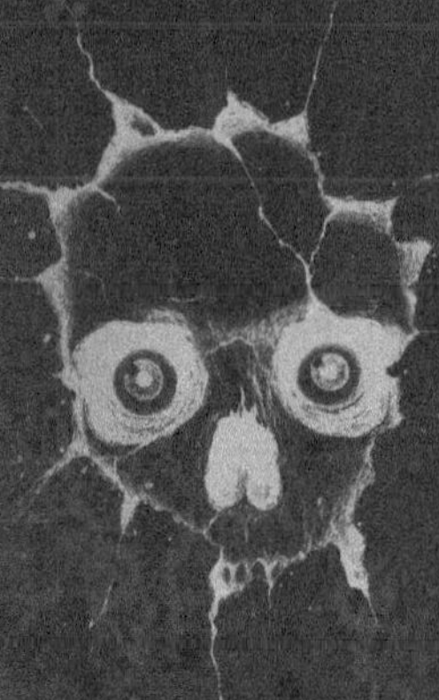

NINETY-TWO

AMETHYST

I can't believe it's over. Xero's people stormed the apartment, took Camila out on a stretcher, and gathered up the men in suits. They restrained Delta like he was some kind of cannibal, injected him with four types of drugs, then loaded him on a hand truck.

We're in one of their safe houses within the Victoria Gardens district, trudging into a bathroom the size of my old kitchen. Morning sunlight streams in through opaque windows and onto slate tiles. The air carries a faint scent of lavender, a welcome change from the stench of carnage.

I'm still wearing the bathrobe when Xero leads me to a shower cubicle large enough to have its own bench. The blood has dried through the fabric, making it stick to my chest.

Xero slips off his robe. The blood on his skin was already dry when the medics checked our vital signs and scanned us for trackers. His platinum hair has formed red clumps, and his face is streaked with crimson.

"Ready?" he asks.

I nod.

He turns the faucet, and warm water cascades down from four dinner-plate-sized shower heads. Slumping on the bench, I close my eyes and let the liquid flow over my skin. Each droplet feels like it's come from heaven, washing away our hellish ordeal.

Xero sits on the bench beside me, his fingers finding their way to my robe's collar. Despite getting soaked, the fabric still clings stubbornly to my skin.

"Give it a minute," I murmur.

"Are you alright?" he asks, his voice barely audible over the roar of the shower.

Swallowing, I nod and lean against his larger body for support. For the hundredth time, my mind runs through my encounter with Dolly and all the things I learned from Locke.

"Do you think I could have saved her?" The words escape my lips before I can stop them, laden with the weight of regret.

"You know the answer to that." Xero wraps an arm around my shoulders and pulls me into his side.

"I don't know... You were a child assassin, and you turned out okay?"

"What I went through was a picnic compared to the years Dolly suffered under Father," he says. "No amount of reasoning can compete with fourteen years of trauma, manipulation, and abuse."

"Yeah," I reply with a sigh.

"My father had her channeling all her anger and resentment onto you for a reason."

I open my eyes and gaze up into Xero's face. The blood encrusted in his hair and skin has gone, leaving him as starkly beautiful as ever, with his pale-blue eyes and chiseled features.

He runs gentle fingers through my curls. "They built you up as a scapegoat to make her cooperative. Maybe that was the only way she could survive. If you had hesitated for a minute with Dolly, you would be dead."

My throat tightens. "Maybe," I reply. "But the animosity started before we even went to Three Fates."

Xero slips his fingers beneath the collar of my robe. By now, the fabric has loosened its hold on my skin, and he peels it down my arms, letting the water wash over my shoulders.

"How was she before your stepfather started framing you for breaking her things?"

"We weren't close before then. She had her friends. I had my books."

"Those men took an innocent girl and twisted her into the type of person who relished other people's pain. They tried to do the same to you, but failed."

I dip my head. They turned me into a killer, but at least I have a moral code.

"Maybe," I say again.

"Let me take care of you," he murmurs, his voice a soothing balm to my frayed nerves.

With tender fingers, he eases off the robe, exposing me to the warm cascade. His gaze roams over my body, lingering on each bruise and scar, and his features tighten with anger. The air thickens, charged with his silent rage.

"What's wrong?" I ask.

"You're injured."

My hands travel to the finger marks on my neck. "It's nothing."

"I did that."

"Xero—" I place my fingers over his lips, silencing his protest. "It was the drugs. You were half-crazed."

"Did I hurt you?"

Shaking my head, I smile. "I've trained with you at your best. It was easy enough to dodge."

His gaze pierces mine, desperate to uncover any trace of concealed pain. "You can't have been successful with those bruises."

"I took a risk and let you grab me to get through to you."

He squeezes his eyes shut. "That was dangerous."

"You thought I was Dolly. I was safe when you realized it was me."

"Don't do that again." Voice trembling, he cups my face, his thumbs brushing away stray droplets from my cheeks.

"Do you plan on going out of your mind again?" I ask.

Opening his eyes, he shakes his head, his lips quirking into a reluctant smile. "Not in this lifetime."

"There you go."

I lean in, my lips parting, and he captures them in a kiss. It's tender, a heartfelt apology that needs no words. I luxuriate in the moment, wanting it to last forever. His hands cradle my face, his touch gentle yet firm, grounding me in the warmth of his love.

When we break apart, he leans his forehead against mine, his thumbs tracing circles on my cheeks.

"Let me wash you," he says with so much reverence that my skin breaks out in shivers.

"Please."

He reaches for a bar of soap and rubs it between his hands, creating a rich lather. Starting at my shoulders, he works the suds into my skin with firm strokes. His touch is methodical, almost clinical, as if he's focused on erasing every trace of those men's gazes.

"You're mine, little ghost," he growls.

"Yours," I whisper. "And you're mine."

"I belonged to you the moment I read your first letter. Hell, the moment I picked up your scent on the paper, you became the keeper of my heart."

As his gaze finds mine again, he glides his hands over my arms, his thumbs tracing the lines of my muscles. "You're so strong," he murmurs, almost to himself. "So brave."

"I don't know about that," I say with a smile. "I spent a long time playing dead."

"Clever ghost. They underestimated you—even my father. You should have seen the horror in his face when you threw him into the glass."

Closing my eyes, I let the praise wash over me along with the water. He moves his hands lower, soaping my chest with careful attention, his fingers skimming the tops of my breasts. I shiver, my nipples hardening.

"And beautiful, too," he says, his voice deepening.

He guides me to the edge of the bench and turns my body to face sideways, so his strong hands can work their way down my back. His fingers knead the knots in my muscles until the tension dissolves, and I melt under his touch. Pulling me flush against his chest, he reaches around to my belly and runs his soapy hands in slow, sensual circles.

"You have no idea how much I love you," he murmurs into my ear, his breath warm against my skin.

"Tell me," I whisper back.

"More than I love the beating of my heart. More than I love blood running through my veins. You are my everything, the air that I breathe, the sun that warms my skin, the moon that brightens my darkest nights."

His words resound through my soul, filling my heart with warmth. A lump forms in my throat, and my eyes prick with tears. No one has ever described me in such beautiful, raw terms. For the first time in my fragmented memory, I don't just feel complete, but completely loved.

"Your words..." My voice thickens with the depth of my emotions. "I... You... God, Xero. You've gotten me tongue-tied."

"Let it out."

His fingers continue stroking my belly, never wandering any lower. My blood hums, my clit swells, and my skin thrums for his touch.

"Xero, I..." My throat tightens.

The last time I said those words, I had a miscarriage. The man I loved stood over my broken body, his expression unreadable, as I cramped and bled and cried.

Xero's lips graze my ear, and he murmurs, "I've got you, little ghost. Your heart is safe with me."

"You saved me in more ways than I can imagine," I say, my voice trembling with the depth of my emotions. "Even when I thought all was lost, it was your voice guiding me through the dark. Xero, you're the other half of my soul. Without you, I'm a shell, drifting aimlessly in an ocean of nothingness."

I turn around to face him, my eyes brimming with tears, searching for him through the haze of water and steam. Our gazes finally connect, and it's like the entire world falls still.

His ice-blue irises, streaked with bolts of lightning, strike me to the core. They draw me in, holding me captive with an electrifying allure.

"I-I love you, Xero," I stammer, my heart fluttering against my chest like the wings of a trapped bird. "I can't even begin to thank you for saving me."

"Promise you'll be mine forever. That's all the thanks I need."

My heart aches with gratitude and longing. That's all he's

ever asked. The part of me that wanted to run away from him now wants to run into his arms.

"Forever," I say. "Forever and the day after that. I promise."

He leans in for another kiss. His hands continue their journey, moving lower to soap my hips and thighs. The intimacy of his touch, the way he handles me with such care and reverence, makes my heart skip several beats.

My legs part in a silent invitation to seal our vows with something deeper than words.

When his fingers trace my inner thighs, my breath hitches. Every muscle in my core clenches in anticipation of his touch, but he pauses, barely grazing my pussy lips.

"May I?" he asks, his voice husky.

"Fuck, yes," I cry, the word escaping my lips before I can think. I want this. I need him.

He slides off the bench and drops to his knees, and my eyes widen.

"What are you doing?" I ask.

"I'm kneeling at the feet of my goddess, worshipping her sweet altar, getting the closest taste of heaven this sinner deserves."

My lips part with a gasp, but my thighs relax. Xero separates my legs and growls against my sensitive skin. Water cascades from above, yet his breath feels so much hotter. He kisses a slow path along my inner thighs, punctuating each press of his lips with licks and gentle nips, until I'm slumped backward, whining and trembling for his tongue.

After what feels like an eternity, his hot tongue slides over my sensitive clit. A jolt of ecstasy shoots through my core like an electric shock, causing my hips to jerk. It's as if every nerve in my body gets dialed up to eleven.

"Xero," I gasp, my voice choked, my fingers tangling into his wet hair.

He hums against my folds, the vibration sending waves of pleasure through my core. His tongue circles my clit with deliberate slowness, then explores every inch of my pussy like he's committing its contours to memory.

"Relax," he murmurs, his voice infusing me with tingles. "Let me take control. Let me give you all the pleasure you can handle. I want you coming apart on my face, baptizing me with your sweet nectar."

I melt against the wall and bench, my hands trailing over his broad shoulders.

Xero alternates between gentle licks and firm, swirling motions, then adds gentle sucking that has my eyes rolling to the back of my head.

Stars burst through my vision, and the world spins in swirls under his ministrations, threatening to cast me adrift from reality completely. His sinful mouth feels like it was made for my pleasure, his clever tongue shaping itself around my folds with an ease that could only come from the depth of our connection.

"Look at me when I'm making you come," he growls into my pussy.

I meet his eyes, which are dark with arousal and hunger—voids of black pulling me into his soul.

His fingers slip into my entrance, delivering a stretch that detonates a body-wide explosion of ecstasy. I arch against his mouth, my hips moving in counterpoint to his tongue.

"Just like that. Let go for me," he says.

I teeter on the edge, every nerve ending on fire. His tongue flicks and licks and swirls, adding to the building pressure. Pleasure coils tight within my core, making my movements erratic. His hands grip my hips, anchoring me in place as the world narrows down to the sensation of his mouth on my clit.

With a final, desperate cry, I shatter, the orgasm ripping through my core with the force of a storm. Body trembling, my nails dig into his shoulders as I ride the waves of pleasure.

He doesn't stop, his fingers and tongue drawing out every tremor until I'm a boneless, blissful mess. When I fall limp, he pulls back, his lips glistening with my arousal. I've never seen him look so beautiful.

Pulling him up, I wrap my fingers around his shaft. "Fuck me," I moan into his mouth. "I need you. Right now."

"You want it, little ghost?" he murmurs into the kiss. "Tell me how much."

"Yes. More than anything," I moan.

"Dirty girl, gripping me so tight. If you want more, then you'll have to beg."

"Please, Xero," I murmur. "Give me your cock."

He pulls back with a wicked smile. "Since you asked so prettily, then take what you need."

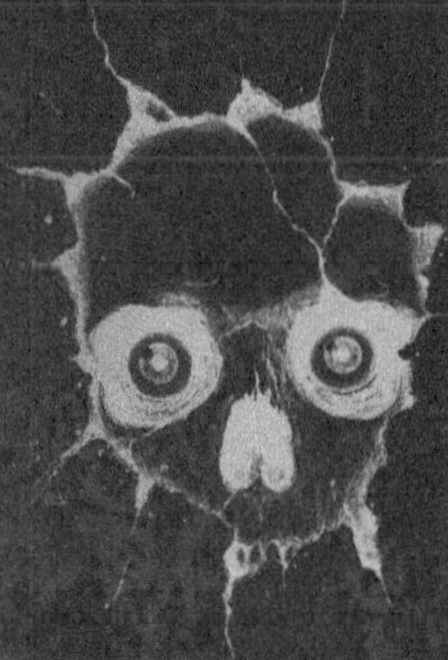

NINETY-THREE

XERO

I want to lose myself in Amethyst's sweet cunt, forget the world exists. But after the shit I put her through during that drug-fueled rampage, I'm in no position to push. She needs to set the pace. Take control.

Amethyst scrambles onto my lap, her delicate hands pushing on my chest. I lean against the wall, gazing down at my reason for living. With her cheeks flushed, her full lips parted, and wet curls framing her face like a dark crown, she looks more goddess than ghost.

I grab my shaft by the base, positioning it at her entrance. Her lashes flutter against her cheeks, and she takes a deep breath before lowering herself onto my crown. She inches down, taking me in at an agonizing pace, her tight heat swallowing my cock. Groaning, I throw my head back against the wall and fight the urge to thrust.

"Fuck, baby, you're so tight," I growl through panting breaths.

Lips curving into a smile, she digs her nails into my shoulders. I hiss at the biting sting, which contrasts with the pleasure of her muscles pulsing and squeezing like they want to milk me of every drop of cum.

Once she's fully engulfed my shaft, she pauses, her chest heaving as her walls adjust to my girth. The hands on my shoulders tremble in time with my shallowing breaths. The feel of her tight heat enveloping my cock is almost too much to bear.

I cup her full, round breasts, and trace my thumbs over her thick nipples, only for that sweet cunt to clamp even harder.

A strangled groan tears from my throat. My hips buck, making her moan.

"Please," I groan, my voice thick with need.

"Tell me what you want, Xero," she murmurs.

"Ride my cock. Take what you need. It's yours."

Her pretty face lights up with a wicked grin. She rises, letting my length slide almost completely out of her cunt. Just when I think she'll leave me aching, she slams down, forcing me to exhale a guttural groan.

"Oh God," I hiss, my hands finding her hips, my fingers tightening around her soft flesh.

"Oh, goddess, you mean?" she says, her voice light with amusement.

"Yes," I say through gasping breaths. "Make me come, little ghost. Ride me until I fall apart. Make me your cock slave."

Her eyes sparkle with triumph. "I didn't know you could be submissive."

"Only for you, baby," I say, meaning every word. "You hold the power over my soul."

At my declaration, she rolls her hips. Slowly at first, with movements as fluid as a dancer's. My breath hitches. Having her here is more exhilarating than I imagined from the videos she sent of herself taking my dildo while I was in prison. The crushing warmth of her pussy enveloping my cock far surpasses my hand, which was all I had in those days.

She's all around me—in my mouth, on my lap, in my nostrils, around my cock. Her breasts bounce as she picks up the pace, her nipples brushing against my chest.

Her hands roam over my shoulders, tracing the lines of my muscles. Each stroke is purposeful, driving me to the brink of insanity with the slow, drawn-out torture of her movements.

But I don't break, and I don't buck into her, no matter what the voices in my head demand. Instead, I let her keep control. Her rhythm is erratic, yet maddeningly perfect. Each rise and fall of her hips delivers pulses of pleasure that drive me wild.

"Good girl," I groan. "You're taking my cock so well."

She shivers and gasps, her rhythm quickening, her moans becoming more urgent. Our lips meet and I swallow the sound of her pleasure.

"Xero," she moans into the kiss. "I'm going to come again."

"Then let go, beautiful. I've got you."

She buries her face in the hollow of my neck, her muscles tightening, her hands clawing at my back as she rides me to the brink of climax. Her cries muffle against my skin as tremors ripple through her small frame, and along the walls trembling around my cock.

My pleasure builds. Her muscles clench and spasm around my shaft, driving me closer to the edge. The sudden constricting sensation causes me to cry out. Her body quakes with her release and that sweet pussy grips my shaft. Then her keening cry has me teetering over the edge.

Hands tightening around her hips, I hold her down as I thrust up into her wet heat, each stroke harder, more desperate. The pressure within my core intensifies to the point of suffocation, setting every nerve alight. My world narrows to the feel of her around my cock, the heat, the tightness, the slick slide of her flesh against mine.

"Fuck, little ghost," I growl, my voice strained. "I'm so close."

Her nails dig into my back, sending sparks of electricity that power my thrusts. "Come for me, Xero," she whispers, her voice breathy and broken. "Fill me up."

Her words, the desperation in her voice, the pussy pumping me to insanity pushes me past the point of no return. Every muscle in my body tightens, my breath catching in my throat as the pleasure peaks. It's like exploding fireworks, an intense, almost unbearable sensation that breaks me into a million pieces and reconstructs me into the man Amethyst needs.

My orgasm surges from the base of my spine, spreading a fiery wave of pleasure that leaves me destroyed. I bury myself deep inside my love, my cock pulsing as I release, filling her with jet upon jet of cum.

I make a silent vow never to conceal information, treat her like she's fragile, or underestimate the depths of her strength. She's transcended beyond the girl I strove to protect to a fierce warrior skilled in strategy, subterfuge, and survival.

Amethyst isn't just my equal, but my perfect match.

Finally, the tremors subside, leaving me breathless and spent. I pull her close, our hearts pounding in unison. "I love you to the very marrow of my bones."

She smiles against my lips. "And I love you to the last thread of my soul."

~

The next afternoon, I walk beside Amethyst through the hallway of our medical facility, all traces of euphoria giving way to gnawing guilt. She clutches my arm, her grip reassuring, but I won't relax until I see my little sister.

I push open the door to the same room I occupied after the fire, greeted by the familiar blips and beeping of monitors. Camila lies on the cot, pale and motionless, almost unrecognizable with her dark curls no longer slicked back in a bun. They spill across the pillow like she's floating on water. I can't remember the last time she looked so tiny.

Amethyst squeezes my arm, offering me a burst of comfort. "Talk to her."

Swallowing hard, I edge toward the bed. "Camila," I whisper, my voice hoarse. "It's me."

Her eyes flutter open, and she cracks a tiny smile. "Xero," she rasps, her voice warm. "We did it."

But at what cost? I force a smile. "How are you feeling?"

"Fine, just a bit sore," she says with a wince. "Where's Amethyst?"

"Here." She moves to my side, placing a hand on Camila's shoulder.

My sister closes her eyes and exhales a happy sigh. "Good. We all got out in one piece."

I take her hand. "I'm so sorry. I swore to protect you, and I let you get hurt."

She squeezes back. "I'm not a child anymore. I'm just the same as any operative. Besides, you couldn't have stopped me."

A sigh escapes my lips. I lean down, kiss her temple, and whisper against her skin, "You're not just any operative, you're my baby sister."

The door opens, and Jynxson walks in, clad in a pair of boxers and a rib binder. Apart from his tousled dark hair, I wouldn't guess they had to dig him out of a collapsed tunnel.

He pulls me into a tight hug. "I was worried about you for a minute there, man."

"You have a count of five before my fist lands in your balls," I say.

Snickering, Jynxson tightens his grip around my shoulders. "Then I'd better make this hug count."

I relax in his dubious embrace. Jynxson might be the most annoying asshole to have ever existed, and flouting an inappropriate relationship with Camila, but he's the closest thing I have to a brother. And not just because I murdered the others.

He releases me before the non-existent countdown and wraps his arms around my little ghost. As predicted, he catches my eye. The possessive rage that usually surges at the sight of another man getting close to her is absent. Amethyst's love for me is absolute.

Jynxson draws back and pats Camila on the head. "Glad you're back."

My brow pinches.

Camila glances at me and chuckles. "We broke up before the blast."

I turn to Jynxson, my eyes narrowing. Before I can remind him of the threat I made about breaking her heart, he raises his palms and says, "She dumped me."

The door swings open, and Isabel strides in holding a tablet. Her white coat is crumpled, and her hair is arranged in a messy bun, but she offers us a tired smile.

"Did you get any sleep?" I pull her into a hug.

She yawns. "Not until after the surgery, which went extremely well. The bullet nicked a rib, but missed all vital organs. With proper rest, Camila will make a full recovery."

A weight lifts off my shoulders, and I exhale a long breath. Last night, her injury looked life threatening. "Thank you."

Isabel steps back to address Amethyst and me. "Dr. Dixon needs you both to book thorough medicals. Especially you, Xero, after being involved in another fire."

Before I can respond, Amethyst steps forward and blurts, "I'm sorry. It was me who set the crawl space alight. Will Xero's lungs ever recover?"

I wrap an arm around her shoulders and pull her into my side. "I already said you were forgiven."

Eyes softening, Isabel closes the distance between us and takes Amethyst's hand. "You've saved Xero in more ways I can say by helping us capture Delta. Just take care of his heart."

My gaze drops down to my little ghost, whose eyes shimmer with unshed tears. The three women I love most in the word exchange smiles, filling my chest with a profound sense of ease.

"Has he said anything yet?" Isabel asks.

I shake my head and grimace at the events of the morning. Father isn't just a Moirai trained assassin—he's its founder. He took great delight in explaining that our interrogation techniques would fail.

"It'll take a while to break his silence, but I made sure he can't escape. I extracted all his teeth and scanned him for trackers. The stubbornness will fade once it sinks in that he's fully trapped."

I bask in triumph for a few precious moments with my family before the reality of our victory fades. We still have one more enemy to vanquish—the Moirai. Even if Father releases the names of its management team, we still have to track each member. The only reason we found Father after a decade of searching was because Amethyst unlocked some vital memories.

With a sigh, I steer us toward the door. "I need to excuse myself. We need to attend a funeral."

"Whose?" Jynxson asks.

"My mother's," Amethyst replies.

"What about Dolly?" Camila asks.

"Her body is also in the crematorium. Dr. Saint identified Dolly's corpse as mine, so I can be declared dead," Amethyst says, her lips twitching with a smile.

Isabel looks at me, her brows rising. "There are rumors flying around online that you killed her."

I grin. "Let them think what they want. As long as the police stop hunting Amethyst."

As we leave Camila's room, we bump into Tyler in the hallway.

"Hey, Xero. I have a lead on Dr. Forster."

"Really?" Amethyst says with a gasp.

He nods. "He changed his name to Corvelle after getting struck off following the raid. I tracked him down to a private practice outside Victoria Park. Should we bring him in?"

Dr. Forster was her mother's therapist who sent Amethyst to the asylum and administered those inhumane treatments. The thought of my girl torturing another bastard from her past makes my heart thrum.

"What do you say, little ghost?" I ask.

"Bring him," she snarls.

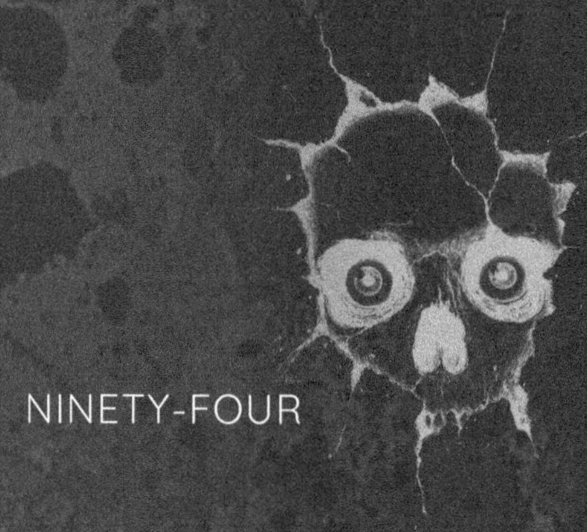

NINETY-FOUR

AMETHYST

My heart pounds as Xero pulls into the Newton Crematorium parking lot. At this time of the afternoon, the sun is at its strongest, drenching the brick building in light. He exits, walks around the hood, and opens my door.

Stepping out of the car, I crane my neck to take in its twin chimneys. "I've lost count of how many times I've walked past this place on the way to the supermarket."

Xero wraps an arm around my shoulders. "I hate to be on team Melonie, but she had a good reason for keeping you away from your father's side of your family."

A shudder runs down my spine at the reminder of my paternal grandmother, who forced Mom to work as some kind of escort. "She never had a moment of happiness, did she?"

Xero sighs. "Do you remember writing to me about unreliable narrators?"

I turn my gaze away from the crematorium to meet his eyes. His hair is dark blond today, with bronze skin that makes him look more like Vinzent from the vineyard. "You think she exaggerated?"

"People lie to themselves all the time, even in their own diaries. There was no mention of her affair with Dr. Forster until she was facing its consequences."

"No one deserved that kind of punishment."

"Agreed." He gives my shoulder a reassuring squeeze. "Ready to go in?"

Nodding, I inhale a deep, shaky breath.

We step through a set of double doors, greeted by the mingled scents of disinfectant and lilies. The receptionist is an elderly woman with pencil-thin eyebrows and a tight gray bun. Her spectacles hang low on the bridge of her nose, held in place by a delicate metal chain draped around her neck.

She scrambles to her feet, her eyes widening. "Amy?"

Gulping, I study her features, wondering if she's Mother Salentino. "Yes?"

"Oh, my dear." She rounds the desk, her eyes welling with tears. "You look so much like Melonie."

My throat thickens, and an ache spreads down to my chest. I swallow hard and lean into Xero's side. "You knew her?"

"She used to drop off items for the twins—"

"Thank you, Angela," says a sharp voice.

The woman stepping out of a door behind the reception desk is tall, with long dark hair cascading down her shoulders in gentle waves. She's in her mid-thirties, wearing a full face of dramatic makeup to enhance her stern features. Her gaze sweeps over Xero before settling on my face.

"Amethyst," she says, her voice softening. "Come in and meet your aunt."

I glance at Xero, wondering if this is one of the Salentino twins. As if sensing my silent question, he nods. The woman disappears behind the door, letting it swing shut.

Gulping, I round the desk with Xero, wondering if turning down their invitation for dinner was a mistake. I thought meeting my paternal aunts at their place of business would be far less intimidating than entering their mansion near the top of Alderney Hill.

There's an entire mafia militia at its summit, protecting the Montesano and Salentino families. According to the diary, they brought me to their mansion after rescuing me from the asylum.

Besides, I'm mostly here for closure. Mom's body has been resting here since the day of her murder. She and Dolly need a funeral. I want to close that chapter in my life and move forward.

I step into an elegant office of black furniture, overlooking the cemetery gardens. The woman from earlier stands by the windows, while another rises from behind the twin desks. She's almost as tall as the first one, with short hair, but dressed in a man's tailored suit.

My gaze darts back to the other, who shares the exact features. I've never seen identical twins looking so alike yet so distinct.

The short-haired twin walks around the desk, her eyes lighting up, and scoops me into a tight hug. "It's so good to finally meet you in person. You look just like Melonie did at that age."

"Hi." I relax into her embrace, trying not to cringe at the implication that she's seen my viral videos.

She draws back, places both hands on my shoulders and drinks me in. "Are you okay? We were both so worried when Xero told us you were taken. I'm Aria."

I gulp. "Pleased to meet you, and I'm fine."

Aria flicks her head toward the femme fatale standing by the window. "That's Elania. We're twins, but not identical."

"Oh."

I glance back at Elania, who rolls her eyes, confirming that Aria is bullshitting. The only differences between the two women are their hairstyles, shoes, and make up.

"If there's anyone showing you disrespect, you let us know," Aria says. "Your aunties will take care of the assholes and leave no traces."

"Thanks," I say with a nervous laugh.

Elania steps forward. "We'd like to apologize for keeping our distance. Your mother wanted to protect you from our line of business."

"Now that you're old enough to take care of yourself, you're more than welcome to join the fold," Aria says with an earnest nod.

I rub the back of my neck and try not to squirm at the prospect of working for the mafia. "Actually, I prefer to write."

"Leave the girl alone." Elania offers me a manicured hand and a warm smile. "It's good to finally meet you, although we hoped to have more involvement in your rescue."

She shoots Xero a filthy glance, which only makes him grin. Aria claps him hard on the shoulder. It's a gesture that would knock most people forward, but Xero just stares at her with raised brows.

"Elania's going to take Amy to the chapel, so she can say her goodbyes," Aria says. "Take a seat. Tell me if there's anyone we need to kill."

"I'm staying with Amethyst," Xero says.

"It's okay," I reply. "I need to face them alone."

He gazes down at me, his brow furrowed, and I respond with a reassuring nod. Cupping my cheek, he leans down and gives me a soft peck on the lips. "I'll be here if you need me."

Nodding, I leave with Elania, who guides me through the crematorium's stark hallway. The click-clack of her heels on the marble floor reminds me a little of Dolly. The walls, devoid of decorations, save for the occasional cross, echo her steps.

As we round a corner, two large men in body armor step into our path. Elania simply lifts a finger, and they straighten before stepping aside to let us pass.

"Don't worry about Xero," she murmurs, her voice low. "He's perfectly safe with my sister."

My lips twitch. "Shouldn't you be worried about Aria?"

"We did our research. Contrary to what the media says, Xero Greaves isn't a deranged psychopath. At least not compared to some assholes we know."

I bite down on my bottom lip. "Like my father?"

She snorts. "Compared to Giorgi, Xero is a saint."

As we stop at a wooden door, a lump forms in my throat at the reminder of what I read in Mom's diary about being held captive by my biological father. The Salentino twins would have been about ten at the time she ran away with us and just turned twenty when she returned for help.

A shudder runs down my spine at the thought of having inherited his psychopathic traits.

Elania pushes the door open, letting out a gust of cold air laden with the heavy scent of lilies. The lights are dim, and the decor is mahogany with muted shades of gray that do little to dull the pain throbbing in my chest at the sight of the twin caskets.

"Take as much time as you need." She squeezes my arm.

"Thanks," I rasp, still hovering in the doorway.

It takes several moments of soaking in the atmosphere before my body will allow itself to move. My aunt stands in the hallway, offering me silent support.

After what feels like an eternity, I step forward on trembling legs, not knowing what I'll find. The last I saw of Mom, her neck had been slashed open. She'd died with her eyes wide with terror. Dolly's violent death hadn't been much different. When I stabbed her through the chest, her features were frozen in shock.

But when I reach their caskets, it's nothing like I dreaded. Mom looks softer than I remember, without the perpetual pinched annoyance. Dolly looks like a wax figure, made up to resemble a sleeping angel.

I pause, waiting for an outpouring of grief or fury or even numbness, but all I feel is relief. The weight of their animosity lifts off my shoulders, making me stand taller.

Taking in a deep breath, I step back to address them both. "I understand why you did what you did," I say, my voice wavering. "Not that I agree with the way you made me a scapegoat, but I'm moving on."

I pause, giving them a moment to absorb my words. It's futile, since they're dead, but I still can't deny the primal part of my psyche that was forced to believe in ghosts.

"You two made my life hell, but you also led me to my soulmate. I guess that makes us even."

There's so much more I could say, but they were really just pawns. The key players are still awaiting us in Xero's interrogation rooms. Besides, I don't want to waste any more time on two people who treated me as if I were a problem that needed to be eliminated.

"Safe journey to the other side, and I hope you both rest in peace."

I walk out of the room, the marble floor echoing my footsteps. Elania rises from a bench in the hallway, her features flickering with surprise.

"Finished already?" she asks.

I nod. "Is there a place I can store their ashes?"

"Of course." Her brow furrows. "You don't want to keep them?"

"I want to start afresh. That includes giving back the house on Alderney Hill," I say.

Her brows pinch. "But you're my brother's only child. This is your inheritance."

She walks me back to Xero, explaining that my birth father was the only sibling in the family with a surviving child. Neither Salentino sister wants to get married, so if I don't take over the house and businesses, then their assets will revert to their cousin, Cesare Montesano—Myra's former boss, and the younger brother of Xero's fellow cellmate on death row.

This time, when she invites me over for dinner, I don't refuse.

It's strange to have family members who don't want me disconnected or dead.

Xero waits for me at the reception with Aria, who gives me another hug goodbye. She's the warmer of the pair, despite her tough exterior.

"Ready to go?" he asks with a soft smile that makes my heart melt.

"Yes," I reply and take his hand.

As we exit the crematorium, Xero leads me to his car and opens the passenger side door. My phone rings, and we lock gazes.

"Hello?" I ask.

"It's me," Myra says. "Do I have your permission to publish the Rapunzelita trilogy?"

I frown. "Yes. Why?"

"Your death drove a lot of traffic to my videos. Publishers are clamoring for your unfinished manuscripts."

My heart skips several beats. "Okay," I reply, my voice breathy. "I want to tweak the sequels, but the first book is ready to go."

"What about the erotic ghost story?" Myra asks.

Xero steps closer, his hand resting on my lower back, his

fingers grazing the base of my spine. His breath warms my ear, making me shiver.

"Give us a few more weeks to fine-tune the spicy scenes," he murmurs.

Myra squeals, promising to negotiate a hefty advance before she hangs up. As I slip my phone into my pocket, I turn back to Xero.

His gaze locks onto mine, filled with an intensity that makes my knees weak. He pulls me close so we're standing chest to chest, his mouth brushing against mine in a slow, deliberate kiss.

His lips are warm and insistent, infusing me with delicious heat. "Congratulations," he says, his voice breathy with pride. "I always believed in your talent. And in Rapunzelita."

The kiss deepens, his tongue teasing mine, and I lose myself in the sensation. Every touch, every caress ignites a fire within me that goes straight to my core.

"Let's celebrate," he murmurs against my lips.

"How?"

"The Spring brothers just transferred Dr. Forster to a holding cell. We can give him a painful welcome before dealing with my father and Charlotte."

My lips curve into a smile. By the time I've finished with Charlotte, she'll be the one seeing dead people. I plan on sticking Delta's worthless dick up his ass and making him swallow his own balls. Dr. Forster will experience every unnecessary medical procedure he subjected me to while I was at the asylum. When his mind shatters and he no longer remembers his name, I'll hunt him through the catacombs and drown him in a puddle.

Rocking forward on my tiptoes, I give Xero a peck on the lips. "Sounds like a plan."

He pulls me into a tight hug, filling my nostrils with his signature scent. Citrus, spearmint, and cedar wood blend together in an intoxicating mix that has me melting against his strong chest.

"I love you so much," I murmur.

"And I love you too, little ghost," he replies, his fingers teasing my curls.

My chest releases a happy sigh. If someone had told me the man behind the mugshot would be my happily ever after, I would have scoffed. And if they said I'd fall for the grim reaper chasing me through the graveyard, I'd have thought they were crazy.

I relax against Xero's larger body, luxuriating in this new sense of connection and belonging. He isn't just a lover or a savior, but the other half of my soul.

For the first time in my adult life, I see clearly, and I've finally found my place in the world.

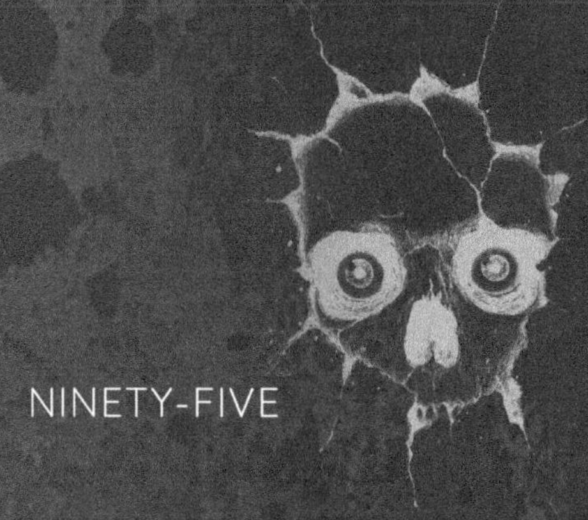

NINETY-FIVE

XERO

Now that Amethyst has said goodbye to her parent, it's time to welcome mine to the final stage of his existence.

I park outside the safe house's double doors and turn off the engine. At this time of the afternoon, the sun paints the gardens with vibrant bursts of color, but nothing is as enchanting as Amethyst.

She stretches in her seat and yawns. "Any update on Dr. Forster?"

I pull out my phone and check my messages. There's a status report on the new prisoner and a link to the live camera feed to his interrogation room.

An unconscious red-haired man in his sixties slumps in a chair. He's naked, with his genitals obscured by his hanging gut.

"Is that the psychiatrist?" I show her the screen.

Her face pinches. "A flabbier version of him, yeah. When can I see him?"

I navigate to another screen to review his records. "He's still sedated, but he should be awake in three hours. Delta is in the cell next door. We could pay him a visit while we wait."

"No," she replies, her face paling. "Give me a few weeks. I'm not ready."

My brow furrows. "Are you alright?"

She gives me an eager nod. "It's been a long day. I'd rather get the Rapunzelita manuscript ready for Myra."

"Do you want company?" I ask.

She leans in, pressing a soft kiss on my lips. "I'll be okay on my own."

As she draws away, I cup the back of her head and pull her closer to deepen the kiss. With a soft moan, she kisses back, her body melting against mine. I hate the moments when we're apart, but my presence is needed for the first few days of Father's captivity.

I pull away at the thought of that bastard, which lets Amethyst catch her breath. Pink tinges her cheeks and the corners of her mouth lift with a relaxed smile.

"Send Delta my regards," she says, and opens the passenger-side door, filling the car with a burst of fragrant air.

She steps out, blowing me a kiss before walking down the gravel path toward our little cottage. Her hips sway, making my blood heat. I watch her, mesmerized, as she disappears around the corner. Then I make my way to the interrogation room.

~

Father hasn't been a captive for twenty-four hours, yet he's barely recognizable. Gone are his hair and beard, and the lower half of his face is still swollen from having every tooth extracted.

Despite being naked in a darkened cell with concrete walls, he sits in his interrogation chair like it's a throne. Wires connect his body to a polygraph machine through a blood pressure cuff, fingertip sensors, a chest band, and a mass of electrodes.

Isabel sits at a table by the door, watching needles scratch data onto a strip of paper. I step inside, inhaling cool, damp air carrying a whiff of blood, and lock gazes with my sister.

"How is he?" I ask.

Her shrug tells me everything I need to know—Father is still being uncooperative.

His eyes remain closed in a semblance of deep meditation, yet the monitors attached to his body betray the spike in his vital signs. They go haywire, displaying enough erratic readings to suggest he's on the verge of panic.

I snort. "You can't hide from us, Delta."

He opens his eyes, fixing me with a glower of defiant contempt. "What's wrong, old man? You looked so at ease when I was the one attached to the chair."

Father flares his nostrils but doesn't speak. If he thinks he's wearing us down with silence, he's sorely mistaken. Every operative we liberated holds a deep-rooted grudge, and we have more volunteers eager to tend to Father than there are hours in the day.

He will break. The only question is when.

"I've been thinking a lot about our past. About your lessons. About how you taught me that pain builds character."

A muscle in his temple flexes.

I close the distance, bring a cup of water to his mouth. A few drops fall onto his lap, making him finally open his eyes.

"Thirsty?" I ask with a smirk.

He gazes up at me, his eyes flickering with rage.

"Camila's going to make a full recovery," I say. "Your little charade with Dolly failed. No matter how many drugs you used to alter my perception, I will always recognize the woman I love."

Father remains silent, his swollen mouth locked into a tight grimace. His eyes, however, burn with impotent malevolence.

I pull away the cup. "You taught me about power and control, but you never grasped compassion. Or even love. And now, it's time for you to learn from me."

Shaking his head, he releases a dry chuckle. "Obviously, I failed to teach you the fine art of interrogation."

The corner of my lips lift into a smile. "Why waste time asking questions you won't answer when I can have revenge?"

His Adam's apple bobs. "Psychological tricks?"

"Don't mistake me for a man who makes veiled threats."

I walk to the table, pick up a needle, and dip it into the water. Once it's wet, I slide it into a point on his hand, watching for the slight twitch that confirms it's in the right spot.

The bastard doesn't even flinch. Neither do his vitals.

Rage simmers in my veins, but I hide my fury beneath a calm façade, dunking another and targeting a point on his lower leg, pressing it into the muscle. Each needle goes in with precision, tapping into the acupuncture pathways of pain and control.

With every insertion, his vital signs begin to fluctuate, accompanied by a faint twitching in his brow. His stoic façade cracks, and his grimaces morph into a full-on wince. Sweat gleams on his brow, and he clenches his fists as I place them into points on his inner leg, forearm, and foot.

Isabel appears at my side, attaching small crocodile clips onto each needle.

"Electro-acupuncture?" Father asks, his voice incredulous.

"With a twist." I motion for Isabel to return to the table and switch on the current.

The lights flicker as a surge of electricity floods through the wires. Father's body goes rigid, his eyes widen, he tightens his jaw.

"Do you think this will break me?" he asks.

"Isabel."

She turns up the dial, making Father grunt. His breath quickens, and the veins on his temples bulge. His fingers claw at the armrests.

"Feel that pain?" I ask. "It's directed at your nervous system. The low-level electric currents can keep you in agony while maintaining your sensitivity to pain."

"To what end?" he snarls.

"So you can taste the suffering you inflicted on others," I say.

Turning back to Isabel, I indicate for her to raise the current again. A low growl reverberates in Father's chest as his muscles tighten.

"You were always too emotional, Xero," he says through clenched gums. "That's the difference between you and me. Focusing on forgotten bygones instead of gathering intel."

"That's why you turned your back on your family as I slaughtered them," I reply. "Because there was no profit in saving their lives."

"Putting sentimentality over the pursuit of power will be your downfall."

"Yet you're the one strapped to this chair about to lose everything."

He sucks in a sharp breath and snarls as Isabel increases the current.

"What do you want?" Father says.

"What else were you running, apart from the snuff movie studio, Three Fates, and the organ trafficking ring?" I ask.

He answers with pained grunts, his body going taut. Agony flashes in those cold eyes, his defiance battling with fear.

Father's silence is no surprise. I endured years of misery before I finally broke. However, we don't have that kind of time.

I pick up a scalpel and crouch in front of him, my face close to his. "Days without food and water," I murmur, tracing its blade along the lines of his jaw. "Days of humiliation and pain. How long will you last?"

He doesn't respond. I press the knife harder, making a shallow cut on his forearm. A thin line of blood appears, and he flinches, but barely perceptible. "By the time the other operatives finish, you'll be nothing but a husk."

Alarm flashes across his features. "I thought you'd keep it in the family."

"Absolutely not. I have operatives, medics, cleaners, and maintenance staff waiting to extract their pound of flesh."

"Call them off or I won't share a shred of information."

I draw back. "My people have captured at least twenty of your accomplices. We're overwhelmed with data."

A guttural noise escapes his lips, part laugh, part snarl. "You're bluffing."

"They have my permission to inflict any amount of degradation and pain, but to leave you intact. Amethyst is the only one who gets to cut off body parts."

Father stiffens. It's finally dawning on the old bastard that I'm here for revenge. "Then consider us even for killing my wife."

Isabel turns up the electricity once more, infusing him with a surge of pain.

"She was a bitch," she snaps.

Father hisses in, his breath coming in ragged gasps. "What's wrong, boy? Can't cope with a little competition?"

I move the blade up to his ear, making another shallow cut. His breathing labors, and he trembles from the effort to remain still. Leaning into him, I lower my voice to a whisper. "Do you know what Dolly said to me before you called her away?"

His eyes dart to mine with the tiniest flicker of curiosity.

"She hoped I would be a better fuck than you."

Father purses his lips, looking like he wants to spit. Instead, he spreads his lips in a toothless grin. "It won't last. Infidelity is in her blood. Amethyst is still just like her mother. And her sister."

Laughter bubbles up in my chest. I draw back and rise to my full height. "Cheap psychological tricks only work on helpless children. Next time I check in with you, I'll ask you to repeat those words to Amethyst."

The smirk vanishes. "Is this your idea of an interrogation?"

With a snort, I turn to Isabel. "I'll leave you to decide how many operatives he can handle for today. Make sure he's ready in the morning for a full day of visitors. We have over eighty people scheduled for the week."

Nodding, she turns the dial, adding a touch more power to Father's electric shock.

"Xero," he rasps. "Where are you going?"

"Don't worry," I say, tapping the flat of the blade against his cheek, "There'll be plenty of time for us later."

With a last, lingering glance, I turn to the exit, leaving Father screaming at me to return. Part of repaying him for his past includes giving the others he wronged their chance of retribution.

No amount of torture could ever make up for the trafficking, rapes, and murders, and I intend to spend the next several months hunting down his accomplices and saving his victims.

I step into the hallway, inhaling a deep breath. The air is cooler, cleaner, free from that bastard's stench. A knot in my gut loosens at the prospect of Father finally facing the consequences of his actions.

Soon, Amethyst will have her retribution, and I will have my closure.

As I continue past cell after cell holding investors, instructors, and all manner of individuals who took part in Father's empire, a weight lifts from my shoulders. Ahead lies a future free from the shadows of the past.

Justice will be served. I will have my reckoning. And the woman I love can finally begin to heal.

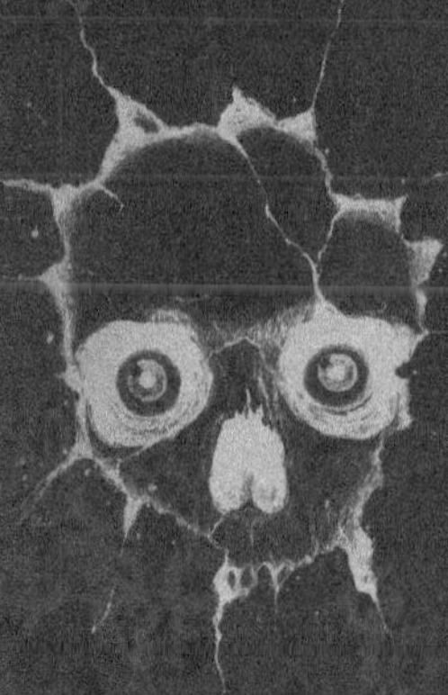

NINETY-SIX

SIX WEEKS LATER

AMETHYST

Dr. Forster is dead. Drowned by the same ice bath he used for my mind conditioning.

I pull him out by his hair and glare into his lifeless gray eyes. Eyes that bored into mine during countless painful experiments. Eyes that haunted my recent nightmares. His skin is burned from the scalding hot bath that still simmers from the adjacent tub. In the end, he was too weak to withstand his own torture.

Mom was only one of his many victims. The doctor had a list of complaints against him longer than his forearm. His specialty was violating vulnerable women and reinventing himself in a new town when the complaints grew too loud. Now, he has nowhere to run.

Before he died, he admitted to torturing me for revenge. Somehow, in my addled state, I had admitted to killing Heath. The stupid bastard believed the words of a grief-stricken child who had been tortured to the brink of insanity.

I spare one last glance at the doctor's lifeless form before turning away. He was part of a past that felt more like a distant dream. The abuser I'm about to face is more recent.

I step out of the interrogation room Xero's maintenance

people set up to mirror an asylum and into a darkened hallway. My footsteps mingle with the thud of flesh hitting flesh.

My skin tightens as I approach the door at the end of the hallway, but I push back a surge of dread. It's been six weeks since Delta and Dolly abducted us, and I'm ready for my revenge.

I step into the room, pausing at the entrance to catch my breath.

Xero stands over Delta, shirtless, revealing the hard lines of his chest. The dim light casts shadows across his sculpted muscles, highlighting every sinew. His face is a mask of sadistic pleasure, pale eyes gleaming with cruel intent. For a moment, all I can see is the raw masculinity of his form.

He's sliding needles under Delta's fingernails, making him flinch. The older man sits bound and naked in a chair, his chest rising and falling with rapid breaths.

Six weeks of intermittent starvation has reduced Delta's presence from menacing to meek. His once-powerful shoulders are now hunched, his skin sickly. His eyes, though sunken and framed by dark circles, still hold a defiant glint.

Despite his weakened state, he struggles against his restraints, the muscles in his neck and arms taut against the leather straps.

Delta's gaze shifts to me, and I stiffen. For a second, I'm stuck in that white tent, pinned beneath his powerful body. My heart skitters across my chest, but I refuse to let him see my fear.

Xero draws back, capturing my attention, and the tightness in my chest loosens. I'm no longer powerless. I'm safe here with the man I love. And in a minute, Delta will regret having stuck his penis where it didn't belong.

"See how she looks at me?" Xero asks, his words low with menace. "She's mine."

Delta's eyes harden. "Don't forget, she was mine first."

Xero flashes his teeth. "How fitting for you to take pride in claiming ownership of an innocent child."

Delta's dry chuckle sets my teeth on edge. "Every time she sees you, she'll be looking at me."

"You're wrong." I storm into the cell, closing the distance between us, every nerve ending crackling with fury. "All a man like you can ever do is take. You're not good for anything but inspiring disgust."

The older man's features twist in a rictus of fury. He pulls at his bindings, his face reddening with futile exertion, but the straps are taut against his chafed skin.

Xero grins, baring his teeth in a wolfish smile. "When you were busy trying to break my little Amethyst, she was hallucinating a version of me to buffer herself from you."

Delta flashes his gums. "You can't erase the past, Xero. I will forever haunt your little ghost."

The use of my nickname ignites a surge of fury that has me charging across the room. Xero punches his father so hard, his chair falls backward with a sharp crack. The impact has Delta wincing and groaning.

My pulse quickens, and a dark thrill settles in my core. I step even closer to Xero, soaking in the intoxicating rush of his dominance. The room seems to shrink around us, the air thick with tension and the scent of fear.

"I taught you better than to lash out," Delta snarls from the floor, his nose streaming with blood. "This anger is a sign of weakness."

Xero laughs, a low, dark sound that sends shivers down my spine. "Yet you're the one groveling at our feet."

"Because I still hold power over you," Delta rasps.

The words hang in the air, heavy and charged with danger. My gaze darts to Xero. Six weeks aren't long enough to erase years of trauma and abuse.

Instead of recoiling, he scoffs and pulls me into his arms. His touch is electric, charged with a dark energy that leaves me breathless.

I gaze up into his eyes, exchanging unspoken words, the silence between us broken only by the sound of Delta's harsh breaths.

"Want to show this soon-to-be-dead bastard who's in control?" Xero asks.

I glance at the older man staring at us, his gaunt face twisted in a mask of hatred. "I'd love nothing more."

Eyes darkening with a predatory gleam, Xero pulls me into a

rough, passionate kiss, his hands roaming possessively over my body, demanding my surrender with every touch.

"Wait here," he says, unchains Delta, then punches him hard in the stomach.

With a groan, Delta doubles over, and Xero arranges him on the floor. A smirk pulls at my lips as Xero spreads his father's arms and legs wide, attaching the shackles on each limb to brackets drilled into the concrete.

Then, Xero eases me down so we're kneeling beside Delta, who stares up at us, his eyes burning with resentment. It's the most emotion I've noticed on the bastard's face.

Maybe he sees his son with his wife. Maybe this is the first time he's seen a woman in the throes of pleasure. Either way, I don't give a shit. Delta is about to discover that the power he once wielded over us was nothing more than a delusion.

"Take off your dress," Xero growls into the kiss, his voice a rough whisper.

Shivers skitter down my spine as I comply, pulling the fabric over my head and tossing it to the floor.

"Those cuts you made into her skin healed nicely," Xero says. "Soon, all traces of you will be gone."

"She'll always remember me," Delta snarls.

I turn to him and snort. "You barely registered the first time, but I'll make sure to remember you now."

Pulling away from Xero, I crawl to the side, pinning Delta's shoulders with my knees. The old man glares up at me, his lips twisting with defiance.

"What are you doing?" he asks, his voice going hoarse.

Xero positions himself at my back, moving me forward so my crotch is directly over Delta's face. He reaches down, pushes my panties to the side, and exposes my pussy.

"Look at her," Xero commands, his breath hot against my neck. His fingers circle my swollen clit, making me moan. "Watch closely. See how Amethyst responds to my touch because she's mine."

The muscles of my pussy spasm. We discussed this before. Having Xero make me come in front of Delta is exactly what I need to erase the haunting memories of my rapist.

Delta's eyes widen, his breath quickening. "This is how you prove yourself, Xero? Using her to show your power?"

Xero laughs. "Before you die, you should witness a woman's pleasure at least once."

The older man stiffens, making me smirk. It's a bluff. We need to keep Delta alive long enough to extract information about his other operations, and he also needs to witness the downfall of the Moirai.

Charlotte gave us several leads on the organ trafficking operation, which is proving to be a complex web of corruption and deceit. Unraveling Delta's empire will take months, but we plan to use that time to prolong his torment.

Xero parts my wet folds with his fingers. "See that arousal? It's all for me."

I groan, my nipples pebbling against my lace bra cups. Rolling my hips, I writhe against his touch, eager for more.

Delta's tongue darts across his cracked lips. I gaze into his blood-shot eyes, no longer seeing the headmaster of Three Fates or the suave psychopath who held me captive.

"Xero," I rasp. "Stop teasing and give me your cock."

The older man's eyes widen, and I hide a smirk. Something tells me he never once made a woman beg. Beg for mercy, perhaps. Beg him to stop, but never beg for his attention.

Xero continues teasing my clit, not giving me an inch of satisfaction until I'm dripping. Arousal slides down my inner thighs and a drop falls onto Delta's upper lip. Eyes flickering with surprise, he licks it off.

"How do I taste?" I ask with a grin.

Gaze never leaving mine, his stoic mask fades long enough to reveal a tangle of emotions—fury, resentment, disgust. Beneath it all is a flicker of excitement.

By the time Xero positions his cock at my entrance, I'm quivering with anticipation and already teetering on the brink of release. His presence behind me is intoxicating.

He pushes into my pussy with agonizing slowness, stretching me inch by delicious inch. My clit now feels like twice its usual size, throbbing to the frantic beat of my heart.

Delta's eyes are fixed on the spectacle, his gaze unblinking.

He swallows hard, the tendons in his neck taut with suppressed emotion. The old bastard's features are a mask of humiliation and rage, which has me laughing under my breath.

He watches, transfixed, and squirms in his restraints, his breath coming in ragged gasps.

Xero draws back, making me moan. He leans in, his breath hot against my ear. "See how he can't keep his eyes off you, little ghost? That's because he could never touch someone so unique."

"Bullshit," Delta snarls. "The whole reason you're fucking her in front of me is proof that I got under her skin."

"Don't talk like you did something special when you're a rapist," I snap.

Delta flinches, his lips tightening.

"He doesn't understand real power." Xero drives into me with a thrust that steals my breath. His fingers tighten around my hip, making me cry out. "He doesn't understand what it's like to be chosen. Or how it feels to be wanted."

"Oh, fuck," I moan.

"You were never his," Xero adds. "Every look, every touch belongs to me. In a moment, the last thing you'll remember of Delta is an emasculated husk."

"She's your stepmother's identical twin," the old man rasps.

"So, what? I killed the last one."

I shouldn't laugh, but I can't help my reaction to Xero's words combined with the sight of Delta laid out beneath us, his dark beard splattered by my juices.

Delta's lips tremble with fury, but he holds his tongue.

Xero pounds hard, his cock driving me to new heights of pleasure.

"My father can't keep his eyes off you," he says. "Because you're so beautiful when you take inches away from his face. I love making you come undone," he says.

My core spasms around his girth, the pleasure intensifying. "More, Xero. Please, don't stop."

"Father, you don't know what you're missing. She's so hot, so wet, so tight," he growls, his breath hot against my ear.

I jerk backward, increasing the friction, my nerves singing.

My eyes roll to the back of my head as he continues to give me pleasure.

"Tell us how much you love my cock."

"I love it, Xero," I moan, my voice trembling with need. "It's the only one that satisfies me. I need it. I need you."

"Good girl," he murmurs, his voice dripping with satisfaction. "You're doing so well. Come for me. Show Daddy dearest how a good girl gets her pleasure."

His words push me closer to the edge. Pressure builds in my core, and every nerve ending thrums. My body tenses, then a climax crashes over me in waves. I cry out, the sound echoing off the dungeon walls. The intensity of the moment is magnified by Delta's helpless presence and bitter, burning gaze, driving me to heights I've never known.

Xero tightens his grip on my hip, his movements quickening as he rides out my climax. "That's it, little ghost. Let it all go."

My breath comes in ragged gasps, my body quivering with the aftershocks of pleasure. Beneath me, Delta grunts and thrashes.

As I come down from my climax, Xero pulls out and helps me off Delta's shoulders. I sit on my heels, gasping and panting through the aftershocks.

Xero straddles his father, his lips twisting with a cruel smile playing on his lips. I lean forward, reveling in the pain in Delta's eyes.

Positioning himself over Delta, Xero grabs Delta's hair, holding him in place. "Look at me, Father."

Delta's nostrils flare. "Don't think a display like that could ever break my spirit."

Xero's chest rumbles with a low growl. With his free hand, he strokes his length, his eyes never leaving his father's. The tension mounts before he comes with a roar, shooting spurts and spurts of cum over Delta's face.

The older man's features harden with rage, his lips tightening.

"This is a low blow, even for you," he spits, his voice trembling with fury. "This is how you treat your father? I must have damaged you more than I thought."

Xero sits back with a satisfied smirk. "You have no idea. This is just the beginning."

As Xero rises, Delta's Adam's apple bobs, betraying a glimpse of dread. I pick up a knife from the floor and scoop up the trails of cum toward his lips. "Feeding time."

The hatred in his eyes gives me a surge of empowerment that goes straight to my core. Delta finally understands he's about to lose everything, including his dignity.

"Waste this lovely cum and I'll slice off your left testicle," I snarl.

Delta tenses, his brow breaking out in a sweat. He glances at a spot over my shoulder and grimaces. He's sorely mistaken if he thinks Xero will show him mercy.

A large hand lands on my shoulder. "Let me show you how to tie a testicle tourniquet."

"Xero," he rasps.

Something stringy lands on my lap. I pick it up and wrap it around Delta's testicle, my gaze never leaving his.

Delta whimpers, a barely audible sound that makes my nerves thrum with satisfaction. He licks Xero's release off his lips, a broken man, willing to debase himself for mercy.

"There. I'm doing it," he rasps.

"Too late." I tighten the tourniquet, pick up the knife, and position its blade against the base of his left testicle.

Delta breathes hard, his chest rising and falling like bellows.

"Tell me, Father," Xero drawls, "how does it feel to finally taste defeat?"

He screams, the sound ringing through my ears.

The power is mine now, and I revel in it.

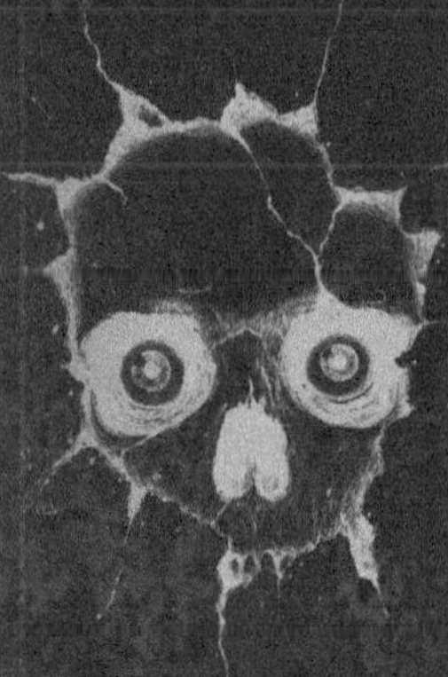

NINETY-SEVEN

ONE YEAR LATER

XERO

I push open the heavy iron door with a loud creak, letting out the mingled scents of decay and filth. The cell is damp, dark, and despondent, reflecting the time I spent under Father's control.

He lies on his back, chained to the floor, twitching and flinching with each drop of water from an overhead pipe connected to the septic tank. Every bone in his body protrudes to form a perfect outline of his skeleton, and he looks like he's in his eighties instead of his late fifties. More importantly, he's devoid of his nipples, testicles, and a penis.

I walk around the cell's perimeter, unclipping his chains from the rings on the wall. They clink as Father pulls himself up to sitting.

"Xero?" he rasps, his voice barely more than a whisper. "What else are you taking from me now?"

"Your life," I say.

He chuckles, the sound more like a cough. "You wouldn't let me die. Not when you can prolong my misery."

"I have something you need to see."

After attaching a chain leash to his collar, I yank him up, eliciting a satisfying groan. I drag him out of the cell and into a dim hallway, making him crawl after me on his hands and knees.

The catacombs remained compromised until we obtained the names of Father's outstanding associates. With the right cocktail of truth serums, he helped us locate the instructors who were absent during the raid, along with all his contacts at the police department and FBI.

Our entire team of operatives coordinated numerous simultaneous assaults, striking them down in a single night. Shortly after, we returned to the Parisii Cemetery and restored the catacombs as our headquarters.

I continue through the hallway, with Father panting behind me like a hound. Months of torture have broken his body, but his spirit remains intact. Part of him clings to the hope that I'll overcome my so-called daddy issues and we'll bond.

"Xero," he says through labored breaths. "Slow down."

I quicken my pace, my heart soaring as the walls echo with his pitiful cries. Finally, we reach our destination, a chamber where Amethyst awaits on a stone bench with a box of popcorn and a projector.

A double dog bowl sits on the floor, with one section filled with fresh water and the other a thin gruel containing every vitamin, mineral, and antibiotic required to sustain Father through his captivity.

He recoils at the sight of my little ghost, his chains rattling. "What's she doing here? You told me her vengeance was complete."

My lips twitch. After Amethyst took his left testicle, she forced it down his throat. The following month, she took his right and stuffed it in his ass. She spent weeks keeping Father in suspense, letting him linger in paranoia and terror of when she would take his penis.

When she finally ended the old bastard's wait, she made it a spectacle. His screams shook the catacombs but were nothing compared to the misery he'd inflicted on hundreds of innocent children.

I thread my gloved hand into his hair. "You no longer hold her interest. This little outing is about something else."

Amethyst picks up her popcorn. "You're safe with me. I've moved onto bigger and better things."

Father's gaze darts between us, his haggard face contorting with confusion. "Then why am I here?"

"It's movie night." I take my seat beside Amethyst and gesture at the dog bowl. "We even brought you a snack."

Stomach rumbling, he crawls to the bowl and laps at the water, then moves on to the gruel. As he gobbles the pale liquid with noisy gulps, I take my seat beside Amethyst and enjoy the show.

Father's pride has dwindled to nothing. It's a combination of torture, semi-starvation, and facing his sins. Every operative in our organization has had the chance to visit his cell and dole out their own form of retribution. Isabel, Camila, and Jynxson were the first in line, as they had been some of the longest affected by his manipulations.

Amethyst flicks a switch and the projector hums to life, casting an image onto a screen that spans the entire space. It's footage from a data center deep within the Moirai headquarters.

Father sits back on his haunches, panting like a dog. "What is this?"

"Yesterday was the last Friday of the quarter," I say through a mouthful of popcorn.

As predicted, he flinches.

"Your debt bondage scheme was a mistake. Instead of making people subservient to the Moirai, it created an entire class of employees who would do anything to gain their freedom."

Face paling, his eyes dart between us and the screen. "I don't understand."

"The last Friday of the quarter is the only time when the Moirai's entire management team crawls out from hiding to gather in a single location," I say, my chest swelling with satisfaction.

"Graduation," he rasps.

"After the number of graduates I poached over the years, the arena is now so heavily guarded that HQ is virtually empty."

He turns to me, his eyes widening, his lips trailing streams of gruel. "Xero, what have you done?"

"Maintenance staff on my payroll seeded explosives into the

building's stairwells, elevator shafts, and along the eleventh, twelfth, and thirteenth floors," I say, relishing his terror.

"That won't be enough to destroy it."

"Which is why we paired up with the Montesano family to deliver a truck full of Mercury nitrovolucite into the Moirai," I continue.

Panic floods his features, and he shakes his head from side to side. "They wouldn't..."

"Look." I point at the screen.

The movie switches to drone footage of a pair of trucks driving past an empty industrial estate and down the long stretch of road that leads to the Moirai headquarters.

On the outside, it looks like an abandoned parking lot, but inside are multiple elevator shafts that lead down to a ten-story basement with three additional secret levels, containing living quarters and servers the management team wants to keep hidden from their assassins.

"Call it off," Father croaks. "You were supposed to take control of the Moirai, not destroy it. Use poison gas or something that won't damage the AI servers!"

Annoyance prickles at my skin, and I curl my fists. "You don't get it. I was never power hungry like you. All I ever wanted was freedom."

The trucks enter the seemingly deserted parking lot, and the Moirai lowers shutters to the entrance, trapping the Montesano brothers.

Father's eyes bulge, watching the scene unfold, his knuckles turning white from gripping his knees. Amethyst fast-forwards the footage to where one of the vehicles bursts out and reverses down the road.

Seconds later, the camera shakes as the parking lot implodes. It disappears into a sinkhole, which swallows the surrounding road and buildings. The truck reverses out of the chaos, barely avoiding the expanding chasm.

Father wails, his hands clutching at the sides of his face. "My legacy... You've ruined me. Everything I worked for is gone!"

My chest thrums with satisfaction. I smirk at the impossibly large crater that now forms under what was once the largest firm of assassins in the United States. When Father set it up with a rag-tag group of disgraced FBI agents, he expected a dynasty, an empire that would span generations. But now, it's been reduced to rubble.

The drone zooms in on the carnage, showing twisted pieces of metal and debris that were once the foundation of the Moirai headquarters. The thirteen-story underground basement is now nothing more than an enormous cavity.

"Hurts, doesn't it?" I ask.

His mouth opens and closes. "Hundreds of millions of dollars... years of research!"

Amethyst snorts. "Watching your creation get destroyed is nothing compared to all the lives you and your partners ruined."

Father crumples to the floor and sobs, his shoulders heaving with each wretched sound. I turn to Amethyst, our gazes meeting in a moment of shared triumph. Satisfaction glitters within their green depths. I take her hand and bring it to my lips.

"Is it time?" I ask.

She gives me an eager nod.

"Inform all the operatives. Tell the maintenance team to bring the chair."

As she leaves the chamber, I approach Father's trembling form. Sobs wrack his broken body, echoing across the stone walls. I pick up his chain and drag him toward the projection screen, which rises to reveal a second chamber.

Taking pride of place in its center is an electric chair.

Father recoils with a scream. "Don't do this, Xero. I'm sorry. I'm so sorry."

Ignoring him, I hurl his carcass onto the wooden seat and secure the straps around his wrists. He kicks and thrashes, his screams echoing across the walls.

The maintenance team enters, pushing along a cart carrying a high voltage generator. It hums to life with an ominous drone that makes my spine tingle with anticipation. As I secure the electrode cap on Father's head, the chamber fills with operatives, who form a semi-circle around the chair.

Father jerks backward in his seat, his eyes widening. "I can't die yet. We have unfinished business."

"We've stripped your bank accounts, killed your investors and accomplices, exposed your members, destroyed your former partners, liquidated your businesses, and divided your personal assets among your illegitimate children."

"No..." he moans.

"We took your teeth, nipples, and genitals."

A few people in the crowd of operatives chuckle, but it's drowned out by Father's screams. "But I didn't tell you about the organ business."

"Charlotte already bartered that intel in exchange for a quick death," I say, my lip curling.

Father convulses, his eyes darting with disbelief. "She lied."

The information she gave us was incomplete, but we tracked down the ringleaders of Father's organ trafficking ring to a warehouse in New Jersey, where we found cells containing eighteen former child assassins. They, along with the others, are now in our safe houses, receiving therapy.

I place my hands on his bony shoulders and gaze into his tear-filled eyes. "Any final words before we dispatch you to hell?"

"Sorry," he cries, his features twisting with anguish. "Please, just give me another chance."

Amethyst pushes her way through the crowd and stops at my side. Camila joins us with Isabel, Jynxson, and a few other boys who were at the underground facility when I was young.

Father's gaze snaps to Isabel. "You can't condone this. I never hurt you. You're a medic."

Isabel spits in his face and walks away.

Camila approaches Father and punches him in the jaw. His head snaps backward, his metal cap hitting the back of his chair with a clang.

I turn to the operatives. "Each of you has a chance to say goodbye to Delta. No more head injuries."

Stepping back, I wrap an arm around Amethyst's shoulder. She leans into my side and sighs.

"Are you ready for him to die?" she asks.

"His ending is the second thing I want most in the world."

She directs her pretty green eyes to me, making my breath hitch. "What's the first?"

I drop my gaze to her soft, pink lips, hungering for another taste. "You. It's always been you."

A radiant smile spreads across her delicate features that makes my heart soar. Holding onto my shoulder, she rises up to her tiptoes for a kiss. The warmth of her touch and the gentle press of her lips against mine drowns out the chaos of the operatives taking turns with Father.

The world falls away, and all that's left is me and the woman who's always been the missing part of my soul. Amethyst tastes like freedom, like victory, like sweet salvation. I thread my fingers through her curls, holding her in place. Her body presses against mine, making me wish I could claim her once more while the bastard fries.

A loud cheer breaks the moment, making us part. I turn around to find Jynxson connecting electrodes to his legs. Behind the chair, Tyler attaches the cables to the generator and gives me a thumbs up.

It's time.

By now, Father is a pitiful mess of blood and sweat and saliva. He jerks back and forth within his restraints, mumbling an incoherent string of apologies.

"Any last words?" I ask again.

His answer is a puddle of urine that elicits a round of applause.

After waiting for a member of the maintenance crew to mop up the liquid, I pick up the thick rubber cord linking the chair's electrodes to the generator. Silence descends across the chamber, a collective holding of breath, coupled by anticipation so solid that the molecules in the air vibrate.

"This is for my mothers."

I plug in the cord, and the world lights up with his screams. The sound is brutal, raw, drowning out the hum of the generator. Father's body convulses, his eyes bulging. The sweat and saliva on his skin evaporates, then turns into smoke, and finally, burning flesh.

As the chamber fills with his stench, I pull Amethyst close, my heart swelling with gratitude. "Thank you for making my dreams come true."

She turns to me and smiles, her eyes shining with love. "Always."

Father's body jerks one last time before slumping on the chair, a hollow shell.

And in that moment, I know I'm finally free.

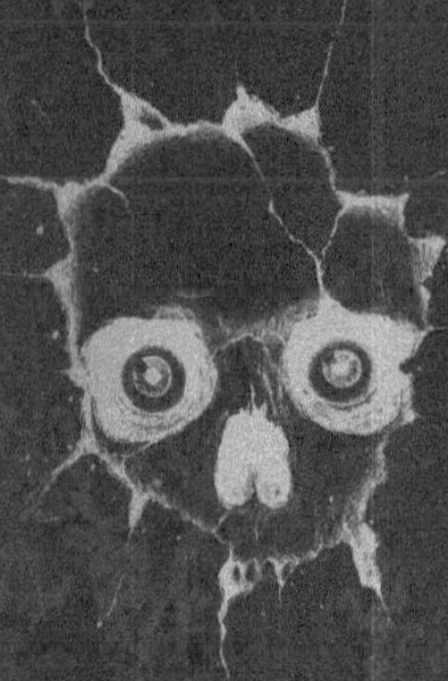

NINETY-EIGHT
EPILOGUE

THREE WEEKS LATER
AMETHYST

I lean over the mezzanine, staring down into the bookstore Myra inherited from her aunt. It's crammed with customers, some of whom I recognize from the book fair.

Today is the launch of Rapunzelita, which Myra published under her new imprint. My notoriety and my best friend's relentless publicity efforts have propelled my book to the top of the charts.

Myra's store is the only one selling a limited edition with bookplates containing my signature. She claimed to have found a large box of them after inheriting my possessions. Now she's created a retail frenzy.

Xero's arms wrap around my waist, pulling me back against his solid chest. He presses a kiss to my neck, sending a shiver down my spine.

"How does it feel to be a bestselling author?" he murmurs against my skin.

"Bittersweet," I reply with a sigh.

"Why?" he asks, his lips brushing my ear.

"I should be down there." My gaze drops to the fans clamoring for a hardback of my book. "I want to sign autographs, not be honored posthumously."

His grip around my waist tightens, and he grinds his erection into my ass. "Want me to cheer you up?"

My breath catches, and I push against his hardening cock. "How?"

"Look straight ahead."

I obey, my gaze locking on the crowd below. Myra stands on a small podium, delivering a speech about our decades-long friendship. Xero's hand slips beneath my skirt, his fingers tracing a path up my thigh. Shivers run down my spine, and I turn my head.

"Do it, or I'll stop," he growls.

"A-Alright." My teeth clamp down on my lower lip.

His fingers continue their journey, sliding along the lace of my panties. The pulse between my legs pounds hard, drowning out the excitement below. Each touch sends a rush of heat to my core, and my folds become slick.

"Are you watching the crowd?" he asks.

Gulping, I force my gaze back down to the bookshop. "Yes."

"Good girl."

He pushes my panties aside, exposing my pussy to the cool air. When his fingers slide up my slit and find my swollen clit, I want to scream.

"Xero," I say, my voice strangled.

"Shhh... Show some respect for the book launch."

Swallowing back a moan, I relax into his embrace. My body thrums with anticipation as his digits tease my needy clit with slow, deliberate circles. Pleasure rolls through my core in delicious waves, making it impossible to focus on regrets. Breathing hard, I roll my hips and concentrate on the moment.

"Stay still," he whispers, his voice thickening with desire.

"Fuck." I force my body to go rigid.

He chuckles. "You're doing so well. Keep watching your fans while I make you feel like a queen."

His fingers continue their relentless teasing, driving me closer to the edge. My legs tremble, and my lips part with a throaty moan.

"Don't make a sound," he murmurs, his breath hot against my ear. "You're going to take my fingers like a good little ghost."

The thrill of his words add to the sensation, and I stifle a whimper. Public sex has always been my weakness, and it's even more illicit with the oblivious crowd below. Xero and I are supposed to be dead, yet here we are, getting off at my author debut.

His fingers slide down to my opening, teasing the slick moisture there before plunging inside. Molten ecstasy surges through my core, making my knees buckle. Xero keeps me upright, his strong arm an anchor around my waist. His fingers move in a rhythm that has me gasping for breath, and pleasure mounts with every thrust.

"Look at them," he purrs into my ear. "They adore you and your words. You're an artist in your own right, just as I always believed."

It's true. Xero was the first person to fall in love with my manuscript. He even asked for more books. And even during that lull when I still thought he was a ghost, he read through my work, giving me inspiration at night.

Pressure builds around my clit, and his fingers increase their pace, stroking and thrusting until I see stars. My pussy clenches around his digits, the pleasure becoming nearly unbearable, his words fueling my desire.

"Remember how it feels to be adored, to be wanted. That's how it's going to be from now on."

His fingers rub a spot that makes my inner muscles convulse. Then his hot breath fans across my skin, sending shivers down my spine. "Now, come for me, little ghost. Let go."

At his command, he takes me to the edge, then the thumb stroking my clit presses down, and I explode. A climax tears through my system, white and hot and all-consuming. Electricity sizzles across my nerves, making my body shudder.

"That's my girl," he growls, his thumb tracing gentle circles, heightening the intensity of my pleasure. "You feel so good, spasming around my fingers."

The crowd launches into polite applause before forming orderly lines to the cash register. I lean my forearms over the railing, panting and gasping through the aftershocks.

Before I can fully recover, Xero pulls his fingers out of my pussy, yanks down my panties, and bends me over the balcony railing. The rush of cool air makes the skin on the backs of my thighs erupt into goosebumps.

Gripping my hips, he runs the crown of his cock along my wetness, coating it in my arousal. His Prince Albert bumps against my clit, detonating delicious sparks. As he nudges at my entrance, my need for him becomes unbearable.

Whimpering, I push back, desperate to be filled.

"Patience," he murmurs against my ear and pulls back.

I brace myself, my heart racing with anticipation. "Please," I whisper. "I need your cock. I need you."

"When you put it like that, how could I deny my talented little ghost?"

He enters me with a slow, deliberate thrust, lavishing me with a spine-tingling stretch. I grip the railing, my knuckles turning white, as he buries himself to the hilt. A low moan escapes my throat at the delicious torture.

"Feel that?" he whispers, his grip tightening on my hip.

I nod, the movement frantic. "Xero. Please. Move."

"You're so adorable when you're needy." Chuckling, he draws back his hips before delivering a sharp thrust that makes me gasp. The burst of pleasure he delivers sends all thoughts of being caught scattering to the wind.

Each drag of his cock fires needy sparks across my nerve endings, making my toes curl. He sets up a slow, teeth-grinding pace, making sure to hit that sweet spot inside me with every stroke.

"You feel so fucking good," he hisses, punctuating each word with a deep thrust.

His hand snakes around my waist, pinning me against his chest as he strokes my over-sensitized clit. The combined sensations are too much, bringing on the approach of another climax.

Each move is powerful, possessive, controlled. His lips find my neck, peppering my skin with kisses. The sensation of his lips and teeth grazing my skin only heightens my arousal. He bites down on my shoulder, the pain making me whimper and clench around his shaft.

"Look at them," he snarls. "Look at your adoring fans while I fuck you senseless."

I stare down at the bookstore, where the first dozen purchasers stream through the crowd with their bags. Xero's pace quickens, and I push back, matching his rhythm, our bodies moving in perfect sync.

"You like this, don't you?" he asks, his voice rough with desire. "Fucking beneath their noses with the danger of exposing your dirty little secret."

"Yes," I gasp, barely able to form the word. "Don't stop."

Hands tightening on my hips, he thrusts deeper. "Never. Because you're mine. You belong to me, Amethyst. Every pretty little inch."

The bustle of the bookstore fades, leaving only Xero, the railing, and the way he pounds into me with raw intensity. An orgasm builds up again, the tension coiling tight within my core.

Loud footsteps echo up a set of iron stairs leading to our mezzanine. I glance down to find Myra approaching, clad in the same white shirt and leather skirt she wore to the book fair.

"Xero," I say, my words choked. "Someone's coming."

The finger thrumming my clit falters for a heartbeat, then moves faster. "Let them come. Let them see who you belong to."

Terror explodes across my chest, making every nerve ending thrum. The thought of nearly getting caught sets off an explosive climax that seizes control of my limbs. My walls clamp and convulse around Xero's cock, making his shaft swell.

"Fuck... I'm coming." Spurts of warm cum hit my cervix, filling me with a delicious heat.

Xero's grip on my hips tightens, his movements becoming more erratic as he pounds through his own release.

I collapse against his chest, gasping through my climax. When the footsteps grow louder, Xero pulls out, letting my skirt fall back into place.

Seconds later, Myra appears at the top of the stairs, her shoulders sagging. Strands of red hair fall across her face, making her look drawn. When she raises her head and we lock gazes, her expression brightens.

"Amethyst! Xero!" She advances toward us with a broad smile. "The special edition is selling like crazy. We've already sold out of the first batch."

"That's fantastic!" I pull her into a hug. But as I draw back, her forehead creases. "What's wrong?"

Her smile falters, and her shoulders droop. "Martina sold her share of the store."

"To who?" I ask.

"Gavin," she whispers.

My gaze snaps to Xero, who scowls. I turn back to her and ask, "Gavin from school?"

She nods, her features twisting with annoyance. "He turned up one morning, saying he owned the store. When I called my sister, her assistant told me she'd sold her share online."

"Wait. How is that even legal?"

"Martina got an expert in inheritance law to look through the contracts," Myra replies with a grimace. "There's nothing else I can do."

Xero steps forward, his shoulders expanding. "Does this guy need to lose five more fingers?"

Paling, she shakes her head. "No, he's a friend who's become an annoying asshole who won't leave me alone."

It takes a second for the reason to register. The reason why Gavin was always such a creep. The reason why he tattooed BDSM on his fingers. "Don't tell me it's because of *that*."

Her face tightens.

I lean forward. "Seriously?"

When her gaze darts to Xero, I wrap an arm around her shoulder and walk her to the other side of the mezzanine. Xero remains in place. I'm sure having two sisters has gotten him accustomed to giving women their space.

"What happened now?" I ask.

"Don't laugh."

I give my head a vigorous shake.

"Do you remember when I told you about taking him to the Wonderland playroom when he was depressed about never being able to find a sub?"

Nodding, I school my features into a neutral mask.

"Well, he's decided I'm his Domme."

"Shit. No!"

"Shhh!" She places a finger to her lips. "He's become obsessed."

I lean in close and whisper, "Do you want us to have a word with him? If you don't want Xero to do it, I can pay him a visit—"

"No, no! He's harmless, just annoying. He's spent a fortune refurbishing the shop and excavating the basement for more storage."

"Where did he get the money?" I ask.

"Computer stuff," she replies with a shrug and returns to where we left Xero.

I follow her, my brows pulling into a frown. Gavin is more irritating than dangerous, but he also rented Xero's execution video from X-Cite Media. His name didn't come up under the list of members, and he didn't rent any snuff movies. Nobody bothered to investigate him any further because he was insignificant.

Xero approaches us, his expression grave. "We're going to be out of action for a few weeks. If this man is causing you trouble, say something now, and he'll be gone before morning."

"Do you have a mission?" she asks, her gaze darting from Xero to me.

Excitement bubbles up in my chest, and I grin. "Xero is taking me on a trip to France. We'll be staying at a vineyard in the Armagnac region, then moving on to Paris to explore the catacombs. After that, we're taking a train to London for a Charles Dickens tour."

Myra's eyes soften with a wistful smile. "I wish someone would take me on a romantic vacation."

Footsteps creak up the metal stairs, making our gazes snap to the direction of the sound. Myra rushes at a fire door and pushes it open. "You'd better go. He'll recognize you both immediately and call the cops."

Xero's jaw tightens. "Let me deal with him."

I tug at his arm, pulling him towards the exit, but it's like trying to drag a great oak. "Come on, let's go."

The footsteps quicken, and I release Xero's arm and step outside into the night, knowing he'll follow. Sure enough, he scoops me off my feet, making me squeal, and jumps off the fire escape like a superhero.

My stomach lurches during the one-story drop, and my mouth opens in a silent scream, even when he lands in a perfect crouch. As he races towards the car, I ask through panting breaths, "Are we late for the airport?"

"Private jets have no boarding times, but I'm in a hurry to introduce you to the mile-high club."

An hour later, we arrive at the airport, where Xero holds my hands as we ascend the steps of a private jet. Heart pounding with excitement, I lean into his side, reveling in his quiet strength.

We settle into the plush seats, and Xero refuses the flight attendant's offer of champagne, eager for a speedy takeoff. I glance around the luxurious cabin, at the cream leather seats, polished wood accents, and the door leading to what looks to be a bedroom.

I'm so excited for this trip that I barely hear the captain's announcement. The hum of the plane's engines forms a soft undercurrent as we soar into the night sky. Xero shifts in his seat and reaches into his jacket pocket. "I have something for you."

"What?" I ask.

He hands me a small red envelope, containing something solid. "Don't tell me it's another body part."

"Take a look," he murmurs.

I tear open the seal. Inside is a delicate silver locket I've only seen in pictures. My breath catches, and I turn to Xero. "Is that—"

"My mother's locket that your assistant intercepted," he says with a smile. "I've been waiting for the right moment to give it to you."

Gratitude swirls through my chest, making my eyes sting with tears. I pull it out, along with a delicate silver chain. "Oh, Xero," I say, my voice thick with emotion. "This is perfect. Thank you."

I lean in, brushing my lips against his for a slow, lingering kiss. This moment is perfection. Receiving this locket from him in person is a thousand times better than getting it in the mail.

When we finally pull apart, he reaches into his jacket again, this time extracting another envelope.

"There's more," he says, his tone teasing.

My brow furrows. What could be more meaningful than the locket? I take it from him and ease open the seal. Inside is a worn page. When I pull it out and unfold it, it's the sex contract I'd sent him while he was in prison.

"But I thought it was destroyed in the fire." My voice trembles.

His smile widens into a grin. "I kept everything. Every letter, every memento. They're the most precious things I own."

My heart swells to bursting, rendering me speechless, overwhelmed by his thoughtfulness. I cup his face and kiss him again, slow, deep, and full of promise.

When we break apart, he brushes his lips against my ear. "There are still a few things in that contract we haven't yet tried."

My pulse quickens, and warmth spreads across my core. "Why don't we start with the mile high club?"

"You don't need to ask me twice," he growls.

Now that Delta is dead, along with all the other ghosts of our pasts, Xero and I can finally focus on the future—one filled with everything we've earned and all the things we're yet to discover.

THE END

Dear Reader,

Thank you so much for joining me on Amethyst and Xero's story! I hope you enjoyed reading about them as much as I enjoyed writing them.

In the future, I hope to expand the story work with tales from my favorite characters in the duet. While you're waiting, please enjoy a short story from Xero and Amethyst's trip to France.

Love,

Gigi

P.S. Get the story at www.gigistyx.com/france

P.P.S. Xero, Dr. Saint, Officer McMurphy, the Montesano brothers, Salentino sisters, Martina Mancini, and even Myra appear in my Morally Black series, which starts with Taming Seraphine.

ALSO BY GIGI STYX

Morally Black Series

Taming Seraphine

Snaring Emberly

Breaking Rosalind

Stalking Ginevra

Pen Pal Duet

I Will Break You

I Will Mend You

Standalones

Am I A Liar?

ABOUT THE AUTHOR

Gigi lives with her husband and two cats in London. When she's not crafting twisted dark romances with feisty heroines and the morally grey villains who love them, she's cuddled up on the sofa with a cup of tea and a book.

Sign up for Gigi's updates at:
www.gigistyx.com/newsletter

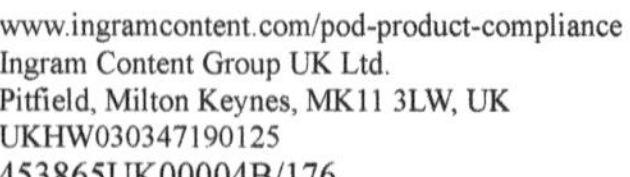

www.ingramcontent.com/pod-product-compliance
Ingram Content Group UK Ltd.
Pitfield, Milton Keynes, MK11 3LW, UK
UKHW030347190125
453865UK00004B/176

9 781965 738016